(un)**verified**

(un)verified

a novel
by kristin giese

Printed in the United States of America
First Printing, 2019
ISBN 9781733992701

www.allmoxie.com

For Shantelle.
Stop trying to change the spelling of your name.

PROLOGUE

Margo watched Matt's chest rise and fall as he lay sleeping on the living room floor of their just-rented home, the glow of her phone screen lighting up the dark room. Her eyes traveled from Matt up to the vaulted ceiling and its white beams. This house was their first move together as a couple. Her phone blinked 3:30 a.m. and her mind wandered back over their evening.

"You two look mighty sharp. Big night out?"

Margo turned to find the eyes of their Uber driver looking at her in the rearview mirror.

"We had a party to go to," she answered kindly.

"Musta been fancy." The driver turned, nodding toward her outfit.

She smiled, as she smoothed the front of her vintage Halston jumpsuit. She looked back out the window of the car, watching Matt through the glass of the pizza shop, his head down looking at his phone screen. Her inbox dinged. *They put ham on our pizzas. What are we, serial killers?* Margo smiled, then typed, *Do only serial killers get ham on their pizza? Cuz I kinda don't hate it.* Three dots appeared on her screen. Then, *What kind of monster are you?!* She laughed out loud.

"Your boyfriend seems like a wise guy."

Margo's gaze returned to the rearview mirror and the crinkled corners of the driver's eyes. "He's okay," she offered, warmly.

"You two just got a place, huh?" he peeled off a Mento and offered her one as he popped his in his mouth.

She shook her head no in polite decline, turning to see Matt exit the shop, pizzas in hand.

"Well, I'd tell you good luck," the driver said, "but you don't need it. I can always tell the ones who are gonna make it."

"Are you watching me sleep?" Matt whispered in the dark, startling her back to their empty living room.

"No," she denied, blushing at the recall of the driver's words. "But, even if I were, isn't it considered sweet for a girlfriend to watch her boyfriend sleeping?"

Matt rolled toward her. He lay on the chevron wood floors, four feet away. She was atop a blow-up mattress, the only piece of furniture in the empty room. "I guess it could be considered sweet, but seeing as we're actually strangers, I think it reads a bit like the start of my Lester Holt, 'And Then He Vanished,' Dateline episode."

Margo laughed out loud as she kicked at the scarf she was using as a makeshift blanket. "Seeing as I've only known you a day and a half, Lester's not exactly on speed dial just yet."

"Well, that's good," Matt yawned. "I'm actually more a Katie Couric man, anyway."

CHAPTER 1:

Matt

"Run it again," Matt said, hiding his annoyance behind a forced smile. "Please," he tacked on to appear congenial.

"I did. Twice. It says it's been declined, Bud. If you want this beef jerky and Pedialyte, you'll have to pay for it another way," the cashier observed with obvious judgment.

Matt smiled, grabbed his card, and walked out of the shop dialing Rob Rolle as he did. He got his voicemail. "Rob on a Rolle," Matt boomed over the line, using the nickname he'd given his father's wunderkind of a CFO when Matt was 21 and Rob was 30. Rob on a Rolle hated that nickname, which is exactly why Matt kept calling him that. Matt hated Rob. "It's me, Matt. I was just trying to buy some," he paused grappling for a word other than "garbage at the 7-Eleven" and landed instead on, "groceries and my card got declined. Give me a quick call."

He hung up and told himself it was a fluke. The pit in his stomach said it was more than that. The card in question was his debit card linked to his savings account, which drew directly from his trust fund. Each month money appeared there, and Matt vacationed, partied, and surfed his way through it. The thought that his father might finally have made good on a longstanding threat to freeze it made him dizzy, or was that hunger? He was starving, *and still a little drunk,* he thought. He reached in his pockets searching for cash. He didn't even have enough to go back in and buy just that Slim Jim. *I'm screwed*, he decided.

His phone rang. It wasn't Rob. It was Leandra Jennings, the head of business services for his father's company, Milles-Lade Enterprises. He thought about not answering, but knew it was Rob's way of saying he wasn't going to call back. *Fuck you too, Rob*, Matt thought vehemently.

"Hey Lee, what's new?" he said, forcing optimism into his voice and putting on all his charms, which wasn't hard. Matt Milles-Lade was all charm.

"Rob just rang saying he wishes he had a moment to chat, but"—Matt and Rob both knew that was a lie—"he and your father are on their way to Zurich. He wanted me to pass along some updates. Hate to be the bearer of bad news, Matthew, but they've frozen your trust. Don't worry though, they've instructed me to set up a stipend for you, $4,000 a month."

Matt grimaced in actual physical pain at the amount. *How am I gonna live on that?* he thought.

"Rob said your father plans to reinstate your funds once you accomplish a few things on a checklist he's emailed you...."

Matt pulled the phone away from his ear to look at the screen. Sure enough, his inbox blinked back at him. He opened the email.

"Son, I've frozen your trust. I'm happy to give you your access back, but first you'll have to do the following,

STOP BEING SUCH A FUCK-UP. Get a job. Drink less. Care more. Basically, be the sort of human that doesn't have to be extorted by their own father to get their act together. Dad"

"Matt, can you hear me? Maaatttttt?" Leandra's voice floated up from the phone in his hand.

"Yeah, sorry, bad reception. I'm here," Matt said putting the phone back to his ear.

"Right, like I said, I've funded the account. You'll have to come in to get the card and pin."

Shit, Matt mouthed up to the sky as he wrung his shirt collar. A card and pin meant he'd have to wait until tomorrow to have any cash.

"Rob thought you might need me to organize parking. He wasn't sure if you'd have the cash flow, which I thought was nice of him to think about. You know Rob...."

Cutting her off, "Oh, I know Rob, he's a real peach," Matt said, saccharine sarcasm dripping from his words. "Listen Lee, I gotta go, I got some things going on over here," he said as he stood in the middle of a gas station parking lot at 4 p.m. on a Tuesday, latently drunk from the night before, having just gotten up 20 minutes ago. They hung up and Matt looked around, his plan of grabbing cash and snacks now derailed. He pulled up Uber and ordered a car. After a minute of searching *Please update credit card on file,* flashed on his screen. Matt forced all the air out of his lungs in frustration and pinched the bridge of his nose. He texted Charlie: *Need a lift. Just down the hill.*

For 22 of his 26 years on this earth, Charlie, his dad's driver, had driven Matt everywhere, including their first trip together, Safety Town when Matt was four. Other kids had beamed back at their moms and dads, Matt had gotten a solemn head nod from Charlie in his shiny, three-piece, polyester suit. When he'd failed to tell the difference between a yellow light and red light, it was Charlie who comforted him on the ride home. "No worries, Mr. Matt, I drive you wherever you need to go."

Just not today, Matt thought reading Charlie's reply as he started to walk. *Sorry, Mr. Matt. Mr. M says I'm not available to you.*

An hour later, dripping in sweat and filthy dirty from the dusty, dry canyon air, Matt rounded the final hill to his house. *No wonder no one walks in LA,* he thought miserably. Halfway up his phone had died. It was like a mini episode of *Survivor*, minus the low-level dysentery. He crashed through the gate and made a beeline to the garden hose. Despite its steady gush, it felt like the water couldn't come fast enough for him to guzzle down.

"Jeez, Matty, manners much?" Tiffany chided behind him, using the nickname she knew he hated.

The only person allowed to call me Matty isn't here, he thought crabbily as he raised the hose up above his head, letting the shockingly cold water drench him.

She arched her eyebrow and pouted as he ignored her. "Don't think for a second you're walking into *my* house dripping water all over the place. I'm having the girls over in an hour."

He shook off like a dog spraying water everywhere.

"Maatttyy," Tiff screamed, jumping back to avoid the muddy spray. "I'm wearing white!"

From what Matt could tell, Tiff's main goal in life *was* to wear white, specifically on the day she achieved trophy wife status. Landing Brooks Milles-Lade, Matt's father, put that goal in sight. She knew it. Matt knew it. Hell, even Brooks knew it.

"Well, son, when the sex is this good, I'm happy to give the girl a trophy—you know what I mean?" Brooks smirked as Matt grimaced.

"Yeah, Dad, I got it, and I should remind you I'm your son."

For years, Matt had hoped his Dad would stop the endless stream of women parading through their home.

"Don't you want to have something real?"

"No, son, I've had enough real life. I'm into escapism these days."

Matt added it to his already long list of things he and his father disagreed on, but this one was surprising, mostly because Matt was no monogamist. On more than one occasion he'd had Zinny, their housekeeper, hustle a woman out of *his* bed. He'd call her from the shower, hissing, "You have to come get her out of here, Zin. She hasn't taken the hint. She thinks we're going to brunch for Christ's sake. What next, our wedding?"

Zinny viewed it less as saving Matt and more as rescuing those helpless girls. She'd arrive to his room, a to-go cup of coffee, warm wash cloth, and breakfast sandwich in her hand. "Time to waaaake'yyy," she'd trill in her Russian accent, throwing open the curtains. "Mr. Matt is in the shower. He's a weak man. You are too good for him. I'm doing you a favor, saving you from falling for him. Because, you will. He is a doll, but he is also a dog. I should know, I raised him. So, let's get you up before you get broken."

They'd protest, but Zinny—as she was known to Matt—was actually Zinaida Katerine Bobrova, a proper Russian woman who had grown up behind the Iron Curtain. These girls were no match for her blend of cold war charm. She could snap them like a twig, not physically—Zinny was petite, like the adorable tiny center of a Matryoshka nesting doll—but emotionally. She instinctively had the skills of the Russian secret police. She'd politely strong-arm them into a car, close the door, and lean into the window. Matt never knew what she said to them, but no girl ever called, so he didn't question it. Then she'd head upstairs to change Matt's sheets.

"Make sure to wash your penis, you disgusting boy," she'd always say as she gathered his clothes off the bathroom floor. "I'll get rid of the evidence."

Over the years, Matt had become certain she'd delivered that line long before him.

"Did you hear what I said?" Tiff asked sharply, shaking him back to the front lawn

Matt looked at her briefly. Not that his dad had taken his advice, but Brooks Milles-Lade *had* allowed Tiff to move in. At first, Matt was relieved. *No more random women*, he'd thought. But then something worse happened: Tiff believed Brooks was faithful. After all, he'd given her the keys to the castle. Matt knew better. There *were* other girls. Despite himself, he felt bad for Tiff.

"Yeah, I heard you. The real trophy wives of Beverly Hills are coming over. I've got things to do anyway," Matt said, snaking the hose back onto its reel.

"I bet you do, like figuring out how to live *without* a trust fund?" Tiff smiled smugly as she swirled a strand of what Matt could only imagine was the fake portion of her hair.

Come to think of it, maybe I don't feel so bad for Tiff, after all, he thought.

CHAPTER 2:

Margo

"Kirby, when do you move in?" Maureen Melon shrieked as Margo walked into the kitchen. "Did you hear that M&M? Kirby bought a house!"

"Wow," Margo said flatly, greeting the news with the same enthusiasm as dental work.

"I close next week. And then after that," Kirby trailed off, lost in a haze of euphoria before exclaiming, "I'm gonna be a homeowner at 24! Can you believe it?"

They both looked at Margo with stars in their eyes.

"I can't," Margo echoed dryly.

Timed to be born in September, because her mother had read that babies born in the ninth month were smarter and more successful, every move Margo Melon made had been a revelation for her parents. Kirby—her younger sister by two years, intended for September but born in November, "the month when most serial killers are born," Margo had shared with her at age seven—wasn't quite *The One Minute Manager* material Blanchard and Johnson had written about. In the Melon house, cerebral acrobatics reigned supreme. And Kirby just couldn't quite keep up, something they'd all silently registered when at age 15 Kirby asked over a bucket of Costco chicken, "But, how did they know the rotisserie breed would be the delicious ones?"

Margo had gone to Brown and been the editor in chief of the *Brown Daily Herald.* She'd graduated top of her class. Kirby had studied fashion merchandising and dropped out. "You know that's not a real degree anyway, right?" Margo had asked as she watched her sister glue-gunning a fantastical wool and fiber installation as a final exam. "We'll see," Kirby had chirped sunnily.

"It's small," Kirby continued, pulling Margo back to their little Castle Heights kitchen. "Tiny. Up in The Hills. I just...Blush & Bashful was, like, a side gig. I can't believe how much it's grown. It's, like, I don't even know what I'm doing. And, David, well, he's courting investors who want to explode our platform into a channel!"

Margo sneered to herself as she turned with the stack of plates her mother had handed her. *A side gig that landed you on the Forbes 30 Under 30 List,* Margo thought jealously.

"Set the table," Maureen cheerily directed of her eldest daughter. "And you get the Champagne. We're going to toast," she said to Kirby.

"With tacos?" Margo grimaced.

Margo had moved home as a stopover after a failed stint at *Popler*, the holy grail of fashion magazines, but that was four years ago now. She'd nabbed the position her senior year and crammed her entire world into two checkable duffel bags and flung herself across the country to a rundown studio in Harlem. In real life it was 246 square feet of worn walls and sloping floors. *Perfection,* Margo had thought the moment the door swung open. Her first day, she arrived ready to run the place. But, after eight weeks of only filing, running errands, and fetching coffee, she surmised she wasn't being used to her fullest. So, with an abundance of entitlement that she mistook for confidence, Margo marched into her boss's office. Lennox Stanton sat before her picking apart a vegan burrito like a vulture clad in Balmain as Margo launched in: "People say you have to start at the bottom, but I don't think that applies to everyone. Some of us are meant to start several rungs up. I'm happy to get your coffee every once and a while, Lennox, but I'd like to be given more challenging duties if I'm expected to remain in my position."

Five minutes later, Margo was on the corner of 45th and Times Square holding the contents of her desk, three packages of Little Debbie snacks, and a fake cactus. Lennox Stanton had fired her.

Her parents had encouraged her to bootstrap a way to stay in New York. "I'm not just taking any job, Dad," she'd protested. "I wanna write, not wait tables." The next day, she bought a ticket home. "It's fine. I'll take this time to write," she informed her parents as she hefted her suitcase off the baggage carousel. Their worried glances said they weren't so sure.

Kirby, on the other hand, skyrocketed. While waiting in line for coffee in between her classes Kirby had met a coding student, David, from the technical school across the street. Together, the pair formed a resale fashion start-up, Blush & Bashful, selling Kirby's vintage finds. Surprising even to them, it took off and took them with it. Kirby went from a girl with no professional drive to driving a Mercedes in two short years. As far as Margo was concerned, that ride, metaphorically and literally, was supposed to have been hers.

"Earth to Margo!"

Margo shook free from the memory to find her mom passing Champagne flutes through the window that connected their dining room and kitchen and robotically grabbed them. She lapped the table placing one flute at each seat.

"What do you mean a channel?" she asked as Kirby joined her relay team, falling in rank behind her, placing napkins at each stop.

"I mean a channel, AN ACTUAL CHANNEL. I've already started shooting videos for the site, and we're changing my title to editor in chief and style director. Can you believe…"

Margo halted. Kirby smashed into her back. "What?" Margo asked indignantly. "You're an editor in chief just because some coding school dropout gives you the title?"

Kirby's face crumpled.

"MARGO!" her mother reprimanded. Silence stood like soup in the room.

She knew she should stop but didn't. Couldn't. "I'm the writer. Not you. What have you ever done? I mean, really, Kirby? Seriously?" she asked, each word punctuated with accusation. "You made eyes with a guy in a coffee shop who wanted in your pants and somehow you parlay that into a self-professed editor in chief title. You're such a fake. And…."

"THAT'S ENOUGH!" Hank Melon boomed from the doorway. "Margo Valentine Melon, you will not speak to your sister that way. What has happened to you? You're the one who quit. Not me. Not your mother. Certainly not Kirby. You. *You* gave up. *You* threw in the towel. And yet here *you* are trying to hang all of us with it. I don't think so, young lady."

His words stung, mostly because they were true. Margo wanted to yell at them, like a child who drops their ice cream and then shouts at everyone standing around for what was their own mistake. She bit her lip to keep it from trembling, placed the remaining flutes on the table, and rushed out.

"Margo?" Kirby started behind her.

"Give her a minute." Maureen grabbed Kirby's arm.

The sliding door made a shushing sound as Margo closed it. She leaned her head into the cool glass as she felt her chest hitch. Shame washed over her. She turned and sat at their outdoor table. Melton, their yellow Lab, hefted himself up and lumbered over, placing his head in her lap. Margo leaned to kiss him as a full sob escaped her chest and tears flooded forward. "Oh, Melty, I don't know what to do anymore." She sat there for several minutes, resting her forehead to his, smelling the sun on his skin.

She heard the door slide open but didn't look up. Her sister placed a Topo Chico on the table and sat down across from her.

After a pause, "Why do you think I'm so shocked about what's happening with me?" Kirby asked as she took a sip from her own bottle of mineral water.

Holding Melton's head in her hands, her fingers under his jaw, Margo traced circles around his closed eyes with her thumbs. "I don't know," she said quietly.

"I'm surprised, because none of this was supposed to be mine. Success was reserved for the *amazing* Margo," Kirby began, almost hanging a cape on the word *amazing*.

"Whatever, Kirb," Margo's head shot up, defensively.

"Whoa. Let me talk." Kirby raised her hands and Topo Chico in surrender. Margo lowered her gaze back to Melton, absent-mindedly still tracing his face. "Success was always yours, Margo. I didn't need it. I didn't crave it. But, now that I have it, I see why you fell so hard when it went away. It's..." Kirby searched for the right word. "Electric. It literally lights you up."

"I know," Margo hushed, surprised by her sister's understanding. "Why do you think I'm falling apart? I don't know how to get it back, Kirbs." She wiped away a tear before looking back down at Melton.

Kirby stared out into the yard. "Well, I know one thing for sure, you're not gonna find it here." She gestured around their parents' cinderblock backyard. "What you're doing isn't working, M. You've locked yourself away, waiting for success to what, find *you*? I know you never had to chase it before, but you have to now. You have to put yourself out there. You're not meant to play safe. That's not your story."

Margo raised her tear-filled eyes to Kirby's searchingly. "Yeah, so what is?"

"I don't know what *it* is, but I know where it begins. It begins with you standing on your own two feet again." Kirby smiled. "You're a boss, Margo. Start acting like it. Or fake it. I don't care, but I need my sister back." Kirby held her gaze until something dawned on her. "I think you should get your own place." Kirby's eyes darted back and forth as she considered what she was saying. "That's exactly what you should do. Get your own place, Margo. It'll force you to do whatever it takes to make it work."

Margo's heart zinged at the thought of escaping her childhood bedroom for her own digs. "And how would I afford *that*?"

Kirby sipped her drink. "Well, I need someone to help me move. I know we agreed living together would result in a double homicide, but we never said I couldn't hire you—not full-time, but a freelancer. That would put money in your pocket for a deposit. From there, we'll figure it out. *You'll* figure it out. You might have forgotten you're brave Margo, but I haven't. And, probably neither has Paul Schiffer, who you decked for trying to put his hand up my shirt in the fourth grade." Kirby stood and walked over to Margo. She hoisted her up into a hug. At first Margo resisted, but then she leaned in. It felt good to lean on her little sister again.

"Okay," she said softly.

"Okay?" Kirby pushed Margo back by the shoulders to search her face.

Margo nodded.

Kirby swept her back up into a hug. "Great, let's go eat tacos, and definitely *not* tell Mom and Dad."

CHAPTER 3

Matt

"Honestly, he's a loser. He's lazy, doesn't have a job, and a parade of women pass through his bedroom. Last week I caught one here. I mean, horrible.... Brooks told me he's at the end of his rope. He doesn't want him here either. But, what can I do? It's his son."

Tiff's condemnations floated up to where Matt stood in the kitchen making a sandwich. *Oh the irony,* Matt thought. Tiff didn't have a job either. And the girl? The one she'd caught in the house? She wasn't *here* for *Matt.* His father had just stood there stone-faced as Tiff laid into him. Mr. Fortune 500 media mogul had let his own son take the fall for what was his dalliance. And later? Not even a "Thanks, son" for covering for him. *Typical,* Matt decided.

As for the rest of it, Matt didn't want to admit how deeply Tiff's words cut. *He doesn't want him here either,* echoed in his ears. Honestly, that had been true for Matt since he was 11. Up until that point Brooks had been World's Greatest Dad-written-on-a-mug material, playing catch in the yard, surfing on weekends, camping trips in the summer, *Hallmark card shit*, he thought. But, that year everything shifted. He knew why, but he wasn't going to pry that door open tonight, especially not for Tiff.

As he put the mustard in the fridge, Tiff's last jab grabbed him. "Anyway, we're selling the house. Brooks wants to move. At some point Matty's stuff's gonna end up on the lawn."

Fuck, I hate when she calls me that, he scowled, further annoyed to be caught off guard by Tiff's breaking news.

He walked down the hall to his room, sandwich in hand, and launched livehere.com. He shook his head to himself as he reached for the remote. *Newsflash, Tiff, I don't want to live here either.*

CHAPTER 4

Margo

As soon as dinner was done, Margo bolted to her room. Her father thought she was pouting. In reality she was planning. Before the tacos had even hit her plate, Margo was 18 pin boards deep in her mind designing the apartment she didn't yet have with money she hadn't yet earned. *Whatever, details*, she decided. She knew in her gut her sister was right. She was ablaze with the notion that she had to stand on her own two feet, NOW, even if it took her holding down two jobs to do it.

She flopped down on her bed and opened her phone. Grid.it popped up. She swiped it away. *No time for social media now*, she thought. *It's so depressing anyway.* Her feed was an endless scroll of how amazing her friends' lives were and how far behind she was falling. Try as she might to make peace with her sister's success, she was still jealous of her, and of them, honestly. She'd become a pro at avoiding all of it. Yet, she couldn't delete the app. Grid.it was the hangnail that hurt, but Margo couldn't stop picking at. She just had to look. Instead, she launched livehere.com. She'd spent enough time on the app daydreaming about the home she'd one day buy. Today, Margo plugged in what she thought she could actually afford, $1,850, and held her breath. A list populated. She began opening them. Each one was worse than the last. Her heart sank lower and lower with each listing.

Her phone dinged with a text from Kirby.

Glad about 2nite. Felt good having my big sis back. 2mrw be at 9551 Cedar Lake Dr. 8am. BTW, Ford asked about u....

What do you mean Ford asked about me? When? Where? Spill.

Nope. 2mrw. Sleep tight M&M. xx

She stared at her phone. *Ford asked about me? What did that even mean? Why did he ask? How did it even come up? Fucking Kirby,* she thought. Kirby knew that Margo's stalking of Ford Van Hewitt, the very handsome social and digital director at B&B bordered on an arrestable offense. Margo had even created a fake Grid.it account so she could watch his Grid.Vids without him knowing. As far as Margo knew, Ford didn't even know she was alive.

And yet, I guess he does, she realized.

Her nervous excitement about his inquiry quickly morphed into terror. His asking *after* her meant he might find out *about* her. *That can never happen,* she decided. She'd made an artform out of ensuring she remained an enigma to Ford. He was handsome in a way that made her suddenly very aware of her vagina. For him to find out that she still lived in her childhood bedroom with the same large Smurfette sticker that she'd stuck to her headboard when she was eight would be a fate worse than death. In fact, her mother had almost killed her for that very sticker when she'd first found it. She'd hauled Margo down the hall, furious, upon discovering it while stripping the bed. "Margo Valentine, what is this?" Margo knew better than to answer her angry mother's rhetorical question. Instead, she'd done what every child does under any parental interrogation, shrugged. "I did not raise you to ruin your things. I hope you and Smurfette are very happy, because you'll be sleeping together until you can afford to buy your own bed, young lady."

All these years later, Maureen Melon had remained true to the threat she'd made to her daughter 18 years before. Every night peering over Margo like a blue guardian angel stood Smurfette. The one time she'd attempted to have sex in this bed that little blue cartoon had been along for the ride, a smurfing ménage à trois. Her college boyfriend Kipp had come to visit on summer break. With her parents at work and Kirby at cheer camp, they'd started messing around. When they pushed the pillows off the bed, Smurfette made her sultry debut. At first it was what it had always been. Kipp's fumbling hands. Missionary position. Him eager to come, not even pondering how he'd get Margo there too. But, the sight of Smurfette changed him. Kipp amplified his duties. Margo, however, wasn't so sure it was for her. It seemed to be for Smurfette. He stared intently at her six-inch buxom blue frame, draped in a white dress with those poorly rendered white chunky heels, while jackhammering into her, his little smurfberries about to explode. *Un-fricking-believable,* Margo thought, unsure whether to laugh or cry. Needless to say, she and Kipp broke up that weekend. But, try as she might with Goo Gone, acetone, and turpentine, that slut Smurfette stuck around to this very day.

I have to get out of this room, she sighed.

She sat up, relaunched livehere, and reloaded her search. Nine listings blinked back at her. She opened each one, hoping to find a gem. What she found instead were quite possibly the Nine Circles of Hell that Dante had written about, and that was putting a smurfing spin on it.

CHAPTER 5

Matt

"I didn't even know you were single, buddy," Matt said aloud, his thumb hovering over the screen as a bandana-clad Bret Michaels stared up at him. "Or a woman," he observed, noting the marker drawn in goatee of the Halloween costume donned by SeeMargoDate in her profile picture. Matt swiped right and waited for the page to load, when a text interrupted the scroll.

Beverly Crest house got an offer. Officially off the table. Got another property if interested. Pocket listing in Woodland Canyon. Could show right now. LMK. Cheers. Paul

Fuck, Matt thought. Out of all the listings he'd flagged, the Beverly Crest house had been the one he'd hoped for the most. The fact that it, too, was now off the market, was just another hiccup in an already disastrous day.

"What's that?" Matt grimaced, at his first walkthrough, pointing at the thick green film of algae growing across the pool. "*That's* the reason the rent's so cheap," the realtor snipped as he slapped a property sheet to Matt's chest and walked away.

At the second property an older woman with a face made of what appeared to be melted plastic toys greeted Matt from her kitchen island perch. "Got two offers raising the rent by $1,500. If you wanna be in the running, you'll need to ante up," she informed him without even looking up from her phone. Matt had no idea a listed rent was just a jumping off point. Midday he downgraded his rent threshold and switched from homes in the hills to apartments and duplexes in the flats, deciding the swap would give him and the $15K he'd cobbled together between his stipend and his bedroom safe, some negotiating room.

"Where's the rest of it?"

"The rest of what?" the bathrobe-clad landlord asked, feigning ignorance.

"The rest of the bathroom," Matt said flatly at his third walkthrough.

"Ooooh, the toilet?"

"Yeah, the toilet...."

"It's down the hall. It was an illegal build so I had to get creative, but you get used to it."

"Do you?" Matt sneered, as the man shrugged sheepishly. "Or, maybe you just pee in the sink?" Matt pondered aloud.

Shaking off his morning of mishaps and forgetting the dating app entirely, Matt texted back: *On my way,* plugged the address of the Woodland Canyon home into his GPS, and pulled out onto Mullholland.

CHAPTER 6

Margo

"Whose house is this?" Margo's voice echoed off the heavy slab, white marble of the foyer.

"Mine," Kirby shared nervously, her voice rising at the end, making her answer a question.

"Wait. What? Yours? This place is ginormous, Kirbs! You said it was small, in the hills?"

"I know. I couldn't tell Mom and Dad the truth." She looked apologetic, in her high-waisted jeans and vintage Chanel bolero.

I was already jealous of that jacket and now this house, Margo thought, defeated, her face showing her obvious shock.

"Hey, girls," David chimed from the doorway. Then, "Hey, baby." He leaned in and pecked Kirby on the cheek.

"What's going on here?" Margo folded her arms across her chest, her eyes darting between David and her sister.

"We have some news."

"Clearly," Margo retorted as she gestured to them practically holding hands. Kirby rolled her eyes.

"David and I are living together and we're going to run Blush & Bashful out of this house." Kirby winced as she said it.

"You two are dating?" Margo asked, surprised, her brow furrowing.

"Maybe," Kirby said trying to read Margo's face.

"Babe!" David exclaimed.

"Okay, definitely dating," Kirby admitted. "We didn't tell anyone because we thought, maybe, it was just a thing that happened a few times. We didn't want it to get weird if it didn't work. But it's working, and we figured between his house, my house, and our offices we were spending a *ton* of money that, could be put to better use. So, we crunched the numbers and it made sense. We'd been renting locations all over town for shoots, which costs a fortune. When we walked in here, we knew this house could work for all of it. We can shoot, live, and work here. It just made sense."

And it did. It made total sense to Margo. She realized she'd always known that David adored her sister and revered her artistic talents. He let Kirby be Kirby. Margo liked that about him.

"Why keep it a secret? You don't think Mom and Dad would approve? You do know they lived together before they were married, right?" Margo asked, swapping her hobo bag to the other arm.

"Yeah, but this is different. We're not just living together. We *bought* a house together, and you know Dad. He would never approve of *this* house. He's going to be furious that we're leveraging the business before it booms. I just didn't want all his judgment," Kirby offered.

"I know how that is," Margo agreed, continuing to take in the scale of her surroundings.

David removed their lattes from the cardboard carrier he'd walked in with. "It's risky, but we have some big things happening and some heavy hitters coming to the table to invest. So..." He trailed off.

"Who's the last coffee for?" Margo asked as she took hers from his hands.

"Me," a whiskey-toned voice said behind her. Margo didn't need to turn around to see it was Ford. Her vagina was confirmation of that, like some sort of labial homing pigeon, it dinged whenever she was near him. "I wondered if you'd be here on our first big day, Margs," he said, dragging his feet across the welcome mat.

Margs, is that his pet name for me? She was certain if anyone else called her that she'd correct them immediately, but somehow her name, in any form, falling out of Ford's mouth was permitted.

He stood momentarily in the doorway, the blue of his denim shirt matching the indigo of his eyes. When he grabbed the frame above his head and leaned in, he looked like a Hemsworth brother in a GQ spread. Margo's breath caught in her chest at the sight of him.

"Guilty," she said, trying to sound casual as she took a sip from her latte. Driblets fell down her chin and onto her white tank top.

"Oh, you're spilling," Ford observed, immediately grabbing a napkin from the tray David was holding.

Margo waved him off, dragging the back of her hand across her chin. *Stop being such an idiot, Margs*, she cringed inwardly.

He smiled and brushed past her, Margo's eyes following the worn edge of his back pocket and the brown leather wallet that was peeking out—her mouth watered. *Man, does he smell good,* Margo thought. *Like what you'd imagine Brad Pitt would smell like, sandalwood and success*, she decided. Her knees went weak.

"Shall we?" Ford gestured to David. The two of them turned to head toward the back of the house.

"We'll get the office set up. It's gonna be awesome, babe." David winked at Kirby.

Kirby beamed back at him and then turned to Margo shaking her head. "Smooth move, Ex-Lax," she chuckled.

Margo gave her the finger as she took another sip of her latte. Then, "I'm proud of you, Kirbs."

"I'm proud of me too, M&M," Kirby hushed.

"But you do know Mom and Dad are eventually going to come over, and," Margo gestured around the space as if to say, "*figure out that you're lying.*"

"I know, but I figured it's easier to ask forgiveness than permission. It's pretty impressive, right?"

Their gazes traveled around the room. "Yeah, it's pretty impressive," Margo agreed.

CHAPTER 7

Matt

"Traffic must have been horrific," Paul observed as he stood in front of the home's double French doors, his Chicklet-white smile blinding Matt nearly as much as his sharp, chocolate brown pinstripe suit.

Matt smiled. "You know LA."

Paul knelt down, unlatching the left French door from its floor bolt. "That I do. Let's get you in to have a look around." As he stood, he pushed both doors open and stepped off center so Matt could see the room fully in frame.

This is the one, Matt knew instantly.

"Well, then, come on." Paul gestured for Matt to walk inside.

Matt complied and crossed the threshold. His eyes traveled through the space and up to the ceiling, where a large lantern hung down over an entrance table stacked high with books and an urn filled with flowers. To his left, a dining room. To his right, a sunken, grand living room with vaulted ceilings and dark wood Spanish-style beams. It stretched out before him for a good 40 feet, with a wall of glass doors at the opposite end. Two sofas sat facing each other with a heavy wood coffee table in between. He walked down the three steps that led into the room. On the far wall stood a white brick fireplace. Directly opposite, floor-to-ceiling built-in bookcases.

"It's old," Paul said in a hush, honoring the quietness of the house. "Hasn't been touched in years. No AC, but you get great breezes off the hill when you open the doors. Got screens last year to keep the mosquitoes out. Never had those buggers before in LA, did we?"

Matt realized he was smiling more than a sane person should.

"The owners are Swedish, a couple who moved here for work but then relocated to London. We had a tenant, but he booked a series. You live alone?"

Matt nodded.

"A right proper bachelor, then are we? This house suits you. I'm good at matching the house to the man." Paul looked around the room, nodding his approval at this potential real estate marriage. The level of relief Matt felt standing in the living room was immense. "Go wander around," Paul encouraged.

Matt took off down the hall. The rest of the house wasn't big, but it had charm. The hall that stretched past the kitchen housed the master suite and guest room, with a bathroom just across the hall for guests.

"There's a powder room off the foyer," Paul shouted from the kitchen. "I updated the MLS, but it doesn't show."

Matt walked back into the room.

"Oh, here I am shouting after you and you're here. So, what do you think?"

"I'll take it."

"Yeah?" Paul asked.

"Yeah," Matt said definitively.

"Great let's get the paperwork done. You won't regret it. This house is a major steal."

CHAPTER 8

Margo

"Margo, your sister's calling." Chelsea peered around her computer, from the other side of the farm table they shared as a desk.

Margo's head popped up. She looked toward Kirby's office, which was actually the larger of the guest bedrooms in the main house.

"Thanks, Chels." She smiled and started to gather her things.

Chelsea had become her first friend at work—really, her only friend at work if she didn't count Kirby, which Margo didn't. Chelsea was the Blush & Bashful graphics intern. She hadn't graduated yet. She had a few more credits to meet her requirements, but already her résumé trumped Margo's. On scholarship to NYU, Chelsea worked two jobs to stay in school and still maintained a 4.0 GPA. Blush & Bashful was her third internship in just two years. Old Margo would have hated Chelsea; moreover, Old Margo would have been jealous of Chelsea. New Margo, however, decided to get to know her and, dare she say, learn from her. Margo was quickly realizing her reflex to make every man, woman, and child her competition—be it for a job, parking spot, or place in line at the fro-yo counter—was an approach that hadn't served her, or the five-year-old crying behind her in line at Pinkberry, well. She was determined to take on a new skin, one that said, there's room for everyone at the top, even those, like herself, who had previously so valiantly failed.

Forty-seven days had flown by since Margo agreed to help her sister move both home and office into her Beverly Crest house, which was more of an estate boasting a four-car garage, two-bedroom guesthouse, pool, four-bedroom main house, and a bonus artist's studio that had become Blush & Bashful's prop closet. Kirby's promise of a part-time freelancing gig had organically grown into a semi-permanent position, for which Margo wasn't about to complain. Truth was, it felt good to feel like a professional again—or feel like a professional for the first time, seeing as she'd never really gotten her career off the ground for her to be revisiting it. Each day brought something different, and she arrived ready to work, thrusting herself into any task that came her way. She coveted the editorial desk but didn't dare speak it, instead doing whatever was asked of her.

She still lived at home, but thanks to her hours at B&B, housesitting for the Sneels, Parkers, and Cochrans and a few hours here and there nannying for the Nelsons, she'd managed to scrounge together more money than she'd ever seen in her bank account, save for those few instances when her scholarship money transferred in so she could, in turn, write a check to the Brown registrar's office for her tuition. *This* money was different. She had earned it, and each time she looked at her account she found herself in awe. Every red cent of that money and the money yet to be earned was dog-eared for her eventual apartment.

"Are you over there looking at your account again, counting that money like Johnny Depp in *Blow*?" Chelsea asked, one cheek puffed out to accommodate her sour apple Blow Pop addiction as she clacked on her keyboard.

Sitting across from Chelsea, Margo had quickly learned, meant sitting across from all of Chelsea's clicks—keyboard clicks, nails on a phone screen clicks, teeth against a Blow Pop clicks, bubble gum bubble clicks, LaCroix can opening clicks, and, of course, as the only other nice girl in the office, Margo's literal clique.

"I gotta print that money if I'm gonna move out, Chels," Margo answered with mock reverence.

Chelsea rolled her eyes and shifted her lollipop to the other cheek. "I don't get it. Why don't you live *here*?" her eyes looking around the room to punctuate her point before shifting back to Margo. "You are, after all, the boss's sister. Isn't that one of the perks of a successful sibling? Sponging off them?"

"She gave me a job, that's enough of me to ask of her." Margo continued tossing things into her bag as she spoke. "Hey, do me a favor, look at the calendar and tell me where I'm going." She was beyond excited for their company-wide 1:00 p.m. creative meeting, the very one she'd waited for all week, scheming with Chelsea for her big plans.

"Ummm, conference room Rose. Ford's leading." A conspiratorial smile crossed Chelsea's face, "And, you're gonna blow his mind with your idea—maybe something else if you'd ask him out already."

Margo ignored the bait Chelsea was dangling to dish on her crush. "Not Dorothy?" she asked.

"Nope, IT has Dorothy on lock."

They both sighed. Who would have thought that naming the Blush & Bashful conference rooms after *The Golden Girls* would have had such a lasting impact on the entire office? For Kirby and Margo, it just made sense. They'd never mistake a meeting with Sophia for a call with Rose. The staff had taken it to a whole new level. They'd made cardboard cutouts and monthly cheesecake Fridays were set on the calendar. Kirby and David encouraged it. "We're not just creating a company; we're creating a culture."

She wasn't lying. In the 40-odd days since Margo had been there, they'd already turned to her to amp up the cleverness for the staff and their consumers. "We want them in on it too. This isn't some bank where the CEO is some rich white dude who gives investor updates on a mass conference line to their shareholders. It's me, and I'm just like the girls who buy our things."

What shocked Margo most was that as the girl who dreamed of covering wars and the refugee crisis, she oddly loved the creative challenge of it all. When Kirby asked her and Chelsea to dream up themed sticker sheets to go in each order, Margo was pleased as punch. They'd done 12 of them—Margo art directing and concepting, Chelsea drawing and laying them out. Her favorite so far was an entire sheet dedicated to the "men we love and the animals we'd love to cuddle," as Kirby had put it. They'd done Ryan Gosling's head on a gosling body. Chris Pratt's face on a wolf pup. Adam Levine on a lamb. They were ridiculous and ridiculously cute. *The same cannot be said for famine*, Margo thought.

"You better get going. You don't want to keep lover boy waiting, especially not when you're about to wow 'em." Chelsea smiled coyly. "And seriously even if I had to float in that pool on a pool raft, I'd just tell Kirby I wanna live here."

"Stop calling him lover boy," Margo admonished, looking to see who was within earshot.

"Go," Chelsea commanded, pointing her Blow Pop toward the conference room. "Knock 'em dead!"

CHAPTER 9

Matt

"What do you mean, my car payment didn't go through? What car payment?" Matt howled into the phone while aggressively gesturing a stop signal to the flatbed truck driver, who was attempting, and succeeding, at repo'ing his car. Putting his hand over the phone mic, "Hold on man, I've got the woman on the phone who's going to clear up this entire mess."

"I got orders, buddy," the coverall-clad man said continuing to use the truck joystick to lower the flatbed to the driveway apron, fully ignoring Matt's meltdown.

"I'm sorry, Mr. Milles-Lade, but I'm not the woman who can clear this up," the cotton-candy toned customer service rep said politely into his ear. "All I can tell you is that six months ago your card started declining the payment and our attempts to notify you of the issue went unanswered. I wish I could help you, but even if you pay me today over the phone, I have a feeling that man in your driveway is hauling your car away no matter what. There's just no authority I have at this point to stop him."

Without even hanging up, Matt let his hand with the phone fall to his side. He watched, helplessly, as the flatbed engine whirred into gear hauling his Mercedes G-Wagon up into position on the back of the truck.

The past 47 days had sucked, an endless succession of shit sandwiches all served up to Matt on a silver platter, with each one of them depleting his bank account.

For starters, the house on Woodland had turned out to be a steal...literally. Excited for his new start and determined not to let another listing slip through his fingers, Matt had signed the paperwork on the spot and immediately withdrew the $5,000 cashier's check Paul required to make the house his. As he handed it over, "This security deposit allows me to take the listing off the market with one click," Paul purred in his lush, indistinguishable accent.

On the ride home, Matt blared Creed's "With Arms Wide Open," his go-to hype song. With the windows down and the breeze on his face, he felt liberated, like he'd just won the big game. *Not even Tiff is gonna bring me down*, he thought.

Paul said he'd get the lease countersigned by his clients in Sweden that night, grab the tenant keys from his lockbox, and run Matt's credit report. "Protocol, just to have on file, mate."

They agreed to meet the next day at noon to hand over the keys and finalize the paperwork. Matt arrived and waited. No Paul. He called the number. No answer. He waited some more and tried calling again. He texted. Undeliverable. Then, the call just stopped going through. Matt's uneasiness shifted into annoyance. *I paid that motherfucker $5,000,* he thought, *where is he?* After an hour he got in his car and drove to the house next door. Parking on the apron of the drive, he got out and walked to the call box.

A man's voice crackled over the line. "Just leave the packages at the door."

"Um, I'm not the delivery guy, sir. I had a question about the house next door."

"And," the nameless voice said through the speaker, annoyance hanging on the edges of his tone.

Matt bent forward, hands on his knees, talking directly into the call box, "I rented it, but the agent hasn't shown up...."

"Call Airbnb."

"What's Airbnb got to do with this?"

"Didn't you rent it through them?"

"No, I rented it through an agent named Paul. A real estate agent. To live here."

"What do you mean live *here*?"

"Well not *here*, THERE. I mean live *there* as in move in next door to you."

Matt heard a clatter, then a click. *Did this douche just hang up on me?* He stood and peered over the hedge. A silver-haired man walked out the front door, clicking a remote. The heavy gate lumbered open. Matt extended his hand to shake. "Hi, I'm Matt, your new neighbor."

The man looked confused. "Which house?"

"That one," Matt said gesturing to the 1940s Spanish Revival home he'd leased the day before.

"That one?" the man repeated, nodding his head in the same direction of the same house Matt had just pointed at.

"Yes, that one."

"Son, you didn't rent that house."

"What?" Matt squinted in confusion and then snorted a laugh. "I certainly did."

"No, you didn't. That house has been owned by the Donahue family for decades. When Mr. Donahue died two years ago, Mrs. Donahue decided to go live in Bordeaux. Took up painting. I made sure her gardeners mowed and took care of the yard while she was gone. Then, her grandkids talked her into listing it on Airbnb. She's made a killing renting it out ever since. Goes for $500 a day. It's booked solid. You didn't rent *that house* unless you rented it from *her*."

Matt's head was on a swivel, turning back and forth between the house he thought was his until 2.3 seconds ago and the man trying to tell him he'd been swindled.

"What?"

"Son, I think we should call the police. You have your phone?"

Five days later after multiple calls to Bordeaux, four trips to the police station, and two visits from FBI agents Tack and Martin, Matt had a much clearer picture of what had happened. Paul, the realtor with his haughty Thurston Howell accent and pinstriped suit, was actually Daryl Brigget of Bernice, Louisiana. Daryl had a real estate license and a record for petty theft and grand larceny. He was a con artist. His scam was easy. He posted a listing for a home on livehere.com. Livehere checked the legitimacy of the listing. It cleared. Why? Because it was an actual listing. It's just that it wasn't Paul-slash-Daryl's actual listing. So when Matt messaged him about that house, Paul responded and said that the house he was inquiring about had already been leased, but he had a second, pocket listing that he could get Matt in to see right away. Matt jumped on it, went to Woodland Canyon, and fell in love with the house. Bada-bing-bada-boom, Matt gave

Paul-Daryl 5Gs and signed his fake fucking lease. Quite the scam in a hot market. Finding a last-minute listing is like striking gold. Matt didn't think twice about turning over the money. And for anyone who did, Paul-slash-Daryl had his grifter girlfriend waiting in a rental car. Parked three doors down in a beat-up Honda Civic and decked out in a faux fur with an even more faux Birkin on her arm, she was one text away from rushing in waving a check, threatening to steal the house out from under any mark who might have cold feet.

Matt hadn't required that. He'd fallen for the con, hook, line, and sinker, the minute the door swung open. Now his bank account was $5,000 lighter and his dad was still holding strong on withholding his trust.

"Sign here," the repo man demanded, shaking Matt back to reality.

"No, I'm not signing anything."

"Don't matter much to me, buddy," Karl said, the name on his work shirt declaring his identity. "I got what I need." He gestured toward the car with his head. He gave Matt a salute, got in, and drove away.

"Sucks to be you, Matty."

"Don't call me that, Tiff," Matt growled, his back to her as he watched his car pull out of the drive and onto the road.

"Forget to pay the bill?" she asked syrupy sweet. "What a shame. No trust fund. No car. Your social life is really taking off."

Matt ignored her, walked inside, and headed to his room, or what was left of it. Last week, Tiff and his dad listed the house. A team of stagers had arrived and hauled his things out, replacing everything in his room with the entire contents of the Restoration Hardware catalog, complete with requisite metal airplane propeller on one wall and a giant clock on the other. It was awful. "The house'll sell better if they don't think it comes with a man-child living in the upstairs bedroom," Tiff had informed him in front of her army of interior ninjas.

Matt was running out of the time and cash he needed to find a new place. So, he entered a realm he never thought he'd have to, the roommate section on livehere. As the page loaded, he gave himself a pep talk. *You don't have to hang out with them. They're not a friend, they're just a means to an end.* The screen came into view. He clicked on the first one.

37, single after divorce, covering costs for 2 homes and 2 kids has me pinching pennies. Having a roommate will help me meet my monthly budget. Will share whole home. Applicants must be well kempt and kind. A sense of humor is preferred. Not looking to be friends, buddies, or bros. APPLICANT #3457

He seems normal. Maybe it's good that he's a bit older than me, Matt thought as he proceeded to the real estate images of the home, clicking through each one. It was a simple duplex in West Hollywood with three bedrooms. It was basic but not terrible. *Fuck it*, Matt thought. He clicked apply, punched in the applicant code and a message box appeared. TYPE MESSAGE HERE. ACCEPTED APPLICANTS WILL RECEIVE A RESPONSE FROM THE LISTER. Matt typed.

Hi, I'm Matt. 26. Born and raised in Los Angeles. Graduated UCLA. Looking for a roommate to cut costs as well. Definitely have a sense of humor. Let me know if the room is still available.

Matt put his phone down—*one submission's enough, for now*, he reasoned. Just as he put his feet up, his phone dinged. It was from livehere.com. He opened the app to find a message from Applicant #3457. It read, "Show me a picture of your feet."

"Well, I think we know why you got divorced, buddy," Matt said aloud.

CHAPTER 10

Margo

Margo entered the conference room. Rose had floor-to-ceiling retractable doors on one end that were easily pushed back, making its patio, appropriately entitled Shady Pines, the spill-over seating needed for this company-wide meeting. She carefully selected her seat. It was important to her that she carve out her own space in the company. "I don't want people thinking I didn't earn my spot just because I'm Kirby's sister," she'd told Chelsea over happy hour.

She laid out her notebook on the conference table. Using her best GOOP-learned breathing technique she centered herself. She hadn't shared her idea for this inaugural editorial shoot with anyone, save for Chelsea, whom she'd told just four hours earlier as they sat by the pool working. They often gathered there in the morning, working before the day got hot, and they were forced back inside. Chelsea's wild enthusiasm for her idea had bolstered her confidence. She felt prepared. She wanted to wow her sister and Ford. More importantly, she wanted to feel that *thing* again, that surge she got when she knew she was killing it in a pitch meeting. This was her chance.

Kirby walked in with Ford directly behind her and David on his tail. They each said their hellos to the group. "Today is a big day, because it marks the moment we're moving beyond just retail concepts to reach our true north, editorial. But, we aren't going there alone. We have all of you," Kirby announced as she looked around the room. Buyers, social, IT, PR—everyone was here. "Brainstorms like these are something that will set us apart. This isn't about your title or time here. It's about the best idea in the room winning. So with that, I turn it over to you to wow us. Topping our board today is our inaugural shoot. The pool party shoot. Go!"

Margo felt herself soar on the inside. Immediately, she raised her hand to go first. She'd have given anything to have had this meeting include the interns, so Chelsea could be there cheering her on. She knew she wasn't just raising a hand; she was raising the bar on her role at Blush & Bashful with this idea. A smile spread across her face, and a confidence brimmed in her heart as she waited to be called upon. She opened her mouth to speak, to say out loud she'd love to kick it off when a voice from the back of the room boomed.

"I don't know if there's a talking stick we pass around, but I got to jump the line. I can't keep this one to myself."

Margo's hand fell. Her head pivoted, although she already knew who was speaking, the one woman on the team that Margo despised, her boss. But, even Margo didn't expect what came next. This villain stood and began to evangelize what was, up until 3.2 seconds ago, *Margo*'s idea for Blush & Bashful's editorial debut. As this idea-thief spoke, Margo's jaw hit the floor. Her blood began to boil. She was dumbfounded, appalled, enraged as Margaux, her nemesis by the same name, but spelled with an 'x,' began to present what was *hers* to share just moments before.

Seething, Margo called upon every cellular fiber in her body in an attempt to metaphysically will this traitor, Fake Margaux, as she and Chelsea referred to her their first week on the job, to look her way. Of course, clad in a pale pink, crushed velvet duster, '80s inspired floral jumpsuit and, while it pained Margo to admit it, very cute shoe-booties, Fake Margaux's doe eyes fell everywhere in the room but upon Real Margo.

When she was done speaking, Ford spoke. "Well, look who showed up to play."

He nodded appreciatively at her and her fake *fucking* idea. Real Margo reflexively glared at him for his unknowing betrayal. Fake Margaux, however, responded to his praise, flashing her brilliantly bleached white teeth and tacking on a dose of phony humility—an emotion she evoked by blushing on command and coyly tucking a tendril of her loosely beach-waved hair behind her ear as she cast her chin down and her eyes up at Ford.

Oh, she's good. I'm gonna put bleach in her Swell bottle, Margo thought.

The moment they'd met this same-named imposter, Chelsea called it.

"I can't wait to work alongside you both," Fake Margaux said, exuding the kind of cheer reserved for someone on methamphetamines.

"Me too!" Chelsea replied boisterously, matching her cheerleader-level enthusiasm. As Blush & Bashful's new hire with the same name walked away, Chelsea leaned towards Margo, "That girl's a serial killer. I feel it."

And by all accounts, Chelsea was right, but this display in the conference room took her skills as a corporate sociopath to a whole new level.

Her full name is Margaux Dubois, which sounds really French—shocker, it's not. "I'm from a little town in the middle of a big corn field in Iowa, but not big enough for my dreams," she'd shared.

Chelsea had glanced at Margo with a look that said, "Do you want to kill her or should I?" Margo's sweet smile responded back, "I just had a mani. You got this."

She'd been hired a week after real Margo and much like *The Bachelor* franchise, which customarily nicknames anyone who shares the same name—à la Ashley I or Becca K—her name had been immediately appropriated. Margaux Dubois was tagged Margaux X by Ford, bestowed with a deep bow on day one. By day two, Ford had flirtatiously shortened it to X Factor. Day three, Tavis, Blush & Bashful's head of fashion styling, declared her, "The Divine Lady X," when Brad in IT did what every IT guy does, mislabeled her workstation X, Lady. So, Brent, Fake Margaux's junior assistant on her integrated marketing team, rebranded her X Marks the Spot to solve the snafu. Soon thereafter, thanks to a call sheet error by a photo intern where she was infamously titled MX Dubois, the nickname Mix was born and stuck.

"Well done, Mix," Ford said as he looked to Kirby for confirmation of her unspoken agreement, which she gave in the form of a head nod. "Right out of the gate and looks like we've got our winner—one that's going to require all of us to pull it off." Ford beamed, looking mouth-wateringly handsome in worn vintage Levi's, a white button-down, and brown combat boots. "It's shoots like these," he continued as he looked around the room at the entire social and marketing teams that reported into him as digital and marketing VP, as well as all the other departments present, "big ideas, like these, are the perfect bridge between the blogosphere and social media. And with these visuals they'll not only be drooling, they'll be resharing and reposting our campaign all across Grid.it and social. I think I speak for all of us when I say you killed it, Mix! Bravo!"

He applauded and the room followed suit. Mix preened under the praise. Margo couldn't tell if her head was still on her body or if it had exploded all over the room. What struck her was how easily Mix had presented what was Margo's brainchild. She hadn't even paused as she shared it. She launched in as if she'd woken up that morning, yawned, and found Margo's entire plan scrolled across her Dreams notebook on her bedside table.

What a fool I am, Margo thought. She'd shared her entire plan with Chelsea that morning as they sat out by the pool, feeling confident for the first time to do so. She hadn't noticed that Mix was even there. She and Chelsea were under an umbrella. Mix was tucked inside a cabana, headphones on, scrolling notes in her notebook, quiet as a church mouse *or a terrorist,* Margo thought. Even when Margo had spied her, she'd thought that Mix, with her headphones on, hadn't heard. *Man, was I wrong,* her eyes now narrowed upon Mix in the B&B conference room as she recalled the morning.

"Oh my gosh, M, it's so good. They're gonna fall out," Chelsea had gushed that morning.

"Do you really think so?" Margo asked, fishing for compliments and approval.

"Absolutely. Tell me again, from the top what you're seeing, just so we can make sure you sell the visual impact of it. It's so good! This is gonna be your first shoot. I know it! How did you not tell me this idea until now? They have to give it to you! *Have* to!"

She and Chelsea had grabbed hands like two girls do when one tells the other she's engaged. Chelsea was Margo's unexpected ride or die at Blush & Bashful, and Margo was beginning to think well beyond the office walls as well.

"Okay, well, we all know Kirby named the site Blush & Bashful both as a tongue–in-cheek jab at Millennial Pink and in honor of our undying love for all cinema of the '80s and early '90s. We've been building our level of editorial, but this shoot marks our first real transition from a retail site to a full editorial platform. So, like Shelby's wedding, in the movie *Steel Magnolias*, drenched in her colors of Blush & Bashful, we'll turn the water blush, the Astroturf bashful, the umbrellas, the bathing suits, the pool floats, the Speedos and swim trunks, the drinks, the lawn chairs, the vintage Mercedes that we'll pull up by the fountain, which we'll pack full with pink sequins, the dog, all of it in our colors of blush and bashful for a shoot. It'll feel Slim Aarons iconic and Blush & Bashful branded. We'll rely on the '80s for hair, big like Truvy's, barrel curls like Shelby's, mullets for the boys and girls too. We'll tuck in all kinds of takeaway that we can digitally capture as content on our channel—our choosing of the perfect pink for the Mercedes, how we got the pool pink, the mix of the martini, the hair for all the models, all of it will be shareable as tutorials. Not only that, we can create ancillary content like how to develop a theme for your event or best fashion of the '80s. We'll use this shoot not only to launch our editorial, but be the foundation for our first cooking, entertaining, beauty, and lifestyle segments. Since this is digital, we'll be able to bring it to life here. Then, host a party featuring some of our most favorite Grid.it influencers. They'll do the heavy lifting on getting us noticed once it all goes live. Every inch of this lawn will be a Grid.it paradise. Everyone else will be doing beer Koozies in red, white, and blue, while our Founding Fathers will have on pink powder wigs and be bowing down to today's modern woman, after all, the future is female. This company proves that. It's a lot, but I've already started mapping it out. Now we just need to come together to get it done."

"Nailed it!" Chelsea exclaimed.

"Yeah?" Margo asked unsure.

"Yes," Chelsea confirmed.

Now, four hours later, sitting in the conference room, blindsided by Mix's stealing of her idea, Margo's blood had gone from boiling to cold as ice and her heart from beating out of her chest to black as coal with anger. She sat frozen in disbelief.

"Looks like Margo's in a state of shock," Ford said, shaking her back to the room.

"What?" Margo croaked.

"Are you shocked or just planning how you're going to murder this shoot?" Ford asked jovially as Kirby and the rest of the room looked at her expectantly.

"Something like that," Margo laughed. Her chest heaved like the little girl in *The Exorcist*.

She and Mix made eye contact for the first time across the room. Mix raised one deceitful eyebrow. Margo had a vision of herself climbing across the desks like a rabid animal and tackling her to the floor.

"Great job, Mix!" Kirby boomed, both girls turning to look at their chief creative officer and founder.

Mix's smile grew as she crossed her hand over her chest and bowed her head reverently in thanks to Kirby. Margo smiled on the outside, while her vision on the inside grew from a headlock to her literally dragging Mix by her hair across the room as she screamed for mercy.

"Get with Margo after the meeting. She'll run second on this project." Margo's heart literally stopped as she took in Kirby's words. "She's so great at bringing an idea to life, Mix, you'd almost think she thought it up herself."

CHAPTER 11

Matt

Matt weaved his way down the hall into the kitchen. The smell of coffee rich in the air. He grabbed a mug and reached for the coffee carafe when a note stopped him. "Make your own damn coffee. Love, Tiff," with a heart dotting the *i*. Matt cursed under his breath.

He hadn't slept well last night. After Applicant #3457 had asked to see his feet, he'd pinged Matt with a series of dick pics, shirtless selfies, and a dozen sexts that would make even the seediest of bathroom walls—and grammar teachers everywhere—cringe.

So, this is what girls put up with, Matt thought grimacing, noting Applicant #3457 had taken the time to cut his head out of frame but not the overflowing ashtray and empty Red Bull cans that sat atop his dresser. *Classy*, Matt observed.

When the first dick pic arrived, Matt had literally jumped back from the screen. He'd seen dick pics, but this one was alarming. Matt turned his phone clockwise, and then counterclockwise, trying to understand how *this* dude had gotten *that* angle.

The penis really isn't photogenic. Hard or flaccid, the angles just are not good, Matt observed.

Out of fear for what might arrive next, Matt searched "how to block someone on livehere.com." He then immediately fell down the digital rabbit hole entitled 'my livehere roommate destroyed my life.' At 2:30 a.m., he forced himself to power down both his phone and the idea that he was roommate material, solemnly swearing to never return to livehere's roommate section again, unless he got vaccinated for gonorrhea.

Matt yawned and shuffled to the pantry, pulling down the coffee canister. It felt light. He opened the jar. Inside, a second note: "But first, you'll have to buy it..." Matt's head fell back. This time he cursed aloud.

"Fuck livehere, I already got a nightmare roommate in Tiff," he growled.

"You want eggs?" Zinny asked behind him, the *w* sounding more like a *v*.

He turned to see her standing with a bag of groceries resting on her thrust-out hip.

"Coffee," Matt said as if he'd been marooned in the desert for days.

"Yes, I make. I see Miss Tiff dump coffee just to be rude. So I go to store." She had a look of disgust on her face, her mouth in a downward frown mirroring Robert De Niro's scowl.

"Zin, you're the best." Matt took the heavy bag from her arms and placed it on the island. His phone dinged as he slid a carton of eggs into the fridge. A text from Ian

Where you at?

Matt paused, even though he and Ian had hardly seen one another in two years they remained tight from rooming together at boarding school and then college.

At home, why?

Planning a trip between installations in Madrid and Rome. Come so we can party.

Matt's fingers hovered over the screen. Ian's life was far more interesting than his. Ian was an artist, but in school, his father, a record exec in LA, had forced him to study what Mr. Kehai described as an "actual job." Ian complied but upon graduation, he'd gone rogue. Following his gut, he combined his art with his business degree for a combination that landed him on the Forbes Young Millionaires list by the age of 24. Wisely, he'd kept the contacts he'd made interning for his dad's label. He approached them, asking for some space on their concert grounds to create a mammoth art installation. The placement resulted in his work getting splashed all across Grid.it, which led to his concert pop-ups touring on their own as standalone traveling installations. So far they'd grossed millions for Ian.

His first one, *Danica,* was an homage to Ian's childhood crush. Ginormous banana clips the size of hammocks and walls covered with bow barrettes greeted attendees. Giant My Little Ponies with enormous Pegasus wings stood proudly at the entrance. Ian covered the gallery walls with their pastel, synthetic hair, and turned their now-large combs into swings that begged to be swung upon. Puffy stickers the size of giant flat-screen TVs adorned the walls. One room was entirely dedicated to Little Debbie Snacks. The installation, like their muse, smelled softly of grape bubble gum and Love's Baby Soft, with corresponding scratch and sniff stickers sold in the gift shop. *Danica* was a living breathing Grid.it utopia, and girls, especially, were drawn to it like moths to their childhood flame.

Money's a bit tight. Not sure I can swing it.

WTF. M$TT?! Brooks strikes again? Whatever it is, tell me when you get here. I'll cover you. You just get to the airport.

Matt hesitated. His muscle memory was to avoid responsibility. Ian was giving him a chance to do just that, but Matt didn't want to run this time. He wanted to stay. He wanted to show his dad—and himself, he was starting to think—that he could stand on his own two feet. When he was in school, his dad's money made him cool. It was the reason he got into trouble and how he paid to get out of it. But what once made him cool, was now a source of shame, of hushed whispers. "He's just a trust funder." He saw the respect that Ian got. Ian had done it himself, in spite of his father. *Time for me to catch up*, Matt thought as he stared at the screen.

Sorry buddy, gotta sit this one out. Catch you next time?
You better.

Matt felt a sense of pride, like maybe this tiny step showed something was changing inside him for the better.

"Oh shit. I go to store for coffee and forget it," Zinny said, the word *shit* sounding like *sheet*.

Matt looked up from where he was leaning, his entire torso resting atop the marble island, his feet casually crossed as he stood.

"Nope, you already went once. I'll go. Give me a few to get dressed." Matt stood.

"You sure, because," Zinny began.

"Zin, I thought we discussed this. You're on the payroll of Mr. Milles-Lade and me, not his son," Tiff said walking into the room. "Your time is to be dedicated to the duties that further *our* household." Tiff's tone decidedly declaring Zinny the help.

Zinny didn't respond, her face was the picture of calm. Matt could tell on the inside she was using the spatula in her hand to cut out Tiff's tongue. Her espionage-level poker face would not betray her, by showing one iota of the disdain Matt could only guess she held for Tiff.

"Fuck you, Tiff!" Matt boomed from his spot at the end of the island.

"Do not speak to me that way in this house. In MY house!" Tiff shot back, her eyes aflame.

Matt chortled. "Your house? I don't think so, Tiff. Until you met my dad you were living in an economy apartment in Ventura. So, dial back the lady of the manor shit, why don'tcha?" He began to walk toward the door. "Zin, I'll be back with your coffee. Don't worry about my egg. I'm a big boy," he said with a sugar cane smile directed at Tiff.

"A big boy who depends on daddy for everything," Tiff said smarmily as she set her baby blue Birkin on the counter, along with a Fred Segal shopping bag.

Matt stopped in the doorway and turned back to face her. He walked back toward her. "You know what, Tiff, I don't think you should throw stones. Last time I checked there's no ring on that finger. So, when Daddy Warbucks drops you, I hope you can fit as much cash as you can into that bag before you go. You'll need it."

Tiff's eyes narrowed. Then with very little thought for her actions, she raised the glass water bottle that remained in her hand and threw it directly at Matt. He ducked as the bottle hit the wall denting it before it fell to the floor and shattered.

Matt slowly stood, he looked at the wall and then back at Tiff. She held herself defiantly, as if in a fighter's stance.

"What the actual fuck, Tiff?" Matt's volume at a shout.

"Get out!" she spat at him as she took her first step toward him.

Zinny stepped in her path and slowly shook her head, raising her hands up to halt her. "Now, now, Miss Tiff. We stop. Mr. Matt, you go get coffee. Ms. Tiff and I stay here and talk."

Time froze. Matt turned and walked toward the door, shedding his robe as he went, grabbing clothes off the dryer as he walked out. With his car repo'ed he took the guest Volvo. He was halfway down the hill when a text came in. He waited to read it until he pulled into the small corner parking lot of the café that resided halfway down the hill from their Bel-Air home, Coyote Café. It was one of the rare remaining canyon coffee shops. On any given weekend, all manner of celebrities could be found there, bedhead and all. There was no place for the paparazzi to stand and snap their picture on the way in or out. It was a hidden gem that only locals knew about. Their hours were strange, but their sandwiches were amazing, and yet Matt couldn't remember the last time he'd been there. It was a hole in the wall that lacked any real décor but made up for it by the way they took care of their customers. As Matt idled in the lot, he read the text.

You're out of chances, Son. Find a new place to live.

Matt's blood boiled as he waited for a sliver of parking space to open. He slid the car into park when a text from Tiff arrived.

You did this to yourself.

In that moment, the petty part of Matt wanted to tell her about the other girls, to get revenge, to ruin her life like she seemed dead set on doing to his. Just as he began to type the one line that would bring her world crashing down—*My dad's cheating on you*—his phone dinged.

Applicant #3457 was back at it, "Fucking A," Matt said aloud.

He opened the app and its corresponding inbox. A message blinked. It read: *I'll show you mine if you show me yours*. Matt let his head fall back on the headrest. A part of him was grateful he hadn't hit send on his text to Tiff. Matt was many things. Mean was not one of them. Knowing he couldn't be cruel, he decided to seek revenge more cleverly. He reopened livehere and his message from Applicant #3457 and responded.

Sure, text me instead tho…

Then he typed in Tiff's cell phone number.

Send more pics please. [rainbow emoji].

With that, he threw his phone on the dash and strode in for coffee.

CHAPTER 12

Margo

"Canyon, now!" Margo demanded as she dashed past Chelsea, carelessly throwing her bag onto her side of the desk causing its contents to spill out onto the floor.

Chelsea's face lined with worry as she jumped up to grab at the falling items. With her headphones still on, her head jerked back as if she'd been clotheslined. "Shit!" she said, yanking the headphones off. "Margo?" she hissed after her friend.

Margo didn't hear her or didn't care about the mess she'd just made, behavior completely uncharacteristic of this girl who organized her desk daily.

"I can't function if there's clutter," Margo had said day one, eyeing Chelsea's side of the desk.

Chelsea had immediately attempted to bring her Polaroid and Instax cameras, stash of crystals, rainbow stapler, caticorn pencil cup, and sushi erasers back into order. Even now she wrestled daily to rein in her Post-it and paper clip obsession, all in the name of Margo, whom she'd known was a soul sister the moment they met. Now, as she frantically hoisted Margo's laptop, notebook, and pens back up onto her desk, she couldn't fathom what had gone wrong in the morning meeting to cause this obvious meltdown. Choosing the worry for her friend over the spilled contents of the bag, Chelsea shoved the remaining items under the desk and started after Margo. Margo turned to make sure Chelsea was in her wake. When she saw Chelsea wasn't, she hissed, "Now, Chelsea!"

"Coming," Chelsea shot back, picking up her pace. She was half walking, half running, mimicking the stride of an aerobic mall walker, arms swinging, hips jutting side to side. Now within striking distance, Chelsea shout-whispered, "Margo, what's happening?"

Margo stopped and swung to face her so fast that Chelsea recoiled to avoid slamming into her. Margo spat out one word, "Mix," an intense loathing in her voice. She wagged her finger in Chelsea's face, an almost rabid setting of her jaw. Then even more wild-eyed came the word "mine," before ending on a definitive statement of "that bitch." Margo pointed defiantly in the direction of Mix's office.

Chelsea reflexively pushed Margo's outstretched arm down. "Margo, stop," she said, as Margo spun out of her hold and yanked the door open as if she were pulling it off its hinges. Chelsea looked back, feverishly, hoping no one saw them. When the door slammed shut behind her, she yelped. She turned and flung it back open, crashing out onto the pool deck in the process. Tavis, confused, looked up from his seat. Feigning normalcy, Chelsea smiled and casually tucked her hair behind her ear as if it weren't on fire. Tavis went back to what he was doing. Chelsea turned, searching for Margo, finding her already climbing toward the upper deck patio that hung out into the canyon. She shot across the cement, now taking long strides like a pole vaulter bounding toward her friend.

"Margo, wait, hold on," she said more winded by her concern than the climb to the patio. "You're scaring me."

Chelsea crested the green grass of the terrace patio— called the Lanai, for its cluster of green and pink striped daybeds and banana leaf–patterned umbrellas all resting atop the patch of mountain that hung out over the canyon. It was the most coveted of the gathering spots for the staff. Chelsea, afraid of heights, had seen the Lanai on her new employee office tour. She had vowed never to set foot on it. Clearly, *this* was an extenuating circumstance that required her to lift her embargo. She may have only gotten to know Margo a few months prior, but the importance of their friendship had already shifted her DNA.

Chelsea had always been a lone wolf, never needing a pack. She never had many girlfriends. Even as a kid she was happiest reading on the hammock in her backyard. As she got older, she never desired to fit in or follow the crowd. She'd had an artist's soul and was more focused on using her spare time to create than conform.

In high school when all the other girls were at the mall, Chelsea was at the art store. When her classmates spent Friday nights getting drunk in the field behind Stellt Farm, Chelsea was holed up in her room reading about French Modernism or Alex Katz. She went to prom in black leather combat boots, a sequined high-waisted pencil skirt, and a fitted T-shirt knotted in the back. Like Andie Walsh, Molly Ringwald's character in *Pretty in Pink*, Chelsea had dreamed up the outfit herself, and then spent weeks making that skirt and the most exquisite statement earrings Lititz, PA, had ever seen.

Her mother, forever encouraging her individuality, had helped her purchase everything she needed, including the two tuna-can-size acrylic hoops and quarter-size buttons, to make the clip earrings. With TLC's "Waterfalls" booming through her stereo speakers and her mother making tomato and cheese sandwiches in the kitchen, Chelsea had turned the dining room into her atelier. She'd cut the fabric for the skirt—a decadent sapphire blue—and then painstakingly affixed all the sequins, tacking on a silk taffeta train and bustle off the back that would have made Rodarte drool. She arduously made dozens of small clay roses, each about the size of a pencil eraser, to adorn to her custom clip earrings. After they'd set and dried, she painted them an ombré of pinks. Then she glued them to the pieces of acrylic, placing pearls in among the roses. The final touch was a fringe of shocking-blue raffia adhered along the bottom. When she placed them in her ears, she and her mother gasped. Tears had sprung to her mother's eyes.

"You're beautiful, baby girl," Patricia Rogers declared, in awe of her daughter's creative beauty and yet wistful that her two full-time jobs hadn't allowed her the extra cash to buy Chelsea a real prom dress.

"Mom, stop," Chelsea said with an eye roll. "They are pretty great, though, right?"

Her mother gave a definitive nod.

"And, light as a feather," she observed as her mom started to ugly cry, "Moooom!" she crooned.

Her inspiration had been a pair by Ranjana Khan, designer and wife of Naeem Khan, also a fashion luminary. She'd obsessed over them, immediately trolling the Khan's respective Grid.it accounts deciding how she'd construct her own. She knew her mother didn't make enough money to foot the bill for the $495 pair she was in love with, so she didn't even ask for them as a prom splurge. In Chelsea's book, she'd take a well-made accessory—that could be worn again and again—over a cheap prom dress—worn once—any day. Besides, Chelsea loved the challenge of styling herself. Secretly she'd always wanted to style someone else.

"Mom, let's do a makeover this weekend. It'll be fun."

"Oh, Chels, I'm tired. I'll be lucky if I stay awake standing in the checkout line," her mother had replied with a yawn as they grabbed pizza fixings at the grocery store.

As she and her mother stood looking at her handiwork in the dining room mirror, she felt pride swell in her chest. She didn't say it out loud, but she thought her work rivaled the real deal.

As prom crept closer, Chelsea made her mother, who had sworn she could deliver a drop-dead up-do for prom, a mood board of the exact messy topknot she envisioned to complete her look. It was mostly a series of pictures of Claudia Schiffer from her Guess campaigns.

"Fashion was so good when you were in college, Mom."

"Yep, all bra tops and high-waisted jeans. Major," Patricia recalled sarcastically.

Then they watched Janet Jackson's "Love Will Never Do" video a hundred times, the one where she dances with Antonio Sabato Jr. on the beach.

"He's certainly handsome," her mother sighed each time he appeared on-screen. It was the first time Chelsea recalled hoping she'd be successful enough for the both of them, so her mom, who had given up everything when she found herself unexpectedly pregnant with Chelsea, could pursue her own great loves.

The day of prom, Patricia Rogers did Janet Jackson proud. She'd managed a perfectly messy topknot that sufficiently said, "I just rolled around in bed with Antonio Sabato Jr himself."

Her makeup, also done by her mother, had given Chelsea a pink-flushed cheek and dewy sheen that had "just been shagged" stamped all over it. Her mother, of course, saw neither of those references when she looked at Chelsea. Patricia Rogers only saw what a stunner her daughter was. But, Chelsea wasn't quite sure what she saw. She loved all the pieces and parts of her look but standing in front of the mirror she felt daunted by the night ahead.

"Come on then, let's take selfies and get you on your way, Cinderella," her mother said in an attempt to bolster her daughter's confidence.

When she walked into prom, solo, jaws hit the floor. For one brief moment the air left the room and there was only Chelsea giving everyone life. Of course, that lasted only a minute because, well, high school girls will be high school girls. Green with envy that they immediately guised with ridicule, the mean girls of Lititz High whispered and made snide comments. But deep down, they knew that Chelsea was spectacular. It's why they had to immediately ferret her out freshman year and remained unrelenting in the quest to tear her down. She was a threat. Chelsea was *that* girl in high school who was intrinsically cool, wickedly funny, and wildly interesting, and those girls knew it. Thing was, Chelsea didn't. She knew only what the girls wanted her to know.

They'd bullied her all four years of high school. Chelsea had no idea that underneath their spray tans, *Toddler & Tiaras* blow-outs, and the inappropriate prom cleavage that gave their date's dad a partial erection, these mean girls wanted to be her. She didn't get that each of them would kill for just one ounce of what Chelsea so effortlessly possessed. Instead she had come to believe their insults and the bullying that went on behind their keyboards. And, even today, as she chased Margo out of the office, wanting to be there for her friend, she still hadn't realized the reality of her beauty. The girls from high school were long gone, but it didn't matter because in their absence *Chelsea* had taken up their cause. Their abuse had worked. It had done what bullying was intended to do, soak bone deep and sear into her soul. As a result, Chelsea had become her own worst critic, with the ravaged shreds of her self-esteem to prove it.

Stealing herself from her fear, she stepped forward onto the patio, at first hunkered down like someone running toward a helicopter, crouched to avoid the blades. She white-knuckled the daybed before her, making her way around it toward her friend. "Margo, what is happening?"

Margo swung wildly back around to face her, "That bitch stole my idea!"

"Whaaaaaatttt?" Chelsea hissed. She shot upright, forgetting her fear, and walked directly toward Margo. "Who?" she asked deeply confused.

"Mix!" Margo exclaimed. "Mix, that monster! That fucking monster!"

"Wait, what in the actual hell are you talking about, Margo?"

Chelsea was utterly confused.

"Sit down and tell me everything. EVER-REE-THING," Chelsea said annunciating each syllable.

"In the meeting, word for word. She presented my idea for the Fourth of July campaign. My sister kicked it off and asked for our best ideas. I raised my hand to go and suddenly Mix chimed in from the back row—some shit about how she had to hop the line and then she launched headfirst into *MY* idea."

Chelsea's mouth opened and then closed, like she wanted to speak but couldn't form any words. "Wait, what?" she finally got out.

"I saw her when we were by the pool this morning, Chels." Margo's eyes were full of regret. "*After* I told you my idea, I saw her. She had her headphones on. I assumed she hadn't heard because we weren't talking loudly…" Margo trailed off, momentarily. "*Obviously*, I was wrong!"

"I'm so confused. Mix gave your *exact* idea, as if it was hers?" Chelsea asked as if trying to understand quantum physics for the first time.

"Yes, Chelsea. My exact idea," Margo said, impatiently. "I mean, we knew she was a bitch, but even I didn't think she could sink this low. What the hell do I do about this? Do I tell Kirby? Do I accuse her directly?" Margo searched Chelsea's face for answers.

"What did *they* say?" Chelsea asked, desperate to catch up to the crisis.

"They loved it. I mean, it's good to know that they liked it. But they think its hers. This is a nightmare. A fucking nightmare, Chels."

"I'm so shocked. I mean, this is bonkers, Margo."

"I know!" Margo bellowed. "I mean, what are my options? I tell Kirby? I tell Ford? I run her over with my car? Please tell me I get to run her over with my car. I mean, what do I do?" she pleaded for the second time.

"Okay, just hold on," Chelsea calmed, "we need to think this through. On *The Bachelor*, whenever one of the girls is deceitful, all the other girls lose their shit over it. Without fail one of them goes to the bachelor and complains, but he never sends the conniving girl home. He always cuts the tattletale loose," Chelsea said in a gush as she looked up at Margo for agreement.

"Chelsea, this is real life, not the fricking *Bachelor*!"

"First of all, *The Bachelor* is real life, thank you very much. Second of all, I'm not a social butterfly, Margo. I don't have a string of girlfriends to use as my go-by for girl code. *The Bachelor* is as close as I come to knowing what *Lord of the Flies, Girls Gone Wild* edition looks like, okay? And here's what I know, every season of *The Bachelor* there's a villain. Mix is ours. We need to play this right. We can't Corrine or Taylor this situation, you know what I mean?" Chelsea looked at Margo for validation.

"Not in the slightest," Margo said flatly.

"Point is, they didn't win. We need to win. So, we just have to figure out how to do that."

Margo nodded in agreement.

"First, Mix was your sister's *big* hire. She lured her away from Barney's. She's not gonna be so quick to attack the woman that she brought on to give B&B some clout, especially since it's outlandish that she took the idea. Second, is it your goal to get Mix fired?"

Chelsea stared down Margo.

"No," she continued answering for her, "it's to get credit for your work. Well, we can still do that even if she pretended if it was her idea. Heck, maybe by not immediately selling her down the river we come out even further ahead. Maybe in the end, you'll be an even bigger star for making it happen, even though Mix's intent was to claim that prize by being the one to share it first. Oh my gosh, she'll *hate* that!"

There was a devious glint in Chelsea's eyes.

"Third, and this is key, based on everything I have ever learned from reality television, we don't need to take Mix down. We need *Mix* to take Mix down. Her ego's so huge. If we play it against her she'll do the dirty work for us. I know it. She's a total Dorit."

Chelsea looked resolute.

"I don't know who the fuck Dorit is but, Chels, you're a genius!" Margo hugged her friend who beamed with pride.

"So, what do we do now?" Margo prodded.

"Well, we toy with her a bit, to see how she's going to play this. She's going to expect us to run to mommy or melt down. We're not gonna do either. We're going to let her think she's safe, that she has the upper hand, that she has all the power, lull her into a state of complacency. Then we make our move. She knows that we know that she knows, you know?"

"Actually, for the first time in this conversation, I do know," Margo said with a smirk.

"Could you not make fun of me of Margo? You have enough enemies," Chelsea mocked. "Besides, we have to go to our 3 p.m. and read the room. I bet she's already set the stage with your sister, laying the groundwork to protect herself. Going to Kirby in the wrong way might play right into her hand. She's very good at this. We can't underestimate her, Margo."

Margo frantically looked at the calendar on her phone, "3 p.m.? What 3 p.m.?"

"The Grid.it team is coming. Didn't you get the invite?"

"No. When did *that* happen?" Margo scrolled her emails looking for a missed schedule request.

"Oh, she's good," Chelsea admired as she thumbed through her emails. "Mix invited their entire development team to take us through their next big initiatives so we can increase our engagement." She turned her phone to face Margo, showing her the screen. "She didn't invite you. You know that's on purpose, right?"

Margo stared at the phone. Sure enough, the entire team had accepted the calendar entry, except Margo. She hadn't been invited.

Chelsea locked her phone and stood. "So, we go, act normal, like you were meant to be there because you clearly are! I mean, I'm just an intern and *I* got invited. Mix is going to know you crashed. Might freak her out a bit. Consider today, day one of *sweep the leg*."

"Sweep the leg?" Margo asked puzzled, blocking the sun from her eyes as she looked up at Chelsea.

"Okay, really, did you grow up in a cave? I mean, not watching *The Bachelor* hurts my feelings, but if you haven't seen *The Karate Kid* you're dead to me."

Chelsea eyed her friend. Margo grimaced.

"Margo," she boomed, yanking her friend to her feet, pulling her back toward the offices. "We're fixing that this weekend. You're about 16 years behind the rest of us who pretended our pillow was Ralph Macchio and made out with it. But it's okay. It's never too late to fall in love. I promise I won't Grid.Vid you dry humping my sofa cushions."

Chelsea checked her phone for the time once they reached the door. "It's 2:53. You grab your laptop. I'll grab us each a La Croix. We'll meet back up in the conference room," Chelsea directed as she opened the door. "And remember, sweep the leg," she whispered as she shoved Margo inside.

Margo hustled back to their desk as Chelsea's words rang in her ears. "My guess is she's already gotten to your sister." Margo felt the hair on the back of her neck spike. Kirby would never knowingly betray her, but she could unknowingly be played by Mix. Margo wasn't just looking out for herself. *I have to protect Kirby too*, she decided. Margo felt her phone vibrate. Looking down it was a text from Chelsea.

Sit where I put your La Croix.

Less than five minutes later, Margo found Chelsea's can of key lime soda water holding her seat at the conference room table. To its left sat Mix. To its right sat Ford.

"Wondered where you ran off to? Everything good?" Mix purred as she sat.

Margo flashed her brightest smile. "Just had a quick call."

"Hm, busy little bee, aren't we? Well, this should be a good meeting. *Not* to be missed."

Margo forced her smile to reach her eyes. "Wouldn't dream of it," she purred right back.

"We got our work cut out for us," Ford offered, leaning toward them. Heat crept up Margo's neck as his chest brushed up against her arm. "Thought we should get some planning meetings on the books."

"Agreed," Mix murmured, "Margo, why don't you coordinate calendars? That seems like a great first task for you. Give us plenty of time—I've got all kinds of ideas for the campaign to share." Mix's eyes bore into Margo, ready to soak up any signs of a reaction.

Margo held her gaze, unflinchingly, and smiled. "I can't wait to hear all about them."

"Great," Mix replied, the tiniest glimmer of confusion registering in her eyes at the fact that Margo had yet to acknowledge what had happened in their staff meeting. It was just a flash, but Margo saw it.

And....

Margo looked down at her phone to see the text from Chelsea. She moved her chair back from the table to better disguise her screen. Over the next hour, she and Chelsea texted back and forth, half listening as the Grid.it team revealed their top-secret plan to anoint their own next wave influencers.

"It's our list of the 25 Must Follows, relative unknowns selected by our team, Verified on Grid.it and made famous overnight. It's going to change the digital DNA," revealed their marketing VP.

As she spoke, Margo realized that she, too, felt a seismic shift. She was changed by what had happened today, suddenly seeing something she'd been too angry to realize earlier. The idea she had hoped was good enough to *share* had actually been good enough to *steal*. And even though she was disgusted by Mix, she suddenly felt an odd satisfaction that a woman—with eight more years on her résumé and the titles to show for it—had not only recognized Margo's good idea but had been desperate enough to take it.

Margo glanced in the direction of her boss, who sat dripping in 18 pounds of Cartier Love bracelets, Jacob the Jeweler–encrusted bangles, and airbrushed-on Dior foundation. Mix was actually just an empty promise, a fraud, Margo decided. It dawned on her that she did have what it would take to outfox a phony like Mix and climb to the top. *I'm good at this*, she thought looking around the room and her fellow Blush & Bashful staffers, and the respect she'd forged in just a few short months. She'd lost sight of her capabilities these past couple of years, but they were coming back into focus now.

"So that's it," Margo heard Grid.it's VP of channel development say, a sign the meeting was wrapping up. "Soon, we're changing the entire game. And, when we do, mark my words, we're going to sweep the competition."

As applause broke out in the room, Margo's eyes slid from the Grid.it exec to Mix. Mission Sweep the Leg was in full effect.

CHAPTER 13

Matt

Matt sat at a table in the back of the clubhouse, slowly sipping an iced tea. Over the past few years, he'd avoided coming to the Riv with his father. If only he could have escaped that fate today when Rob asked Matt to meet him here. The Riviera Country Club, or the Riv as it was commonly called, was located on Capri Drive in LA's posh Pacific Palisades neighborhood. With an initiation fee of $250,000 and monthly dues that would make any member of the middle class choke on their Arnold Palmer, Matt's dad relished the country club life. Matt had never gotten the appeal.

"Can I get you another iced tea, Mr. Milles-Lade?" a server asked, interrupting his thoughts.

Matt looked down, not realizing he'd had the entire glass. "Please, call me Matt. And, yes, I'll take another."

"Great, and Mr. Rolle's assistant called. He's on his way, but won't be here for about 20 more minutes," the server shared before swiftly disappearing.

Matt shook his head in dismay. Rob Rolle, always the showman, took his self-appointed part as a power player very seriously. He could have texted Matt to say he'd be late, but having his assistant call the clubhouse to then have a waiter pass along the message was straight out of the rich asshole playbook. And Rob Rolle was every bit a rich asshole.

Matt pulled up his phone. He started to scroll Grid.it, but his mind immediately drifted back to that morning. Tiff throwing her gem water bottle with its cylindrical center of amethyst right at him might have been her most surprising move yet. It sure as hell shocked the shit out of him. And he was fairly certain it had shocked the shit out of her too. It had exploded against the wall with a force that he didn't think she had in her and then gone off like a transcendental grenade against their marble tile.

"Sorry, no social media posting in the clubhouse, Mr. Milles-Lade," the server reminded as he set Matt's drink down.

"Sorry," Matt replied, honoring the rule by putting his phone on the table.

As he stared out at the green waiting for Rob, he thought again of the scene he'd walked in on when he returned home from his coffee run. Expecting to see a pouting or even passive-aggressive Tiff, her two most frequent modes, he had been surprised to find her with her eyes red and swollen from crying. She'd jumped up when he entered the kitchen, backing away from him as if he'd been that morning's aggressor.

"Don't come near me," she'd said with fear in her voice, grabbing Zin's shoulder to hide behind her. "I'm not kidding, Matty. I will call the police."

Matt was surprised that, instead of immediate anger, it was sadness that flushed to his face at Tiff's apparent fear.

"Tiff, what are you talking about? You threw the bottle at *me*." He turned his arms upwards toward the ceiling, his shoulders sagging, not even rising to her use of his nickname.

She spoke, a waver to her voice, "Your father and I have decided you need to be out of the house by the end of the month." Tears spilled over the rims of her eyes and stained her cheeks. "I'm not kidding, Matty. I will not have violence in my house."

Matt could feel the low simmer of annoyance in his gut at her insinuation. In a flash it got the best of him. "Are *you* moving out then?" he asked, sharply. "Because, *you're* the one who threw the bottle at *me*."

Tiffany straightened her shoulders, a move undermined by the quiver of her lip, which she bit down on willing it to cease. "Next Friday, Matty. You're gone by next Friday."

Matt's head fell back as he let out a gust of air. His jaw tightened, and he looked back toward her. He was surprised at how defeated and suddenly fragile he felt. Unexpectedly, his chin quivered. He looked away. He could feel his emotions getting the best of him, tears threatening to spill over. He wouldn't let them. He wouldn't give her that satisfaction. "I don't get it, Tiff. What have I ever done to you?"

Tiffany Bettina Ray was born just outside Elsa, Texas, in an old motel that had been converted into economy apartments. Her father had walked out on her when she was seven. The last words he'd said were, "Don't be sad, Tiffy Ray, I'm not your real dad anyway."

She'd never seen her dad again and, thanks to his admission, realized she'd never seen *him* in the first place. Her mom, Brandi Ray, wasn't like the moms she watched on TV, giving out hugs indiscriminately, telling their children they were special. Brandi Ray had taken a harsher approach to child rearing, "The world's ugly, Tiffy Ray. You better toughen up if you want to survive it."

Making her daughter tough, it seemed, required never saying a kind word to her. When Tiff was eight, she got an A+ on her science project. That night at the fair, her teacher pinned the blue ribbon to her chest. Elated, she ran to her mother. Brandi Ray just looked down at her daughter and said, "Unless they started taking blue ribbons at the Stop & Go, that ribbon's no use to us." When Tiff made cheer camp at ten, Brandi Ray observed, "Thought they only took the pretty girls?" When Tiff was 13, her mom taught her to drive so she could pick her up at the bar. "I got one DUI. Not gonna risk another 'specially when I got a daughter whose never been no use to me 'til now."

Tiff would wait outside in the car until her mom stumbled out, always with a different man in tow. They'd sloppily make their way to the car, groping one another relentlessly in the process. They'd crawl in the back seat, and as Tiff drove them home the men always leered at her in the rearview mirror. When they arrived, Tiff would head straight to her room and lock the door, pretending not to hear each man's pathetic come-ons through the cheap wood fiber of the frame. "C'mon. Let me in, Tiffy Ray. I promise, I just wanna talk."

Their behavior made Tiff sick. Eventually her mother would coax them back. "That girl don't know what to do with a real man. Get back in here."

As Tiff got older though, she realized her mother was wrong. She did know what to do with a real man. She lost her virginity to the husband of her high school drill squad, Hollis King. She caught Hollis looking at her each time they practiced in her coach Rachel's backyard on Saturday mornings, the football field already obligated to the football team's practice.

Hollis would stand at the kitchen sink and pretend to do dishes so he could stare out the window and watch her. He wasn't like the men her mother picked up. Those men were deadbeats, they looked at Tiff like she was cheap, but Hollis King looked at Tiff like she was a queen. He was 32, had a job, had money, had taste, and he noticed Tiffany. She could tell because while he was different, the look in his eyes was the same as the men in the rearview mirror.

"Rachel's not home," Hollis said when Tiffy dropped by.

"Oh?" she mused, but she knew Rachel taught cardio-kick at the YMCA on Thursdays. "No worries. I'm just here to grab some pink tape to rewrap my wooden gun."

"Oh, sure. Come on in. Tape's probably in the office." Hollis held the door open.

Tiff stepped forward, purposely brushing her breast across his chest and stopping. "Mmmm, you smell good," she said innocently, standing decidedly too close to him.

"Thanks, Rachel got me this cologne for Christmas," he said nervously, daring not to move closer to her but definitely not wanting to step farther away.

"You should wear it more often." Tiff pouted sweetly. "I wonder what it would smell like on me," she contemplated, as she bit the corner of her lip.

Hollis sharply sucked in a breath.

"Why don't you put a little on me. Right here." She smiled, demurely touching the nape of her neck right below her ear.

Hollis cleared his throat, "How?" he asked hoarsely, then swallowed hard.

Tiff smirked devilishly. "You're the man, silly, you tell me." She let her pinky finger brush the back of his hand.

"What are you doing?" Hollis looked down at her pinky finger touching his. He looked panicked and yet his skin seemed to be smoldering.

"Nothing yet," Tiff cooed.

Hollis's eyes flew to her face. Tiff winked. With that Hollis lunged toward her, crushing his lips to hers. In a tangle of arms and sighs, he picked her up and carried her into the next room. And while his wife Rachel taught cardio kick at the Y, Hollis King crowned Tiffy Ray a queen on their dining room table.

"Can I see you again?" he asked, smitten, as he pulled up his sweats.

Tiff flirted, "If you're a very good boy."

His eyes flared with lust. She felt on fire by the obvious pull she had over him. She left that night on a high, feeling powerful for the very first time in her life. Tiffany Bettina Ray had dominated that man. He had eaten out of the palm of her hand, and as the weeks unfolded, he'd move his meal to the crux of her thighs. Her mother, who had been pretty once, let liquor line her face and body. Men like Hollis didn't want the Brandi Rays of the world. Tiffy decided she would never let that happen to her. She had a powerful gift, which men would pay greatly for. It was her superpower.

After that night, everything changed. She saw the world as what she could have by who she'd allow to have her. Once she unleashed it, she could feel men were intrinsically drawn to her, and women indelibly threatened by her, including her own mother.

On her 17th birthday, Tiff sat on their secondhand, blue velour sofa as her mom crashed about in the bathroom getting ready.

"Where's my blue mascara?" Brandi Ray shouted.

Tiff looked up momentarily to see her mom standing in a short miniskirt, wedges, and a dingy pink bra. "How should I know?" She looked down and continued texting Mr. Anders.

"You better not have stole it!" Brandi Ray shouted back, now in the bathroom rifling through their makeup bin.

"As if I would. I don't want hepatitis," Tiff shot back. A text from Trent dinged in her inbox.

Can't stop thinking about you...

Trent Anders was 39. He wasn't the most handsome guy. He had a beer gut and a receding hairline. His skin was red and blotchy. His build, carby. He spent his time playing video games and watching online porn with takeout containers and pizza boxes littering the coffee table of the home he'd inherited from his diabetic mother. Tiff was his fantasy come to life, and when she shyly cornered him in the chem lab he'd almost started the school on fire. Tiff felt a rush of power. But, she wasn't with Trent just because. She had a had a bigger play in mind. She was confident that after a few more weeks of Trent's sluglike tongue, she'd clinch the keys to his dead mother's Ford Mustang.

"I need my uniform for tomorrow." Brandi Ray was now standing in the kitchen, cigarette in hand.

Tiff continued to stare at her phone, paid for by Hollis King.

"Tiff?" Brandi Ray demanded.

"Fine," Tiff relented. "Leave me quarters," she demanded as she texted a tongue emoji to Trent.

Her mom smacked down several dollars' worth of change on the counter and opened the door.

"Stop cutting your shorts so short, Tiffy. I can see your vagina from here."

"Ditto," Tiff replied flatly noting her mom's miniskirt as Brandi Ray headed out the door.

Reluctantly, Tiff gathered her mother's uniform, a blue and red smock for the Buzzies Gas Station. She wasn't even upset that her mom had forgotten her birthday for the seventh year in a row. She swallowed that bitter pill ten years ago when Brandi Ray had forgotten it for the first time.

"Maybe I'm done celebratin' a day that ruined my life in the first place," Brandi Ray blamed.

Tiff cried that night, but she hadn't cried since. She knew that crying over spilled milk or Brandi Ray never did any good to clean up either mess.

With the laundry done, she placed the sheets in the hall closet. When she closed the door, Boone Pickens was standing on the other side. Tiffy jumped.

"Fuck off, Boone," she said, brushing past him and walking to the kitchen.

Once there, she reached for a Fanta out of the fridge. Boone grabbed her hips and ground into her from behind.

He'd hit on her many times before and it always made her skin crawl.

"I could have you anytime I want, Tiffy Ray."

Tiff stood up, turned and slapped him across the face, hard. "Get your hands off me, you pig," she spat.

A look came across Boone's face. Tiff had seen that look before in other men. She lunged for the door, but Boone grabbed her by the hair and yanked her back toward him. She fell to the ground but was only there a second before he pulled her back up and thrust her across the kitchen counter. Smashing her face into the Formica, his breath hot on her cheek as he ground into her. "I'm about to teach you a lesson, girl," he hissed.

Tiff fought and clawed to break free, pushing his hands away from her hips. Boone struggled to hold her still as he reached for his belt.

"What's going on here?" Brandi Ray's voice ricocheted through the tiny apartment.

Boone immediately released Tiff. "Your slut of a daughter was coming onto me," he drawled.

Tiff jumped up and away from the counter. "That's a lie," she protested, wiping at the blood dripping down from the corner of her eye. "He was attacking me," she shouted.

"I've heard enough, get out!" Brandi Ray shouted behind her.

Boone didn't move.

"Get out!" Brandi said again.

Still Boone stood there.

"Girl, didn't you hear me? I said get the fuck outta my house."

Tiff swung toward her mother. "Mom," the word muffled by the swelling of her cheek.

Brandi Ray stood defiantly.

"What are you doing?" Tiff asked again, betrayal like gravel in her throat.

"Something I shoulda done a long time ago. I didn't want you the day you was born. I don't want you now. Get out."

Tiff straightened her shoulders and stepped toward the hall. As she did, Boone jerked out an arm to grab her. Tiff recoiled, a moment of fear hot on her skin.

"Hah, made you flinch," he jeered.

She hardened herself, so she could walk past him to her room.

"Be quick about it. Boone and I got things to do," Brandi Ray cooed as she walked by.

Three hours later, Tiff boarded a bus for Los Angeles. Her Grandma Ray lived just outside Palm Springs. Each year she'd sent Tiff $25 on her birthday. The card was always mailed to Mrs. Noland next door, which told Tiff that Grandma Ray knew her own daughter would steal her granddaughter's birthday money in a heartbeat. And the fact that Mrs. Noland told Tiff to hide the money meant she knew too. On that bus ride, Tiff said goodbye to a lot of things, her mother, Elsa, Texas, Tiffy Ray, her birthday... She'd never go back to any of it.

As Matt stood before her today, tears in his eyes, she realized she had let the tiniest sliver of Tiffy Ray back in. She'd thrown that bottle at Matt just as much as she'd thrown it at Boone Pickens and Brandi Ray. They'd threatened her chance at survival then. Matt was threatening her chance at it now. He clearly thought she was a fool, that she didn't know that Brooks was cheating on her. Of course, she knew. Brooks wasn't that clever, and she wasn't that dumb. Tiff didn't care. She wasn't with Brooks for love. She was with him because he was the furthest thing away from Boone Pickens and Elsa, Texas, as she could get. He was everything Tiff had boarded that bus for, everything she had worked for. She had sat at cafés and hotels and studied the women in California. She had gotten the tan that was less orange and more bronze, the blonde that was more Swedish and salty air than brassy bottle. She had lost her accent and swapped super short skirts for skintight pencil length that said, "I'm country club, not strip club." She had gotten her GED and learned the language of older men. Scotch. Cars. Dangerous sex. She had Brooks Milles-Lade in the bag all but for his son, Matt. She would be damned if this brat who had been raised with everything and still managed to fuck it up would get in the way of her happily ever after. She was one well-drafted prenup, followed by a few good years of marriage, away from her total emancipation from Tiffy Ray.

"Hey, Matt. Sorry, I'm late," Rob said as he grabbed the seat across from him.

Matt, suddenly shook back to reality by his arrival, had still been thinking about Tiff's expression that morning. He didn't trust her, but in a weird way he also felt sorry for her. Honestly, he didn't care if she married his dad. They deserved one another. She was using Brooks. His father was using Tiff. They were a matched set as far Matt was concerned.

"No problem," Matt lied, leaning back in his chair, "I had a bit of free time today."

"Heard there was a scuffle." Rob raised an innocent eyebrow.

"Tiff," Matt answered as if her name explained it all.

"Right, well, I wanted to talk to you about your dad. I like to think I'm the son he never had so ...."

"You do realize I'm his son, Rob?" Matt cut him off dryly.

"Of course, but you didn't exactly turn out like he'd hoped, right?"

They stared at one another.

"What's your point, Rob?" Matt asked sharply.

"Maybe I'm mucking this up, not saying it properly," Rob continued, mustering an apologetic air, but Matt knew he wasn't sorry. Rob, forever clad in Tom Ford, was often cruel only to pass it off later as if Matt had misunderstood. Rob knew exactly what he was saying. He was one of the most calculating men Matt had ever met.

"So far you haven't *said* anything," Matt replied looking directly at Rob, not wanting to go another round with yet another person whispering into his father's ear on the same day.

"Your dad talks to me all the time about you, Matt. I wish he didn't, but he does. And I think to myself, *this fucking kid has the dad of all lifetimes and he's throwing it away.* And it's killing your father. You know that right? Now, he's deciding who to pass the company down to..."

Ahhhh, there it is, Matt thought. *My father's dropping hints about handing the company off to someone and Rob on a Rolle wants to look like the golden boy who tried to help his boss's son not be such a fuck-up.*

Rob continued, "and I want to make sure you and I are doing all we can to support him. I'm worried your dad might make a choice that he really doesn't want to make."

"Oh yeah, what's that, Rob? What's got you up at night?" Matt asked bitterly, crunching the last bit of ice left in his glass.

"I'm worried he'll leave you the company out of obligation when really, in his heart, I know he wants to leave it to me. He knows I'm the better man. So, I wanted to say, do the right thing, Matt. Tell your dad you don't want it. Do one good thing and let him off the hook, because lord knows you've caused him enough pain."

His tone implied empathy, but both he and Rob knew he was cruelly gutting Matt like a fish right in the Riv clubhouse. Moreover, they both knew he was enjoying it.

Matt stared at Rob, not even attempting to hide the hatred he felt for this prick of a man. Matt stood.

"Well, Rob, thanks for the refreshing iced tea and the riveting conversation. I've got someplace to be, but I promise you," Matt continued as he leaned into the table, towering directly over Rob, "You aren't the better man, and I don't need any advice from you about my father, my family, or the company he built."

He pushed his chair in and headed for the door.

"Matt?" Rob called after him, as he stood, tossing a handful of wasabi peas and nuts into his mouth.

Matt turned back to Rob to see him wiping the crumbs from his hands.

"If you don't need any business advice from me, Matt, what about some real estate tips now that you've been kicked out of your house?"

The people around them pretended not to hear. Matt knew they had. He also knew every single one of them knew he was Brooks Milles-Lade's son.

"Have a great day, Rob." Matt turned and walked out of the restaurant toward the valet.

Between Tiff and Rob, Matt was done with this day. It had begun with Tiff getting him kicked out of his house and had ended with Rob threatening to get him kicked out of his birth right, his father's business. He seethed as he stood waiting for his car to pull up, desperately trying to ignore the entitled woman standing beside him, her young face already bloated with enough Botox and filler to de-age half a senior home. *Jesus, her lips are like a floatation device,* Matt thought.

"I left my Chloe sunglasses on the dash and need them immediately. What is so hard to understand about the word *immediate?*" she berated, as the poor valet over-apologized for what was her mistake in the first place.

"Perhaps if I said it in Spanish? *Rápido, rápido,*" she said, wearing her racism on her silk Versace sleeve.

Man, this town really is full of pricks, Matt thought as he tipped the valet double.

"So sorry you have to deal with that, Diego," Matt conceded as he slid behind the wheel of the Volvo.

"It's okay, Matt. There's just enough of you good guys to make up for all the assholes, even the pretty ones." Diego winked as he shut the door.

Matt buckled his seatbelt just as one of the valets ran past with the woman's Chloe sunglasses in hand. Matt looked in his rearview mirror to see if she would tip only to find that, instead, Rob had rushed to her aid, kissing her as he walked up. She snatched her glasses and walked off in a huff with Rob in tow. Neither tipped Bruno. *Boy,* Matt thought, *do they ever deserve one another.*

CHAPTER 14

Margo

"I feel like that's perfect for Margo's list, don't you think?" Mix looked at Margo and Ford as the trio sat on the Lanai going over logistics for the shoot.

As if anyone else's opinion but yours even matters, Mix, Margo thought.

Over the past week, Mix had already assigned every grunt job, administrative headache, and logistical nightmare to Margo, which basically meant Margo was doing everything for the shoot while Mix basked in the glow of the credit. But, in keeping with Margo and Chelsea's sweep the leg plan, Margo had accepted each duty with dedication and a smile on her face.

"That's the thing about power," Chelsea said as she and Margo lay on the floor of her teeny-tiny, one-room studio apartment in Highland Park drinking rosé, attempting to numb the toll that Mix had taken on them over the course of the past week. They were sprawled atop large Moroccan floor pillows, staring up at the ceiling fan. "It's an illusion, really. Right now, Mix thinks she has all the power, and, maybe she does, but only because we're allowing her to. Each day, her false certainty that you're afraid of her grows and so does her cockiness, which means she'll just keep climbing farther and farther out onto that limb, and as they say, when the bough breaks...." Chelsea smiled knowingly at her own words.

"How are you so sure of any of this?" Margo asked, continually suspicious of their plan.

"*Can't Buy Me Love. Clueless. Mean Girls.* Need I go on?" Chelsea asked as she twined a fruit tape around her finger, only to place it in her rosé like a chemical-laden straw.

"*Yes*, go on, because those are just movies," Margo replied, "They're not actually credible footnotes for your argument, Chels."

"Excuse me?" Chelsea said in mock outrage, sitting up to face Margo. "*Just* movies? They're not *just* anything. They're the classics, thank you very much, and they have informed everything about my life thus far. We've been over this. Mix is classic villain vibes. For days. And just like in each of those movies, we can predict her behavior and her fall from grace, which is going to happen. She's gonna be so busy patting herself on the back that she won't even see us coming with the saw. I promise. Trust, Margo. I have a long history with mean girls. I've seen every play in their playbook, plus I've seen every episode of *The Real Housewives*, from *every* city, including Potomac. There's not a single thing Mix can do that we won't see coming. She's Brandi Glanville basic. Look how we've already played her so far."

Chelsea did have a point. In the past week alone, Mix had edged further out onto that branch. She started first by swirling in her own ideas for the Fourth of July shoot, and they were not good. Tuesday morning, she made the request for pink ponies.

"Mini and full-size, we need a spectacle."

Margo's immediate inclination was to be critical. She opened her mouth to say, "Nothing says spectacle quite like horseshit on pink Astroturf."

But before she could tamp down the idea, Chelsea pressed her knee into Margo's under the table and interjected, "Wow, pink horses! Talk about a Bianca Jagger meets Blush & Bashful moment. Love it. Tongues are going to wag."

Wednesday, when Mix said she wanted pink pyrotechnics to go off in the background of the shoot, Margo instantly saw the breaking of fire safety and prevention laws with the hillside ablaze and an exorbitant tally for the animal licenses, wranglers, fire marshals, and pyrotechnic experts needed to make it all happen. But instead of saying any of that, she just innocently asked, "What budget do you want to put behind it?"

When Ford arrived, Mix gushed, "I'm expanding my vision to make sure we get the internet talking."

Margo kept her eyes downcast and envisioned the internet talking in the form of a Grid.it & Hit.it newscast headline read by Maria Menounos. "*George Washington's pink powder wig went up in flames on the set of a Fourth of July shoot for the fast-growing fashion retailer Blush & Bashful. When their hillside set caught fire, the shirtless model playing George, who was wearing only a wig and a pair of pink, skintight britches, suffered second-degree burns to his neck, pecks, and six-pack abs. The fire commissioner was quoted today as saying, "Good thing George can't tell a lie because we're investigating who's at fault here.*"

When she raised her eyes to look at Ford, she saw that he looked pleased with Mix's declaration.

Obviously he'd didn't catch Maria's breaking news, Margo thought.

As she and Chelsea drove to lunch that day, Chelsea exclaimed from the passenger seat, "What kind of idiot sets off pyrotechnics in the hills of Hollywood? It's like a tinderbox up here."

Margo laughed, but in line at Chipotle cautioned, "But for real though, this is my sister's company. I'm not going to torch Hollywood like Mrs. O'Leary's cow just because Mix told us to," her eyes strict and serious.

Chelsea snorted a laugh. "Of course not, but you are going to price the pyro guy, the fire marshal, the animal wranglers, and every other harebrained idea of hers so you can innocently say to Kirby, 'I guess I didn't realize your marketing budgets allowed for all these other things.' When Kirby sees the list, she's going to fall out. Mix is going to look like the pink horse's ass she just tried to have you hire."

Despite Margo's desire to tell Kirby, Chelsea forbade her. "You can't tell Kirby. I get it, she's your sister, but in this moment that doesn't apply because she'd take this news as your boss. She won't *hear* what Mix did to you as it relates to *you,* her *sister,* she'll hear what Mix did as it relates to Blush & Bashful. No good can come from telling her. It just puts her in a bad position. Pinky swear, Margo."

And Margo had pinky swore, something previously she'd only ever done *with* Kirby. It felt strange to now be swearing to keep something *from* her sister. But while it made her uneasy, she knew it was time she fought her own battles.

Each day, she and Chelsea showed up to the office, chipping away at their massive workloads, following Mix around like ducklings imprinted upon a wild hyena as Mix continuously doled out new and outrageous duties for them to tackle. Surprisingly though, work was good, more than good, actually. Margo was enjoying herself. Though it had been hard at first to look at Mix without calling her out every second of every day as a fraud, it had gotten easier, mostly because there was too much to be done. As long as Margo didn't think about the things she wasn't telling her sister, she was fine.

That got put to the test on Thursday at their weekly Melon family meal.

"Grab that corner," Kirby directed across their parents' Castle Heights dinner table.

Margo tipped forward, reaching for an edge of the tablecloth.

"Remember? You pinky swore not to tell Mom and Dad about the house."

Both girls looked toward the kitchen where their mother was rooting through the silverware drawer. Of course she remembered promising, it was part of the reason Margo felt like she was lying to everyone.

"Margo," Kirby hissed, bringing them both back to the table, "or about David and me. Remember?"

Why are we hiding this? What's the big deal? Margo lamented internally.

"Margo?" Kirby demanded, as their mother moved on to squeezing lemons from their tree out back for lemonade, the whir of the juicer covering up their discussion.

"I remember."

"Good," Kirby said, a relieved smile touching her lips as they each smoothed out their side of the cloth. "I have to say, it's been great having you at work. I don't want you to take this the wrong way, but I was worried there'd be drama. You've always been the star, and I was...," Kirby paused searching for the right, and perhaps, least offending word she could think of as she parceled out her stack of plates, lapping Margo. "I was concerned about being your boss, especially since you're in such a junior position."

Margo, placing cups at each seat, willed her younger sister to stop talking. She could feel her ego lumbering to stand in defiance. But Kirby kept right on going, completely unaware of the epic tailspin she was igniting on the other side of the table.

"It seems so silly now, but I was really worried it would be too much, that you might not be able to set your pride aside and just focus on the building blocks and this chance I'm giving you."

There it is, Margo balked to herself. *The chance you're giving me?!* Her feathers were fully ruffled.

"But you really showed me," Kirby said, looking admiringly at Margo, beaming at her in fact.

The rational part of Margo knew Kirby was coming from a good place. Of course, the reasonable part was dwarfed by a much larger portion of herself that was undeniably bruised by her sister's words, her ego. She knew Kirby was the boss, but she didn't feel like the lackey Kirby was describing. Up until this very minute, she had felt like a hired gun.

Guess I was wrong about that, she thought, but instead said, "It's been wonderful, Kirb." She smiled at her sister, beating any emotion except gratitude back down with a lead pipe, hoping her comment appeased her.

"Have you been looking for a place?" Kirby stared at her expectantly. "I mean, I don't wanna get ahead of myself, but Mix told me she'd love to have you on her team as an assistant. I mean, she did say your ideas can be a bit more basic since marketing isn't your forte, but with her guidance and mentorship she thought you'd flourish."

Kirby looked pleased as punch at the idea as she carried her mother's pitcher of just-made lemonade in from the kitchen. Margo, on the other hand, felt like she might momentarily black out or, worse, shout, "Work for her? Are you kidding me? That bitch stole my idea!"

Instead, Margo walked into the kitchen. She briefly white-knuckled the edge of the island, leaning her weight into the countertop to regain her composure.

"Did you hear me, M?" Kirby shouted toward the door.

"Wow," Margo replied, reentering, now carrying napkins.

"Would you want to be on Mix's team full-time?"

"I don't think I ever stopped to think about *that* as a possibility," Margo said feigning normalcy by folding napkins.

Chelsea's going to die when she hears this, she grimaced inside.

"Well, that's what happens when you make a good impression," Kirby marveled at Margo. "Honestly, M, I'm so proud of you."

Margo paused, mid fold. She looked at her sister. "Me too," she agreed, surprised by an unexpected moment of honesty.

And, Margo *was* proud of herself, *really* proud to be exact.

"Well, anyway," Kirby continued as she placed a low centerpiece of palm fronds cut from the backyard, in the middle of the table. "Like I said, I'm probably getting ahead of myself. I know writing is your thing, but it would be really good for you to learn under someone like Mix. She's great at her job and for you to be proving your worth to her, wow!" Kirby's eyes melted with admiration like two glazed donuts left on the dash of a hot car, oozing with esteem for Mix. "I mean that idea she had for the shoot is a game changer."

As Margo folded the last napkin, she could feel Kirby looking at her for agreement. She forced her features into a smile. "Absolutely," she said raising her eyes to her sister's.

Before she could spin off her axis, her parents entered the room.

"There's my career girls," Hank Melon boomed carrying a plate of fresh-off-the-grill barbecued chicken, Maureen trailing behind him with a bowl of roasted sweet potatoes, both radiating pride.

As they sat down to dinner, her parents began asking Margo all about the small house on the hill that Kirby had purchased.

"Is it so cute?" Maureen asked with the wonder of a child who's about to meet Elmo for the first time. "We're dying to come over, if someone would stop canceling on us," she playfully chastised her youngest daughter.

Kirby pretended to plate up food in lieu of acknowledging her mother's admonishment. The weight of Margo's mistruths weighed on her. She was lying to her sister about Mix and lying to her parents about her sister. Even after Kirby left, her parents kept peppering her with questions about work and the house, gushing over Margo's new employment and Kirby's ongoing success.

"What are you doing?" Margo asked as she watched Chelsea dump ice into her glass, wiping the memory of their Melon family meal away for now.

"What do you mean, what am I doing? I'm drinking wine, same as you."

"No, I'm drinking wine. You're making a fruit salad in your glass."

Margo nodded at Chelsea's drink, which now contained a melting fruit roll up.

"I don't like wine," Chelsea blurted out, as her shoulders slumped forward in defeat. "Everyone wants rosés and frosés these days. I don't get it," Chelsea admitted woefully. "I never really made it out of the fuzzy navel stage," she added as she reached for a Blow Pop from the counter candy dish.

Margo took Chelsea's glass and dumped it along with hers before pouring them each a new drink.

"What are you making?" Chelsea asked, hoisting herself up on her countertop, mystified as Margo took over the role of bartender.

"Truth be told, I'm not a big drinker either." She dropped ice into two, mismatched tumblers. "Partying was more Kirby's scene. But, I did make up one drink."

Chelsea watched as Margo poured two tall Jack Daniels mixed with the fresh pressed apple juice they'd just picked up at the Friday afternoon farmers' market near Chelsea's flat. "They're dangerous if you have too many, so don't," Margo warned, as she handed Chelsea her drink. "Cheers. Here's to us getting everything we want!"

They clinked glasses.

"And, cheers to summer Fridays, Saturdays off, and no Mix on the weekend," Chelsea added before taking her first sip, then giving an impressed smile.

"Thanks, but I do have to work," Margo groaned. "We're casting the models tomorrow."

"Oh, that's right! With Ford...ooh la la," Chelsea said as she fell back dramatically on the floor pillows, her hand to her forehead like a '50s movie siren.

"Stop it," Margo chided, hitting her with a pillow. "Ford hasn't even noticed me."

"Of course, he has," Chelsea replied, outraged, with a tone that said, *don't be naive.* "Now you just have to get him to act on it."

"And how does one do that?"

"Beats me. My last date was last year," Chelsea admitted, her nose scrunched in dismay.

"Well then, we have to fix that for both of us," Margo declared.

"Amen, sister," Chelsea shouted as she clinked her glass to Margo's.

"Chels, what would you say if I said I'd never seen *Gossip Girl*?"

Chelsea gasped as if she'd been burned. "I'd say we're going to be here for a while." Immediately she began hunting for the remote control to the Apple TV. "You better order pizza. We'll need sustenance for you to meet Chuck Bass."

The next morning Margo woke bleary-eyed from their seven-hour crash course into all things Serena van der Woodsen. Too tired to drive home, she'd slept at Chelsea's. As Chelsea danced around the kitchen, making Margo a green shake from their farmers' market haul, Margo realized how intensely grateful she was to have Chelsea as a friend. Balancing her makeup on her lap, Chelsea's tiny bistro table too laden down with her computer and art supplies for Margo to eke out room, she realized that she couldn't go to work in the same clothes as yesterday. Not only was she seeing Ford, but they were casting ten male models for their upcoming shoot.

"Chels," she shouted.

Between the juicer and Chelsea singing into a carrot, Chelsea didn't hear her. Just as she hit the chorus of the club mix of "Only in My Dreams," Margo tossed her makeup sponge at her.

"What?" Chelsea laughed as she stopped the juicer.

"I can't go to work in the same clothes, and I'm a giant compared to you," Margo lamented.

"Girl, I got you. First, I live to style people. Second, any real fashionista knows you have to have clothes that range from your size to five sizes bigger depending on the look and the layer. I'll be right back."

Chelsea stopped at the sink to wash her hands.

Margo looked around. "Ummm, where are you going that I won't see you?" she asked furrowing her brow. "You live in a one-room studio apartment."

"Storage locker, third floor, end of the hall. Have we not discussed this?"

"No," Margo replied.

"Ahhh, come with me. You're in for a treat." Chelsea opened the door and bowed for Margo to go first.

They walked down the hall to the elevator and rode up one floor, exiting to the right, walking along the back of the building with its pool reflecting water spots on both sides of the courtyard below. One lone door stood at the end of the hall. Chelsea unlocked it and then dramatically turned to face Margo. With her back to the door, she placed her right arm languidly above her head, then with no warning, she let the door fall open behind her, with her falling into the room along with it. Margo's jaw hit the floor.

The room was narrow but deep. One small window stood on the back wall, below it a chair and a table holding a sewing machine. Racks of clothes flanked the walls. In the corner stood a dressmaker's form draped with the most exquisite pink wool military jacket.

"Chelsea," Margo gasped, actually clapping her hand to her heart in reverence.

"Are you impressed?" Chelsea asked nervously, looking between the room and Margo's face.

"*Impressed* is an understatement."

Margo turned to Chelsea. Her face haloed by a glow of wonderment, "Did you make all these?" she asked, stepping into the room.

"I did," Chelsea said humbly in a hush. "Have I not told you that I'm a closet Christian Siriano?" She then gestured to the fact that they were standing in a closet and added, "literally."

"No, you didn't!" Margo marveled as she spun into the room. "Why haven't you told me this?" she demanded, lovingly reprimanding her friend.

"Truth is, I've never really told anyone. I love to sew, but people mostly made fun of me for my style choices...."

Margo stopped mid-spin and gasped, "You have the best style, Chels. I could never pull off what you dream up!"

"Well, the kids in high school made fun of me and I just thought maybe this," she gestured toward the clothes, "was too risky to take what little money we had and spend it on an uncertain career in fashion. But it's always been my first love, my pipe dream."

"Oh no, Chelsea," Margo said as she delicately touched the clothes, almost petting them, "What's in this room needs to be seen."

Chelsea looked both relieved and worried at the same time. "Well, as of today they will be. I've never had any friends to style until you, so we can talk my career change later. Right now, we gotta get you warrior-ready to cast some models and get your man."

Margo laughed. Chelsea started pulling items off the rack, constructing the look she wanted for Margo, as Margo approached the dressmaker's form and the pink military blazer. It was the cut of a jacket a soldier in colonial times might wear if he were going to a party in 1985, short in the front, long in the back, epaulettes on the shoulders, a stash of '80s gem-stone Maltese crosses on the chest.

"What is this?" Margo asked, astonished by both its beauty and its construction, delicately holding one of its sleeves.

"I've been so inspired by the shoot, I thought why not make us *each* a killer jacket."

"Shut up!" Margo boomed. "You're making *each* of us one of these?"

She turned to Chelsea, her eyes gleaming with excitement. Chelsea smiled and nodded.

"Where will we wear them?"

"Girl, where won't we wear them?" Chelsea answered with attitude. "Celine Dion would wear this to grab milk at the grocery store."

Margo laughed. "I love you, Chels," she said as she put her arm around her friend.

"Enough of that. Come here. I've got your look. The jeans are your own, but I think we should cut the knees. We're the same size shoe, so you'll wear my nude oxfords, the ones you love," Chelsea continued as Margo nodded, her eyes getting big at the thought of borrowing Chelsea's beloved vintage McQueens. "This nutmeg bralette will be your top," she said as Margo's brow furrowed. "Don't furrow your brow, you'll get wrinkles," Chelsea quickly corrected. "And for the record, I hate the fact that you're five feet taller and we still have the same boob size." Chelsea pouted for impact. "Then, it's this oversized white button-down, which we'll knot and layer. So, don't worry if it looks like a tent now. It won't by the time I'm done with it," she concluded, handing Margo the hangers as she reached for jewelry. "I think a pile of thin gold necklaces will add a flair of St. Tropez that we'll top off with a messy braid and a linen ribbon bow for just a touch of Coco Chanel from the '40s."

Chelsea turned to face Margo, who hadn't moved.

"Put it on," she commanded.

Margo started with the russet colored bralette as Chelsea leaned down to hack apart the kneecaps of her jeans, perfectly tattering them.

"Are you sure about this?" Margo asked concerned. "The bra thing fits. I don't know why I couldn't wear my own. But you're right, this top makes me look like I'm wearing a tent."

She looked down at the mass of white fabric that hung to her lower calves as she fastened the last buttons. Without responding and without hesitation, Chelsea slit the side hems of the long white shirt all the way to Margo's waist. She stood and turned Margo back around, so she was facing the mirror. The newly created back tails of the shirt hung down as Chelsea reached around Margo and unbuttoned the buttons she'd just done up.

"I don't know about this," Margo whined.

"Just hold on."

Chelsea grabbed the front tails of the shirt and tied them in a clever long knot that instantly made the shirt elegantly fitted in the front. Margo suddenly understood the bralette top. It was right out there for the world to see. As Chelsea layered on the thin gold chains, Margo asked in a hushed uncertainty, "Can I wear this?"

She covered her chest like Baby in *Dirty Dancing* when Penny's fitting her for her costume. "This half shirt bra thing is really out there."

Chelsea stood and peered over Margo's shoulder from behind. She reached around and lowered Margo's arms. "Can you wear this?" Chelsea repeated. "Girl, you should wear *only* this. Look at you! You look amazing."

Margo remained suspicious.

"Okay," Chelsea said, making eye contact with Margo in the mirror. "First rule of style club: don't question your stylist," Chelsea said, her eyes encouraging Margo. "You're everything in this. Trust. Celine Dion wouldn't ponder *this* outfit. She'd already be in line for that gallon of milk and be feelin' herself so much she'd have gotten a dozen eggs and some bacon to go along with it, my queen."

Chelsea smiled, her tone dripping with empowerment. Margo turned to face her friend.

"Okay, I'll wear it. But when I'm done with work, we're vision boarding the shit out of our Saturday night, because if Christian Siriano can come out of the closet, so can you."

She raised one eyebrow just like Lucy Liu does in every film, letting her costar know, *we're doing this my way now.*

"Shut up," Chelsea said as she pushed Margo out of the room. "You're gonna be three Apple Jacks deep with Ford tonight if I did my job right."

As Margo drove to work, she noted the effects of her outfit. It certainly put her assets on display, but not inelegantly. The overall affect was what Victoria Beckham might wear on a lazy beach day while on holiday at Lake Como. Two men at the coffee shop on the corner from Chelsea's house smiled as she walked by; one told her she looked beautiful.

Is this all it takes to hook a man, show some skin? she considered.

She wasn't ever good at getting the guy. Then again, she had never left the house with a top knotted at her navel with a flesh colored bra underneath.

This is uncharted territory, she decided as she feigned confidence.

When she got to work, Mix stared her up and down. "That's a look," pausing, then, "are you trying to cast a model or land one?" she asked smarmily just before Ford entered the room.

"Well, look who turned up for work?" he said, clearly admiring her outfit. "Shall we get this casting under way, ladies?" He clapped his hands like a coach.

Margo smiled. "For sure. Where's Kirby?" she asked.

"She had a giant meeting come up unexpectedly," Ford answered. "I told her we had this. How hard could it be for two women and one very astute man to pick the hottest dudes in the room, right?"

He laughed and then hustled back to his office to grab his phone.

It's not like Kirby to miss something and not tell me, Margo thought. *And it's really crazy for her to have a giant meeting that I don't know anything about.*

"Earth to Margo?" Mix said, shaking her back to reality.

Mix gestured for her to pick up the opposite end of the table she was standing at. "Is that okay with you?" Mix huffed, annoyed at having to repeat herself.

"I'm sorry," Margo said confused as they slowly walked the table to its new spot. "Is what okay with me?"

They dropped the table to the side of the room so that it now flanked the wall.

"I said we'll get started while you go to get us coffee. Sound good?"

Now standing at the next table's end, Mix gestured for Margo to help her turn the table so it would sit at the far end of the conference room.

"Do you mean, *make* coffee?" Margo asked as they pivoted the heavy table clockwise. They were opening the room so that the models could have a catwalk of sorts down the center.

"No, Margo," Mix said, patronizingly, "if I wanted to *make* coffee, I could. I want you to go *get* us coffee."

"I wish I had known. I was just at the coffee shop."

Margo set her end down, clearly annoyed. Mix looked satisfied at riling her and then reached to move one chair in place behind the table. "I'm not sure what that has to do with anything," Mix said as she reached for its twin, positioning the chairs side by side, "but it shouldn't be too hard for you to go back. It would be a huge help." Mix picked up a stray chair and walked closer to Margo with it in her hand, "and isn't that what you're here for, Margo, to help me?" she sneered.

Mix stood directly in front of her.

"I guess so," Margo said sweetly, "I did, after all, *help* you with the idea of this shoot, didn't I?"

Mix's eyes flashed dark with animosity as Margo held her gaze.

Mix stepped in closer, handing Margo the chair she was holding before leaning in. "I don't think I recall that, sweetie, but I do recall giving you my coffee order. Let's hope you remember it since *that's* your job."

With that Mix brushed past Margo, walking out into the hall. Margo stood seething, the stackable chair in her hands, when Ford walked in.

"Here, let me help you with that," he said cheerily taking the chair she was holding, tucking his papers under his arm, his bicep under his Black Watch plaid shirt rippling. He strode to set it behind the table.

"Oh Ford, Margo was taking that chair to the hall for me," Mix said as she reentered the room, a manila folder in her hand of the model pulls Chelsea and Margo had done that week. "We only need two chairs, for you and me. Picking the models is a senior staff decision, not the junior help. Besides, I already spent the week calling in who I thought would be best." Mix set the folder she was carrying down onto the table, retrieved the chair from Ford, and handed it back to Margo with a sly smile. She then turned to go sit, before a thought stopped her, "Oh, and see if they have one of those croissants I love so much, Margo. I'd hate to have you run out twice, that'd be foolish, don't you agree?" she said sardonically.

Margo could feel her blood boiling as she turned for the door. Just as she reached the doorway, Kirby whizzed into the room, almost crashing into her. "Oh hey," Kirby said, before fully registering it was Margo. "Wow, you look amazing!"

She stepped back from her sister taking in the outfit. Margo was still enraged by her interaction with Mix. Catching a glimpse of her anger, Kirby asked, "Everything okay?"

Margo quickly mustered every ounce of her professionalism in an attempt to guise her true emotions. Somehow miraculously a plastic smile appeared on her face. "All good," she said, worried that Kirby, who knew her every expression, would see through it.

"She's just running out to get us coffees," Mix offered behind her. "Ford and I are about to start casting."

"How fun!" Kirby said enthusiastically, not even questioning Margo's forced smile.

Are you kidding me? She's not even going to question the energy in the room, Margo glared to herself behind Kirby's back.

"I'm sorry I'm going to miss it. But you know…," Kirby trailed off, a glint in her eye.

Just as Margo thought, *No, I don't know,* Mix boomed, "We know! Big day!"

What?! Even Mix knows where Kirby's going and I don't? Margo questioned to herself. Anger flushed red across Margo's throat and chest.

"You know I will! Just had to grab my business cards." She smiled, flashed the cards in her hand, and headed for the door. "Alright, I'm off," she said as Margo noted her 100-watt smile.

"Knock 'em dead," Mix cheered as Kirby disappeared into the hall.

Margo rushed out behind her, setting the chair on its stack as she went. "Kirby!"

Kirby stopped and turned.

"Where are you going? What's the big news?" Margo asked.

Kirby walked toward her, her face glowing with excitement. *Thank God, she's going to tell me. I was worried for a moment.*

Kirby clasped her shoulders. "I can't tell you, but it's big!" She looked punch-drunk with joy.

"What do you mean, you can't tell me? I'm your sister, silly," Margo forced jovially, hoping to weed out the weird mix of jealous anger that, even she, herself, could hear in her tone.

"I know, but this is above your pay grade, M." Kirby gave a playful pout. "But, I promise the minute I can tell you, I will."

With that, she swept Margo into a hug, "Wish me luck."

"Good luck," Margo forced as Kirby broke the hug before Margo could even return the embrace.

"Love you, M," Kirby clucked as she headed out the door. "Call you tonight!"

Margo watched her go. "Are you frickin' kidding me, Kirby?" she quietly said to herself.

"Not happy for big sis?" Mix said behind her, saccharine sweet. "Doesn't seem like you, M."

Without looking back at Mix, Margo strode to her desk, grabbed her bag, and walked to her car, leaving 30 deliciously handsome male models in her wake. *I have always been Kirby's confidante, but now I'm not at the right pay grade?! What the fuck does that even mean?* Margo huffed as she yanked her seatbelt into place. Her phone dinged with a text.

I *prefer Starbucks over coffee bean.*

"And, I'd prefer you went to hell," Margo said aloud. "I'll be damned if I'm driving all the way down the hill for you."

Margo punched the word *coffee* into the search of her navigation screen with enough force to crack it. The first place that came up was Coyote Café. *Perfect. Sounds like a hole in the wall.*

Margo was right. Carved into the side of the hill halfway down Beverly Crest sat Coyote Café, a small sliver of an establishment that was easily missed thanks to its hidden façade, so much so that Margo *had* missed it. She had to go down the hill and turn around, driving back up to locate it. She waited for one of the only spots in the lot that her beat-up Bronco would fit into. When she walked into the café, she stepped in a puddle of water. *Damn it! Chelsea's McQueens!*

"Watch out," a small man behind the counter said. "We got a leak."

Obviously, she thought with her right foot sloshing in water. She gingerly stepped around the growing puddle as she took in the scene. A giant water mark scarred the fold of the ceiling and one entire corner of the café had an inch of water on the floor.

"Come on in" the older gentleman behind the counter encouraged. He looked oddly like Tim Conway's brother but with a mustache. She and Kirby watched the Carol Burnett show every Saturday with her parents. She felt her anger ratchet down a few notches at the memory.

"What can I get you?" he asked.

"Are you open?" She looked around the room with its plaster falling from the ceiling.

"Sure are," the man shrugged. "Way I see it, there's always a leak or a problem. Can't quit every time one of those crops up. We gotta keep moving forward. We gotta show up, try, make the coffee, take the leap. That's the human condition."

Margo felt herself relax, the anger shaking free from what had just happened up the hill. "Ain't that the truth," she said, smiling at his positivity.

"What can I do ya for?" he asked.

Margo rattled off her order and paid at the register.

"Take a seat." He pointed to the booth. "I'll get that right out to you. Want any pastries?" he asked, as he began to grind coffee beans, gesturing with his head toward the counter brimming with cake stands. "We make 'em homemade daily. I get up at 4 a.m. just to do it."

Margo looked at the counter and spied the pile of at least ten croissants under an elegant glass cloche. She thought of Mix's request for the flaky and buttery baked goods. "Nope, all set," she said as she took a seat.

As Margo sat in the oversized walnut booth, a flood of anger and uncertainty washed over her. *Universe, God, Beyoncé, Oprah, give me a sign of what I'm supposed to do. I thought I was on the right path, but I don't know. I'm keeping things from my parents. Kirby's keeping things from me. Mix is destroying my life. I just need a sign of what to do next, of where I belong....*

"All done," the man said, breaking Margo's train of thought. As she stood up to reach for the coffee, he gasped.

"Something's stuck to your jeans. Hold on."

She looked down to find that a wet piece of paper was adhered to her thigh.

"I'm so sorry," he said. "This just happened today and I'm here by myself. I hope it didn't stain."

He reached toward the half-dried piece of paper to assist her. Margo peeled it off for him. As she went to hand it to him, she noticed the words, "FOR RENT," in big red letters. She snapped the paper back before he could grab it and stared at its message. It was an ad for a two-bedroom storybook-style guesthouse in lower Beverly Crest with its own yard. The picture, although blurry, looked adorable. The listing price was $2,250.

That has to be an ink run, she thought, *everything's twice that price now.*

Margo's head fell back as she looked up at the ceiling, with its giant wet pock mark. "Thank you, Oprah," she whispered aloud. Then she hugged the man, who was still holding her coffee. He looked surprised. "Thank you too, sir. I think you're right about that leap."

CHAPTER 15

Matt

Matt was momentarily unsure who was speaking to him when he felt the trailing of her fingertips along his spine.

"Wanna get breakfast?" she whispered again, a familiar lilt to her voice.

As the warmth of her frame nestled in close from behind, Matt began to wake up. Her chest pressed to his back, she reached her arm up under his armpit and around his chest, her hand squeezing his peck as she kissed first his back and then the top of his shoulder. Her leg began to twine atop his. Matt continued pretending to sleep as he weighed his options, the oddest combination of dread and an erection settling over him.

"I know you're awake," Bibiana Romano said in the breathy tone she always adopted when seducing a man.

It was a tone Matt knew all too well; he had, after all, lost his virginity to Bibi when he was 15 and she was 19. She was his tennis instructor. And, unlike Matt's first serious attempt at fooling around when Holland Beck accidentally bruised his penis, Bibiana knew exactly what she was doing.

To spite his father, he had quit baseball, the one sport Matt was good at, the one thing he and his father still had in common. But he missed the daily workouts and the camaraderie of sports, so he signed up for tennis. The club had told him Ben would be his instructor, but when Matt arrived Bibiana jogged up.

"Hi! Ben tore his rotator cuff, so you're stuck with me this summer."

Although bruised, Matt's penis immediately stirred as if to say, "Bro, we got this."

Bibiana was a goddess with almond-shaped eyes, sporting both an all-white smile and tennis outfit. Her thick, dark hair was pulled atop her head, haloed by a visor to protect her flawless skin. Matt was stupefied by her beauty. He'd certainly jacked off to the thought of exotic women who looked like her but had never actually been in the presence of one in the flesh. He went to an all-boys prep school, and even though they'd hung out with the local high school girls, none of them looked like Bibi. Anyway, those were girls. Bibiana was a woman.

"You okay?"

"Yeah," Matt said his voice cracking, which he attempted to cover with a cough.

Bibiana smiled, amused at his awkwardness.

Matt couldn't tell exactly how old she was, but knew she was far worldlier than him. Her father, a famous director, had sent Bibiana to a Manhattan school for the performing arts when she was in junior high. Teaching tennis was her layover before entering her freshman year at the London Academy of Music and Dramatic Arts in the fall.

"Let's do some suicides on the court to warm up and then get a look at that arm," she said as she took off running toward their reserved court.

Matt immediately fell in line behind her like a lost puppy.

"So," she asked as they jogged, "How long have you been playing?"

"I haven't," Matt replied, "I mean, today's my first day. I'm a baseball player."

"Oh, what position?"

"Pitcher."

She stopped, Matt nearly running into her.

"And they're letting you play tennis, in season?" she asked surprised.

"Well, I sort of quit," Matt offered.

"Hmm," she said taking stock of him, beginning to jog again. "Okay then, looks like you're my star student."

As they reached the court, she gracefully unlatched the gate. "You're also my only student," she concluded with a wink and a smile over her shoulder as she leaned toward him. She was so close; Matt could smell the softest touch of coconut floating on her skin.

I'm not gonna last the summer, he thought. *Me either, bro,* his penis echoed.

"Starting today, you do everything I ask," she continued with a conspiratorial smile as she handed Matt his racket.

Matt was too inexperienced to realize she was flirting with him, but two weeks later after practice she asked if he'd rather shower at her place instead of the club. On the car ride to her apartment, Matt was entirely unsure of what to make of the situation, but when she stepped into the shower with him, he caught on real fast. His penis had caught on sooner.

"Don't you dare call Zinny in here to rush me out," Bibiana said sexily, knowing all of Matt's tricks as she pulled at his shoulder forcing him onto his back, kissing him delicately along his neck.

Matt, shook back to reality, obliged rolling over as she slid on top of him. She continued to nibble along his jawline as her hips began to grind against him, Matt willed himself *not* to rise to the occasion, which was very hard where Bibiana was concerned. She had a way of bending a man's will or building it as was the case of the current situation.

"Don't you play hard to get with me. You know I can break you, Matthew," she whispered in his ear as she bit his earlobe.

After a sharp intake of breath, "Bibi, I have a ton to do today."

Matt sat up, his left arm wrapping around her waist, as she straddled him, his right hand grabbing her neck with his four fingers resting just below her ear, his thumb tipping down her chin so that her lips could meet his mouth in a languid kiss. As she fell back, Matt came up onto his knees hovering above her. She wrapped her arms up around his waist, pulling him down toward her as Matt took the position of a push-up, his arms on both sides of her head, his back strong and tensed as he held himself there for a long kiss. Just as the kiss deepened, Matt suddenly stood, stepped off the bed, breaking their contact.

"I have to go." He reached for his underwear.

Bibi tsk-tsked as she swatted his naked rear.

"You have to go too," he furthered looking back over his shoulder at her as he pulled on his briefs and then reached for his jeans.

Bibi rolled onto her side watching him dress, the sheets entwined around her waist, not even caring to cover up. From the moment Matt had met her, he had been drawn to her confidence. Bibi never hid in any way, from a friend, a lover, the truth. She always laid herself bare, almost like an exhibitionist, which definitely got her into trouble with men. Over the years, they'd shifted from hot and heavy summer- and winter-break flings to friends with benefits, to best friends with benefits, which had never been the easiest for the people they were dating to make peace with.

"I hate her, and I want you to stop seeing her," Matt's fling of a few months ago had demanded.

Obviously, that hadn't worked out for the fling. It was, after all, Bibi who was in Matt's bed this morning. Over the years, Bibi had changed a lot more than Matt. Matt was somewhat stunted as his college-aged self, while Bibi had morphed, grown, and evolved. She had lived in the world, striking forth toward her dreams. She had gone from tennis coach and starving actress to a small part as a homicidal serial killer on *Luther* that catapulted her career when she unexpectedly got pregnant at 26 by the asshole she'd been dating, off and on, at university.

Matt had been with countless different girls over the years. Bibi, however, had only one ongoing, broken relationship in Alex. *Fucking asshole*, Matt thought whenever Alex's name came up. Alex had skipped out on Bibi the moment she'd gotten pregnant.

"Why can't you get rid of it, love?" Alex had asked, unemotionally and annoyed. "You're just about famous. Don't mess this up for us," he added flippantly.

She told him she was keeping it and then watched defiantly as Alex grabbed a bag and moved out of their flat. She'd slid down the wall to the floor and remained there for hours crying after he'd gone. Matt caught the red-eye to London the next day and propped her back up. Bibi didn't know it, but he'd gone to Alex's place to implore him to do the right thing.

"Come on, bloke. It's on her if she has the thing. I'm about to break big. I can't be there for a kid."

Matt seethed with disgust. "Good thing for you, I can be, you piece of shit," he snapped as he walked out.

Matt swore he'd always be there for Bibi. He kept his word and so had Alex. When Gus was born, it had only been Matt and Bibi's parents there. Matt had been there for every birthday, holiday, family vacation, and meltdown when Bibi didn't think she could hang on one more minute going it alone. Through all of that, the ups and downs, the bumpy start of her career before her steady rise, the fights and eventual breakup with Alex, the baby, the struggle from size 0 to 12 to somewhere in the middle, Bibi never lost her confidence and she never lost Matt. The two had been on again, off again through it all, but their love never waned.

"Where do I have to go?" Bibi asked coyly, as she stretched like a cat across Matt's bed. His mouth watered at the sight of her. "My mother has Gus in Ojai until Tuesday, when my guest spot's done filming on

Handmaid's and it's Saturday in LA. Doesn't that mean it's mandatory that we go to brunch?"

She masterfully flirted with him.

"Bib, I know you're holding out hope for a sweeping romance like Mary Kay Letourneau had with her child groom, but I think we both know I'm still too immature to date an older woman."

Matt leaned in to kiss her again.

"For the record, I didn't know you were 15 when we met," she said sternly, biting his lip in the kiss, "And, I'm not trying to date you," she challenged.

"Ah, but you did know I was 16 when you hooked up with me the next summer when you were 20, officially corrupting a minor. Is that a felony, Bibs?"

Matt shook his head in mock judgment as he sweetly kissed her on the forehead.

"And look at you now, revisiting the scene of the crime, still hot for my bod," he said shaking his head theatrically.

Bibiana rolled her eyes. "At least tell Zin I want one of her delicious breakfast sandwiches. I think we both know I earned that much." She pouted playfully.

"Don't worry, I'm sure Zinny has your order memorized, Mrs. Robinson." Matt walked into the bathroom to pee, leaving the door open.

"As if! I'm only four years older than you, Matthew," Bibi shouted after him.

"Speaking of four-year-olds, when do you and Gus go back to New York?" Matt shouted over the flush of the toilet.

"Not for a few more weeks," Bibi answered as she moved through the room, collecting her clothes. "I have an audition for a part I really want, so we're hanging through that," she said as Matt walked back into the room. "Why don't you stay with us since your stepmother is kicking you out, which, for the record, as a grown man, should have happened years ago."

She smiled as she buttoned her denim shirt, winking at him.

"She's not my stepmom yet," Matt shuddered at the thought as he buttoned his jeans. "But, I'm guessing soon. That'll be a fun wedding for us to wreck," a devilish smile on his face.

"Be nice," she encouraged.

"I might take you up on that," he said as he grabbed her hips, her arms circling his neck, "staying with you, I mean. I was supposed to be out yesterday."

"Let me know. But you know the rules, if you do. Friends, no benefits. It's too confusing for Gussy who already asks everyday why Uncle Matt can't be his daddy. If you get your act together, I might tell him you can be." She smiled.

Before Matt could process her comment, a knock on the door interrupted them.

"Mr. Matt, I come in now." Zinny said, making her statement a question.

"Saved by the bell." Bibiana smiled kittenishly as she poked him in the bare chest.

"Come in, Zin," they both chorused.

The door swung open and Zinny was upon them, coffee and sandwich in hand.

"Good morning," she chirped. "Looking beautiful, Miss Bibi," she continued her smile bright and cheery. "I make coffee just as you like, two Splenda. And I make no meat on sandwich. Is still okay for you?"

"Yes, Zin. Perfect," Bibi replied, gratefully.

Over the years she had come to love Zinny like a mother figure.

"How is Mr. Gus? I miss him," Zinny swooned.

"Oh, Zin, he misses you too. He certainly misses Matt," Bibi said as she leaned in to kiss Matt goodbye.

"Love you," he said in their quick embrace.

"Love you too, babe." Then Bibi turned and followed Zinny out.

Matt reached for his phone on his bedside table before padding out of the room, grabbing a shirt off the floor. He stopped to listen to the quiet of the house, hoping its silence meant that Tiff wasn't home. Optimistic, he continued toward the kitchen. As he sat at the island eating cereal, Zinny walked in from the side entrance.

"Miss Bibi is such good girl." She gathered the newspapers on the island, her tone telling Matt a point was coming. "This is second girl this week, no? I wonder to myself, *Does Miss Bibi' know this?*"

There it is! Matt thought.

Her tone made the question sound like a threat. They held one another's gaze before Matt shook his head, "No, she doesn't know, but she doesn't not know either."

He was aggravated that he felt compelled to answer her.

"What does this mean?" Zinny asked, her accent feeling thicker than usual due to her annoyance with him.

"It means Bibi and I have an understanding. We aren't dating. We're just friends." Matt's tone declared an end to the conversation.

"In Russia we have a term for this," Zinny began.

Matt cut her off. "We do too, friends with benefits," he said pointedly as he tossed his bowl in the sink.

"No, in Russia is simpler. It's just pig. You are a pig, Mr. Matt," Zinny said unapologetically, staring him down.

"For the record, this pig didn't sleep with that other girl."

"No?" Zinny asked.

"No," Matt said firmly.

"Hmm," Zinny observed. "You two just braid one another's hair then?" she asked sarcastically.

Matt wanted to smile but didn't. "Something like that." He smirked at her with one eyebrow raised.

"Okay, you win. Also, Russia is not spying on U.S.A., okay? Now we both lie."

This time Matt couldn't stop the smile.

"My point is, you act strangely after fight with Ms. Tiff. Behaving like old Matt. Drinking. Parties. Strange girls." She was listing his offenses but her tone sounded less judgmental, more sad. "I know she tell you to move out," she continued, "I think this is okay for you. You too smart to stay here, no work, no girl..."

Matt cut her off. "That's not true, you said yourself, two this week."

Zinny threw her towel at him.

"No serious girl. It's time you grow up. I love you like son, but right now you behave like son of bitch." She scowled.

Matt looked down at the island tracing a vein of the marble. "You have place to go yet?" she asked.

"Worse case, I can stay with Bibi for a few weeks."

"Okay." She nodded. "Is okay to do that, but then you have to be a man, the man I know you can be, either be together or let Miss Bibi move on. Is no good you two always coming back together to be apart again. It means no matter how far she goes she is on repeat."

Matt wondered if Zin was right. He and Bibi loved one another, but lately it felt like a record that skipped just when it got to a good part of the song. *Maybe I should just be with her. No more excuses. Just commit.*

"Miss Tiff is on way back. You are one day past her Friday deadline. She circled calendar."

Zinny pointed to the pantry door where the house schedule hung. Sprawled across Saturday were the words free at last. Matt rolled his eyes.

"Is Saturday," Zinny noted.

"I know, I'm going to Bibi's tonight. I'll come back for my things once I find a place. I just can't believe my dad picked her over me."

Tears sprang to his eyes. He looked away. "I'm worried," he said, cutting himself off, afraid he might actually cry.

Zinny walked around the island. "You are son. He will choose you." Her voice was confident and motherly. "He is not always best father, but in end he will come through for you. In meantime, *you* come through for *you*, okay?"

"The fuck," Tiff shouted from the hallway, as Zinny and Matt's heads swiveled in the direction of the noise.

Matt quickly wiped at his watery eyes as Tiff clomped down the hall, her backless Gucci loafers thwacking across the floor with each step. Keys, shoes, and bags fell in her wake. She rounded the corner to the kitchen.

Without greeting them, "I just got a new iPhone and somehow this disgusting pig is still texting me pictures of his balls," she shouted.

Applicant #3457 still coming through for me, Matt thought, a smile playing at the corners of his mouth.

"I mean, look at this," Tiff beseeched them, as she held her phone out toward Zinny and Matt.

There's a visual that's gonna haunt me, Matt thought turning his head counterclockwise to try and understand the amount of red pubic hair staring back at him. *Hmm, a ginger. Didn't see that coming,* he thought.

"How do I get rid of this guy?" Tiff pleaded.

Matt reached out and took her phone, scrolling through what had to be at least 30 very startling dick pics.

This guy's commitment is admirable.

"Mr. Matt can fix this," Zinny offered, giving Matt a prodding look that said she knew he had somehow orchestrated this.

"Probably," Matt offered, bending to Zinny's will.

He clicked to pull up the block number prompt on the screen, his thumb hovering over it.

"Are you sure, Tiff? This guy could be Justin Theroux. Maybe you wanna meet him first?"

"Stop it, Matt," she demanded.

Matt hit the button and handed the phone back to her. "There, don't say I never did anything for you."

He stood and headed toward the hall. "Today's Saturday," Tiff said coolly to his back.

"Sure is," Matt replied, turning to face her.

They held one another's gaze, a stand-off. Matt put his sword down first, reminding himself of his commitment to not aggravate the situation. "I know," he acquiesced,

"I'm going. Today. I promise. Just sorting out some of the details."

Tiff looked suspicious. "Can one of those details be no more girls? I had the unexpected pleasure of meeting Sasha in the hall Wednesday. Do you remember her?" Tiff asked sweetly.

Sasha! That was her name! He'd racked his brain all day Wednesday after Zinny saw her off. Thank God he hadn't slept with her. Zin was right, he was a pig, but not so much so that he ever forgot the name of someone he slept with. *Tiff coming through in the clutch*, he thought.

"I'd prefer that you take the trash out, not bring it back in with you. That includes Bibiana," Tiff said, sourly.

Matt knew that Tiff hated Bibi. She was so threatened by her, especially since Matt's dad was so drawn to Bibi. Brooks adored her. Truth be told, Bibi was the sort of woman Brooks would cheat with if only she didn't have a son. *He already has one of those that he doesn't want,* Matt thought of his father. *No need for another, right dad?*

"Like I said, I've already packed a weekend bag. Once I have my lease sorted, I'll be back for the rest." He turned and left the kitchen.

As he slid into the driver seat of the Volvo, he knew there were no homes in LA in his price range that were even remotely a fit. And for a guy like Matt, whose family net worth put him in the Buffett bracket, living in an economy apartment in Encino wasn't going to cut it. Besides, getting an apartment was only half the battle, according to his father's email. He needed a job, Matt thought recalling that very discussion with Bibi the day before.

"What do you mean, different?" Matt asked last night as he and Bibi sat at Pace having dinner in the Hollywood Hills, discussing that very email.

"I mean different. You've always done the right thing. Always. But now I feel like you *want* to do the right thing, like not just because you know you *ought* to but because you *want* to." Bibi spoke as she sopped up the tomato chutney the waiter had brought with the bread. "Oh my gosh," she gushed, her eyes rolling in pleasure, a mouthful of focaccia. "Taste this."

"What do you mean by 'right thing?'" Matt questioned, ignoring the fact that she'd moaned less in his bed last night than she had over the carb in her hand today.

"I mean, at first you wanted to do what you had to do to get your trust back. But now I don't know if it's Tiff's kicking you out or Rob's threatening you about MLE or that you're just sick and tired of not being the man you're truly capable of being, but you have a fire that wasn't there before. I see it. Your eyes are sparkling." She tore off another piece of bread.

"Are you sure that's not just the carbs talking?" Matt prodded.

"Hah. Hah," Bibi said dryly. "Listen, Matthew. I've known you for a decade. This is the first time I've actually thought that good enough is no longer good enough for *you.*"

Matt felt the lightning bolt of her words strike him. *Good enough isn't good enough anymore,* he thought. *She's right. I want more. I want success, but not from my dad, the kind I carve out for myself. I want to be happy,* Matt realized as he watched Bibi pantomime fainting over her first bite of tagliatelle.

Matt hadn't been happy in a really long time. Yes, there had been epic parties and unforgettable trips, floating in the Mediterranean with 50 friends on an endless booze cruise. However, Matt was certain not a single one of those people would turn up for him unless the words yacht and private plane were included in the invitation. Happiness had alluded him for years. His last true glimmer of it had been when Gus was born.

"Look at him, Matthew," Bibi had hushed in her hospital room, Gus cradled in her arms. "I don't know if I gave birth to him or he gave birth to me because life began for both of us today."

Her eyes glistened with tears, as she marveled at her son. Matt had felt in awe of that kind of happiness. He'd assumed he'd never have it. Suddenly he realized he wanted to *build* it for himself, starting now.

"What can I do ya for?" Sam said behind the counter of Coyote Café, shaking Matt back to his morning.

"Coffee," Matt replied. "Black, one sugar."

"Pastry?" Sam asked.

"No thank you, trying to watch my figure," Matt offered as he sat in the booth along the wall.

"Me too," Sam said patting his paunch of a belly.

Over the past week, Matt had been coming here every day to escape the wrath of Tiff. He'd holed up in the corner booth cleaning up his résumé, writing cover letters, and sending out inquiries to friends letting them know he was looking for a job. So far, it had been crickets, but Matt knew something big was coming. Something was going to fall in his lap and when it did, it would shift his whole world on its axis.

As Matt sat there on his phone, he felt a drip on his forearm. He ignored it, but then he felt another and another. He looked up to see a giant watermark directly over him, the ceiling, sagging beneath its weight.

"Um, Sam," Matt said cautiously pointing up, "What's that?"

Sam's eyes traveled upwards. "Holy cow!" Sam exclaimed, panicked.

He slid around the counter and ran out of the café rounding the building to the side stairwell. Matt heard him bang up the stairs, presumably to knock on the second-floor tenant's door. As Matt stood up, he heard a loud crack before a giant chunk of the ceiling fell, followed by a gush of water that poured down on him.

"Shit!"

Water streamed down the walls and began pooling on the floor. Matt heard footsteps pound overhead, Sam now inside the apartment. Then those same forceful footsteps hurtling back down the stairs, as Sam careened into the cafe. "Oh my lord," he shouted. "The upstairs tenant left the bathtub on!"

Matt was drenched.

"Let me grab a mop and towels," Sam yelled as he flung himself into the closet, buckets and cleaning supplies falling out as he crashed in.

Matt stood there, his arms out, his head down, sopping wet, when he heard another crack. He looked up to see one nail of the giant café bulletin board give way. At least five feet by four feet and filled with years' worth of lost dog notices, found cat posters, lawn care offers, and computer services, the board swung precariously down hitting the chair rail with a bang. Matt lunged to catch it. With its cork now waterlogged, it had doubled in weight.

"Sam, get out here! It's too heavy," Matt's voice strained under the weight.

Sam jumped back from the closet as one listing after another fell to the floor. Just as Matt was about to drop it, Sam hopped up onto the bench and helped to lift it up off its one remaining nail.

What had just been the picture of serenity not less than a minute ago looked like a war zone. The two men, stunned, suddenly started to laugh. An unsuspecting man appeared in the doorway. He took in the scene, turned, and walked back out. Matt and Sam laughed harder.

"I'm so sorry," Sam said.

Matt wrung out the flap of his shirt. "It's okay, I live just up the hill. I'll go change. But first, let me help you," Matt said gesturing around at the chaos.

"No, you've helped enough." Sam shook his head gratefully.

"Listen, I'll stay here while you at least sort out the water valve and call for help. I'm not gonna desert you just like that," Matt offered.

Sam looked relieved. "Thanks," he said again as he dashed into the back room.

Matt started to pick up the debris on the café floor. As he crammed a portion of the ceiling plaster that had fallen down into the garbage, something caught his eye. Sopping wet and resting on the bench was a sign. Red for rent letters at the top of the poster caught his attention first. Afraid to touch the saturated paper, knowing it would tear, Matt bent forward to read the notice. He hovered above it, his hands resting on his knees, as he read. It was an ad for a guesthouse in the Beverly Crest area. "2 bed. 2 bath. Yard and parking." "Price $2,250."

That has to be an ink run. Everything is four times that price these days, Matt shook his head in shock.

There was a number. Matt grabbed his phone and took several pictures of the sopping wet piece of paper.

"Don't you dare pick up one more thing. I got it from here," Sam said behind him.

"Are you sure, Sam?"

"Completely. Get out of here," the café owner urged.

Matt nodded and was already heading for the door, dialing his phone as he walked out

CHAPTER 16

Have We Met?

Margo flew through the gate of Blush & Bashful, coffee sloshing onto her shirt as she shouldered the office door open.

Shit.

She raced toward conference room Dorothy, as the stain on her rust bralette bloomed in size.

"Get here as soon as you can," the odd woman had said in an Eastern bloc accent, followed by something Margo couldn't decipher as Polish or German.

Rushing, she was determined to get there *immediately,* before anyone else could see the place. She'd been looking for months and had yet to find a single, solitary viable option in her budget that didn't look like the crack den Benson & Stabler just ransacked on a rerun of *Law & Order.* Margo knew that storybook home in that ad was meant to be hers. Although slightly beyond her price range, she had a plan. She'd ask Chelsea to be her roommate. Chelsea's studio was a sublet she'd extended month to month when she remained at B&B. She could easily get out of it for July and August, head back to school, graduate in the fall early and return for a position Margo was confident she could talk Kirby into giving to Chels. It was all coming together, at least in Margo's mind.

Margo careened down the hall, passing the 20 remaining men milling about for their audition, not even noticing they were stripped down to their underwear.

"Looks like you got a stain brewing there," Ford said. Margo power walked toward the front of the conference room where Ford and Mix sat, the table full of headshots from the men who had already auditioned. "Here, let me have those," Ford said taking the coffee tray, as he stood. "I'll go get you my Tide pen." He set them down and hustled out.

"In a hurry?" Margo turned to see Mix standing at the white board, her eyes scheming.

"Just hurrying to get you your coffee. Wanted to get it to you piping hot." Then she said, "Sorry, they were all out of croissants," her voice sweet as the butter Sam had undoubtedly used to bake the treats she'd purposely left behind.

"I bet they were," Mix said, deciding Margo was lying. She turned to put the eraser down. "Well, don't think you're rushing back to join us. Like I said earlier, senior staff only."

Exactly what I was counting on, Margo thought.

Had Mix said anything *but,* she'd have been stuck there and not able to make it to the rental property. Now she needed to buy as much time as she could. "You have to make Mix think everything is her idea," Chelsea had told her last night as they watched *Gossip Girl.* "Reverse psychology," she patently diagnosed in between bites of pizza.

"Oh," Margo said, dejectedly to Mix. "Well then, I'll organize the female auditions folder *today,* so that on *Monday* I can take all the clothes in for alterations to Sal's

Dry Cleaning. Hate to ruin this outfit loading a hot car, you know?"

Margo turned to walk toward the door, pretending to be on task.

"Actually," Mix's syrupy voice purred as she took a seat. Margo knew instantly she had her. "Since you already ruined your little outfit," Mix continued, nodding toward the stain, "I think it's best you load the car and run the wardrobe down the hill to Sal's today."

You're so easy, Margo thought, turning back. "And if you can find a way to let her think she's abusing your time," Chelsea had slurred one Apple Jacks later, "then she'll really go for the jugular and do exactly what you want."

With Chelsea's words ringing in her ears, Margo forged ahead, "Are you sure, Mix?" hesitation in her voice, selling it. "Because I still need to grab your lunch, and on Monday we'll have all the girl sizing too. Won't that be a better use of my time to do it all at once? Then I don't have to go there and back twice. This way I can really focus on the casting calls. I think that makes more sense."

Margo looked at her innocently.

"Excuse me, did I ask your opinion?" Mix arched an eyebrow. Then answering herself, "I didn't think so. I want it done today and I want it done this way."

Margo wanted to jump for joy; *this* would give her the few solid hours of freedom she needed to go see the storybook house. Concealing her happiness, she framed her face in quiet defiance making Mix feel certain she'd won this one.

"Fine," Margo said coldly and turned to go load her car, only then smiling so Mix wouldn't see.

As she swung out of the conference room, she ran smack dab into Ford, who had been bent over putting the wrapper to the just opened stain remover pen into the trash, the back of his head coming up and bashing her in the cheek. "Ahhhh," Ford cried with a sharp intake of breath, "Are you okay?" he asked rubbing the crown of his head.

Cradling her cheek, Margo sucked in air. "Yes, I, I'm fine."

"No, you're not fine," he said firmly, handing her the laundry pen, still rubbing his head. "You take care of your coffee stain, and I'll get a bag of ice for your cheek. You already have a lump, Margs."

He looked back over his shoulder and smiled sweetly, to make sure she was following him. Margo could feel her insides melt at his boyish concern. She trailed him dutifully to the kitchen, impressed that the stain on her shirt was lifting. "These things really work," she said in amazement as Ford loaded ice into a plastic bag, only to then wrap it in paper towels.

With her full attention still on the shirt, she wasn't expecting it when Ford reached out and gently placed the small pouch of ice on her cheek with his left hand as he delicately cradled the back of her head with his right, almost cupping her ear.

"Here, this will help." Margo shivered from his touch, not even noticing the ice.

"Thanks." She looked up at him, moon-eyed.

"Least I can do since I almost knocked you out." He smiled apologetically.

Focus, Margo, she told herself.

"Is this okay?" he whispered. "I don't want to mess up your hair."

Margo nodded, realizing her eyes must look like two heart emojis.

"You should wear it like this more often," he said gently touching her braid as his left hand continued to expertly hold the ice in place.

"You smell good," Margo blurted out, her voice oddly loud in the tiny kitchen.

He grinned widely as she turned crimson. "Do I?" he asked coyly.

"I wondered where you two were," Mix said snakelike from behind them.

"I hit Margo's head," Ford offered, smiling past Margo, shrugging his shoulders to show he was helping her. "Here, Marg."

He gestured for her to take the ice. As she grabbed for it their hands touched. She could feel Mix's eyes bore into her.

"Got it?" he asked.

She nodded shyly.

"If it's any consolation, I don't think you're concussed." He winked then leaned in, "But I wouldn't be doing my job if I didn't call you later to check on you. And, just for the record, you smell good too," he said with a lazy smile.

Margo's gaze followed him out and then landed on Mix's savage stare sizing her up. "Sal's," Mix said flatly and walked away, leaving Margo alone and smiling in the kitchen.

A second later, she was off like a shot. She cemented every delicious moment of her encounter with Ford to memory so she could reenact it later with Chelsea. Right now, she had to focus. She had to get the van loaded so she could get to that rental. She ran down the hall and grabbed both racks of clothes set to go to Sal's. They weren't *all* the outfits for the shoot, but they were their first wave of selects—one rack for the girls, one rack for the boys. Circling back for the keys and two drop cloths from the hall closet, she jetted to unlock the van and lay them out, covering the entire floor of the vehicle. Next, she methodically unloaded all the garments onto the now-covered surface. Last up, the vintage leather goods—bags, belts, shoes—that Sal had told her he could fix for their shoot.

Like everything about Blush & Bashful these days, the van, once packed, was a mix of high-end vintage including Gucci, Prada, and Chanel, decade-appropriate vintage in the form of amazing finds from the '50s, '80s, and '90s that weren't labels but were still to die for and a Kirby-curated list of brands that were featured on the site, like Brookes Boswell and Baron custom hats, Big Bud Press Jumpsuits, Lingua Franca embroidered sweaters, Rodarte shirts, Freda Salvador shoes, Midland Shop rompers, Brock Collection anything, and Ulla Johnson everything. She slammed the doors shut and looked at her watch. The van-packing process had cost her 30 precious minutes. She had to bust a move if she was going to see that house and still get to Sal's before noon.

She set her GPS and turned Beyoncé all the way up. As she careened through the hills, she realized how crazy the morning had been. An hour ago, she was ready to throw in the towel on everything, especially Mix. But now she wasn't just back in the saddle, she felt like she was about to own this rodeo. As she turned down the street to the house, however, her confidence waned.

These homes are huge, Margo thought.

Worry crashed over her like waves. She gave herself a pep talk as she exited the van and walked toward the tall hedge. She adjusted her shirt as she walked.

Wow, Tide pen for the win. The stain was completely gone, she noted.

When she looked up, she noticed a boy walking toward her. She smiled politely. "Hello," she said as she moved to the edge of the sidewalk so he could pass by.

But he didn't. Instead, he stopped right next to her. "Hi," he returned just as politely.

Her eyes drifted from him to the buzzer. His eyes followed hers. A pause between them turned into a realization. It was as if in that instant they both knew they were there for the same reason, to rent that house. Margo's hand shot out like a lightning bolt toward the buzzer. His did too. Aggressively, she stepped in front of him. Blocking his connection to the button and his view of the speaker, she firmly shouted, "I got this."

Just to be sure, she jutted her arm out to the side, letting him know he wasn't to take another step. Then realizing how crazy she must seem, *what if he's here to fix the pool,* she thought, she smoothed the wisps of her braid and more calmly said, "Please, let me."

Matt maintained his stance behind her. "Of course. Ladies first," he conceded.

As she turned back toward the speaker, she rolled her eyes. She depressed the button and instantly a rather loud doorbell went off inside the courtyard. After a few bars, Matt asked with uncertainty, "Is that *It's Raining Men*?"

As Margo continued to congenially barricade him behind her, she said, "It is," pretending like it was totally normal for a doorbell to be the dance cult classic of the '80s.

When it ended, they stood and waited, expecting a response. Nothing happened. Margo remained facing the speaker, her arm still outstretched in a block of the boy behind her, while Matt maintained his spot directly over her left shoulder. The awkward silence clicked on. "Do you think I should push it again?"

"Depends. How much do you like disco?" Matt deadpanned.

For the first time, Margo relaxed. Looking over her shoulder she smiled despite herself, "Very funny," she said dryly.

Just as she was about to ring again, the speaker crackled to life.

"Hello," a voice sang through the plastic mesh of the buzzer.

"Um, hi," Margo said quickly. "I'm here for the apartment, the house for rent," she added.

"Of course," the voice boomed. Despite the quality of the speaker, its tone was that of honey bourbon. "I'll buzz you in. Follow the hall straight ahead to the kitchen. Rita, my house manager, will help you."

There was a click as the line went dead. The heavy metal door buzzed. Jumping out from behind Margo, Matt pushed it open before she could, but then stopped himself. "Like I said, ladies first," he repeated with a smile.

Without hesitation, Margo slipped under his arm and stepped into the most over-the-top courtyard she could ever have imagined. Huge white marble columns flanked the front porch, fountains stood on both sides of the path, and a giant lemon tree, laden with lemons, branched overhead. Margo had never seen anything so opulent. It was outdated, but oddly well done. Matt, having been around money his whole life didn't stop for the gaper's delay Margo had. He was already turning the handle of the front door. Margo catapulted herself forward now, reaching toward the center doorknob, which looked like a massive fortune teller's crystal ball, along with him. It clicked open and they pushed in on the white lacquered door. It pivoted in the middle of the frame allowing them to walk through on each side. Laid out before them was a wide and long hallway completely clad in black, white, and pink marble. It extended all the way to the backyard, where it spilled into sweeping views of the canyon.

"Holy marble," Margo said. "I can't decide if it's gorgeous or terrifying," she observed breathlessly.

"I'd go with both," Matt offered.

Ginormous crystal chandeliers dotted their path toward the kitchen. As they made their way down the hall, their shoes clicking on the cold floors, they peered into each room flanking the home's casino-like entrance. Every room was more over the top than the last, with every surface drenched in silk taffeta and animal prints. Margo suddenly imagined that it might be Elizabeth Taylor who lived here, or Miss Piggy. Reaching the kitchen, they turned to see that its expanse ran the entire length of the back of the house. To the far right stood a giant family room with a drop-down TV screen that was playing an old episode of *All My Children*, which was ironic because the house felt just like one of the soapy sudsy homes Susan Lucci's character, Erica Kane, may have won in one of her ten divorces. Matt and Margo took in the space, neither one noticing the small woman slumped over the counter. She was surrounded by the makings of what appeared to be tuna fish salad, one pickle already partially diced. Margo saw her first and gently touched Matt's arm, pointing in the direction of the woman. Matt frowned. Margo shrugged. They turned back to the woman, perplexed. She appeared to be dead asleep, or as Matt worried, *just dead*.

"Rita?" Margo quietly mouthed with a confused frown.

"Maybe?" Matt whispered back.

Unsure of what to do, they stood staring at her. Quiet at first, they uncomfortably stirred. The woman didn't move. They talked louder, hoping to pull the small woman out of her stupor. When that didn't work, Matt yanked the fridge door open and closed, clanking the bottles inside. Nothing. Upping the ante, Matt pushed the line of pots hanging over the counter into one another. They clanged loudly. The woman didn't move.

Feeling a panic rise inside her, Margo asked, "She isn't dead, is she?"

Matt looked stricken, "Lord, let's hope not."

The pair gingerly progressed toward her. Just as they were upon her an extremely loud buzzer from the speakers overhead went off. Matt and Margo jumped. The sudden movement caused this *Weekend at Bernie's* prop body to stand bolt upright and scream, which caused Matt and Margo to scream right back at her. Then, like nothing had happened, the woman stopped and smiled. "You the two I spoke to on the phone about the rental?"

Matt and Margo, who still wore the look of horror on their faces, nodded wearily. Margo's brow furrowed, *The woman I spoke to had a thick accent,* she thought confused.

"I'm Rita," she continued, a leaf of romaine stuck to her cheek from her nap on the counter. "The house manager."

"You have lettuce on your cheek," Margo said. Without even reaching up to remove it by hand, Rita unfurled what appeared to be an oddly long tongue slowly pulling the lettuce back into her mouth, chewing as each bite folded inside, finishing with a smack of her lips. It seemed like an oddly sexual gesture that caused both Matt and Margo to glance at one another with a look that said, "We're in this together now."

"I'm sorry," Margo began, "but the woman I spoke to had an accent."

"I do accents," Rita said, proudly. "Bit of an actress, I am. I'm sure you can tell."

Margo lied with a nod. The woman before her had skin like leather with raccoon tan lines from Oakley sunglasses circling her eyes. She was clad in head-to-toe camo with her hair swirled into a mullet. She looked like a more compact, less attractive Steve Irwin, but with boobs.

"Just couldn't pursue it cause of my sciatica. But, I still audition. Give the people what they want, I say." Rita struck a pose, winking at Matt. "Especially you, big guy."

Matt looked at Margo in a silent plea for help.

"You two look like a cute couple," Rita continued. Their heads on a swivel, Matt and Margo turned back to look at her, surprised by her comment. Before either of them could correct her, she continued, "Boss is gonna like you especially," Rita said clicking her tongue at Margo.

Margo slid an inch closer to Matt, as scenes from Liam Neeson's *Taken* flashed in her mind. "Heck, we forgot we even put those posters up a few years ago. Then today, two calls. What are the odds? I stopped lookin' cuz she," Rita said gesturing upstairs, "can smell a problem a mile away. Rejected everyone. I don't know who else is showing up, but you two look like you've been sent straight outta of central casting. You just might make it through. She always said she thought a cute couple needed to live in that cute house," Rita concluded with a very bad New York accent as she began mixing heaps of mayo into her tuna salad.

Margo's expression was that of someone witnessing a doctor pull a cockroach out of a patient's ear on a YouTube video as she watched Rita lick a glob of mayo from in between her two fingers. The speaker buzzed loudly overhead, causing Matt to jump and yelp. The same voice they'd originally heard through the gate came over the speaker. "Rita, my sandwich," it clipped.

Rita smiled like a mom in a '50s sitcom at Margo and Matt before barking up at the ceiling, "I'm coming already! Lay off that buzzer, you old battle-ax!" Then just as immediately her smile returned. Her face the picture of serenity. "Can I get you anything?" she asked as she spooned her newly made tuna salad onto toast and constructed her sandwich.

"I'm good. You good?" Matt asked nodding at Margo.

"Good," Margo replied.

"Well then, that makes three of us," Rita concurred.

With her plate constructed, she climbed down off the footstool that Matt and Margo hadn't even realized she'd been standing on.

"She likes her tuna tub-side." Rita walked toward them. "Rich folks, amiright?"

She playfully punched Matt's arm, then paused and squeezed his muscle before nodding her approval with a pat. Matt's face was like that of squirrel cornered by a dog, frozen in the hopes that it made them invisible. "Make yourself at home." She winked, then headed down the hall. "Don't steal the silver. Boss makes me count it in front of her each week. You steal a knife one time for a boob job in '97 and you can't live it down, ya know?"

Matt and Margo nodded in return like they did know, but that was just because they were terrified. "Okay, you lovebirds. Wait here. She's a fast eater."

The compact woman spun and headed for the stairs, her Crocs squeaking against the marble, her mullet swaying as she went.

Matt and Margo briefly looked at one another, before turning to see Erica Kane on the large screen cowering from a grizzly bear. *I feel ya, Erica,* Margo thought.

"This place is mine," Matt said, definitively causing her to look his way.

Despite the strange house manager, Margo immediately replied, "I don't think so. Besides, I found it first."

"What are you talking about? We got here at the same time," Matt retorted.

"We'll see," Margo replied before pulling out her phone to ignore him.

"Oh, so you're going to ignore me, is that it?"

"You are smarter than you look," Margo smiled sweetly before pulling herself onto the bar stool to wait.

"Real mature," Matt replied.

As Margo stared at her phone, Matt kept an eye on the hall, planning to spring into action. *If there's one thing I know I can do better than anyone else, especially her,* he thought looking at Margo, *it's charm the pants off a middle-aged woman.*

The pair sat in silence, when suddenly Margo said, "By the way, you get to be the one to tell that kook we're not a couple."

"Why me?" Matt asked, contemptuously.

"Because you're the one she said it to first."

"Oh, is that some rule?" Matt asked. "Besides, she was talking to both of us."

The pair looked at each other narrowly, when suddenly from the back wall on the far side of the kitchen, a door flung open and a woman swanned in.

"*Ciiiaaaoooo, bella,*" the woman behind the bourbon and velvet voice they'd heard over the intercom sang.

Matt and Margo watched as a tall, stunningly beautiful black woman, in a floor-length silk caftan and headdress floated in through the now-swinging pink lacquer door. As silk fabric billowed out behind her, she paraded across the kitchen, her arm already outstretched. Margo stood and reflexively reached for her hand, which she noted was weighted down with the most exquisite estate jewelry Margo had ever seen.

As they shook, the woman boomed, "Rita told me the cutest couple was downstairs to see my little guesthouse, and I instantly got a good feeling about you two. In my heart I've *only* ever wanted a couple to call that place home. I'm Dinah Robbins-Mackey-Salter-Joiner-Jenson," the woman said with a smile that was absolutely captivating.

Margo was entranced by Dinah when she felt the boy, who'd arrived at the gate at the same time as she had, step to her right and place his arm around Margo's shoulder.

"Well, that Rita got it right," he said, pulling Margo in to his chest.

"Well, good, let's get you out to see *my* guesthouse, *your* future love nest."

Dinah clutched her heart in joy. It was Margo's turn to look like that cornered squirrel.

"Sounds good, right, hon?"

Matt peered nervously down at Margo grinning like an insane person as he squeezed her arm, his glance pleading, *Follow my lead.*

Dinah turned to the wall of windows running along the back of the house. "Rita, open," she commanded as the two of them began to slide the doors to one side.

Focused on the task and not paying attention to their guests, Margo pushed Matt away and mouthed, "What are you doing?"

"Just go with it," Matt insisted with a forced smile.

Dinah and Rita, suddenly finished with the doors, motioned for the pair to follow them outside. Margo stood momentarily stunned as Matt fell in line behind Dinah, circumventing the pool. Shaking herself back to the situation, she rushed behind him to catch up, hissing "no way" before bypassing him on the footpath that led to the back house to stop Dinah.

Before she could interject, Dinah, the clear matriarch of the estate, began telling them about the property.

"Now," she said, "in the ad, I played it down a bit. It's actually a full 1800 square feet with two beds, two baths, a den, walk-in closets, its own garage, a lap pool with a side yard, and a private patio all to itself. It's just such a large property and my pool has its own pool house, so I thought why not rent it out. But then, it was one weirdo after the next and I said forget it. Then, out of the blue, six years later, you two call. A couple no less. I love that. I love, love. I've been married six times to five husbands," she said proudly. "And really," she continued, "the timing is quite perfect because my third husband's kids want to send their kids here for the summer. Can you imagine?" she asked as she shivered in terror at the very idea. "Children," she repeated contemptuously. "I'd rather marry my third husband again, and he's dead," she laughed. "So I said I don't think so. But they're such harpies. They won't let it go. Our father would want them to see the city where we grew up," she pantomimed. "Cry me a river, right," she said shaking her head in judgment. "So, having you two as renters puts all that to bed."

The whole time she talked she never once broke her smile, sort of like a Miss America contestant answering questions for the judges about world peace or polar bears going extinct. Not only that, each time Dinah spoke, Margo fell more and more under her spell. She was oddly enthralling, like the human equivalent of a Quaalude. No wonder she'd been married six times. *Men must fall at her feet,* Margo thought.

She was breathtaking. Margo couldn't tell if she was 33 or 79. *I need the number of her dermatologist,* she decided.

"Not like we don't have eight rooms in the main house for those grandkids," Rita said coming up on Margo's left, poking her in the side as she snorted in laughter.

"I heard that, Rita," Dinah said flatly as she stopped walking to face her employee, swatting her away from Margo. "You know I don't like you to speak to the guests."

Rita rolled her eyes dramatically for everyone to see, especially Dinah. Dinah turned to walk again and then stopped dramatically.

"Oh, my goodness, where are my manners?" she asked, correcting herself. "What are your names?"

"I'm Matt and this is my girlfriend," Matt said spinning to face Margo, gesturing for her to hop in. When she didn't, he continued, "My girlfriend, Bug. I call her Bug," he said, nervously with a nod.

"Oh, well, that's hideous," Dinah said, pointedly looking at Margo and shaking her head in shame. "And Buuuuugggg," she said the word as if she were being forced to eat one, "what do you call yourself?"

Both Dinah and Matt looked at Margo expectantly. Margo—dazed from the assault of information from Dinah, the destruction of her dream to have this house for herself, and the lie this guy was trying to wrap her up into when her whole goal was to get away from all the tall tales she was spinning in the first place—looked from Dinah to Matt and back again. Just as she was about to say, "I'm sorry but there's been some confusion," her eyes fell upon the storybook house that stood directly ahead on the path, soaring up between Matt and Dinah's two shoulders. Her breath hitched in her chest and her desire to just maybe have the life that stood on that other side of its emerald green front door reared up.

"Margo. My name's Margo," she said, shocked that she, herself, had just furthered this lie.

"M&M," Dinah said, "How adorable!" Margo winced at her own nickname being used as a moniker for her association to this complete stranger. "I love it! Let's show you *your* house."

What are you doing? Margo thought as they neared the door. *Tell this woman the truth!*

She looked at the stranger that was about to become her faux boyfriend in the name of real estate and thought, *My lies are stacking up faster than this lady's husbands.*

"Rita," Dinah shouted, as she reached for the door handle. "The KEY!" They turned and looked back down the path. Rita was asleep on the bench where they'd just stood talking. Dinah set off an air horn. Matt and Margo hit the deck like a gun had gone off. "Narcolepsy," Dinah offered, nodding toward Rita, who was now trotting toward them with the key in her outstretched hand.

As Dinah unlocked the door, Rita hushed, "Be prepared to be wowed."

And boy, was she right! Margo thought. As Dinah swung the door open, Margo swore light flashes twinkled in the corners and sappy music, like in a home makeover show, swelled. It was gorgeous. They stepped forward to walk inside.

Dinah shouted, "Wait!" They froze. "You have to carry her over the threshold!"

Matt looked toward Margo and Margo looked back at Dinah. With Chelsea's voice ringing in her ears, *Fake it, girl. That's what Mix is doing,* Margo said nonchalantly. "Not until it's official. Don't want to jinx it."

I'm impressed, Matt thought as she walked past him inside.

"We'll let you look around," Dinah offered, signaling for Rita to follow her to the kitchen. As she floated across the living room, she rattled off more features of the house, "as you can see, marble island, Viking appliances, floor to ceiling bookcases, black and white marble floors, iron windows that open all along the far wall, and a fireplace in the master bedroom."

"Bet you two make your own heat," Rita whispered to Matt as she and Dinah walked by, biting the air next to his cheek. Matt leapt back in fear.

Like Julie Andrews in the *Sound of Music,* Margo spun into the room, crashing into Matt. "Now what? She thinks we're a couple," she hissed as he righted her.

"Well, it's not like you corrected her either," Matt shout whispered back.

"Corrected *her*?" Margo said in outrage. "You TOLD her we were dating. Are you crazy?" she insisted.

"You know what I am, I'm desperate," Matt said, laying his cards on the table as they wandered into the next room. "I can't stay where I am. I have to move out. This place is my only option. So, I say we get the place and we sort it out later," he said pragmatically. "Besides, have you seen another property that looks like this at this price?"

Their eyes traveled around the room. Seeing that Rita was trailing them, Margo grabbed his arm and ushered him into the master bedroom closet, shutting the door. "And then what, we live here? Together? You could be a serial killer for all I know," she said outraged.

"Me? You're the one who practically tackled me at the gate."

They stared one another down until Matt lifted his hands in surrender. "Listen, all I'm saying is this solves a problem for me. Maybe it doesn't for you." His eyes grilled her.

Margo stared at him as her tiny bedroom with its Smurf sticker headboard crashed into her morning interlude with Ford and his ice pack sweetness. *Two things that can never meet,* Margo thought as she looked at the built-in cabinets surrounding them.

"Well, does it?" Matt asked impatiently.

"Maybe," Margo admitted reluctantly, "But who's to say I can't get it on my own." She jutted her chin toward him. "Maybe Dinah will have a good laugh at the mistake." She feigned optimism.

"Mrs. I-love-love, married six times? Are you willing to take that risk?" Matt asked, his eyebrows raised. "I'm just saying, maybe we do it for a minute. No one has to know. There are two bedrooms. We make the most of it for a few weeks and then I buy you out," Matt offered.

"Me? Why am I the one to go?" she asked angrily.

"A minute ago you didn't even want to stay," he cried in outrage.

"Well, that was before I saw this closet," she offered smarmily.

"You two joining the mile-high club?" Rita asked through the wood slats of the door, her lips pressed against the wood.

Matt and Margo froze and watched as Rita snaked her tongue in between two of the slats. Margo grimaced. Matt looked like he smelled something bad. "Because you want to live here alone with Rita?" Matt asked cheerily.

Margo looked dismayed before plastering a smile onto her face and flinging the French doors open, "We're already members, you silly goose," she admonished as Rita fell into the room. "Just excited about that closet space. This one's got a lot of shoes," Margo said gesturing at Matt as she walked back toward the living room.

"Does this mean we're doing it?" Matt smirked as he caught up with her in the hall.

Margo kept walking. As they rounded the corner to the kitchen, Dinah echoed Matt's question. "So, are we doing this?"

She and Matt both stared at Margo. Margo's eyes floated up around the room with its exposed wood beams and sumptuous amount of good light.

"Yes, we're doing it," she said, shocked to hear own voice saying those words.

Dinah squealed and so did Matt.

"Great, let's get the paperwork," Dinah swooned.

"What do you two do, anyways?" Dinah asked as they walked toward the main house. Matt and Margo shared glances.

"We're influencers on Grid.it," Margo blurted out. She regretted it immediately.

What the hell, Matt thought, although slightly relieved since he didn't even have a job to declare. The fact that this girl did was a good thing, he decided.

"I mean," Margo continued, realizing that even if she started their feed this very minute, they'd maybe get five followers by the time Dinah looked at it. "We're just starting. We're taking that leap, you know? Got to build that influencer base, which takes time, but we're really excited."

Dinah nodded as if she understood. "I have no idea what you're talking about, darling," she said looking at Margo. Then turning to Matt, "Is that even a real thing?" She looked between the two of them before turning and continuing down the path. "I swear, kids today just make up jobs. Don't worry, Rita will show me later. She's really up on all the pop culture. She knows every member of that cute boy band, Menudo, by name."

Dinah stopped and looped Matt's arm through hers. "But more importantly. You're so handsome, Matthew. Is your father single? I know you're taken." She winked at Margo.

Matt and Margo smiled at Dinah's charm as she ushered them into her office.

"He is actually," Matt answered.

"Well," Dinah said as she gestured for them to sit, "not like that's ever stopped me."

Dinah sat down behind the large, high lacquered lavender, Louis XIV desk that sat in the middle of the room. It was laden with crystals and the same shade as the walls, carpet, and drapes. Rita appeared, dropping a manila folder, which was also lavender, in front of her. She bowed and then went and stood in the corner, almost instantly dozing off. Matt and Margo stared at her in wonder.

"You get used to Rita," Dinah gestured toward the elfin woman.

"She seems nice," Margo whispered.

Dinah let out a laugh that cascaded through the room. "Oh, no, she's horrible, but I can't fire her. She's been with me since husband number two, who was, ironically as titled, a real piece of shit."

"Don't talk 'bout daddy that way," Rita said from the corner.

While holding Matt and Margo's gaze, "Rita, don't you have things to do?" Dinah asked, her perfectly white smile never leaving her face.

Rita walked out slamming the door behind her. "Anyway," Dinah continued, "you two just fill out this paperwork, attach your financials, and get me your personal and work references, which I guess for you two *is* you *two* since you're Grid.it Gone Wild," she laughed.

Following her cue, Matt and Margo laughed too. "And then, we'll get you the keys and get you moved in. Sound like a plan?"

"Totally," Matt affirmed.

"Buuuuug?" Dinah asked, using her just-given nickname, then grimacing as if it left a bad taste in her mouth to speak it.

This is a horrible idea, Margo thought to herself. "Totally," she said with a forced smile, both Dinah and Matt looking back at her elated.

"Ready, boss?" asked a hollow-sounding Rita from behind them.

The trio turned to see the cherub-like woman standing with what appeared to be a white welder's mask on.

"Time for my chakra wax," Dinah boomed. She stood, gesturing for them to stand too. "Rita will show you out."

"Thanks," Matt said, as he offered his hand for a handshake.

"Stop, we're huggers in this family."

Just like that, Dinah took Matt and Margo under each one of her arms and walked them to her office door where she deposited them in the hall. "This is going be great. I can feel it," she said, smiling.

"Follow me," a muffled Rita commanded, her mask making her look like a little kid dressed up as Darth Vader for Halloween. They walked the labyrinth of the house to the front door. She bowed deeply as they walked out and then swung the door shut as she jeered, "See ya laters, alligators!

Matt and Margo stood on the front step inside the courtyard, dazed by what had just happened and what they'd just agreed to. They walked silently to the gate and exited out onto the sidewalk, neither certain of what to do next when Matt turned to Margo and stuck out his hand.

"Hi, I'm Matt," he said.

Margo looked down at his outstretched hand and then back up to his face. She extended her arm to shake.

"I'm...," she paused. "I'm sorry. I think I've made a big mistake. I have to go." With that she turned and headed toward her van.

CHAPTER 17

Sweet-Talker

"Wait!" Matt shouted as he darted after her. "You can't just leave. We have to talk about this."

"There's nothing to talk about." Margo searched her bag for her keys, practically dumping its contents in the process. "I made a mistake, that's all."

"A mistake?" Matt echoed. "No, you made a deal."

Margo spun to face him, "No, I made a mistake."

Her eyes narrowed in on him as her nose scrunched, which Matt noted was cutely buttonlike. "And, now I have to go," she said as she spun and resumed walking in the direction of her car.

"Just like that?" he asked. "You're giving up before we've even filled out the paperwork?"

Margo ignored him and continued trucking up the hill, Matt doggedly in her wake. "Okay, fine. You have to go. I get it," he said, trying to appease her, now half walking, half jogging next to her. "Let's just exchange numbers so we can get this sorted out later."

"Sorted out?" Margo asked as she pushed the button on the key fob to no avail. "There's nothing to sort out. Like I said, this was all just a bungled house tour."

She reached up and pushed the side-view mirror of the van back out from its now turned in position. "We both just got swept up. That's all," she said definitively.

Matt watched as the mirror popped into place with a *thwack* and Margo wiped her dirty hand onto her torn jeans. "Now, if you'll excuse, me..." she said, looking at him expectantly, prodding him to fill in the blank of his name.

"Matt," he answered again.

"Matt," she echoed, indicating for him to step aside so she could key into the door. "If you'll excuse me, Matt. I have to get to work."

Matt stepped back, allowing her to reach the handle. As he did, he noted the company name emblazoned in pink on the side of the white van. "And, work is Blush & Bashful?" he asked, pointing at the logo.

Margo looked at the van and then back to him. She could tell he wasn't going to let her just drive away. "Listen," softening her tone and expression, "I get it. It's been impossible for me to find a place too. I've looked and looked," she said shaking her head then shrugging. "Nothing, but *this* isn't the answer." She gestured back toward Dinah's house. "We both know it can't work. I don't know you. You don't know me. Maybe it was a fun idea for a second, but...." she trailed off, her hand on the door handle, building to the ultimate brush-off that Matt sensed was coming.

He could tell her act to appear casual was forced, much like that of a cashier who just wants to calm an irate customer and shuffle them out of the store. Matt knew he had to play this carefully. If he pushed her too far she'd go to Defcon Eight in two seconds flat and tear out of there. So instead, he matched her mannerisms, breezily leaning up against the van, his arms nonchalantly crossed. "I actually don't know that. I think this could be the universe's way of dropping a perfect solution into both of our laps." He looked wistfully past her out into the canyon, shrugging his shoulders deferentially.

Margo knew exactly what he was doing. *He's trying to win me over*, she thought. *Nice try, buddy. Not gonna work.* She didn't have time for any of this. She wanted to shove past him but instead; she smiled sweetly, trying to read him. It was the first time she'd actually looked at him. In the house she'd been too caught off guard to look him head on. Now, as the sun danced across the morning sky, she noticed his sleepy good looks, enhanced by a tiny scar that sat just above his right eyebrow. *What is it about scars?* Margo thought. As she pondered what childhood stumble had resulted in that former gash, she considered her best escape. Matt arched the exact eyebrow she was looking at. She averted her gaze immediately. She looked out into the canyon.

"What are you thinking?" he asked, playing it coolly. "Because I'm thinking we could make this work, Margo," he said warmly, letting her know he took the time to remember her name.

She could feel her defenses weakening at the thought of that living room and walk-in closets. "For a few weeks at least," he continued softly, "and then both of us come out ahead, without anyone being the wiser."

Margo used the key to unlock the door. The silence stretched out between them when her phone dinged. She looked down. "Shit, I'm late."

"Late for work as an influencer at Blush & Bashful?" he fished for an answer.

Margo looked at him confused. "As a what?" she asked.

"An influencer? Isn't that what you do, what you just told Dinah you do?" that same eyebrow arching.

"I also told Dinah you were my boyfriend. Did you believe that too?" she retorted cynically.

Matt smirked, "No, I just didn't realize that part wasn't true either."

"That's the problem, none of it was true. I didn't know what to say, so I just said that."

She sounded defeated as she stared at her hand on the door handle. "Well then, what do you really do?"

Margo's gaze floated up at the sky. She wasn't sure how to answer that question anymore. For years it had always been, *I'm a writer.* But now writing rarely entered the picture. She sighed deeply.

"Lie," she said, almost surprising herself at the admission. "Apparently, all I do lately is lie."

With that she swung the van door open and hopped in. Matt attempted to stop her, but as the door slammed shut it was either get out of the way or risk losing his fingers at the knuckles. Margo put the key in the ignition and the van rumbled to life. As she put on her seatbelt, Matt bolted toward his Volvo. *Thank God my car's facing the same way as hers,* he thought as he dove into the driver seat to tear out behind her.

Margo headed down the hill. Matt pulled into the lane behind and quickly caught up thanks to the poor acceleration of the cargo van. Margo looked in her rearview mirror to see the black SUV in hot pursuit. *What the fuck,* she thought as she drove down the canyon. *This guy just doesn't know when to quit.* She attempted to lose him when she pulled off Mullholland onto Laurel Canyon, but there he was in the gaze of her rearview mirror. He stayed behind her the entire way, horns honking, tires screeching as he tore through lights, maintaining his spot directly behind her, other cars on the road undoubtedly thinking LA drivers were the worst. When they pulled into the tiny lot of the hillside dry cleaner, he blocked her car so she wouldn't be able to bolt out of the space. "What are you doing?" Margo asked, incensed by his continued intrusion as she hopped out of the van, slamming the driver-side door with such ferocity that she thought the window might shatter.

"What am I doing?" Matt asked angrily. "I'm trying to stop you from fucking this up for both of us," he snapped. "I get it. You aren't interested for *you,* but don't take me down too," he demanded. "All I'm saying is fill out the application. See if we get it. Then decide. I'm about to be homeless and this is my one shot. I'll pay the whole rent. I just need you to help me get it. What does it matter if those two think we're dating? It's a private guesthouse with no neighbors. No one will know. And anyone in your life that might come over in the few weeks ahead will just think we're roommates. Is that so horrible? Lord knows the house is big enough for you to avoid me." His eyes searched hers. Her phone dinged. She looked down. His gaze followed hers to her phone.

How's my patient? Thought maybe I could drop by with wine and pizza. Keep an eye on you tonight. [winky face emoji]

Ford. Margo's heart swelled then haltingly stopped. *You can't have him over! And do what? Sit on the couch and pretend you don't live with your parents.*

She looked back at Matt who was staring at her in anticipation. Then she looked back at Sal's. *If you ever want to have a chance with Ford, Margo Valentine Melon, then you need to do this.* She looked up at the blue sky above. Then, "Okay," she relented.

Like an animal backed into a corner, Matt's body untensed but remained on guard. "Okay?" he questioned, not trusting her sudden agreement.

"But, we do it my way," she concluded, looking up at him defiantly.

"Fine. Yes," Matt swiftly conceded before the situation could shift again, a smile pulling at the corners of his mouth.

His face is perfectly symmetrical, Margo thought. *It's like he's photoshopped but in real life.*

"Whatever it takes, Bug," he said trying to hide his ear-to-ear grin.

"First rule, don't call me Bug." Her eyes went dark and serious as they bore into him. Matt felt a tinge of something he couldn't identify. He pushed the thought aside.

"Got it. That's an ixnay on the nickname bug." He saluted, noticing one of her eyes was slightly more hazel than the other and then immediately wondering if he'd actually ever met someone with hazel eyes.

Margo spoke, shaking him back to Laurel Canyon. "First, we need to go get some things."

"We do?" Matt questioned. "For what?"

"To sell it," she replied, as if that answer should have been totally obvious to him. She looked at the van and then brushed past him toward the back, asking, "What size are you?" He opened his mouth to speak but before he could, she answered, "Doesn't matter. I'm sure we got it." She walked back past him toward the driver door. "Get in."

Confused, Matt stood there watching her pull the door open.

"Get in?" he asked.

"Yes, get in," she said as she swung herself up into the van seat and reached back for the door handle to close it, "We have to go pick some things up at Target and then find a park."

Matt remained frozen as he watched Margo reach for her seatbelt. When the side door didn't open, Margo looked back to see him standing in the exact same spot. Buckled in, she opened the door. "Do you want to do this or not?" she asked exacerbated, "because any second now, I'm going to come to my senses."

"Yes, I want to do this," Matt responded.

"Then move your car and get in," she repeated and slammed the door.

Matt turned to move but then swung around and knocked on the driver-side window. Margo rolled it down. "Is this all a ruse to get me to move my car so you can drive away?"

"No," Margo said, "I'm serious."

Matt arched his brow, his scar followed suit, showing he wasn't buying it. Margo rolled her eyes. "Fine," she cried, looking around for something that would prove her intent, when suddenly she turned off the vehicle. "Here." She commanded him to take the keys. "I can't drive away without them. Believe me now?"

Matt stared at her briefly then scooped the keys out of her hand and jogged to his car. The Volvo darted around her on the road and took the one remaining spot in front of Sal's Dry Cleaning. *Hmm, never noticed this place,* he thought as he grabbed the lavender application folder off the seat. He swung up into the van and tossed her the keys. "Milady?"

Margo rolled her eyes, smiling despite herself, and pulled out.

As they headed down the hill, Margo glanced at the console clock. 9:37 a.m.

"Why Target?" he asked. "Not that I'm questioning you, my liege. Totally doing this your way, but I don't get what that has to do with the application."

"It has to do with the fact that we told her we're influencers," Margo stated.

"Correction," Matt said raising one clarifying finger, "*you* told her we were influencers." He smiled at her sweetly.

"And *you* told her we were in love. Now we have to sell both to her," she replied sweetly with a saccharine smile all her own.

"Touché," Matt replied.

"So, we're going to do just that," she said as she accelerated down Santa Monica.

"At Target? Is this a couple's thing?"

"No," she said, then corrected, "yes. Going to Target is exactly a couple's thing, but that's not why we're going to Target. We're going to get props to make us look like a couple on Grid.it."

"What does that even mean?" Matt asked as Margo leaned out the window, grabbing a parking ticket for the underground garage. "What are we getting?" he asked.

"Stuff," Margo replied forcefully as if this should all be making sense to him by now. "Couple's stuff," she continued, "To be exact, Grid.it couple's stuff."

"And how much is this stuff going to cost?" Matt asked still completely in the dark.

"Don't worry, we're going to return whatever we don't use for the shoot. The rest we can split. I don't think it will take much," Margo assured as she power walked behind the large plastic cart she'd grabbed just off the elevator.

Shoot? Matt questioned to himself.

Within 15 minutes their cart housed a picnic basket, blanket, rosé, wine glasses, some cookbooks, Scrabble, a tray, coffee mugs, beach towels, and at least a dozen other items. They headed for the front. Margo grabbed flowers. In all his years on this earth Matt had never bought any of the items in Margo's cart and really didn't see the point of any of them now. When the grand tally flashed on the cashier's screen, Matt did what he felt was right and paid for the entire cart even though he thought to himself, *What the hell are you doing, Matt Milles-Lade?*

As they loaded the car, Margo looked at the time stamp on her phone. They'd been in and out of Target in 20 minutes. *That's a record*, she thought as she pushed the now empty cart back into the corral.

"Where now?" Matt asked as he buckled up.

"The park," Margo answered plainly.

"What's at the park?" he asked, deeply puzzled.

"A place where we can stage our photos," Margo answered as she navigated the exit gate and the blue Nova in front of her who was behaving like he'd never driven a car before in his life.

"Photos? Photos for what?" Matt asked almost incredulously.

"For Grid.it," Margo exclaimed as if this entire charade should be obvious. As she looked over her shoulder to merge into traffic she asked, "What kind of shoot did you think I meant earlier when I said it?"

"I don't know," Matt said. "How is any of this necessary to us getting a house?"

Margo sighed loudly letting him know his stupidity was exhausting her as she began to drive again. "I told that landlord and her odd middle-aged, step," she paused to search for the best word for Rita, before landing on "woman, that we were moving in together so we could build our business as social media influencers, a career we'd just started with a page we'd just started. That means she won't be expecting a ton of followers, which is good because we won't have any, but we *do* have to have the page with photos that sells our story. Otherwise she's going to think *no followers, horrible photos, fail,* and deny us. We gotta hedge our bets. So, we're going to stage *something* that I can use to craft our story around," Margo concluded as she looked for parking.

She wasn't looking at him, but Margo could tell that Matt's mind was turning this information over and over dissecting its merit.

"Listen," she said in a tone that sounded like a woman who was out of options, as she threw the van in reverse and looked at him, "If we want this house then we have to sell her some way. *This* is the best way I know. I work with social media every day at my company. I know it's all how we position this for her. Besides, I can't have her call my sister for a job reference." Matt remained quiet so Margo bulldozed ahead. "My sister owns Blush & Bashful. What about your boss? What would he or she say if Dinah called checking your employment history?" Margo eyed him for acknowledgment of how horrific that would be.

Matt nodded. *What job,* he thought, not letting on to the fact that the one and only job he'd ever had he'd been fired from. And certainly not sharing that the person who had put in for his pink slip was his own father. "I think I get it now. I agree, I don't want anyone to know either. Too hard to explain. I got enough issues, and *this* would be the cherry on top of that shit sandwich," he said.

"I think you're mixing metaphors," Margo observed as she parallel parked along an empty strip of the park.

Matt rolled his eyes, "You get what I mean. We get the house and then decide who's going to live there."

Margo turned to look at the park from her seat, "Perfect," she said, seeing it mostly empty. Then she turned to face Matt. "For the record, I've decided, I'm not going to move out." She undid her seatbelt.

"Of course not," Matt replied as he exited his side. "Not at first," he continued as she came around to open the cargo side door, which Matt took hold of and pushed open for her.

"No, not even after a few weeks," Margo continued, looking at him seriously. "If I go to all this trouble to stage our story, and then move in, I'm staying to reap the benefits of having my own place. Got it?" Matt nodded. "We'll be roommates, deal?" she offered as she reached out her hand to shake.

Without hesitation Matt agreed. "Deal," he said as he shook her hand in return.

Margo began rooting through the massive amount of clothing in the back of the van, handing him items that he carefully stacked across the front seat.

As Matt watched her carefully debating the contents of the van, he decided it was more than fine for her to stay. *I guarantee in no time she'll be begging me to take over her half of the rent, anyway,* he concluded.

"Okay, here's what we're gonna do," Margo began, as she compared a white button-down to a pale blue sweater next to his skin tone. "We're going to stage a series of photos for our feed. I'm going to tell you what to wear, where to stand, and what to do, and you're going to do it. No questions asked. I may not be an influencer, but I spend a ton of time booking, researching, meeting, and covering them at work so I know what we need. Okay?"

Matt nodded, half impressed by and half terrified of the woman who stood before him.

Looking at her phone, "I have to get back to work, so we have to be focused. Got it?"

"Got it," Matt parroted back, feigning confidence, even though he felt completely unsure.

He watched as Margo opened a blanket in the grass and carefully placed a pair of sandals, a glass bottle of green juice, some books, and a folded *New York Times* along one side. Then she hauled out a tripod with one long arm, which she set up directly overhead, clipping her phone into the stand.

"Put this on," she directed, shoving a pair of jeans and a denim button-down into Matt's arms, directing him to the van.

Matt did as he was told. Then she hopped into the van, herself, and changed. She emerged wearing an all-white dress that came up high on her neck and buttoned in the back, with her shoulders bare. Matt realized as he watched her work how graceful her arms and neck were.

"Lie down," she commanded.

"Normally you have to buy me dinner first," Matt smirked cutely.

"Somehow I doubt that," Margo replied flatly without skipping a beat.

A sense of humor, good, they both thought at the exact same time.

Matt complied kneeling down on the blanket Margo had laid out.

Thank goodness for the location van and the fact that just last week I packed it full of equipment for a Venice Beach shoot, Margo thought as she hauled out a step stool to stand on and a light bounce for the sun. Matt continued to lie on the ground looking completely uncomfortable. "You're going to have to work with me here," Margo said as she loomed above him, her hands on her hips. "You can't look as if I'm holding you hostage. Good Grid.it couples make the stupidest shit look totally normal. And don't sweat in the clothes, they're for a shoot next week. I'll lose my job if we ruin them."

Matt nodded. "You've got a lot of rules."

"Wait until you hear my list of dos and don'ts for boys and bathrooms," she replied as she shifted the camera screen, fidgeting with the lens lock.

"I don't think I'll need 'em. I passed my good hygiene test in second grade," he assured her proudly as he adjusted his position on the blanket.

"Well, so did Bryce Tuttle, I'm sure, but that didn't stop him from shaving his balls in our communal sink in our college dorm," Margo replied. "I call my bathroom list the Tuttle Ten."

She hopped down off the stool to adjust his pose. "I'll have to look ol' Bryce up on Grid.it and let him know the kitchen sink's where it's at for any business with your balls. Better light. Better height. Better hose in case it turns into a crime scene, you know what I mean?" Matt charmed.

Margo yanked on his pant leg as she laughed, "you're disgusting."

She climbed back up on the stool and peered down at him. Matt suddenly felt very self-conscious, like he wanted to do the right thing to impress this strange girl. "Okay, what should I do?" he asked, committing to his role as influencer.

Margo smiled at her phone screen as she watched Matt awkwardly attempt to look cool. Unexpectedly, her breath hitched in her chest as she watched him. *Holy photogenic,* she thought as she clipped the phone onto the ring light.

"Easy, you're just going to lie there while I do all the work." His brows shot up. So did that cute scar.

Margo dramatically rolled her eyes. "You know what I mean."

Matt noted the slightest tinge of pink blushing her cheeks.

"Stay just like you are right now, and I'm going to start the timer and drop into the shot and rest my head on your stomach. Leave your arm tucked up behind your head. Use the other to hold my hand. Don't look directly at the camera. Just follow my lead. This app is gonna take a series of photo bursts timed about 15 seconds apart until

I stop it." She pushed the button. "We'll see what we get and go from there."

Suddenly she hopped down into frame and fixed her dress so it spread out around her and tucked one leg up under the other so her calves were elegantly and effortlessly out. Then she swept her hair to one side as she lay down, their two bodies like a capital T. Without even pausing, she took his hand in hers and held it to her collarbone. Matt noted instantly how natural it felt.

"Don't forget to smile and—pro tip—open your mouth like you're saying *Yeah* with a wide mouth grin. They always do that," she said as the camera started to click.

Matt had no idea what he was doing but was certain he looked like an insane person acting as if someone had just told him he'd won his trust fund back. *I didn't see this coming at 7 this morning,* he thought to himself as he did exactly as Margo had instructed.

As the camera clicked, they went from lying on the ground nervously to Matt casually sleeping while Margo pretended to watch him, to one where Matt pointed up at the sky as if they were looking at some make-believe spaceship hovering just overhead. They stood up, grabbed the phone and scrolled through the photos. Margo deftly zoomed in, cropped, and filtered several before landing on one where Matt held the paper over his head, appearing to read, as Margo coyly looked into the lens, her lip brushing up against their entwined fingers.

"Holy shit," Matt said over her shoulder, "We look legit. I didn't even know that my hand was near your mouth." He looked at her in amazement. "You're good."

"Thank you, kind sir," a humble smile spread across her face. *Holy shit, I didn't even know I'd done that either,* she thought. She felt her pulse quicken at how familiar she had let herself be with a stranger. *He's right about one thing, we do look legit,* she silently agreed, impressing even herself.

For a long moment both Matt and Margo continued to stare at the pictures, distracted by how oddly good they were when Margo called them back to attention. "Okay, we got at least five more of these to go. We gotta focus."

In very fast succession, Margo staged a series of shots in the park using the timer app. There was one where Matt swept her up in his arms and swung her around as she laughed wildly holding a bouquet of flowers. Another taken from behind appeared as if they were just coming back from a baseball game. Both in T-shirts, Matt walking ahead, Margo holding his one hand with both of hers as she coyly looked back at the camera. There was an entire series where Matt took the pictures of them using his long arm to capture just the corner of her face as she nuzzled his neck. She had mussed his hair and taken off his shirt, wrapping a blanket around her shoulders. When she filtered it to black and white it looked like they were naked in bed on a lazy Sunday morning. From there they headed to the local café where Margo tipped the barista, so they could borrow a table and chairs. For that series, they played mock Scrabble, toasted with rosé, and took a picture that Margo quipped was "but first, coffee vibes." Next, were tons of pics of just their hands or bodies close when seated, and an entire moment dedicated to their feet in different outfits as they walked, which Margo shot from above selfie-style, their hands clasped firmly together in the frame. As Matt scrolled through the series of shots, he got what Margo meant by *selling it.* Even he believed they were a couple when he looked at them. As he flipped from one to the next a text bubble popped up. Without thinking, Matt read it.

Where are you? Lunch anytime on the horizon?

"I think you got a text."

With her arms full, Margo looked at the screen as he held it out in front of her. Her eyes widened as she read it. "I gotta go." She foisted everything into the van. "Shit," she muttered as clothes fell onto the ground. "That's my boss, Mix."

"Your sister?" Matt asked.

Margo looked horrified, "God no!"

"I thought your sister was your boss?" he asked confused as he helped her toss clothes and props into the van.

Margo shook her head, "She is. It's her company, but Mix is my direct boss and she's a monster."

She slammed the door and commanded Matt to get in. "We'll have to do the application on the ride back."

"Perfect," Matt agreed as they buckled in.

As they tore through the streets toward Sal's, Matt and Margo were eternally grateful that much like the outdated real estate listing, so was the application. Whereas applications today have countless requirements, this one was a basic questionnaire. They filled it in easily. "Name?" Matt asked as Margo drove.

"Margo Valentine Melon."

"How old are ya, Valentine?" Margo smiled at the use of her middle name.

Within minutes they were done checking through the remaining questions, making up some items as they went along. "So, what should our handle be?"

"What handle?"

"Are you not on Grid.it?" she asked, astounded at the thought.

"I am but I rarely go on. My account's private." He shrugged. "God forbid I be off the grid."

He shuddered sarcastically as she rolled her eyes.

"Well, I guess since we're telling her this is our job, we need a handle that feels obvious. Here," she said handing him her phone, "Open it and let's search some names. Try Matt and Margo or Margo and Matt." His fingers clicked on the screen.

"Both taken," he shared five seconds later. "How about M&M?" Matt asked before Margo cut him off.

"No, that's my childhood nickname."

"Got it," Matt said definitively.

After another extended silence, "What about @MattlovesMargo?" she asked.

He typed it in. "It's available." He smiled.

"It is?" She was shocked at their luck. Matt nodded happily like a golden retriever who'd just been asked if he wanted to go to the park. "Does that work?" she pondered aloud.

"Totally," he affirmed.

"Then, that's it. We have a handle. @MattlovesMargo. While I'm waiting for the dry cleaner, I'll grab it..."

Matt interrupted, "I can't get it unless we have an email."

"Oh, you're already registering it?" she sounded surprised.

"Just because I don't *love* Grid.it doesn't mean I don't know how to operate a basic registration," he playfully chided. "Should I set up a Hotmail account?" he asked, his face now serious.

Margo burst out laughing. "Sure, if it's 2003. Who even has Hotmail?"

"I do," Matt defended himself.

"Well, then there's two of you. You and my Grandpa Pop Pop," Margo laughed. "You two can be pen pals. He'll write back only when his glaucoma isn't bad," she warned.

Matt smiled at her sarcasm. "Whatever, then you set it up."

Margo navigated the turn up Laurel Canyon as she looked at her dashboard clock. *11:48 a.m.* "I'm so screwed," she said aloud.

"No, you're not. I'll unload the van. You set up the account," Matt said supportively.

"Such a helpful boyfriend," she mused with a smile.

Matt noticed her eyes smiled when her mouth did. They hopped out and Margo ran in to introduce herself to Sal, they'd only ever spoken over the phone. As she emerged from the building, "I think he was relieved I was nice. Mix has used him for all her alterations since her Barneys days. He didn't say, but I could tell he likes having her business but isn't so hot on her. She has that effect on people."

Margo sat on the stoop beginning to set up their Grid.it profile as Matt continued unloading. "Sounds like Mix is a real charmer," he said as he transferred their Target items to his car and then returned to deal with the clothes.

"Only if you're charming snakes," Margo warned.

Matt laughed. "We'll have her over first and make sure she gets to know Rita."

"Inside jokes already," Margo said sarcastically looking up from her phone screen, "we better slow this fake relationship down." Matt chuckled.

"You gonna hold those all day and keep flirting, or you want I should help you?" Sal asked gruffly pulling Matt back to his task.

Matt saw that Sal's team had set up two racks just inside the store. He handed the stern, six-foot-tall, dark-haired Italian man the stack of clothes in his arms and grimaced at Margo behind Sal's back.

"Behave, I don't want him to hate me too," she mouthed to Matt.

"Are you kidding me?" Matt offered. "I've never been more afraid of a dry cleaner in my life."

As Margo continued clicking away, Sal and Matt unloaded the entire van. Then, this obvious mobster gave Matt a Fanta with a wink. "He's a gangster who drinks Fanta, which I admire in a crime boss," Matt said as he skipped down the storefront steps, offering Margo a sip. She shook her head no, as she stood and held out her screen for him to see.

"What am I looking at?" he asked as he reached to steady her hand.

"The equation for cellular respiration," Margo replied, as she rolled her eyes.

"Well, I already have that memorized," Matt answered, "So what else you got?"

Margo spun with her back to him, so he could see over her shoulder. She was tall, but Matt was taller. He could smell her hair, the faintest scent of sandalwood and rose.

The feed loaded, and five pictures floated up. "It's our Grid.it account. See?" she pointed to her screen. "Are these pics fine to use?"

Matt looked closely. It was like he was looking at a stranger's life except it was him in the pictures. "Wow, we look happy."

Margo smiled, "Don't we though?" cantering her head up at him with a grin. "But, you know what will make us happier?" she asked as Matt smiled down at her. "To get that house," she answered her own question with the enthusiasm of a musical theater actor, punctuated with jazz hands.

Matt nodded in agreement as he took a swig of his Fanta. "That is until Lester Holt tells the story of how Rita kidnapped and murdered us on the back of a Vespa on *Dateline,*" he cautioned. Margo snorted a laugh.

"Be serious," she demanded her tone solemn. "Rita's too short to see over the handlebars of a Vespa. Dinah will have her in the side car as she drives. Obviously."

"Obviously," Matt agreed as he nudged her waist, immediately regretting how familiar he was behaving with a girl he just met. *Then again, you're about to be living with her,* he thought. "We look good," Matt admitted. "Now what?" he asked.

Margo turned to face him, "Now I write our love story."

Matt physically felt a pang, *or maybe that's gas from the Fanta,* he .thought. He took a step back which caused Margo to shuffle awkwardly. "I mean, the one Dinah would want to hear. She does, after all," Margo paused so that Matt could chorus with her, "love, love."

"Stop," Margo said, as she laughed. "I liked her."

"Me too," Matt agreed, "I could be lucky number seven. Move to the big house," he looked off dreamily.

Margo shook her head at him, laughing.

"You feel confident enough to handle that?" Matt asked, bringing it back to the job ahead. "The writing, I mean."

"I might work in digital, but I went to school to be a writer," Margo shared.

"*That's* good for us," he offered, impressed. "Do me a favor, make me sound charming and witty," he continued as a 100-watt smile broke out across his face.

That shouldn't be too hard, Margo thought as she smirked at him. "Give me your phone. I'll plug in my number. Text me so we have each other's contact. I'll send you the login for our Grid.it account, so you can look at it later to approve it before we send it all to Dinah." Just then, her phone dinged. She looked down.

Hello, girlfriend.

She looked up at him, the sun in her eyes. Matt reflexively moved to block it, creating a shadow across her face. She smiled. "Hardee, har har," she said flatly. *Hello, boyfriend,* she texted right back.

"Okay, we have our marching orders. I'm on returns duty and you're crafting our legend," Matt said. Margo raised an eyebrow, puzzled. "You know? The made-up story CIA officers and FBI agents create when going undercover," he explained.

"I know what a legend is," Margo replied. "I'm just not sure *we* need one." She smirked.

"I'm pretty sure we do. I mean, I did just act like a certified idiot in the park for about hour, smiling like a demented fool with my fake girlfriend. I think the least you can do is let me have my legend," he said urgingly.

"All right," she said, acting as if it were a big give. "You get your legend and I get to pick the better bedroom."

"Deal," Matt happily agreed as they shook hands.

"Text you in an hour, okay?" Margo asked.

"Okay," Matt said and then, without even thinking, he kissed her on the forehead. Immediately he froze, "I'm so sorry, I don't know why I just did that." *What the fuck, man?* he thought.

Margo tensed and then quickly recovered, "It's fine, how else are we going to fool Dinah at our lease signing?" Then, she awkwardly reached up to high-five him.

"Oh no, don't make us one of those couples that high-fives," Matt said with a groan.

"Oh yes," Margo replied enthusiastically, "we're totally a high-fiving couple." Matt begrudgingly reached up and slapped her hand. "Didn't that feel good?" she asked as she swung the van's sliding door shut? Matt grimaced. "It's okay, you don't have to admit it to me right now, but I know you liked it. Feels right for us," she said with a scrunched-up nose and shimmy-shake of her shoulders. Then she grabbed his hand again and forced him to do a second pathetic high five. "Don't worry, no one gets it right straight out of the gate. We'll work on it," she said sarcastically as she went to get in.

Matt shook his head through the passenger window. He gestured for her to roll it down. "Just promise me we won't ever be the couple who dresses alike," he said, pleadingly.

"Oh gosh," she said, as she looked wistfully out of the front windshield and then back to him, "You know I can't promise that, *especially* now that I know you don't want *that* to happen."

She rolled up the window and waved mockingly, leaving him standing on the sidewalk. It wasn't until she was all the way up the hill that Margo realized she was still smiling.

CHAPTER 18

Ask the Editor

After four more hours of Mix barking orders at her over text, Margo was done with the day. She'd headed back toward the office only to be dispatched to the far reaches of Sherman Oaks to get Mix lunch, a macrobiotic salad with mushroom adaptogens. When she returned, only Ford was there.

"Mix had to go. She said you could eat her salad," he offered up as a consolation prize.

Margo looked down at the salad she'd just opened and placed on a tray. It was nothing more than a pile of bean sprouts doused with a grey cocoa. She grimaced as she placed the edible salad container lid back onto the bowl.

"How's your head?"

"Fine," Margo sighed. "This salad, however, might kill me."

Ford laughed. "We found our models."

"That's great," Margo said sincerely.

"Since we know you're not having that salad, wanna grab that pizza and wine?" Ford's blue eyes turned dark.

Ding, ding, ding went the trolley, Margo thought, drinking in his tousled hair and late-in-the-day scruff. Just as she was about to board his love train she stopped herself, *You have to get Dinah what she needs*, she chastised.

"I really wish I could, but I have a commitment." She looked regretful as she said the words. "Besides, how could I pass up eating this container for dinner?" She smiled. Then gnawed on the edge of it jokingly.

Ford laughed. "Surprisingly, those edible containers have a lot of calories. All carbs. My nutritionist said to skip 'em."

Just as Margo was about to make a joke, she realized he wasn't kidding. *So much for that trolley,* she thought.

"But," Ford added quickly, "worth a bite so you can say you tried it, right? Kinda tastes like rehydrated chicken."

Margo smiled. *Who eats rehydrated chicken other than a labradoodle?* she thought to herself. "I'll save it for later. I already ate two cereal bowls and a plate today," she said with a wink.

Ford didn't seem to pick up on her sarcasm. Instead, he just nodded as he put the rest of his papers in his briefcase.

Man is he handsome, she thought as she watched him. *Plaid never looked so good.*

"Ask me again in a week," Margo blurted out.

Ford looked up.

"My calendar's wide open then," she said, the emerald door of the storybook house floating into view.

Margo Melon, you need to write the fakest love story of your life with Matt, so you can have Ford Van Hewitt for real, she thought, her knees weakening as she stared at Ford's chiseled jaw.

"It's a date," Ford said, with a bright smile.

Suddenly, his eyes turned stormy. Margo's skin prickled, and her breathing slowed. He walked toward her and stopped beside her, his arm pressed against hers.

Margo felt a wave of heat flood from her toes to the top of her head. Every fiber in her body took notice in anticipation. He leaned in. He smelled softly of vetiver and wintergreen.

"Don't refrigerate the salad in that container. They fall apart on the shelf." He winked.

Margo momentarily watched her love trolley drive off a cliff. *Whatever,* she thought, pushing away any misgivings. *So, what if he's into his diet? How else would he have that body? I mean that body, are you kidding me?* Her mouth watered, and not because of the edible salad container in her hand. *He's probably not even into you*, she thought as she tossed the salad in the garbage of the kitchen as she passed by. Suddenly she stopped and turned back. *I just kinda have to know.* She walked back toward the kitchenette, flipped on the light, reached into the garbage and snapped off a corner of the salad bowl. She began to chew and regretted it immediately. *Chicken? Is he crazy?* she thought as she scrapped the chipboard-like material off her tongue. *More like dry wall.* She rushed to the sink and put her mouth under the faucet, swishing out the flavor.

"I meant to tell you."

She froze, her head under the spigot.

"Mix left all the models' names on your desk. Monday you can negotiate their day rates with their agents," Ford said from the door.

Margo pulled her head from the basin. She put on her best, I-wasn't-just-eating-out-of-the-garbage-can-and-bathing-in-the-sink-face and turned to face him.

"First thing Monday," she said weakly, wiping water from her chin.

"Great," Ford offered, then he clapped his hand to the doorway, waved, and strode off. Margo remained frozen until she heard the front door click. Her face was still bright red with embarrassment.

With the coast clear, she dashed to leave. As she passed Kirby's office she thought of the major meeting Kirby had earlier that morning, yet, had refused to tell her about. Just as she felt a tinge of anger rise in her chest she realized, *you struck a deal with a man you don't know to be your fake boyfriend to get a house and you're certainly not telling Kirbs about that. Maybe now's not the time to throw stones, Margo,* she bristled as she keyed into her car.

She sped through the surface streets of LA winding her way back to her Castle Heights bedroom. She shouted hello to her parents as she rushed in but couldn't honestly say if they said hello back. She bounded up the stairs and locked herself in her room to craft her Matt loves Margo love story.

On her ride home, she'd grabbed the necessary writing provisions: One green juice, three Stumptown iced coffees, half a leftover salad from lunch (not Mix's), one plum, her giant Hydro Flask water bottle, and, the pièce de résistance, Red Vines. Margo was in full editor mode. She started first by determining how she'd tell their story, and then got straight to work crafting the captions to speak right to Dinah's heart, a certain euphoria taking hold as she wrote for the first time in a long time. She approached the assignment with the same precision she had every story in the newsroom, covering the who, what, where, when, and why, all to hook her audience. After four and a half hours, two coffees, one green juice, three dance parties, and 34 Red Vines, Margo had written what she knew in her editor's gut would hook Dinah's heart.

Grid.it Post 1: Photo: Matt and Margo walking back from a game. Both in Dodgers shirts, Matt walking a bit ahead, Margo lagging behind, holding his one hand in both of hers, Margo looking coyly back at the camera, her hair swept up in a ponytail and smiling from under the brim of a ball cap. Caption: *Hi, I'm Margo and this is Matt. We're new to Grid.it and, if I'm being honest, we're new to one another. We met and fell in love quickly. But, hey, when you're onto a good thing, you got to grab hold. We wanted to ask you to follow along with our love story here, but thought if we were going to do that, we better get you up to speed first. So here it goes....*

Grid.it Post 2: Photo: Margo seated on the ground, leaning up against a tree, Matt leaning up against her in between her legs, her arms tight around his neck as they both give open-mouthed, wild smiles at the camera. Caption: *We met each other and knew from day one that our lives would forever be intertwined. I wanted to run away at first. I always thought I was the kind of girl who knew exactly who she was and who she wanted to be, until suddenly I didn't. It's strange to feel so lost in your own skin, like the things you loved and the goals you'd set suddenly don't belong to you anymore. I must have turned my map around and around a zillion times hoping to find my path again, searching for my safe harbor. Instead, I found him, and he helped me see that I don't have to have my entire course charted in order to chase the beauty on the horizon. He taught me that you can't find new land if you don't leave the shore. So, here I am out of my depth and in the deep end with him.*

Grid.it Post 3: Photo: Matt mussed hair, shirt off, sleepy smile. Margo leaned in close with a blanket on her shoulders, nuzzling his neck. Caption: *This is Matt. He takes life head on in the fast lane. Everything about him is quick. His wit. His heart. His laugh. God, I love his laugh. The only thing he isn't so quick to give away, that he guards carefully, is his love, that he reserves for those who earn the right to receive it. But, once you're in, you're so in. Unlike me, Matt doesn't have a list of yeses and noes, pros and cons, dos and don'ts. He's more a fly by the seat of your pants, see how it goes, somehow it'll all work out type of guy. He lives life by a strict honor code: Show up for those you love and look for those who will show up for you too.*

Grid.it Post 4: Photo: Matt and Margo lying on a blanket in the grass. Matt reading the paper. Margo looking earnestly into the lens as she gently kisses the knuckle of the hand she's holding over her shoulder. Caption: *For years now, I've been fixated on where I was going, the next step, the next goal, the next on my checklist of "good." Get good grades. Be a good daughter. Get into a good college. Land a good internship. Get a good job. All that good and, yet, somehow no matter how many times I added it up, it still didn't equal something great. And then something happened. This boy, with his sleepy grin and tiny scar showed up and showed me that life isn't just about where you're going; it's about who you're going there with. Don't get me wrong, I'm still vision boarding each day, and I'm going to meet all my goals. It's just that now I've got a team in the fight. I have this man who taught me that showing up for the ones you love begins with loving yourself enough to stand at the front of your own line. So, here we both are, at the start of something new, and we hope it's something that you might just love enough to show up for it too. Love, Matt and Margo*

As Margo created each post, she read and reread each one over and over, looking objectively at the arc, and how each caption led into the next. She wanted to not only connect with her reader, Dinah, but pull at her heartstrings, making her root for Matt and Margo and envision them living in that guesthouse out back. *Dinah's gonna eat this up with a spoon,* she thought to herself on her final pass. Satisfied by both the pending posts and the rope of licorice she was chewing on, Margo resaved them and texted Matt.

The posts are in the saved folder. Go in and read them. Let me know what edits you have. xM

Matt responded almost immediately.

I trust you. You're the writer. If you think it's something Dinah will like... [shrug emoji]

I think it is. I basically put up 4 posts that she'll read as our love story. They'll fool her into thinking it's our way of launching the page. I'll go ahead and publish them. Then you can send her the application and the link to the account.

Why me?

You and I both know she's already started writing her name as Dinah Robbins-Mackey-Joiner-Salter-Jenson-Milles-Lade. [tongue out emoji] You're lucky number 7!

Correction, Dinah Robbins-Mackey-SALTER-Joiner-Jenson-Milles-Lade. Honestly now that I typed that, I think I should take her last name. Seems progressive. Matt Robbins-Mackey-Salter-Joiner-Jenson has a nice ring to it, don't you think?

Listen, 7, get the house first. Then, we can hook you both up on Tinder.

Doing it now. Nite, girlfriend.

Night, boyfriend.

Matt gathered the paperwork for the house and scanned them into his Dropbox to send to Dinah. *Seven,* he thought with a chuckle at the nickname Margo had given him as he grabbed the Grid.it link to put into the folder. He went ahead and opened the app to screen-grab the feed and attach as photos in case Rita wasn't there to show Dinah the page. As the page loaded, Matt was shocked again at how real the photos of him and Margo looked, but even more shook when the captions came up. He read each one in full and was floored. He couldn't believe that this girl wrote with such honesty about where she was in her life as well as guessed so many things that struck a chord for him too. *Obviously, she just made this shit up on the fly to get it done, but man does it feel spot on,* he thought. Each time he landed on the line, "God, I love his laugh," he felt goose bumps prickle up his arm. *The fuck, man, get it together.* He texted her.

I'm reading what you wrote. It's really good. You're a great writer. Dinah's gonna melt. Honestly, it kinda made me melt too.

Realllly? OMG! Okay, good! I just guessed on some things. Others I felt kinda fit you. Some I created based on my fake BF I've been dating in my head since I was 10 [cry laughing emoji]. I also tried hard to make some of what I wrote true. We are going to be intertwined. It did happen fast, etc... Cheesy, I know, but I do have a soul that I'm trying to stop myself from selling entirely....

A soul? Don't tell Rita. She'll come steal it in the night as you sleep in the better bedroom...

LOL. Also, true. [cry emoji] PS...still keeping said better bedroom, but nice try.

Margo continued after a pause: *Tomorrow, boyfriend, we get a house. I'm betting my lucky 7 on it. [winky face emoji] Nite.*

G'nite, Valentine.

Matt hit send on the email to Dinah and clicked off the light. He was exhausted. So much had happened in one day. He hadn't even had a chance to tell Bibiana all about it. Out of anyone, she was always his *Guess What?!* call. He lay there in the dark for a few minutes. *Some of it I made up based on the fake BF I've been dating in my head since I was ten,* Matt heard her say over and over. He wasn't sure what it was about that line that jammed him up. *Are you disappointed it's not all about you?* he thought. With that he grabbed for his phone in the dark and went back to their feed. For the next hour, Matt read and reread their love story until he fell asleep, his phone still in his hand, goose bumps still on his arm.

CHAPTER 19

You're In

Matt shuffled downstairs. His phone dinged with a message. It was 11:39 a.m. He looked down to see that Dinah had responded. *My Dearest Matthew, I'm writing to let you know that I've accepted your application for my sweet little cottage out back. I'll expect you and Ms. Melon, or Bug, as you call her (which for her sake and mine, I implore you to stop immediately), tomorrow morning to sign the paperwork, drop off your security deposit, and get the keys. Kindest regards, Dinah Robbins-Mackey-Salter-Joiner-Jenson*

Matt high-fived the air, *"Yes!"* he shouted.

"You get good news on job," Zinny asked from behind him.

"No, I got a place," Matt responded smiling ear to ear.

"Ah, this is good news. I come clean before you move in."

"That would be great, Zin. We'll be moving in tomorrow," he began when Zinny cut him off.

"We? Who is we?" she surveyed.

Matt froze, *What's the lie I'm going with here?* he thought, knowing any delay would cause suspicion. "The landlord felt better about two folks being on the lease, so I went in on it with a girl I met at the showing," Matt said nonchalantly.

"Hm," Zinny intoned, sizing him up. "This is not like you," she observed.

Matt couldn't read whether or not she believed him. He knew she was hoping he'd offer up more information, just as she had taught him years ago. "As a child in Mother Russia, you learn give man rope and he will hang himself. You do same with this annoying boy. You give him rope," she'd told him when he was five years old and being picked on by Tyler Nevin.

Matt knew she was laying out that rope for him, today, just as he'd done for Tyler all those years before.

"You leave this candy bar I bring home from Russia on edge of cubby," she said, the word *cubby* carrying such disdain it made the hairs on the back of his neck stand up. "He is round, this Tyler, and his parents don't allow sugar. Is catnip for him. For us, it is rope. He will take it. I am sure. And, then you pounce. You immediately let teacher know someone stole your special bar and he will be caught red-handed. You make sure he knows if he messes with snake, he will get bit, yes?" Matt nodded. "If this does not work, we take him down other ways," she'd said as she knelt before him straightening his Barney backpack. "Is never too soon to teach man how to treat you." She tousled his hair, prouder to be teaching him espionage than his ABCs. Matt went to school and did as he was told. Tyler fell for it. Matt tipped off his teacher and Tyler went straight to time-out. He cried like a baby while Matt ate that recovered candy bar at snack, staring straight at him, smiling. "That's my boy," Zinny had told him that afternoon over their *own* afterschool snack. Tyler had been no match for Zinny.

As she stood before him in the kitchen today, though, Matt wasn't sure what she was thinking. Zinny had no tells, neither did Matt. They smiled at each other; a volume of suspicion being written between them. Matt grabbed his coffee and headed upstairs to pack, texting Margo as he went.

Good news, Valentine! We got the house! She wants us to sign tomorrow morning! What time works for you?

Margo's phone dinged. She looked down at the screen as she set aside her *New York Times* Sunday Style section. She'd been up since 7:36 and already emailed all the agents Mix wanted her to, securing the talent bookings and beginning their contract negotiations. Then she'd done three loads of laundry and started packing up her room. She didn't want to get ahead of herself, but she *did* want the universe to know that this house was hers. She read Matt's text and jumped out of her seat, high-fiving the air. *Yes!*

Lucky 7 coming through!!!!! This is great news! I have to work. Ask her if we can come at 8 a.m.?

8? Let me guess, you're the morning person in this relationship.

Chipper as a songbird, 7! Get used to it. I even sing in the shower...loudly.

Between this and the high-fiving, I feel like this relationship just hit the skids.

[tongue out emoji] Let me know what she says. How much do we need to put down for our security?

I'll let you know once she confirms. I'll go ahead and write the deposit. You can Venmo me the cash. What type of furniture are you bringing to this party?

Furniture? Margo's mind flashed to her Smurfette headboard and powder blue desk. *None. Just me myself and I.* [smile emoji]

Okay, that's fine. I actually have quite a bit. Matt's mind flashed through the contents of his room and the many pieces he knew Tiff had just put in storage. *I'll get with my dad's girlfriend and see what all I can bring from our stash.*

Stash, Margo questioned, *what type of home has overflow furniture?! We've had the same La-Z-Boy for a decade, and it doesn't even recline anymore.* That's when Margo realized, she had yet to do what was mandatory of everyone her age, Google him. She responded:

Great, keep me posted! I'll get packing!

Putting her phone down, she reached for her computer, typing his name into the search bar. Matthew Milles-Lade. She sipped her coffee as the search pull came into view. The second it did, her jaw hit the floor. *Is this guy loaded*, she thought, *and a douchebag?* She couldn't go to his Grid.it account. It was private. He'd told her that yesterday. Going on Facebook would mean friend requesting him. *Not gonna happen*, she decided. So, she did what every girl has done since the beginning of time, scoured other people's feeds to see what she could find out about him. She unearthed pictures of him partying at Tao in Vegas, spraying champagne from atop the DJ booth, and taking a shot of Jager from between the breasts of a buxom waitress. *Classy,* Margo thought. In another, he was doing a keg stand on a yacht in the Mediterranean, followed by drunkenly hugging a bevy of supermodels. *Seems right on brand.* Next up, she found him drunk—*shocker*—at a Coachella beach house VIP party. The deeper she delved the shallower she realized he was. *You have to stop,* she told herself; *20 minutes ago you liked him just fine. Maybe none of this is accurate or maybe it's all true, but you can't change any of it. Besides, you don't have to like him to live with him.*

"What's wrong, honey?" her mother said entering the kitchen. "You look upset."

Margo looked up and realized instantly that in her mad dash to move out she hadn't factored in how she'd tell her parents.

"No, not upset, just thinking." She paused, "I have something to tell you." Her mother looked at her, her eyes danced with anticipation and a smidge of worry. "I'm moving out," Margo said plainly, praying this news wouldn't lead to 20 questions.

"With Chelsea?" her mother asked, prompting the only obvious option that existed.

Margo knew she couldn't stomach one more lie, so she went with a half-truth. "No, I saw a house that was better suited for a roommate, so I went in on it with a guy friend who's looking to move too. We're the same age. I think it'll be good."

Margo's mom pondered what Margo had just said. Margo could tell she was tempering her response. "Who's this guy? Are you sure he's safe?" Maureen Melon asked protectively.

"My friend Matt. I don't think you've met him yet. He does have some pretty major serial killer vibes, but the house has a pool, so...." She shrugged playfully and smiled at her mom.

Maureen Melon rolled her eyes. "You and your father and your sarcasm. I'll have them put that on your tombstone. Beloved daughter. Good friend. Sarcastic to the end." She threw her linen napkin at her daughter.

Margo giggled and popped a blueberry in her mouth.

"I think this is a good step," Maureen said assuredly. "As long as you're safe, I'm excited for you to be out on your own."

Margo was so relieved to have escaped without a full interrogation that she *almost* forgot about the pictures she'd just found of her apparent party-bus of a roommate...*almost*.

As she bolted upstairs, her phone dinged again. *8 a.m. tomorrow is a go. See you then!* Margo punched back a simple thumbs up emoji, flipped on her fave playlist, and got to work packing. Having moved so many times for school, where her friends arrived with cars bursting at the seams, Margo had become an expert at getting everything into her two giant roller bags and matching duffels. Today was no different. Her phone dinged. It was Chelsea, exactly who Margo wanted to talk to.

Girl, where you at?

Home. Packing.

For what?!

Crazy, but I found a house. I'll tell you all about it tomorrow. I sign the lease at 8 a.m. If I'm a few late, cover for me.

Gaaaaaah, I can't wait to hear about it.

I know! I'll tell you everything. As Margo typed it, she knew that she *would* tell Chelsea everything, and Kirby too. Matt and all. But for now, Margo just wanted to focus on the job at hand. She sent a final note to Chelsea. *I started all the contract negotiations for Mix. If she's on the warpath before I get there you can tell her it's already under way.*

Got it! Bring pics of your new pad. [heart emoji]

[thumbs up] [heart emoji]

Margo spent the rest of the day packing up her things. It struck her how little of her life that played out in this room—trophies, puffy paint picture frames, and high school yearbooks—applied to the home she now hoped to build. She had changed so much, not just since college, but in the recent months since joining B&B and in the hours since agreeing to that house. She fell asleep writing a list of things she'd need to buy like pots and pans. Typically, a move of this magnitude would have stressed her out, but not today. Today, Margo didn't have a care in the world, and tomorrow she knew her whole life would change.

CHAPTER 20

On the Dotted Line

Margo's alarm dinged at 5:38 a.m. She dashed to walk Melton. *I'm going to miss you ol' buddy,* she thought as they lumbered along. *Maybe I should get my own dog*, she pondered. *Or maybe you should slow down a bit,* she decided. She keyed back into her parent's Castle Heights home for the last time as one of its residents, showered, threw on her fave jeans and vintage loafers, and was off to meet Matt.

She pulled into the spot behind him on the winding road and got out. Reflexively they hugged. The world around them was just waking up. There was a haze hanging over the hill and the entire road was quiet. It was only 7:43 a.m. They were both early.

"Look at you, Seven. Early," she said shoving his shoulder.

"What can I say, I'm trying to be a grown-up," he said modestly.

Margo's mind flashed back to the bevy of drunken Grid.it pics she'd seen the night before.

"Well, shall we get this party started? I'll let you do the honors." She gestured toward the bell.

"Why, I'd love to Miss Valentine."

A devilish smile broke out on his face. He stepped back and spun. When he stopped, he fake combed his hair on each side doing his best John Travolta in *Saturday Night Fever* impression, immediately followed by several very well executed hip thrusts—as noted by Margo's cat calls—before landing Travolta's trademark sideways finger points with practiced precision. Suddenly and much to her surprise, he grabbed Margo.

"What are you doing?" she shrieked as he spun them toward the doorbell where he used their now clasped hands to depress the button.

It's Raining Men, boomed out in its doorbell chime melody and they burst into peals of laughter.

"Seven, you have hips," Margo teased.

"Oh, I got the moves," Matt effused with mock arrogance as he popped a fake collar.

"I can see you two assholes," Rita squawked over the speaker.

Matt and Margo laughed harder as they each struck a disco pose.

"Stop it," Rita shouted, "or I won't let you in."

They both straightened up, barely. The door buzzed. They pushed through still laughing, Matt using his hand to graciously guide Margo up the path.

"You do know she's just angry because *she* wants to dance with you?" Margo said grinning over her shoulder at Matt.

Matt waved her off, "There's more than enough of me to go around Valentine. She'll get her turn."

Margo grinned as Rita swung open the door, "Boss is in the study. You two want coffee?" she asked gruffly.

Margo went to speak, but Rita cut her off, "If so, you shoulda gotten it on your way up the hill, cuz I'm not your servant."

She turned abruptly and squeaked down the hall in new green Crocs. It was only then that Margo realized she was wearing a onesie with a mane and tail in the back. Margo grabbed Matt's hand and leaned in to laugh into his shoulder.

"Get a hold of yourself, Valentine," Matt playfully chastised.

"Well, aren't you two the picture of happiness on a Monday morning," Dinah boomed as Matt and Margo swung to face her.

Unlike Rita, who was dressed like a cosplay participant, Dinah looked like Suzanne Sugarbaker in *Designing Women*, clad in a long silk dressing gown, massive updo, and formal jewelry.

"Morning," Margo sang as Matt smiled, his arm still resting at her waist.

"Let's get this lease signed, shall we?" Dinah asked with a clap as she gestured for them to follow her into her office.

Unintentionally, they took up the same seating as last time. Rita entered carrying a silver tray laden with a lavender coffee set. As Dinah dispensed the paperwork, Rita dispatched the mugs and began pouring the coffee. With a warm smile and wink toward Margo, Dinah handed her a lavender pen for her signature.

"Rita, don't you think mimosas would be better since we're celebrating?" Dinah purred as she looked on at Margo perusing the document.

"Sure, why not," Rita pandered, "You're probably still drunk from yesterday, why stop now?"

She angrily dumped the coffee back into the silver pot before loading the mugs, that she'd just passed out, back onto the tray, leaving the room as they aggressively clacked together. Margo was too afraid to admit she had to go to work. Instead, she said, "That sounds delicious, Dinah."

"Doesn't it, though?" Dinah agreed as she watched Margo sign the lease and pass it along the desk to Matt.

Margo, in turn, watched Matt sign. She couldn't stop smiling. Not even Matt's phone, which had rung for the third time could dampen her mood with its rudeness.

"I'm so sorry," he said. "I don't know why I'm getting so many calls this early."

In a growl-like tone Dinah replied, "I like a busy boy."

Margo could feel the giggle rise up in her chest. To tamper it down she pushed her knee into Matt's leg as they sat side by side. The shift in her position caused her bag to flop over onto her shoe. It was then that she realized her phone, too, kept buzzing, feeling it vibrate through her bag onto her foot repeatedly. The first few hits she thought might be Chelsea. She retrieved her phone just to be sure and saw she had 33 text messages and 14 missed calls. She started to panic. *Whatever it is, Margo, just get this done first*, she steeled her nerves.

Rita arrived with the mimosas just as Matt quieted his phone again and handed over the security deposit. Margo feigned attention as Dinah spoke, now terribly distracted by her own phone. *Who could be so desperate to talk to me?* she pondered.

"Well, no good host would ever dream of letting you move in without a housewarming gift," Dinah began, "So, I got you something special. Truly unexpected, even to me. See, I forgot, but one of my horrible step children..."

"Hey!" Rita interrupted, "I know you're drunk, but I'm right here!"

Suddenly, Margo recalled that Rita was the daughter of Dinah's second husband, making *her* one of the stepchildren Dinah was referencing.

Dinah continued, their glasses still raised, "Like I said, one of my *lovely* stepchildren," she corrected with sugar sweetness; Rita nodded her approval. "reminded me that I know someone who has deep ties to Grid.it. So, for your gift, I got you Verified."

Margo's face fell and so did her arm, sloshing mimosa everywhere, "Oh shit," she said, as Matt sprung to help Rita clean up the OJ.

Margo's mind crashed between her 33-and-counting text messages on her phone, the public profile they thought no one would stumble upon, and that fated Blush & Bashful meeting when Grid.it informed the B&B staff that they were planning to choose 25 obscure Grid.it accounts and declare them Grid.it's 25 Must Follows.

"We have to go," Margo said as gravely as if someone had just died.

Matt looked at her and didn't even question her motives. "Yes, we do," he echoed, not even knowing why but reading real trouble on his fake girlfriend's face.

"Wait," Dinah said confused and flustered, and probably a bit hurt that Margo hadn't said anything about her grand gesture. "Just like that. We didn't even cheers," Dinah said with a pout.

Margo looked at her, plastered a smile across her face, and said loudly, "Thanks, Dinah," like an insane person. Then she raised her glass. "Cheers," she gurgled and threw back her drink in one gulp. "We're so grateful." She set her glass down, then added, "Matt and I." Without even skipping a beat, Margo then took Matt's drink and threw it back as well. "Really good stuff," she said as she wiped the excess OJ from her mouth with the back of her hand, hysterically smiling. "Now if you'll excuse us, we have to be going," she said as she grabbed her bag and reached for Matt's hand.

Matt reached out and took her hand, but with the enthusiasm of someone being asked if they want to go into a room with a swarm of bees. The trio all looked at Margo like how Lindsay Lohan's team must look at her in a room filled with reporters—terror-filled smiles all around.

Matt allowed himself to be dragged toward the door. He had no idea what was happening, but he knew enough to follow her lead. "Thanks for the house and the celebration," Matt said as he neared the threshold to the hall.

"We really do have to go. I have a work emergency," Margo said in a strangled voice.

"Okay," he said, as he held onto the door frame with one hand, trying to finish with a proper goodbye, "Thanks again, Dinah. You're the best," he said as Margo swept him into the hall and out of sight.

"What the fuck is happening?" he hissed as he raced after her.

"Load," Margo said. "Loooooaaadd," as she exited into the courtyard.

"What are you doing?" Matt shout whispered again.

Margo swung toward him. "I have 39," she looked at her phone, "Correction 45 text messages and 16 missed calls! How many do you have?" she asked as she continued to beg her phone to "looooaaad."

Matt pulled out his phone "Shit, I have 47!" he said, now alarmed. "What the fuck is happening?"

"I can't be sure, because I can't get the page to load, but I think we just got named one of Grid.it's 25 Must Follows, and they Verified our account!" she cried.

"I don't know what that means," Matt said chasing behind her as she walked down the hill.

"They came to our offices a few weeks back, the Grid.it execs. I barely paid attention, because Mix had just majorly fucked me over. But, in that meeting, they said they were picking 25 random accounts and Verifying them. You know?"

Matt shook his head, "No, I don't know."

"Verifying someone is what they do so you know you're following the real Oprah or real Julia," she said her eyes wild. Matt stood there shocked and confused, so she continued. "Basically, once you're Verified you hang higher in the algorithm. Based on people's likes, viewing history, and some magic of their code these accounts are certain to amass huge followings immediately, like in the hundreds of thousands! They're basically making these accounts Grid.it famous in minutes," she explained with the same intensity someone would describe a meteor coming towards earth.

"Holy shit!" Matt said as he looked down. He turned his phone to face Margo. Their feed had 33,865 followers!!!

Margo fell to her knees. "Oh my gosh," she said, "what are we going to do?"

They stared at one another. Margo stood immediately. "I have to go to work and get to my sister," she said matter-of-factly, a bit like someone who was just in a car accident and is trying to leave before the ambulance arrives to treat the very obvious blood gushing from their forehead.

Matt followed her when he looked down at his phone to see that his father had texted, *Call me right this very minute.*

"Me too," he said, "well not to work but to tell my family. We have to shut this down." Visions of his father going one step beyond freezing his trust to fully disinheriting him flashed into his mind.

They reached their cars and shouted at one another, nearly at the same time, "Okay, call me," Matt said, as Margo cried, "Let's talk in an hour after we've told our families."

They drove off. Margo couldn't get to work fast enough. She tore into the building and headed directly to Kirby's office. As she flew by the main bullpen she saw Chelsea stand up at her desk with such force that her chair flipped back. She didn't say a word, but her face solemnly said, *Don't you dare not come talk to me.* Margo gave the one-minute symbol and mouthed *Lanai*; with that she disappeared into Kirby's office.

Kirby and David jumped up. "Holy shit," David boomed. "Margo, what's going on?"

"Hey, David," Margo said trying to sound calm. "Can I talk to Kirb alone?"

He looked at Kirby. She nodded, and he left the room. As soon as the door closed Kirby rushed to sit next to Margo, "What the hell, Margo?" But before Margo could respond Kirby plowed ahead, "I'm going to kill you for not telling me you were dating one of LA's most eligible sons! I know I've been busy, but, come on, we still tell one another everything!" Margo opened her mouth to speak, but Kirby kept on going. "But, we can get to that later. Right now, this is insane. The meetings I've been having have been with his dad's company. Milles-Lade Enterprises. They're the ones wanting to dump capital into our brand to explode it. Here I am keeping the fact that his father is our lead investor from you and here you are dating his son! This is perfect," she screamed as she threw her arms around Margo. "This is so huge! We've kinda been keeping the same secret," she shrieked as the door flew open and David fell in.

"I'm sorry, I can't stay out there! Did you tell her?" he asked, as he practically panted with excitement.

Kirby nodded yes, with a punch-drunk smile on her face from this happenstance turn of events in her mind.

"I have to go," Margo suddenly blurted and stood.

David and Kirby stood with her, staring at her as if she were some sort of apparition.

"Okay," Kirby said, suddenly confused.

"I have a meeting with Chelsea that I forgot about...for our shoot," Margo said, slowly trying to cobble a lie together that would stick.

"Oh, okay," Kirby said smiling, "We can talk about all this later. My lord, though what are the odds?!" she squealed.

"What are the odds?" Margo echoed flatly, a very forced and demented smile on her face.

Oh my gosh, oh my gosh, oh my gosh, oh my gosh, Margo repeated to herself as she exited the patio to find Chelsea.

Chelsea launched herself toward Margo the minute she stepped onto the Lanai. "Spill! Right now," Chelsea demanded.

In one breath, Margo told her everything. The water leak, the listing, the scam to get the place, the fake shoot to sell it, Dinah getting them Verified, her sister just admitting that Matt's dad is the lead investor considering pouring capital into B&B, and how coming clean could ruin things for Kirby. When Margo finally came up for air a thought dawned on her that knocked the wind right back out of her chest: *if Matt tells his dad, Kirby'll be screwed.*

"Shit!" she cried, as Chelsea's eyes widened with fear.

Fumbling for her phone, she texted Matt. *Meet me back at the house in an hour. Don't tell your dad. Don't tell anyone.*

Matt raced down the hill to get reception. He dialed his father's office. Patty answered.

"Hi, Patty," Matt said, trying to slow his speech and his heart rate.

"Oh hey, superstar. Aren't you the talk of the office?"

"I guess I probably am," Matt conceded, "My dad there?"

"He is, and he's been wanting to talk to you. Let me put you through," she said, as Matt let the words wash over him.

He never wants to speak to me. I'm so screwed, Matt lamented.

"Matt," his father boomed across the line.

"Hey, Dad," Matt said, launching head first into damage-control mode "I...I wanted to apologize. I know you must be pretty upset about the stuff people have been saying, but before you do anything that we both might regret, just hear me out..."

Brooks cut him off, "Matt, I got another call. I just wanted to say that Tiff showed me that page and I don't know what it's all about, but the boy your girlfriend described is the man I'd like to believe I raised you to be. So, son, I'm reinstating your trust. But, don't fuck this up. I got Leandra on it. Okay?" Before Matt could answer he continued, "Patty, put me back through to Tokyo."

With that, the line went dead. Matt stared at his phone in shock. A text bubble popped up. It was from Margo, although he'd plugged her into his phone as Valentine. *Meet me back at the house in an hour. Don't tell your dad. Don't tell anyone.* As Matt read it, he thought, *Don't worry, I'm not.* His head fell back on the headrest of his car when a second thought hitched in his chest. *Wait, why doesn't she want me to tell my dad?* Matt's head started to pound as he put the car in drive. *Could this day get any weirder*?

Just then his phone dinged. He looked down to see a notification from Grid.it. Your account has 17,657 new followers. *Looks like we have an answer*, Matt thought as he turned onto Sunset.

CHAPTER 21

Cat and Mouse

"Where are we going?" Chelsea said, alarmed as Margo swiftly stood and pulled her friend up alongside her.

"I'm going to meet Matt, and you're going to run interference a bit longer, just so I can sort something out with him. I think I'll be back, but if I'm not you'll come there at the end of the day," Margo said as she hauled her friend toward the door.

"Come where? What about work?" Chelsea asked.

"Considering I'm doing what I have to do to save this deal, work will have to believe I took a personal day."

Margo peered down the hall, making sure the coast was clear. "I have to get to my bag and get out of here without speaking to anyone." She grabbed Chelsea's shoulders and swept her into a hug. "Say nothing."

"How could I? I'm still confused," Chelsea replied, her words muffled by Margo's shoulder.

"See you in a bit. I'll text you my address." Margo turned and strode down the hall.

She made it back to Kirby's office undetected. *Praise be,* she thought, when she found Kirby's office empty. She ducked in and grabbed her bag. As she exited, her head down looking for her keys, she ran smack-dab into Ford, head-butting him in the shoulder like a bull would a matador's cape.

"Shit," she said as they collided. Ford flew back from the impact as Margo dropped her bag. "I'm so sorry," she said as they both knelt to collect her things.

"We have to stop meeting this way," he said rubbing his shoulder, with a smile.

"Or start wearing helmets," Margo offered.

Ford's face flushed confusion before it dawned on him. "Oh, right. I get it."

They stood. Ford looked down at her. Despite the fact that Margo was in full flight mode, she was rooted to her spot, frozen under his gaze. Suddenly Ford grabbed her arm and pulled her toward the garage exit just off the kitchen. Margo let herself be led, still stunned that he was holding her hand. The faint smell of stale oil and old wood filled her nostrils as Ford closed the door behind them. Turning to face her he stepped shockingly close to her, his face gravely serious.

"What's going on, Margo? Yesterday you told me *you* wanted me to call you and today you're moving in with your boyfriend on Grid.it." He searched her eyes.

Oh fuck, Margo thought, *he knows. Duuuuh! Of course he knows, the entire internet knows,* she thought as every person she'd ever met in her entire life flashed before her eyes, including her kindergarten teacher Ms. Pringle. *Why are you thinking about Ms. Pringle when the man you want is standing right in front of you?*

When she didn't speak, he kept going. "Am I confused in thinking there's something between us?" he asked.

Margo's spine straightened. *Did he say us? Is he suggesting the attraction is mutual? This can't be happening. The guy I like, finally, just might like me and now I have a fake fucking boyfriend messing it all up?* "Ford, I...," she started, realizing she had no idea what to say next. *Lie? Buy time? Turn him down? Don't turn him down,* she chastised herself. "You're not wrong, but..." she began, when suddenly Ford grabbed her and kissed her.

Unprepared for the contact, her body went rigid. Almost as soon as he started the kiss, he ended it. "I'm sorry. I shouldn't have done that," he looked surprised by his own actions.

He pushed his hand through his hair and shuffled back and forth for a moment before darting out the door, leaving it swinging on its hinges. Margo stood, bleary-eyed and confused, her mouth slack, her eyes glazed. *Did that just happen?* she questioned as she reached up to delicately touch her lips. The sound of the coffee bean grinder whirred her to attention. She looked up to see Chelsea in the kitchen staring at her in shock.

WTF, Chelsea mouthed as she stopped what she was doing and dashed toward Margo. "What are you still doing here?" Chelsea hissed.

"Ford just kissed me," Margo blurted.

"Shut the front door!" Chelsea shouted.

"Shhhhh," Margo said looking around to make sure no one heard.

"It's no wonder you were able to get a boyfriend and a house in 24 hours. You just left me less than three minutes ago and already you started an affair. What next?! You go to the bathroom and come back and tell me you have an illegitimate child?!"

"Stop kidding around, Chels!"

"I'm not even joking," Chelsea said her voice high and hysterical.

Margo grabbed her shoulders, "Just stick to the script. You haven't talked to me yet, okay?" Chelsea nodded. "Good," Margo affirmed as she brushed past her to leave.

Once she hit the pavement, she heaved a sigh of relief. Her car was 20 feet away. She was home free. She strode toward the Bronco.

"Going somewhere?" Mix asked from behind her, a slither to her tone.

Margo stopped, so did her heart. She turned to face her current boss. Mix's feral stare drank her in as she cocked her head to the side. Mix's eyes narrowed and she arched an eyebrow, reminding Margo of the cat she and Kirby rescued when she was in the third grade. Gypsy.

They'd traveled to Big Bear for Christmas holiday. Day one, she and Kirby spotted the cat outside—long orange and white fur, with a torn right ear, and a snaggletooth. That night it began to snow. The girls begged to bring the newly named Gypsy inside.

"Absolutely not. It's a rental," their father replied, but these sisters were not to be deterred.

Insistent on helping the cat, they snuck hot oatmeal outside to their shivering new friend, leaving their scarves behind in the hopes of giving her a chance at warmth. Their parents pretended not to notice. When the girls added Gypsy to their nightly prayers, vocally worrying about the hungry coyotes, their parents remained steadfast. But as the temperatures dipped lower and lower, Hank and Maureen had a startling realization. With the weather report calling for even more bitter cold, they feared Christmas morning might very well begin with a frozen cat, dead on the front porch. Within one hour of that revelation, Gypsy was curled up by the fire, snow melting from her fur.

"Time to open presents," the girls shouted at 5 o'clock a.m. on Christmas morning bounding onto their parent's bed.

"Are you sure you got presents?" their dad teased as the girls ran from the room toward their Christmas morning haul.

"I'll make the coffee," Maureen yawned. "You control the inmates."

Hank, still in boxers and a thin T-shirt, slid on his slippers and stood when screams vibrated through them. Flying to the balcony, he catapulted toward the stairs, shocked at the scene below. The living room was destroyed. The six-foot-four-inch-tall tree had toppled, smashing and shattering the coffee table. The packages shredded, and from the smell, all peed upon. Sitting right in the middle of the chaos was Gypsy, licking her paws.

"Girls get back! There's glass everywhere!" he shouted as he flew down the stairs two at a time.

He grabbed his boots from the mat and scooped up his daughters, delivering them back to the steps. "Daddy, is Santa mad at us?" a tearful Kirby asked.

"No, baby girl," he knelt down in front of them. "Gypsy just had a party. We'll get this all cleaned up and have a great Christmas."

"Daddy, what's Gypsy doing?" Margo pointed past her father in the direction of the cat.

The entire Melon family turned toward Gypsy. Hunkered down low, with her front legs tucked tightly under her shoulders and her rear haunches raised, Gypsy peered at Hank Melon.

"She's still playing. I'll get her back in the pantry, and we can have Christmas morning."

As he reached for her, Gypsy's rear haunches wagged and she sprang upon him like a leopard would an impala. Her razor-sharp claws extending in flight dug into his skin the moment she made contact with his leg. The second Gypsy was on him, she began to climb first his calf and thigh, then his hip, onto his arm, and then around to his back. Hank Melon screamed like a little girl forced onto a roller coaster, his shrieks only outmatched by those of his wife and children. As Gypsy clawed at him, he pawed at her, turning in a mad and fumbling circle trying to get her off him, his skin actually stretching out with her claws still intact. As he pulled at her, he whirred through the room, tripping over pee-soaked boxes that spilled out onto the carpet. Finally, as she climbed up his neck and face, he pulled her free and flung her away from him. She hit the wall and stuck like a flying squirrel, using her claws in the wooden walls of the cabin to climb up to the rafters, yowling as she went. Mr. Melon, huffing like he'd just run uphill for a mile, fell to his knees, the razor thin scratch marks that covered his bare legs, arms, neck and face, all prickled with blood.

"Oh my lord," Maureen shrieked as she launched herself toward her husband. "Girls, go to the bathroom and find towels and a first aid kit. Slowly," she added as the entire family looked up at Gypsy who was pacing on the rafter above, plotting who to murder next.

"Mommy, I'm afraid," Margo whined.

"I know, baby, but go. Mommy won't let anything happen."

Margo and Kirby ran down the hall and grabbed the bin marked first aid. They wrapped bath towels on their heads and around their bodies like capes and walked slowly back toward the living room. Gypsy's ears went back. She hissed at them from her perch. They shrieked.

"Girls, go call the police. Tell them your father was attacked by a cat and we need help." Margo bravely took her sister's hand and did as she was told.

"What kind of cat?" the dispatcher asked with a thick Minnesotan accent. "Anyone helpin' him?"

"Our mom is. She's with him. He's bleeding. Hurry. We don't want our daddy to die," Margo sobbed hysterically into the phone.

"Easy there," the dispatcher soothed, "Help's comin'."

Minutes later sirens howled up the mountainside and five firemen burst through the door, axes raised.

"Where's the cat?" the first one shouted, prepared for an attack.

Maureen Melon turned her face upward toward the rafters; the firefighters followed her gaze. Then everything stopped as they lowered their defensive stance.

"It's a cat," one said in disbelief. "I mean, an actual cat."

Hank and Maureen stared blankly at him.

"Her name's Gypsy," Kirby said softly from the far corner of the room.

All five firefighters burst into laughter. Then tamping down their giggles, they swung into action. It wasn't until years later that Margo realized those firefighters and the 911 operator fully expected a mountain lion to be in that cabin based on how hysterical she had been on the phone.

"What you got here is a feral hill cat. Can't take *these* inside. They're mean as sin," the captain said, using the wad of Big Red cinnamon gum in his cheek to hide his obvious smirk. "You're lucky you didn't lose an eye. You want us to hose the carpet for the piss smell?"

Hank and Maureen, still in shock, shook their heads no. They spent the rest of the day scrubbing the carpet and cleaning all the presents before the girls could even play with them. By 5 p.m., they were bone-tired. They hadn't even made Christmas dinner. As Margo's dad carefully lowered himself onto the sofa, grimacing as the skin stretched across his cuts, the gouges on his neck and face making him look like Edward Scissorhands, he said definitively, "We're dog people from here on out." They all nodded in agreement.

As Margo looked at Mix in the Blush & Bashful parking lot, she saw Gypsy in her eyes. That feral quality that says, "I will rip you to shreds and smile while I pee on your first Cabbage Patch Doll."

"Hey, Mix, just running some errands for Kirby," she managed coolly, hating the fact that this woman's impact on her was obvious to the both of them.

Mix took a step toward her. "Hmm?" she purred, her left arm jangling with Jacob the Jeweler's handiwork, a Capri Slim cigarette in her right hand. "I don't know what you're up to Margo Melon, but I'm gonna figure it out."

Mix's eyes drilled into her. But like a clock whose hands snap into one another at the noon hour, Margo felt something in her reset. *A sliver of Gypsy, perhaps?* Margo thought. She stepped toward Mix, close enough to feel the heat of her cigarette.

"I could say the same to you, Mix. Except I've already figured it out. I see right through you. I just wonder how long before everyone else sees it too." Then she savagely turned and headed for her car.

CHAPTER 22

Don't Ask, Don't Tell

Margo raced through the canyon, not even paying attention to the beauty of her new commute. She keyed into the gate and trotted around the house to the footpath. Her breath hitched in her chest as her new storybook home came into view.

She could see Matt already inside, putting something together. When she crossed the threshold, she heard the whir of the electric pump.

"Thank God you're here," Matt said dropping the pump to the air mattress he was blowing up, the noise ending with its release.

He swept her into a hug. Margo returned the quick embrace, neither realizing how comforting it felt to hug someone they'd only just met 48 hours ago.

"We can't tell anyone," she blurted out.

"I agree," Matt responded.

"You do?"

"I do."

There was a pause between them. Margo used the silence as a tool, the same way she would with a source to get them to share more of their story. *People always want to fill the silence,* her first journalism professor had taught her. *Let them.*

Matt took a different tactic. *If you want the real story, make uncomfortable silence. Rats don't like quiet,* Zinny had told him. *Drop a crumb. They will sing for their supper.*

"I talked to my dad," Matt said as he went to open the patio door, gesturing to the pool furniture to sit.

Margo followed him. "And?" she questioned.

"Annnd, he seemed thrilled that I'd met someone. I didn't want to let him down, since he's easily disappointed in me, so I let him go on believing it."

Margo nodded.

Matt conveniently leaving out the real headline of his trust fund.

"Why didn't *you* want me to tell him?" he asked. "Why did *you* change your mind?"

"It's crazy, but I rushed to the office to tell my sister and she told me that your dad's company is planning to invest in her business. I couldn't risk our lie ruining something for her."

She searched his eyes. *My dad's company,* Matt questioned to himself. It struck him odd that his dad, who saw him as a perpetual fuck-up wouldn't warn him not to mess up this deal too. *Maybe he didn't realize Margo is Kirby's sister,* he thought, making a mental note to suss that out.

"I didn't even know your dad's company did that," Margo continued. "Crazy, right?"

But you do know that my dad has a company? he thought. *Did I tell her that?*

He looked out across the pool. "Completely crazy," he echoed flatly.

He bent forward resting his elbows on his knees as he looked down at the pock-marked cement of the pool deck. "So, now what, we keep lying to everyone...for how long?" he asked.

"Well, not everyone. I kinda told Chelsea," Margo admitted.

"Who's Chelsea?" Matt asked surprised.

Before Margo could answer, a loud crash in the living room interrupted them. They turned to see Rita wrestling with, and losing against, a huge bouquet of metallic balloons. She was flailing and fighting a giant letter M. The M appeared to be winning. Margo and Matt rushed to help her. As Margo gathered the balloons, Matt rescued Rita who clung to him like a baby orangutan would its mother.

"You're my hero," she crooned as she climbed him like a jungle gym.

Dinah coughed from the door before singing, "Knock, knooo0ck," and entering.

She approached the trio as Margo continued to play balloon Wheel of Fortune untangling the letters, realizing they spelled out @MattlovesMargo in separate Mylar balloons.

"We have an invitation," Dinah said waving a heavy piece of ivory cardstock in her hand. "And I see that it has a plus one for each of you."

Margo noted that Dinah knew this because she'd *opened* the card. She read aloud.

"Welcome to the family, Matt & Margo. Tonight Grid.it celebrates you with a kick-off happy hour for the 25 Must Follows. We'll be flying in every person on our list to hang with you and some of the Grid.it stars you already know and love. This is your chance to learn all about the world you've just crashed into. Check your account to find the name of your handler. They'll be meeting you at the door. Car, security, and full details are in the packet you just received. We picked you because you are truly one to watch, and we can't wait to see what you do next. Grid.it."

Dinah's eyes sparkled with excitement. "I just love a good party."

Margo opened the packet finding that the run of show tucked inside listed a full red carpet with press and photographers. She looked at the clock on her phone. It was 1:45 p.m. The party was slated to start at 5 p.m. She looked up helpless at Matt, who instinctively flocked to her side.

"Don't worry, we'll be fine," he reassured.

"Press? Photographers? What am I going to wear?" Margo worried aloud.

"Darling," Dinah boomed from behind her, "Have you seen my closet?"

Rita clapped and squealed, "Makeover!"

Margo looked back at Matt, helplessly.

"I mean, you couldn't be in better hands," he said with a reverential shrug.

"It's Raining Men" boomed over the speakers. Rita turned to the screen on the wall by the door, "Anyone know this dime?" She thumbed her finger at Chelsea's black-and-white image on the monitor.

Margo felt a surge of relief at the sight of her friend. *Oh thank Goodness,* she thought. "That's my best friend, Chelsea," she said, feeling a weight lifting off her shoulders just by her presence.

"I'll let her in," Rita said and trotted down the path.

"Matt, I'd say you're free to borrow a suit from my last husband, but we were married in the '90s. That man liked a boxy cut with some real shine to it. Every time he stood next to a candle, I held my breath. I kept all his suits in the divorce because, well, I'm the one who took him to the cleaners," she smiled brightly at both of them.

"Thanks, Dinah," Matt chuckled, "but I've got plenty of time to head back and grab something from my own closet. Besides, Valentine here is the one who takes more time to get ready," he said appreciatively with a wink. Then, looking back at Margo, "I'll be back in a few hours. There's a salad in the fridge for you. I wasn't sure if you'd eaten." He turned toward the door to see Chelsea arriving wide-eyed and bewildered. "Chelsea," he boomed wholeheartedly walking toward her and sweeping her into a bear hug.

Margo knew he was pretending to know Chelsea because, of course, her boyfriend and best friend *would* know each another, but Chelsea didn't know that. The look on her face told Margo she'd added his hug to the list of reasons she was utterly overwhelmed today. Slots one and two were undoubtedly this house and Rita.

"Oh, hey," she dazedly replied at Matt as Margo rushed in to save her.

"Dinah, I'm just going to eat that salad," Margo said putting her arm around Chelsea. "And then, we'll come over to find something amazing."

Margo escorted Chelsea toward the kitchen.

"Sounds perfect, Valentine," Dinah said winking at Matt, making it known she noted the new nickname and approved. "And when you do, we'll all be getting ready together, since we'll all be going with you," she persuaded.

As soon as the door was closed, Chelsea crowed, "This place is insane! I can see why you sold your soul to get it."

Margo half-laughed, half-cried, as she grabbed the salad out of the fridge. "Don't remind me," she whined.

Turning the cap on the Pellegrino Matt had left, she read his note, *Didn't know what salad dressing you'd want so I got them all.* She opened the little brown bag to find at least half a dozen plastic ramekins filled with ranch, BBQ, blue cheese, Italian, Thousand Island, and French dressings.

"He's cute by the way," Chelsea said, with an eyebrow raised as Margo fished for both BBQ and ranch.

"Is he?" Margo asked coyly.

Chelsea rolled her eyes. "You know he is."

"What I know he is," Margo said, scowling as she began adding dressing to the salad, "is a drunken frat boy with a lot of money."

Even as the words left her mouth, Margo wanted to defend Matt from her own meanness, the oddity of that flashing through her mind only momentarily. "Anyway, we got bigger fish to fry," she continued as she slid the invitation across the island for Chelsea to read. Chelsea looked horrified.

"What are we going to wear?"

Margo sighed loudly and shook her head. "I think you're missing the point. Forget what I'm wearing. I'm arriving with my fake boyfriend to a very real press event. Isn't that the bigger issue?"

"That ship has sailed. What hasn't docked yet is your place on the worst-dressed," Chelsea said, popping a crouton in her mouth.

"Dinah said we could raid her closet," Margo shared, "which means I'm going to show up looking like an extra from *Troop Beverly Hills*."

Chelsea gasped, "You should be so lucky!"

Margo laughed as she shoveled a bite of salad into her mouth, handing Chelsea a fork. "First things first," she said with a mouthful, "we have to put up another post. That's what an influencer would do, and I guess now I'm an influencer."

"No, first things first, you have to tell me about that kiss from Ford," Chelsea demanded as she crammed a bite of salad into her mouth, her eyes eager and wide.

Margo's shoulders sagged, "I don't know, Chels. It's been a weird day. It was," she paused searching for the right words, "it was like I didn't feel anything. Is that bad? It's bad, isn't it?" Margo scanned Chelsea's eyes for assurances.

Sure, doesn't sound good, Chelsea thought, but said, "I'm sure it's the stress of the day. I mean, a lot has happened." To amplify her point, she gestured around the stunning house they were standing in. As Chelsea's eyes traveled around the room, "Is that crown molding?" She marveled at the kitchen, before coming back down to earth. "I mean, what did your parents say?"

At the mention of her parents, Margo's eyes widened, and she choked on her salad, realizing she hadn't even warned them. She began to sputter and cough, when suddenly Rita was there smacking her on the back and attempting the Heimlich.

"Oh my goodness," Chelsea said, both out of concern for Margo and surprise at seeing Rita suddenly appear.

"Good thing I was here. Boss sent me to get you. Can't have you dying on us before we get into that party," Rita concluded.

Chelsea and Margo shared glances, wondering what Rita had heard. "Rita, we have to set some house rules," Margo commanded, endeavoring to tell her she had to start knocking.

"I'm so glad you think so," Rita jumped in. "I like to run a tight ship. I'll get you a list to follow."

With that she turned and skipped down the path, her mullet swinging behind her.

"She can't be for real," Chelsea chortled.

"Unfortunately, she can be and is for real," Margo replied, tucking away the worry about her parents. *I can't deal with that right now. I have a party to get ready for.*

CHAPTER 23

Triple Word Score

Matt sailed through the door of his room and crashed into his closet. He'd already talked to Zinny on his way in.

"Just a girl you meet at the showing, you say to me," she said affronted, "and yet you tell world you are couple. Is interesting, no?"

Matt didn't take the bait. He knew Zinny would see right through any lie and he knew it didn't matter, because even if she did, she would never give up his cover. "I lost these five nails many years ago in difficult conversation with man at border," she'd winked at him when he was ten. "I never give up what I know."

As he tore through his closet, he got a text from Margo. *We have to put up another post. We're doing this, right?* As Matt pondered what to reply, a note from Leandra came in, *Your account is flush again. I show the initial back pay of $77,897 went in already. I'll check for the rest later.* Matt replied to Margo. *Yes, we're a go.*

Fifteen minutes later as he rooted through his shoes, he saw her post. In the picture they were smiling and laughing as they played Scrabble, or rather pretended to on that first day in the park. *You win some. You lose some until one day it's oxyphenbutazone, the highest scoring word possible in the history of Scrabble. According to legend, it's never been hit. But then legend never had a day like today.*

Thanks for making us feel like a triple word score times 10, @Grid.it.

Matt smiled as he read it. *She's good*, he thought. 14,576 likes told him their followers agreed with him.

Matt found four outfit options that he thought could work, depending on what Margo chose to wear. He swung his shoe cabinet closed and jumped when he saw Tiff standing on the other side.

"What the hell, Tiff?! You scared the shit out of me."

"Hey, Matty," she twirled her hair as she smacked her gum.

You know I hate when you call me that, he thought as he glared at her.

"Zin said you might want some furniture. Take whatever you need. We just hired a designer for the new place, so we won't be using most of this stuff. I'm sure your dad will be thrilled to have you use it."

Why is she being so nice? Matt was immediately suspicious.

"Anyway, I heard there's an event tonight...."

Ahhhh, there it is, Matt smirked inwardly.

"I thought maybe you could get us on the list. My girlfriends and I, not your father, he's working," she said sweetly.

Just as Matt was about to dismiss her, he realized he had something he hadn't had in a really long time where Tiff was concerned, leverage.

"We don't know the Grid.it people yet, but I can see what I can do."

He smiled sweetly as he watched a smidge of annoyance flare across Tiff's face.

"Okay," she acquiesced, "you do that. Oh, and now that I think about it, try to keep what you take to only a few items."

There's the Tiff I know, Matt thought as she tossed her hair and left.

CHAPTER 24

In the Closet

After an hour and a half in Dinah's closet, Chelsea was outside of her body with joy. The closet itself had several rooms, with thousands of pieces of clothing all catalogued by era and color and coded by designer with a separate vault for handbags and jewelry.

"I need to be one of her closet people," Chelsea hissed. "I would never leave here. NOT. EVER. They'd bury me in this room, entombed in Chanel."

Until they'd walked into Dinah's shrine of a closet, Margo had no idea there were three additional humans working in the house. Yet, here they were, all dedicated to Dinah's wardrobe and grooming needs. All three loved Chelsea upon sight.

"You are a stylist. Mother can tell," Blanca declared of Chelsea with a snap of her fan opening. "I should know, I have been head of this wardrobe since disco reigned supreme, darling." She then strutted along the far wall of clothes like Naomi Campbell on the catwalk in 1995.

"Oh no Queen, you sell her short. There's a hint of burgeoning designer in there," Eps surmised as he laid out his artillery of hair products.

"Ladies, I don't think a hint," Clark commanded, "I feel her designer singing to the back of this room," he shivered as if the joy of that thought gave him a chill.

"This child is meant to build a catwalk," he said as he prepped his makeup brushes.

Chelsea blushed at Margo, and then ever-so-slyly demurred, "You are correct."

All three of Dinah's glam squad clapped and hooted.

"Well, diva, then let us work," Blanca declared as she began filling a rack of clothes for Margo to try on, gesturing for Chelsea to join her. Before she did, she leaned over to Margo. "Don't be so surprised. I just let my little white lie of being a stylist get in line behind your giant one."

Before Margo could respond, Eps gobbled Chelsea up by swinging a vintage cape over her shoulders and pulling her into the room. Margo smiled at the four of them as they dashed around in a fashion frenzy, randomly clapping and cheering for each pull.

In three hours' time, Margo had been primped and preened within an inch of her life. Yet when she stood in front of Dinah's wall of mirrors she still seemed to be mostly herself, just more polished.

"It isn't about covering up," Eps affirmed as he tousled her hair with spray. "Everything in these rooms, including us, is here to uncover and remind of what already is."

He winked at Margo. She smiled and then ever so carefully smoothed the front of the white Diana Ross–level catsuit Chelsea had chosen. Draped with a long white linen shirt, which Chelsea had cinched with a gold belt, and then bunched at the sides, Margo felt beautiful. She'd never worn anything like this, but secretly always wanted to. Paired with kitten heels, she looked decidedly Blake Lively. Chelsea had been the one to cajole Margo's bravest self to put it on.

"You really are my stylist," Margo said as Chelsea stepped into view behind her. "It's not a lie for you."

The closet coven, as Chelsea had nicknamed them, put Chelsea in a sequined boxy tuxedo jacket dress. It was short and made her petite legs look long. It was the '90s look to Margo's late-'70s Bianca Jagger moment. When Dinah stepped in between them with her asymmetrical dress and shoulder pads, she brought the '80s to their decades.

"Yaaaasss!" Clark shouted as he fainted onto the round settee that stood in the middle of the room.

"We have our suitor," Blanca declared with a clap. All three hopped into formation presenting Margo to Matt who appeared in the doorway.

She suddenly felt shy, but when she looked up, she caught Matt's stare in the reflection of the mirror. "Too much?" she asked softly.

"No," Matt said, mystified. "You look amazing."

Like a wedge of swans in flight, the trio flanked him, primping his suit, adding a pocket square, and hemming his fitted linen pants at his ankle. "Well, I guess that's happening," Matt said as he looked down seeing the needle and thread expertly wielded by Blanca.

Clark gestured for Matt to remove his shoes. He did as instructed. Eps offered him a Gucci loafer.

"You just happen to have my size or did Rita come to my house and measure my feet while I slept?"

"Oh, Cinderella," Blanca beamed, "Rita measured much more than just your feet," she demurred with a wink.

Matt laughed wholeheartedly. Then he slid his hands in his pockets posing in the mirror as Clark and Eps behaved like wild fans at an Enrique Iglesias concert, fawning over him. Margo smiled, happy that Matt, a straight man, wasn't threatened in the least by the gay male vibrato of the two men.

CHAPTER 25

Your Chariot Awaits

Thirty minutes and 25 mirror selfies later, the troupe headed out the door to the waiting limo. Chelsea sat next to Margo; Matt next to Dinah. While Margo was too nervous to notice, Chelsea was supremely aware of the long glances Matt directed toward her best friend and decided she was fine with that.

Upon arrival, Dinah swanned down the red carpet, Chanel No 5 wafting in her wake, as Rita jockeyed for position next to the Grid.it assigned security officer. Twice Chelsea and Margo caught her talking into her wrist like she had a walkie-talkie, which would typically have garnered giggles, were it not for the fact that Margo was in a tailspin about what they were about to do.

The handler explained that they could do the red carpet or skip it, depending on their level of press experience. Either way they had to walk for photos and talk to Maria Menounos for their Grid.it & Hit.it exclusive. As they weaved through the arrivals area, Margo grabbed Chelsea's arm.

"I can't do this. You and Matt are the ones who wanted to go to this party. You're the Cinderellas, not me."

Chelsea, in an attempt to appear casual, grabbed Matt and pretended to groom him. "We have a bit of a meltdown brewing, Matthew," Chelsea sang as she adjusted his pocket square. "Help rein it in."

She swapped to zhuzh Margo's belt, completely aware they were surrounded by prying eyes and listening ears. Matt swung to Margo and a 1,000-watt smile broke out on his face.

"You got this, Valentine. We're just going to have our picture taken. Just you and me. I promise I won't let anything happen. This is just a part of what we signed up for, okay?"

"I don't recall signing up for this," Margo said gesturing to the wall of photographers.

"Good thing for you, you got me by your side," Matt said with a wink as he took her hand.

She clutched his arm with a death grip as he led her into the fray. She was wholly unprepared for the number of flashbulbs that hit her as they stepped to the X in front of the step and repeat. Even more surreal was the calling of their names.

"Matt, Margo, this way."

"Matt, Maaattt, over here."

"Margo, just a small look to this side. Margo."

She leaned into Matt and he effortlessly slid his arm around her waist.

"You're so good at this," she said through a forced and fixed smile, as she leaned her entire body weight into him.

Matt smiled down at her and then whispered in her ear, "You are too, you just don't know it yet, Valentine."

Then he kissed her on the forehead, as a natural and enigmatic smile of relief broke across her face. The intimate gesture caused all the flashbulbs to go off at once.

Next, their handler swept them to the Grid.it & Hit.it show booth.

Maria Menounos boomed their names as they arrived, "America's newest *it* couple has just arrived. @MattlovesMargo. Hi guys! Welcome," she beamed.

Margo wanted to faint. Matt immediately shook Maria's hand.

"We're still a bit shell-shocked. Margo and I thought the hardest choice we'd make today was what's for dinner, not "Do we take a limo or drive ourselves to the red carpet?" he beamed back.

Margo watched as Maria fell instantly smitten.

"Well, looks like you figured it out between breakfast and now because you two look great," she said. "Margo, this outfit is amazing."

Maria didn't inquire who it was by due to the level of terror rolling off Margo. *Newscasters, like dogs, can apparently smell fear,* Margo thought as her knees buckled under Maria's kind gaze.

"Now if I'm reading your Grid.it account right, you two just moved in together. Who gets final say on design choices?"

Is she actually sparkling? Margo thought staring at her.

"I think we know who gets the final say on *all* things," Matt charmed back.

Margo smiled and then shocked them all by speaking, "He says that, Maria, but then why haven't I seen a chick flick in months?"

Margo nudged his waist playfully. Matt surrendered.

"You two *are* cute," Maria quipped. "Come visit us anytime," she said definitively. Then looking back into the camera, "Well, I know the party awaits for these two, and you at home have plenty more time to get to know them on Grid.it. So, follow along!" Then turning to Matt and Margo, "And you two get in there and eat all the eats and drink all the drinks. I hear they have Shake Shack!"

The cameras went dark, and Maria immediately leaned in, "Thank God you two showed up, the other ones seemed lost. You're the real deal, I can tell."

Maria hugged each of them before Matt commandeered them back into the chaos of the carpet.

"Did we just do a press interview that went out live on Grid.it?" Margo asked in shock.

"We did more than that, Valentine. We *killed* a press interview that went out live on Grid.it."

Matt grabbed her hand and forced her into an awkward high-five, which caused her to laugh.

"There's my girl," he said softly acknowledging her smile.

Margo sighed. She looked back at the shark tank they'd just swum through and then at Matt, who had been her Coast Guard through it all.

For the next hour Matt, Margo, and Chelsea soaked up the scene. The walls showed the feeds of 25 Must-Follows.

We're gonna have to get shooting in order to have enough content, Margo thought, looking at their feed scroll across a 14-foot-tall screen. Their current follower count hung at 82,000. Matt and Margo were the only couple Grid.it had chosen, and they were the only true obscure follows. The others already had followings that ranged from 50 to 150K when Grid.it chose them. Margo even knew some of them already. They were pros. Matt and Margo were novices. But Margo could also tell that their followings hadn't leapt like hers and Matt's had.

As Margo, ever the A student, pondered their social calendars, Chelsea people-watched. "Oh my gosh, don't look now, but that's Becca Tilley, Brad Goreski, and Tanya Rad—MY FAVORITES—and they're talking to Alexis Ren. This can't be real life," she fangirled wildly.

Matt leaned in. "It's not," he said flatly.

Chelsea shoved him with mock outrage. "Don't you dare rain on my reality star parade."

Matt smiled. *I see why Margo likes you,* he thought, looking at Chelsea admiringly.

"Look at Dinah," Margo pointed out, as Matt and Chelsea followed her gaze across the room.

Dinah was holding court in the corner.

"Is that Jonathan Van Ness at her knee?" Chelsea asked and then suddenly shrieked. "It is! You guys, this is the best night ever!"

She threw her arms around Matt and Margo simultaneously, Rita boxing her out like a proper security guard.

"No handling the talent," she barked as she fake-shouted for additional security into her invisible wrist-com.

Chelsea and Matt fell out laughing. Margo, despite herself, did too.

You know what? Maybe this isn't going to be so bad after all, Margo thought. She could feel the worry in her chest lessening, her guard lowering when her phone buzzed. She looked down and realized she had spoken too soon.

CHAPTER 26

Guess Who's Coming to Dinner?

We're disappointed on every level, Margo. Call us.

Margo read and reread the text, her stomach in knots.

"What's wrong," Matt asked, concern written on his brow.

Margo turned her phone to face him, the screen lighting up his face in the dark of the party. The instant he saw *Mom* emblazoned on the top of the screen he knew her parents had just found out.

"I'm so sorry. Didn't you get to warn them?"

"Obviously not," Margo said, fighting back tears. "I have to go."

She spun to leave, crashing into a young CW star, then weaving her way through the massive post-work gathering. Matt grabbed Chelsea's arm pulling her through the crowd, in pursuit of Margo, blazing past waiters with trays of crudités, the vintage Volkswagen Bug exploding with flowers, and the 14-foot-tall Grid.it instant camera spitting out bubbles that every selfie-loving guest was taking pictures in front of. Somewhere near the cake pop and mojito tower, they got tangled in a Wells Adams and Nick Viall *Bachelor* sandwich.

"Leave me here," Chelsea swooned.

"Take the car home!" Matt shouted above the music. Chelsea waved happily, unaware of the drama unfolding as she pulled Wells into a selfie, almost against his will.

"Margo, wait!" Matt yelled, rushing outside to catch her.

"You can stay. It's a great party," she said, peering back into the elaborately decorated room and then down at her killer outfit, both of which were about to go to waste.

"As if I'd want to," he replied, already locating an Uber.

"I have to go see them. Tonight's Melon family meal and I totally forgot."

Matt checked his watch. The happy hour had started at 5 p.m. All told, they'd only been there for about an hour.

"It's still early. Only 6:12. Invite them to our house for a meal. We can get pizza. I can win them over. Parents love me," he said reassuringly.

Margo knew her parents would be well into their meal prep, and Kirby would probably be on her way to their Castle Heights home. She looked at Matt. She was torn.

"It's better than not going or not trying," Matt said.

Margo picked up her phone and stepped away to call. Matt watched her from where he stood, feeling an urge to protect her. He hadn't felt that for a long time where a woman was concerned, other than Bibi.

"Okay, they're coming," Margo said sounding only slightly reassured. "I think they felt relieved to see me being responsible. That's how they know me. Steady. *This,*" she said as she gestured about, "is way off course for me. *This* is more Kirby. I invited her too. *Kirby.* She's bringing David, who's her business partner and boyfriend, but they don't know that. I mean they know he's her business partner but not her boyfriend. Oh, and they think the B&B offices are a tiny house up in the Hollywood Hills. It's actually a massive house in upper Beverly Hills like where we live," she blurted out in one breath.

"Tell you what, I'll focus on the lie we're telling, not Kirby's. You know, I like to be a one-lie type of guy," Matt said with a wink.

Margo knew he was trying to make her feel better, but it didn't help. It just made her realize that today's lie to her parents was only the tip of the iceberg of the ways she'd been misleading them.

"I wish I could say the same," she said feebly.

Matt flagged their car and shepherded Margo into the back, explaining to the driver they had one stop to make. As Margo stared worriedly out the window, he called in the pizza order. He muffled the receiver, "At least tell me you aren't someone who likes Hawaiian Pizza because that's a storm we can't weather, Valentine," he said with mock concern as they careened down Sunset.

Margo held the gate open as Matt navigated through with the large pizza boxes. As they neared their storybook cottage, they saw the lights on and the door ajar. Music was wafting out.

"What the heck?" Margo strode in to find Rita with the blender going and a spread of charcuterie on the island.

"Well, lookie who showed up? Bonnie & Clyde. You two gave me the slip," Rita admonished, wagging a finger at them as she poured her first frozen blend into a glass and offered it to Hank. "I rushed back to find you and instead found these two milling about."

Rita winked at Maureen.

"I see you two met our house manager, Rita," Margo said.

"We did," Maureen Melon replied, a lightness to her tone that Margo knew was forced.

The doorbell went off and disco chords bounced off the walls.

"I'll get it," Rita chimed as she jumped down off the stool she must have dragged over, along with the board, plates, and glasses.

She was still wearing her shiny silver suit. It made her look like an extra from *The Office.* The entire room watched her go.

"She's a strange bird," Hank observed.

"You have no idea," Margo said flatly, realizing she had yet to introduce Matt, who was still holding the pizzas.

You better just dive into the deep end, Margo Melon, she thought as her stomach churned. "Mom, Dad, this is Matt, my boyfriend," her smile both optimistic and apologetic at the same time.

Matt put the pizzas down and extended his hand to shake, "Mr. and Mrs. Melon, hello. So lovely to finally meet you."

After an awkward pause from her parents, the parties reached out and shook hands, sharing niceties.

"Lovely to meet you too, Matt," her mother said, coolly.

"Gang's all here," Rita warbled, Kirby and David tailing her.

Margo hugged Kirby and then David, who whispered in her ear, "Don't worry, we'll help you get through this."

Truth be told, it was the first time Margo thought of him more as a boyfriend to Kirby than just a business partner. They continued the helloes with Margo introducing Matt to Kirby. As they broke apart, Margo realized Rita had joined in on the intros.

"Hi, I'm Rita," she said nodding to David who wholeheartedly clasped her hand in a handshake.

As a silence settled over the room, their guests assumed Rita would beg her farewells. Matt and Margo knew better.

"So, we have too many for Yahtzee, but charades is a real pleaser," Rita offered with a clap.

Kirby's eyes widened with amusement.

"Rita, I'm sorry, but family dinners are a tradition for just *family*."

"Got it! Gentlemen, shall we?" She nodded toward the door.

"Sorry, Rita, but the boys are staying."

Rita frowned deeply. "Hmm, I see how you Melons are," she said as she took one entire pitcher of margarita, dropped in a straw and left the room.

"Is she real or a character from a Wes Anderson film?" Kirby asked as the door closed.

"Both," Margo answered.

Everyone laughed, which was just the icebreaker the room needed before the roof cracked from the pressure.

"Let me get the plates," Margo offered, as Matt reached to open the pizza boxes.

"Are you gonna eat pizza in an all-white catsuit?" Maureen asked, pointing at her daughter's outfit.

Margo looked down.

"Of all your poor choices today, I might argue that's the most dangerous."

Margo could hear the edge in her mother's voice. So could Matt. He closed the boxes. A silence settled over the room.

"So," Maureen began after a pause, "you two are boyfriend and girlfriend?"

Margo nodded.

"And you're living together and thought it was a good idea to tell the internet before telling us?" Hank asked, his eyes drilling into both Matt and Margo.

"It seems so," Margo began.

"And now you're Grid.it famous," his voice rising at the end making the statement a question. "Busy Monday for you both."

Margo looked crestfallen at the disappointment in her father's eyes.

"Mr. and Mrs. Melon, if I may," Matt began.

"You may not," Hank boomed, a death stare directed his way.

Matt's mouth moved like a guppy, opening and closing trying to decide if forging ahead would win him points or be the nail in his eventual coffin.

"Dad," Margo exclaimed. Then she jumped in. "I know this is a lot. We actually didn't intend for *anyone* to find out. We've each been looking for our own place and this spot came up and the owner is weird...."

"We noticed," Maureen scoffed.

"That's not the owner. Rita's the house manager and stepdaughter to the owner, Dinah."

"Dinah's the landlord, she's a little eccentric," Matt jumped in "and on our tour she let us know how much she wanted a couple and we thought it was a sign that we should move in together."

"We used our personal pictures," Margo said picking up the story, "to sell her on the influencer thing because I didn't want her to call Kirby and confirm my job. If she did, I'd have to explain that I was moving in with a boyfriend that you all hadn't met yet. It just seemed awkward, so we hatched the influencer idea on the spot. I created the page thinking she'd be the only one to see it, but then somehow she got us Verified and the world found out about Matt before you."

Her parents looked stiff and unsure.

"So, you've had a boyfriend and even *that* you didn't tell us, Margo," Maureen asked. "Why keep that a secret?"

Just as Margo was about to speak, Kirby hopped in. "I can't let you both go after Margo without telling you that I asked her to keep a secret for me too."

Their parents stared at Kirby in confusion.

"David and I are dating," she continued.

"We were wondering why he was at our family meal. No offense, David," Maureen said flatly.

"None taken," David offered softly.

He put his arm around Kirby and then nodded at Margo. *So this is what he meant,* she thought, relieved that she wasn't the only one with a target on her back. *Safety in numbers.*

"What?" Hank asked, angry and confused.

"We've been dating for a while, and the house we bought together. It's bigger than what I may have led you to believe. I asked Margo to keep it quiet. I think my desire to hide David might have weighed on her, and she didn't think she could tell you about Matt."

Kirby looked at Margo apologetically. *Well, at least that strikes two lies off the scorecard.* Relief flooded over Margo and she jumped in.

"Oh, Kirby, I didn't *not* tell you all about Matt because of that."

Her mother cut her off. "So, that's why you stood me up for every house tour and office meet-up? You didn't want me to see that you've *both* been lying," Maureen observed, both sad and angry. "Is this what we do now in this family?" Her tone rose letting the room know anger was winning out as she looked between her daughters.

Hank put his arm around his wife. "No, it is not," he said matter-of-factly. "Girls, this is not who we are. Why suddenly is there a sense that you can't tell us things?"

Matt who had been standing next to Margo reached out and took her hand. He looked at her face, wanting her to know that he didn't know how to help or what to say, but he was there for her. Margo squeezed his hand back.

"Dad," Margo began, "It isn't that. It's that I've been failing, for like four years now, and I didn't want *this* to be yet another reason you look at me like I've let you down."

Tears wavered on the rims of her eyes. She willed them not to spill over. Matt's thumb brushed back and forth on her hand.

"Is that how you feel, Kirby?" Hank asked.

Kirby looked at David who squeezed her arm. "Kinda," she said, "I'd always been the one to fail and now I was succeeding. I didn't want you to look at me and think, *We always knew the other shoe would fall.*"

Hank who had been holding his wife's hand, let go as each parent strode to either side of the island, sweeping their respective daughters into a hug. "Girls, you could never let us down," he boomed.

"Or at least not in a way that means we won't love you," Maureen added.

Without hesitation, after hugging Margo, Maureen swept Matt into a hug before continuing around the island to hug Kirby and David. It caught Matt off guard. It had been a long time since a parent hugged him like that, with a strength that felt like it could stop a tornado. He felt honored to be welcomed by them and conspiratorial to be deceiving them. *They're so nice. They don't deserve to be lied to*, he thought.

"No more lying, okay?" Hank said looking directly at Margo.

"Okay," she said softly.

She looked at Matt with a glance that said *I'm a horrible person,* because they both knew they were still lying to her parents. Matt squeezed her hand again as if to say *stay strong.* She inhaled deeply and forced a smile onto her face.

After their respective admissions, Kirby's real, Margo's really well constructed, there seemed to be a sense of resolution that rose up in the room. The fear that Margo felt in her chest lessened. Matt opened the pizza boxes and Margo handed out plates.

"Are we good?" she asked as she sidled up to her mom, a plate outstretched.

"We're not, *not* good," her mother offered, "We'll be worse if you spill on that amazing outfit before I get any pictures of you in it," she said sternly.

Margo smiled. This time for real. "Good thing for you we took a zillion pictures at the party."

Her mother hugged her, and Margo inhaled the familiar smell of lavender and lemon on her skin.

"I'm gonna change," she whispered to Matt.

He nodded, "I'll have them eating out of my hand by the time you get back."

I bet you will, Margo thought as she strode across the kitchen. Kirby winked at her. *Thanks,* Margo mouthed back. Kirby nodded.

"Is this Walton's shit done now?" Rita asked gruffly from the living room. They all turned to find her sprawled out on the mattress, her hat dipped down over her eyes like a cowboy sleeping against a tree. "I mean, good night already, John Boy," she said dramatically. "And, for the record, I'm the rich one."

Both Matt and Margo's faces registered surprise at her declaration and what she might have heard. The rest of the evening, though, went off without a hitch.

"Margo, you better show us this house right now," her mother demanded as Matt cleared the plates. After the tour, which took two minutes since they didn't have anything, they sat outside on the pool furniture, laughing and telling stories of when the girls were little. Matt found himself falling in love with Margo's family and the ease of the relationship between these parents and their daughters. He could feel the love Mr. and Mrs. Melon had for Margo, Kirby, and David, and he could tell that the vines of that ivy were already reaching out for him as well.

"So, Matt," Kirby said as they washed dishes, "did Margo tell you about our investor?"

"What investor?" Hank asked as Kirby handed him a plate to dry.

"Margo's been secretly dating Matt, and I've been secretly dating Matt's dad."

"What?" Maureen barked, sloshing wine on the counter and then mopping it up.

"Well, kinda. Matt's dad is considering investing in Blush & Bashful," she exclaimed.

Every set of eyes in the room registered surprise and then fell upon Matt.

"What did you think of my dad?" Matt asked casually.

Kirby answered just as nonchalantly, "I actually haven't met him yet."

Matt's hands froze on the plate he was drying. *In the entire history of my dad's career he has never once, not ever invested in a company he didn't know. When Syb next door wanted $25 bucks to start a lemonade stand, dad demanded to meet her first. "Never give your money to someone you haven't looked in the eye," he always said*. Matt's mind raced.

"So, you're pretty early in the process?" Matt pressed lightly.

"Ummm," Kirby pondered as she scrubbed at some caked-on cheese. "We're pretty far along," she concluded.

Matt made a mental note to get to the bottom of that. "Keep me posted." he said brightly guising any suspicion he had with a smile.

"Well, you boys just survived your first Melon family meal," Hank said, smiling, "but by the looks on my daughters' faces it won't be the last."

Maureen hugged Margo, "You know," she said as she brushed Margo's hair back, "I recall your father grabbing my hand that way when we told my parents we were moving in together. I can tell he loves you."

It was like the air had been sucked out of the room for Margo. She was instantly relieved and repelled by the idea that her mother believed the lie they'd told her.

"Thanks, Mom." She smiled weakly.

"Tomorrow I'm coming to that office and we're talking what happens next for both of you," Maureen said sternly and proudly to both her daughters.

"Speaking of what happens next," Kirby jumped in as she slid into their hug zone. "I thought it could be super smart to cast you and Matt in our upcoming campaign."

"What?" Margo was dumbfounded.

"Well, you two are the hottest couple on the internet and we're trying to shoot the hottest campaign. So... I still have to talk to Mix about it. It's her shoot, after all," Kirby continued as Margo cringed at the mention of Mix still owning the campaign. "I want her buy-in. But good thing for you, M&M, I get the final say," Kirby winked.

This was something Margo hadn't seen coming. Mix may have taken the idea, initially, to grab the spotlight, but Margo being cast would *make* her the center of attention and when *that* gets them even more eyeballs, Margo would be undeniably credited for its success. *Mix is going to hate that,* Margo thought. "Sounds great."

"Yeah?" Kirby questioned, surprised at the easy sell.

"Yeah, I don't know what part we'll play, but okay," Margo said definitively.

The trio hugged when they felt Rita cozy up in between them and awkwardly join in. They all giggled.

CHAPTER 27

Legendary

As soon as the door closed, Matt did a touchdown dance. He swung his arm up for a high-five. "Don't leave me hanging, Valentine. You're the one who made us a high-flying, high-fiving couple," he shouted.

Margo laughed. She raised her hand to return the gesture.

"And the crowd is on their feet. Waaaaahhhhhh!" Matt mimicked the noise of a stadium gone wild. "We killed that," he declared jubilantly.

"We did, but..."

As she said the word, Matt fell to his knees dramatically, "Noooo. I won't let you kill our vibe with a but."

"But," Margo said authoritatively looking down at him, "David was asking me all kinds of questions about you and me. He's more of a girl than Kirby, and I realized I didn't know how to answer them. That's not good."

Matt smirked devilishly.

"What's that look for?" Margo said suspiciously.

"What I think you're saying, here, is we need a legend."

Margo rolled her eyes. "Okay, Jason Bourne, I give in. You win. Let's review our legend and nail down this history."

Matt did another end-zone hustle and then dashed to the kitchen.

"What are you doing?" Margo shouted after him.

"All good spy tradecraft requires Red Vines," he said with a wink as he walked back into the room.

Margo's eyes widened. "How did you know?"

"How'd I know what?"

"That Red Vines are my favorite," she said stealing the bag.

"I didn't, but now that I do, we can put that in the legend. See what I did there?" he said with a wag of his brows.

She laughed and he stole the bag back, cramming one entire piece into his mouth.

Matt and Margo stayed up all night talking and laughing, telling the stories of their childhood, Gypsy the cat, senior prom, losing their virginity—which led Matt to cautiously share his friends-with-benefits relationship with Bibi.

"So, you still sleep with her?" Margo asked trying to appear unfazed.

"Yeah, sometimes," Matt said trying to sound noncommittal.

"What about you? Are you...is there...?" he trailed off, oddly hoping the answer was no. *Why would I care if she's sleeping with anyone?* he thought.

"Not exactly," Margo said interrupting his thoughts.

"Do you know how sex works," Matt asked ponderously, "if the penis is in or near the vagina, that is sex. So how does *not exactly* work?"

Margo hit him with a pillow.

"I mean, I kissed someone today," she blurted out as she held that same pillow up to hide her face.

Matt felt like someone had kicked him. "Oh," he said, not even the remotest part of him expecting that. "Today?" he questioned, then hearing the disappointment even in his own voice he recovered. "Today, today?"

Margo lowered the pillow. "Sorta," she said with a punch-drunk smile on her face.

"*Sorta?* Again, do you know how kissing works, if the lips are on or near or about the face it is a kiss," Matt said instructively.

Margo hit him again with the pillow. "Ford, this guy I've liked for a while saw the news on us and, I guess, it confused him because he kissed me, which surprised him. It *certainly* surprised me," she said, embarrassed to be explaining this to anyone other than Chelsea.

Ford, Matt thought, *sounds like a douche canoe.*

Somewhere around 2:30 a.m., they fell asleep. They'd covered all the bases:

"He was in fact, having sex with Smurfette. Every boy's thought it," Matt declared as Margo confirmed, "giving Applicant #3457 Tiff's cell phone number, with the expressed intent that he would harass her makes you complicit in a sex crime, no matter how deserving she may have been of receiving those poorly manscaped dick pics."

Her assessment caused both of them to break out in fits of uncontrollable laughter.

"I like how you say dick pic. Like it's hurting you. Say it again."

Margo complied and they literally cried with laughter.

They woke up entwined on the blow-up mattress the next morning, sharing the top sheet and the large white linen shirt Margo had worn the day before as their only blankets, to the sound of a whirring blender and the smell of coffee. Margo could tell from his breathing that Matt was awake as he spooned her.

"Are you pretending to be asleep because you're afraid of Rita?"

"You bet your ass, Valentine."

She laughed. "Morning, Rita," she sang as she stood and hopped toward the kitchen, "I thought we talked about privacy?"

Rita nodded as she slid a cup of coffee across the island to her. "We sure did, Valentine. I haven't even looked your way. And, if you two started having sexy time, I woulda snuck out." Then after a pause adding with a smile and a wink at Matt, "eventually."

Matt looked stricken. He slid to stand behind Margo.

"Don't leave me alone with her," he begged in her ear as he reached around her for a slice of bacon.

"Sorry, Seven, I gotta work. You'll have to be a big boy," she said patronizingly as she spun toward him, stealing his half-eaten slice of bacon and heading toward the shower.

Margo stood directly under the spray of the rain shower, letting the water beat the top of her head before cascading down her body.

"I'm coming in, babe," Matt said loudly as he swung the door open and entered.

Margo yelped. "Get out of here, Matty," she demanded.

"Shhhhh," Matt insisted as he walked toward the shower, his eyes closed, feeling his way along the wall. "Be quiet, she'll hear you," he demanded as he tripped over the bathmat and fell into the tile. "I need a rape whistle to live in this house," he hissed, now standing with his back to the glass shower stall as Margo inched closer into the spray, covering herself as best she could. "I told that little fire hydrant I was coming in here to shower with you to escape her."

"I guess we can share that rape whistle then," Margo said sarcastically.

"Hardee har har," Matt replied flatly his head turned over his shoulder but his gaze directed away from her. "I called Chelsea from the pantry."

"You what?" Margo hissed.

"I called your best friend, get over it, Valentine. She and I can be friends too. It's modern times, Jane Austen," he shout-whispered back. "Anyway, she said check your email. Kirby let the entire office know that she's over the moon for us and, in light of your growing social influence, we'll be joining the shoot. Care to tell me what shoot we're joining?"

"I didn't know it was happening for real," Margo said as she hung her head out of the shower reaching for a towel, which Matt grabbed off the wall and handed to her. She shut off the water.

"Hey," Matt yelped, hopping around her now towel-clad body into the stall. "I told that ninja of a sex predator I was showering too. I have to walk out with wet hair."

He reached up over his head with one arm to remove his shirt. Margo, momentarily distracted by how alluring that move by a man always is, watched as Matt tugged at the back of his neckline and pulled his shirt straight up and off.

"Anywho, the email goes on to say that given your need to cultivate your social audience, the prop closet and Travis..."

"Tavis," Margo corrected.

"Right. *Tavis* are at your disposal to shoot content."

She realized she was staring at him through the steamed-up glass and turned her back just as he was about to suds up.

Matt feeling her stare popped his head around the corner of the shower as he shampooed his head, "You and Rita are like living with *To Catch a Predator,*" he said smiling as she gave him the finger over her shoulder. "What does she mean, *content*?" he asked rinsing the soap from his hair.

Margo, still rooting through her bag looking for a comb, bemoaned aloud, "I have to go get my things today."

"Oh, that reminds me, Zinny and I coordinated movers to bring a ton of stuff—like a ton," he said leaning out from around the shower again. "Like the entire Restoration Hardware catalogue is going to show up today. I can go get your suitcases while you wait here for Chelsea."

"She's coming?" Margo asked, spinning to face him and seeing him completely naked in the stall door. "Matty," she reprimanded tossing him her just-used towel now that she had on the white linen shirt.

"Have you been listening?" he asked catching the towel. "She's coming with Tavis to capture content. Even though, I still don't know what that means." He toweled off his hair.

"It means we need to be posting three to five times a day on our feed. That's what good social influencers do. So, we need stuff—pics, tips, moments, to craft our story around."

Matt accepted her answer as he came up behind and grabbed her just-used comb.

"I don't know how we're going to afford all that," she contemplated, catching his eyes in the mirror.

Matt steeled himself from saying anything about his trust fund, just like he had last night, offering instead, "Did you see our DMs?"

"What DMs?" Margo slapped on some coconut oil that she found floating in her bag.

"In our Grid.it feed. There has to be 100 offers for us from brands. Some of 'em are interesting. I had no idea how much shit some of these influencers get," he answered as he stole her Secret deodorant.

Margo scowled. "They get 'em all the time. Trick is to find the ones that pay. All these brands want to do *trade out*," she said, putting the words trade out in air quotes, as she took her deodorant back. "Mentions for stuff. Which, if you ask me, likes don't the pay the rent."

Matt smiled. "Oh, Valentine, you're a baller. I like this side of you. Mogul queen," he said with a snap of his fingers.

"You two almost done in there? I want to shower too," Rita said, her mouth was pressed up to the door frame.

Matt shook his head emphatically at Margo in the mirror as she laughed.

"No. Absolutely not," Matt whispered. He swung open the door. "Rita, this room is off limits. You have your own shower." She went to speak. "No," he said shutting her down. She turned and walked out in a huff. Matt turned to Margo and said in mock outrage, "Rape whistle."

CHAPTER 28

Bulletproof

Margo put up a post as she stood in her kitchen sipping coffee and waiting for Chelsea. Then she perused the list of offers in their inbox. Matt was right, there were over a hundred. Margo found the usual suspects like Fitalicious Boxes and The Length Doctor Hair Pills hoping to sign them up for their affiliate marketing programs, sharing that some of their top influencers earn upwards of 25K a month hocking their items. Yet, there were others that she hadn't expected like Target, Amex, and Sur La Table.

As the likes poured in on her post, a picture taken by Margo that showed her and Matt from the chest down, seated side by side, her in pale pink, him in pastel mint, at a café table with two expertly placed coffee cups. Her left arm was looped through his right, which was holding the handle of his cup. Her hand was casually resting on his forearm, sugar carefully sprinkled and made to look like an accidental spill on the table. *Out late and up early makes it a double pot sort of day.* The likes tally was already well past 20K, which Margo knew meant they were climbing higher and higher in the suppressive Grid.it algorithm. Last night their follower count had been well past 124,000. Today, thanks to Maria's glowing recap on the Grid.it & Hit.it list, that number was climbing. *We're gonna need more pictures fast,* Margo thought, reviewing the handful they had remaining from their day-one shoot to get the house. She carefully shot a boomerang declaring *but first, MORE coffee* as she tipped creamer into her mug, the whiteness of the milk swirling into and back out of the cup for her Grid.Vid.

With that done, she filled her cup for the second time and clicked on @BO$$x10, an organization drawing attention to the fact that out of all the companies on the Fortune 500 List, only 24 have female CEOs. "We want to increase that by tenfold," founder Harper Moon informed her in a DM, inviting Margo to join a panel helmed by Peabody Award–winning reporter, and one of Margo's icons, Maria Shriver. *How did I do it, Maria?* Margo envisioned herself seated on the panel, mic in hand, talking like someone high on bath salts. *Well, Maria, I'm a liar and fraud.* She sighed. *If they knew, they wouldn't want me*, she concluded, deciding she could never sit on that panel, no matter how badly she wanted it. It's what she'd hoped she'd be doing at Brown all those years before, but even though the offer was there, Margo knew it wasn't possible.

Her phone dinged with a text.

At your parents. They're plying me with pancakes before I head back. Like I said, parents love me. [winky face emoji]

Margo smiled as she put her phone down. When it dinged again, she expected to read another note from Matt.

Can't stop thinking about our kiss. Heard you're not coming in today, maybe not coming back after the shoot. I have to see you.

Margo's heart stopped dead in her chest. *Ford, I haven't even had time to think about you.* Her heart leapt.

"Heeeellllooooo?" Chelsea shouted as she walked in the door.

"Hi," Margo returned coming around the corner to see Chelsea and Tavis. She tucked away her thoughts of Ford.

"Um, yes queen of this house," Tavis said, sassily. "You did *real* good, and I don't mean just the house. Ahem, I mean that man you've been hiding."

Margo flushed red at the reference to hiding a man, in light of the text she'd just gotten from Ford.

"Where do you want this?"

Margo turned to see a floating stack of garment bags, Rita undoubtedly underneath them.

"Put them on the island," Tavis directed.

Rita dropped them right where she stood. "I can't work under these conditions," she said dramatically, before swanning out of the room like Nathan Lane in *The Birdcage*.

"Is she..." Tavis began.

"She is," Margo said cutting him off, knowing whatever he was going to say would most likely apply, as they fell out laughing.

"What are these clothes for?"

"Word on the street is that you and your mister are about to be the stars, child, of our little Fourth of July shoot. So, we got to *work* that tailoring to get you set by Friday's camera click. Mix has her claws out so we got to do what we can to make you two bulletproof," Tavis dished.

"What do you mean 'claws out'?" Margo asked, feigning naïveté to the Blush & Bashful style director.

"Girl, don't you play dumb, it's not your color," Tavis admonished. "We all know she hates you."

Margo felt like she'd been kicked. She looked at Chelsea with a glance that said, *did we know this?! I mean, we hate Mix but did we know that Mix hated me?!*

"I think what Tavis is trying to say is she feels competitive with you," Chelsea offered.

Tavis leaned in as an aside to Chelsea that he clearly wanted Margo to hear, "Is that how you handle this one? Cuz she hate her." Chelsea swatted him away.

"We have work to do. We have to plan for the shoot this week that you're now in, which thank the lord we got the propping and all the set builds done for. Those are going in today, which," Chelsea continued as she raised her hand to head Margo off at the pass of her impending protest, "I know, ideally, you'd be there to participate, but I assure you, you are exactly where you need to be. The entire team at the office has that under way, and Topher is fully in charge of his set team. He's the best in the business. Kirby and David hired him away from Anthro because he's so good. Tomorrow we can go in early and do a walk-through of all the details we pored over."

Tavis is right, looks like someone knows how to expertly handle me, Margo thought coolly looking at Chelsea with admiration.

"So, today Tavis will fit you for the shoot, and then we'll capture as much content as we can for your feed from what I've brought from my own styling closet," she said with a wink. "Where's Matt? We have to fit him too."

"Yaaaaasss, where is he? Bring him to me," Tavis said striking a pose.

Margo laughed. "I'll put on another pot of coffee."

"Oh girl, no, we OOO, out of office. You go in that kitchen and make us mimosas," Tavis said as he scowled, handing her a paper bag with champagne and OJ inside.

"Aye, aye, Captain." Margo saluted.

"Ohhhhhhh, and she make me feel butch too. I like," he smiled as Chelsea rolled her eyes at him.

Margo reached for the champagne flutes Rita had undoubtedly brought by as she hollered for Chelsea's help. With Tavis setting up rolling racks, Margo mouthed, *look,* to her friend and slid her phone across the island. Chelsea read the text from Ford and her eyes grew large.

"I don't know what to reply," Margo hissed as she prepared to uncork the champagne, wincing prematurely for its impending *pop.*

"What do you want to do?" Chelsea whispered back. "Do you want to see him?"

"I think so," Margo said, "I mean, I don't want this fake story Matt and I are spinning to get in the way of a real chance with Ford. Maybe if I told him the truth…"

Chelsea looked horrified. "You can't tell him, we don't know him well enough to trust him," she said, *and honestly the fact that he wants to date you even though he knows you're dating someone else tells me he isn't to be trusted,* she thought but didn't say. After a pause, "You don't have feelings for Matt?" Chelsea asked.

"What? Seven? I just met the guy. This isn't one of your romance novels, Chels." Margo scoffed as she filled the glasses with Veuve Clicquot. "Why would you even ask me that?" She scowled, now carefully topping each glass with OJ.

"I don't know. You two are cute together, that's all."

"You've seen too many episodes of *The Bachelor.*"

"Whatever," Chelsea admonished as she picked up Margo's phone and began to type, *I'm not sure how I feel and not sure meeting would be a good idea. I didn't expect that kiss and I don't want anyone to get hurt.*

They each stared at the screen. "Are we sure this is the reply?" Margo asked.

"No, not really, but it feels like the right thing to say for now," Chelsea offered.

Margo took the phone and clicked send before she could overthink it, passed a glass to Chelsea and then carried hers and Tavis's into the living room.

CHAPTER 29

The Bachelor Tell All

As Matt loaded Margo's bags into the car, his phone's FaceTime ring rattled in his pocket. He retrieved it. *Bibi, thank God,* he thought, punching connect. The screen came into view, but all Matt saw was chaos on the other end as he heard Gus clacking and clanging with the phone.

"That's enough, truck driver Gus," Bibi said as she hefted the phone out of the Bruder dump truck Gus had placed him in.

"Did you see that, Matt?" Gus said dragging the phone back down to his face, holding it much too close. "You were driving my dump truck and I was driving the front loader," he shouted.

Matt could see his tiny teeth and yogurt smears on his chin.

"I did, buddy." Matt smiled.

"When are you going to come over and play trucks with me?" Gus asked.

"Soon, buddy. I'm moving today. Hey, I had to rent a semi-trailer," Matt said.

Gus pulled the phone away to look at Matt, his eyes sparkled with excitement. "What color was the cab?" he asked.

"Red, I think."

"You think?" Gus said appalled. "Don't you know your colors?"

Matt smiled. "It was red, Gustard McMann."

"That's not my name," Gus howled.

"It's not?" Matt said in mock confusion.

Gus fell out in fits of laughter as Bibi tickled him shouting "Gustard McMann!" Matt's heart swelled. He loved them both so much.

"Hey," Bibi said, pulling him back to the conversation.

"Hey." Matt shut the trunk and slid in behind the steering wheel.

"I don't want to split hairs, but two days ago you said you were going to be homeless and now the *internet* tells me that you're wifed up with some girl named Margo. If I wasn't so confused, I would be very angry, Matthew," she said matter-of-factly.

"It's a long story," Matt started.

Bibi cut him off, "Make it short."

Matt looked out the window, realizing he was still sitting in front of Margo's parents' house. "Hold on. I'm double-parked. Let me get to a better spot."

Just as the team was placing the last item of clothing on the collapsible rolling racks, Matt returned, pushing a luggage cart with all of Margo's bags and Rita perched atop it.

"Yaw, yaaaw," she cried like a cowboy on a horse.

"Is this girl for real?" Tavis said snarkily as he stared out the window at the spectacle.

"Yes, and she has keys to my house," Margo said dramatically.

"Boo, I will wear my best Dolce & Gabbana to your funeral." Tavis bowed dramatically as Margo laughed.

"Hi, babe," Matt reflexively said as he dragged a suitcase in and down the hall.

"Hey," Margo said in return, then tacking on, "babe," for good measure.

When he came back out to grab the next suitcase, he introduced himself to Tavis and hugged Chelsea.

"Your parents say *hi* by the way. Can I see you in the bedroom?" he asked, grabbing two more bags.

"Absolutely," both Rita and Tavis chorused at the same time answering Matt's question, each with a devilish smile.

Matt shook his head and smirked, while Rita glared at Tavis.

"Maybe I'll wear that Dolce & Gabbana to *your* funeral first," Margo said nodding toward Rita's angry stare, smiling at Tavis as Matt pulled her toward the hall.

"I have to tell Bibi," Matt said as soon as he closed the bedroom door. His urgency caught Margo off kilter. "You got to tell Chelsea. I need to tell her. She's my…"

Margo cut him off. "Fine," she said, her voice carrying more heat than she expected. "I mean, I get it. You love her."

Matt felt a pang when she said it. "I do love her," he began.

"Good. Got it," she replied as Chelsea entered the room.

"Got what?"

"Nothing," Margo said, looping her arm through Chelsea's. "Let's go get me fitted. Matt needs some time to get organized."

As they left the room, she gave Matt a smile hoping to send the message that she was happy for him to have Bibi. *He should tell Bibi,* she thought as she walked down the hall. *She's the woman he loves. Why wouldn't I want him to tell her?*

After an hour Matt emerged, looking less stressed than when he'd arrived. Margo eyed him over Tavis's shoulder and he gave her the thumbs up. *I guess that went well,* Margo thought.

"You're up next, Mr. Milles-Lade," Tavis flirted.

"Sure thing. I just need to grab Valentine."

"Ooooh, Valentine, as I live and breathe. I love this nickname on you," Tavis swooned at her feet, fixing a hem.

She rolled her eyes as she followed Matt out to the pool. The doorbell chime kicked in. "Well praise be, this place gets groovier by the minute," Tavis hooted as he grabbed Chelsea and spun her into a dip.

Matt slid the doors shut. "Okay, I told her. She can't wait to meet you."

"Oh, we're meeting?" Margo asked, worriedly, "I don't think we need to meet."

Matt hovered for a moment, not sure what to say.

"I mean, our goal is to do this thing for a few weeks or so and then have a breakup fight or something, right?" She paused. "I guess what I mean is, meeting parents was *necessary* because they don't know, but Bibi *knows* we're a lie."

Matt nodded. "Right," he said, noncommittally.

"And she's fine with it, so why complicate it?" Margo pondered.

"Matt, you're up next," Tavis said sliding the doors back open. The pair turned to stare at him. "And that cabbage patch doll of a woman says the movers are here."

"Uuuuhhh, a bed," Matt said as he let his head fall back. "Finally, no more sleeping on the floor, Valentine."

"Ooooh, sex on the floor, so *Fifty Shades,*" Tavis said flirtingly at Matt, who mock scolded him.

"Babe, you direct the movers where you want it all. Tavis, I'm all yours."

Tavis clapped with glee as Matt followed him in and stood on the fitting platform. Rita barked orders at the army of movers as Margo pointed where things should be placed. "You weren't lying, this is a ton of stuff," she said as the room filled up, shedding the unease of having to meet Bibi.

Matt shrugged. "Like I said, my dad's girlfriend hired a decorator for the new place. So, Zinny and I just redirected all this from the storage facility."

Margo was actually relieved. She was dreading another night on a blow-up mattress, clinging to her half. In just the few minutes she'd been standing in the doorway, she caught two mattresses heading down the hall to the bedrooms. *One less thing for me to do,* she thought, although she loved decorating. As she stood there admiring the clean modern lines of the white linen sofa, Chelsea grabbed her hand and pulled her to the rack she had set up. Margo ran her fingers along the clothes.

"Hey, Tavis?" she asked.

"Hmmm?" he said as he carefully adjusted a white slim-cut suit that Matt was quite possibly going to wear for the B&B campaign.

"Could I wear this for the shoot?" she asked pulling out the pink wool military jacket she'd first seen in Chelsea's sewing closet. Chelsea inhaled sharply out of surprise.

"Ooooooh, what is this?" Tavis's face illuminated with lust at the sight of the finely tailored jacket. He grabbed it off the hanger and put it on, sashaying around before draping it over Margo's shoulders and then bowing down like she was royalty. As he rose, "It's a definite possibility." He gestured for Margo to spin. She complied, catching Chelsea's eye, who beamed back with pride.

CHAPTER 30

Jet Set

By noon, Tavis was packing up his clothes while Rita flailed about with the collapsible cart.

"Darling, you're going to break it or puncture a lung if you keep at it," Tavis said with a wag of his finger.

"Blanca never uses a collapsible rack, like some sort of peasant," Rita sneered.

"You're more dramatic than *I* am," Tavis crooned, "and that's saying a lot."

After they'd gone, Matt, Margo, and Chelsea got down to shooting content. They staged at least 15 wardrobe changes for Margo and then an entire series of couples' shots. They fake laid on the outdoor cabana, fake grilled, fake floated in the pool, fake made coffee, fake made drinks, fake made the bed, fake, fake, fake.... And yet, as Chelsea framed them in her camera viewfinder she couldn't help but see the real chemistry. When they moved on to boomerangs, Grid.Vids, and b-roll, she found herself even more charmed by them.

"You guys are really good at this," Chelsea observed. Then, after a pause to watch back a video, "Like really good. Are you sure you're faking it?"

Before either could answer, the disco doorbell went off. *Saved by the bell,* Matt thought. Two minutes later Rita power walked into the room.

"Special delivery," she crooned struggling with two giant vases of flowers.

"Oh my gosh, they're gorgeous," Margo cooed as she took one square vase, laden with all white hydrangea, as Matt grabbed the one with roses. Drenched from carrying both, Rita walked off in a huff. Margo read the first card aloud, "Matt & Margo, Thank you for coming last night! We can't wait for all that is it to come. Grid.it."

"That's nice," Margo said. Matt nodded in agreement.

Matt opened the second one and read it to the girls. "Welcome to the family, Margo. Matt's father and I are so excited to meet you. Tiff & Brooks"

"Is she for real?" he said venomously.

"I think it's nice," Margo offered. Matt stared back at her incredulously.

"This is all a ploy," he huffed.

"You don't know that. Maybe your dad *does* want to meet me."

Matt put down the card as it if were laced with poison.

Margo chuckled, "You're such a child."

"Did you see these DMs?" Chelsea interrupted, her feet propped up on the newly arrived vintage coffee table.

"Are you in my DMs on my phone?" Margo asked.

"I am and you two have all kinds of offers."

"We know," Margo said defeatedly as she and Matt flopped down, flanking Chelsea on the sofa. *Please Lord, don't let Ford text me right now,* Margo prayed silently, looking at Matt out of the corner of her eye.

"Just looking at the ones that give their budgets, you're talking about more than $15,000 worth of deals. What are you guys going to do with these?" Chelsea demanded as all three of them watched her scroll through each offer.

Margo sighed. "What would we do with them? We're already lying on the internet, I don't think we should add fraud to our list of crimes," Margo shared.

"Is it really fraud, though?" Chelsea asked. "I mean, we don't even know yet what they want."

Matt pondered what Chelsea was saying. "I kinda agree with Chels. What harm is there in finding out what they want?"

"Say we find out? What does it matter? How would we shoot more than we are now? Today took forever and I have to work." Margo grabbed her phone back. "Look at this one from Jimmy's Subs. They want a game day–themed post. Who's taking that picture, getting all those props, finding our outfits?" she looked at them expectantly.

"Me," Chelsea answered flatly. "I can shoot and style. You can write. Matt can do the deals."

Matt hopped in. "We can pay her." He looked at Chelsea. "Of course we would pay you, Chels." Then looking back at Margo, "Jimmy's Subs has a budget of 4K. If these people want to hire us, I say we let 'em. That's what everyone else does. That's what influencers do."

"Yeah, but should I remind you? We're not *really* influencers," Margo replied flatly.

"Our quarter of a million followers would beg to differ with you, Valentine," Matt said sarcastically.

Margo looked from Matt's face to Chelsea's and back again. "I don't know," she said hesitantly.

Matt grabbed her phone. "What's the Phame thing?" he asked opening the top message and reading aloud.

"Phame at Sea sets sail next week. Keep an eye out for your invite. A great group has already booked and gobbled up most of the first-class seats, but don't worry. That's what jets are for. Can't wait to hear what you think." He looked up, awestruck "I mean, forget Jimmy and his bush league subs, amiright?!"

"Right about what? We don't even know what it means," Margo sniped.

"Well, I can tell you what it means." Chelsea grabbed the phone and pulled up Grid.it, scrolling through the pages of Anine Lee, Joanna Chen, Dree Von Valle, and Manuela Carrillo. "These girls go on almost every Phame trip. If we stalk their feeds, it'll tell us where they're going." She scrolled quickly. "Collectively they wield more than 39 million followers on Grid.it." Her long fingernails clacked over the screen. "Jackpot!"

Matt and Margo craned over her shoulder.

"Manuela is getting a spray tan for Bora Bora, and Dree is packing for, and I quote, *French Polynesian Fashun.*" Chelsea looked at them proudly. "You've just been invited to Bora Bora!" she cried

"How do you know that?" Matt asked.

"They're both getting ready for the same *destination*. That has to be Phame, and it makes sense they'd invite you. They always invite someone that's exploded onto Grid.it. I'd say you qualify."

"I can't go to Bora Bora," Margo hissed.

"Why not? Isn't this the sort of thing we *should* do?" Matt pleaded. "They want to fly us to Bora Bora with the who's who of Grid.it fame. Private jets, spas, five-star experiences...how is this not something you're jumping at?" Matt looked stunned.

"This is what you signed up for, Margo, when you went along with the verification. You said, you wanted to sell this for a few weeks before you break up. You said that to me," Chelsea demanded.

Why do I feel like I'm being handled again, Margo thought?

"This sets the stage—romantic locale, fun in the sun, then a little trouble in paradise. Perfect timing," Chelsea concluded.

"I knew we were right to hire you," Matt exclaimed as he swung his arm around Chelsea, referencing the decision to offer her a job just three minutes before.

"This isn't going to be our thing," Margo said, narrowing her eyes at them, "where you two gang up on me. I have not agreed to this," she warned.

"No, you have not. But Chelsea and I, or as I like to call us now Team Bora Bora..."

"I was thinking more Bae Watch—B, A, E—has a nice ring to it, don't you think?" Chelsea interrupted.

"Oh, that's good," Matt said proudly as Margo shook her head in dismay. "Honestly, Chels, we can't go wrong either way." He smiled. "Good thing we'll have nine hours on a private plane to figure it out."

"You two think you're cute, but you're not," Margo said coldly.

"We're kinda cute," Matt said, pulling Chelsea to her feet, wrapping her in a hug as they both stared at Margo.

"It won't work," Margo said flatly. "You can't wear me down." Their eyes pleaded with her like that of two little kids asking to keep a stray puppy.

Margo blinked.

"She's cracking," Matt mock whispered to Chelsea. "Can you cry on command?"

Margo burst out laughing. Matt and Chelsea started to jump up and down while still in an embrace. "I don't know why you two are celebrating, I haven't agreed to anything. And, have you forgotten, we haven't even been officially invited?!" Margo defended when the doorbell chimed.

Matt swung Chelsea into a disco pose. Chelsea laughed.

"Aren't you gonna get that?" Margo looked at them.

"Why? Rita's probably already attacked whoever's there," Matt said has he dipped her friend.

As if right on cue, Rita careened into the room carrying a white box with a bright turquoise bow. "Jeez Louise, you two are a pain in the ass," she said as she set the box on the coffee table.

"Open it," the ladies directed of Matt.

He lifted the lid. They all peered inside to see a glass jar filled with a tiny art installation of people sunbathing on the beach. Matt knew instantly it was the work of his best friend, Ian. *Of course he would be on the Phame trip,* he thought. *He's one of the founding partners and investors. And he practically put Grid.it on the map with Danica.* He carefully lifted it out and read the letter in the bottle.

"Matt & Margo, come sail away with us to Bora Bora." Matt, Chelsea, and Rita looked at Margo expectantly, all three holding their breath.

"How will I get out of work?" she asked. "How will *you* get out of work?" she asked again, pointing at Chelsea.

"Same way I got out of work today. Your sister wants this for you and I'm just an intern who now happens to be your stylist and editorial director. Don't worry about me. I got this covered."

"And our shoot?" Margo admonished.

"Will be done," Chelsea said quickly. "As of this Friday, it'll be shot."

Margo looked incredulous as all three sets of eyes drilled into her.

"This is kind of perfect. Think of all the photo possibilities," Matt prodded. "Not to mention, setting the stage," he furthered with a *hint, hint* tone.

Margo's resolve weakened at the idea of escaping to white beaches with friends, and the editor in her knew he was right about the content potential. "Okay," she began. The room broke into cheers. Matt actually sweeping Chelsea off her feet. "But," Margo said loudly, "I have a few ground rules."

"You two listen to this buzz kill's ground rules, I'm gonna get a bikini wax," Rita said matter-of-factly as she headed for the door.

"You're not going Rita," Matt shouted after her.

Rita just twinkle waved goodbye from the doorframe and blew Matt a kiss.

Matt dramatically shivered. "She's not going," he declared, turning to Margo.

"Babe, do you seriously think I'm going to let Rita go with us to Bora Bora?"

Matt looked at Margo worriedly, but Chelsea looked at her with surprise. *That babe sounded real, REAL* she thought.

CHAPTER 31

She-EOs

"I'm sure he can figure it out, Margo. It's not exactly rocket science." Mix's tone struck like a dagger.

"Of course, I just meant it might help you visualize how you want us, if we were both here. I could call him."

"Ford, be a dear and stand in since Margo doesn't think I have enough vision to figure out my own campaign," Mix said dismissively, as she peered over the photographer's shoulder at the framed shot, not even looking Margo's way.

This shoot can't end fast enough, Margo sighed inwardly. She chewed the inside of her cheek as Ford, in all his Ralph Lauren glory, strode toward her. *How am I going to pretend not to like him—especially in those jeans?*

Today was the first time she'd seen him since the kiss and the first time they'd spoken since his text and her subsequent reply.

"Hey," he said quietly, a sleepy sexiness on his brow.

"Hey," she offered, timidly, glancing up only briefly. *Don't look at him. What are you, steel? You aren't strong enough for that,* she chastised.

"Let's have you two step out onto the platform," photographer Simon Aadland directed.

The Norwegian-born photographer had been specifically chosen because of his background shooting highly stylized fashion photography for *Popler*, *Vogue,* and *Porter*. Mix knew him from her days at Barneys.

As the Blush & Bashful shoot approached the concept had grown. Margo's original vision of every surface being pink, still stood. However, two weeks ago Kirby had the brilliant idea to shift from just a Fourth of July shoot to using the Fourth of July as the kick-off for a series of campaigns. The lead shot remained "The Founding Females," and the stage behind them had been set to capture that vision, with the pool dyed an opaque turquoise and every inch of the pool deck ombréd in pink, including the cushions, chairs, umbrellas, and curtains. Even the cement and back walls of the house had been shellacked with a barely there pink iridescence.

After Kirby's first wave of changes, Margo and Chelsea decided to go for broke. "I say at this point we just go for it, share our ideas, take ownership of everything from this point on. What can Mix do?" Chelsea considered as they sat eating sushi at SugarFish.

The very next day, Margo had made a suggestion to swap out the female models for actual female founders. Mix had looked at Margo like she might use the Poland Springs water dispenser to water board her as she keyed up her idea. "This campaign is growing and we're missing a big opportunity if we go live with a headline declaring our founding females but feature photography that doesn't include any. I know we can get this booked."

Kirby and Ford loved the idea. Mix's glare told Margo she felt differently. She looked like she might cram the white board eraser she was holding in her hand down Margo's throat. "The women chosen will be titans in their own right, and I think we should dress them in a power wardrobe of white to stand out against all the pink and your dress of deep magenta, Kirby." Mix clutched the eraser even harder.

They'd approved it on the spot, and Brent, Mix's beleaguered assistant, had been offered up to help them wrangle the fiercest female execs and activists they could secure, including Jen Atkin, Jane Goodall, Cleo Wade, and Gloria Steinem. Brent got so excited at one point he openly high-fived Margo across the conference table. Mix had immediately summoned him to her office.

"Poor Brent," Chelsea observed as he dashed out. "Yesterday, I heard his walkie-talkie going off in the bathroom two seconds after he walked in. He can't even pee without her barking at him."

Margo and Chelsea were being brazen in the sharing of their ideas. Yet, while they'd been conscientious about going around Mix, they had not gone above her. She was, after all, still their supervisor. So, they shared ideas with her in the room, just making sure more people were present to hear them. The end result was that they were now getting accolades for their own work.

On Tuesday, Margo had presented the idea of placing Kirby on a special platform floating in the center of the pool. Circular and painted with a pink and white cabana stripe it harked back to "La Concha Beach Club," photographed by Slim Aarons in 1975. Margo had shown the image to Kirby and, much to Mix's chagrin, Kirby had directed Topher to build it. The art direction was set.

But then on Wednesday, when Matt and Margo were being fitted at home for their own series of photos, Kirby had shocked the team at B&B by stepping out. "Margo and Matt should be on that platform. She's our ace in the hole, given what's happened this week. She's our megaphone. They should be in the launch campaign. I'm going to take a lounge chair with our other amazing women. The Founder's Row, all of us in white, that's where I'll sit."

Mix argued that, as the founder of Blush & Bashful, center stage should remain Kirby's, but Kirby was not to be dissuaded.

"Mix, that's the point of this campaign. Competition isn't what matters in the climb, inclusion is. Margo has a bigger draw, and we become more powerful by allowing other women to own their power."

Mix left in a huff, sniping to Brent on the way out, "Don't you dare leave until all the bookings and call sheets are done. I want them in my email inbox tonight."

Brent gave a terrifying nod and called his friends, canceling his own birthday dinner, which Mix knew had been booked for weeks. When he called Margo and Chelsea on Wednesday evening, long after their excitement over Bora Bora had died down, to tell them of the shift, they could hear that he'd been crying.

"You okay, Brent?" Margo asked.

"It's been a day, but I'm fine. I have some news. You'll be on the platform with Matt, Margo."

Margo had gasped and started to protest.

"Don't argue, it came down from on high. Kirby made the request herself. So, your outfit will be changing— Matt's too. We'll need to refit you. Be here at 6 a.m."

Margo and Chelsea arrived the next morning, right on the dot, with coffee and donuts to surprise Brent. He'd been so touched he teared up, then immediately waved them off. "Don't be nice to me in front of Mix. It makes my life harder," he'd sniffed as he quickly hugged them.

With the shift for the featured shot, Matt and Margo were now going to be in the foreground, sitting on the platform floor itself, Margo dramatically wearing a voluminous, off the shoulder, pink evening gown—think Princess Diana's wedding dress—with its fabric train spilling out around her, unfurling across the water with the male models in their colonial jackets and pink powder wigs holding the fabric up above the water line, as they stand in the pool. Matt, now seated behind her, will be wrangling a dog and a cherub-faced child on his lap in a pink slim-cut '60s-style suit.

After her fitting, the entire team did final looks on all remaining sets. Each of their initial concepts had been enhanced with updates made by Topher and his team. The fountain full of pink sequins now had a fantastical menagerie of handmade birds and tall sweeping branches laden with pink paper flowers to support Chelsea's idea of each woman reading Maya Angelou's *I Know Why The Caged Bird Sings* among a swirl of avian magic. The final edit would undeniably be a statement against racism and sexism on every scale. The pink Mercedes convertible, which initially was going to be filled with models road-tripping for the 4th, would now feature Gloria Steinem behind the wheel and a group of She-EOs standing in the car, pointing ahead like the famous painting *Crossing the Delaware,* a banner reading CEO replacing the American flag. They'd added shots, too, like a white box room with hundreds of pieces of pale pink acrylic on fishing line made to look like shards of glass raining down to serve as the backdrop for each founder sharing their story of shattering the glass ceiling.

Margo couldn't believe how the concepts had evolved and how timely it all felt.

She was in awe of what Kirby was building. "I love every element of this campaign, except the part where I'm in it," Margo said woefully as she and Chelsea steamed clothes.

"What? You're amazing in it. Besides, you aren't in it because you're meant to be as far along as them; you're in it so you can get the word out. Eventually you'll be right up there with each of these ladies," Chelsea argued. Margo wasn't so sure. "Just get through these next few weeks. You'll see," Chelsea bolstered.

A few weeks, I just want to get through today, Margo thought. A feat she almost accomplished when Ford stopped her in the parking lot. "I know you said you were confused. I don't want to pressure you, but just so you know where I stand," he said as he leaned in and kissed her. She was more surprised by the fact that he was kissing her than the kiss itself. He broke away. "Don't keep me waiting long," he said as he walked past her toward his car.

Margo stood, stunned, the heat still on her lips.

"You two sure are friendly. I wonder, does your boyfriend, Matt, know about this?" Mix purred behind her.

She really is a feral cat, Margo thought turning around to glare at her. Mix smiled sweetly.

Margo's skin crawled. "Night, Mix," she said coolly and walked to her car without another word.

When she got home, she found that Matt had left one light on, spotlighting a note.

Valentine, May I present to you Bibi's what to eat, drink, and do before a shoot? Hugs, Seven

Next to it Margo found a stash of face masks, serums, a water bottle with Moon Juice powder with chlorophyll drops, and a cooler with a Sakara clean dinner inside. Margo crunched on a bell pepper from the meal and bristled, *As if I want advice from your girlfriend.* Not even an ounce of her wondered if her annoyance was just jealousy in disguise.

CHAPTER 32

Never Nude

The next morning, Matt woke her at 5 a.m. by placing a green tea on her bedside table. "Gooood morning, Valentine."

Margo sat up, her eye mask riding high on her forehead, her hair a mess.

"Someone looks grumpy," he chirped as he tossed open the curtains.

"I'm supposed to be the morning person, remember?" she said gruffly.

"Well, you're falling down on the job, so I gotta take up the slack. Brent called. He said you're to wash your hair but not dry it. I started the shower already." He left the room. Thirty seconds later he was back, throwing the covers off her.

"Hey, I could've been naked," she yelped as she clamored to grab them.

"Oh, Margo, I'd actually peg you as a never nude."

"What does that mean?" she asked irked by his judgment.

"C'mon, have you ever just been totally naked out in the wild?"

She crossed her arms to try and hide the fact that she didn't have on a bra.

"I bet you stay partially dressed at all times?"

She stared at him as he arched his right eyebrow, his cute scar following suit. She huffed a protest. He reached to drag her off the bed.

"Well, this might be hard for you to hear, but you have to take off all your clothes to shower," he drawled sarcastically.

"You're so annoying," she said as he pushed her toward the bathroom door.

They arrived 42 minutes later. The team was already in full crisis mode. The cherub-faced child model booked for the shoot had hand-foot-and-mouth disease. He was out. Brent was in a panic.

"I could just go down to Sunset and pick up a baby somewhere," Matt offered.

Brent looked hopeful.

"That's a crime, Brent," Matt said, grimly. "We can't steal a baby."

"The crime is what's going to happen to me when Mix finds out," Brent replied flatly.

"Maybe we just skip that part," Matt offered. Brent stared at him blankly.

"Is he having an aneurysm?" Matt asked of Margo as they stared at him.

"I think so," she confirmed.

Matt's phone rang. It was Gus on his FaceTime. "Hey, what about Gus? He's not a baby, but he's cute and he loves me," Matt said.

"Show him to me," Brent declared, "Now!"

Matt spun his phone to face him.

"Yes! Book it!"

"Let me see what I can do." Matt stepped out to speak to Bibi. *Great, my fake boyfriend's bringing his real girlfriend to my job, fanfuckingtastic,* Margo thought as she sat down in the hair and makeup chair.

"Fix this," Brent said patronizingly of Margo's hair. "Every minute that goes by we're losing light."

Chasing light is a hot topic on every set. But, due to the position of the canyon, it was especially important on this one. Simon suggested they start the day shooting the pool and platform and then move to shoot the founders later when the sun moved across the sky. "I'll marry the images in post," he'd determined.

Matt returned five minutes later and declared that Bibi and Gus were on their way. "I can't wait for you to meet Gus," he said looking down at Margo.

I kinda can't wait to meet him either, she smiled and thought but didn't say.

Kirby, who had just arrived, let out a sigh of relief.

"How's it going with my dad?" Matt asked as Kirby leaned in to hug him.

"Good. I mean, I haven't met him yet, but the team's great!"

"Well, keep me posted," Matt said, immediately pulling out his phone to text Leandra. *Got a question for you. Call me,* he typed before slipping his phone in his pocket. *It just doesn't make sense,* he thought.

"Matt, this is Ford," Margo said.

Matt looked up to see a cliché frat boy standing before him. *Ah, the douche canoe,* he thought as he reached out and shook his hand.

Margo couldn't be sure, but she thought they were sizing one another up. *What does she see in this guy?* Matt thought, feeling oddly possessive of Margo.

"And this is Mix," she continued.

Ford stepped aside so that Mix could lean in. The minute Matt laid eyes on Mix, he knew he'd met her before. "Hi," he said politely.

Mix's face lit up like a Christmas tree...*a fake Christmas tree*, he thought.

"We're so happy you're here," she said shaking his hand.

"Do I know you?" he asked. "Where did you go to school?"

For the next few minutes, Margo watched Mix and Matt banter back and forth in search of their apparent common history. Matt was certain there was an overlap. "Hmm," Matt said after about ten minutes of it, "I guess we haven't met before."

"At least not in this lifetime," Mix said with a wink.

Puke, is she flirting with my boyfriend, I mean, my fake boyfriend? Margo thought as she stared at Mix.

Yes, I am, Mix telecasted back to Margo with a glance, as if reading her mind.

Over the next hour, Matt and Margo got primped and preened for their starring roles. *Wow,* Matt thought as he watched Tavis help Margo into her dress. The amount of fabric was insane, but she looked gorgeous, and he knew everyone in the room agreed with him, even Mix, whom he knew would never show it.

"Brent, where are my sunglasses?" Mix spat out as the sun moved across the sky. Brent handed her a pair of black frames. "Those aren't mine," she said with disdain, "Are those Michael Kors? I don't think so. *Mine* are Chloe," she said bitterly.

In that instant, Matt knew exactly where he'd seen her before. *The Riv,* he thought, *when Rob came out to grab her.*

He looked at Margo. "Can I speak to you...alone?" he asked impatiently.

"I'm kind of wearing 80 pounds of silk taffeta that can't touch the ground," she said gesturing to the three other people helping her hold it up, "so, alone isn't really possible right now," she said sarcastically.

"MMMMMaatttttt!" Gus shouted as he crashed in between them.

"Hey, buddy," Matt said picking him up. "I want you to meet someone really special. This is Margo."

"Hi, Miss Margo," Gus said brightly.

"We shoot in Atlanta. All his teachers are Miss this and Miss that," Bibi said sweeping in behind them, wrapping Margo in a hug. "This dress is insane," she cried. "You look stunning!"

Reflexively Margo hugged her back, realizing the embrace actually felt real. Then she reached up and kissed Matt on the cheek, "Hi, lovie," Bibi said with a wide smile as she wiped her lipstick off his face with her thumb. Margo watched Matt look down at her. *I wonder if a man will ever look at me that way,* she thought. *If Ford will ever look at me that way.*

"Oh my, you're Bibiana Romano," Mix said, interrupting Margo's thoughts.

"The one and only."

"We had no idea you were Gus's mom. Margo didn't tell us *that*," Mix said apparently apologizing for Margo.

Why is this on me? Margo thought as she stood there grappling with the 18 pounds of dress that was her portion to hold. Instantly, Mix took Bibi under her arm and shepherded her off.

"We'd love it if you wanted to be in the shoot too."

"Oh, I don't know about that," Bibi replied, looking back at Matt with a *help me* glare.

"She's going to swallow her like a snake would a mouse," Margo observed.

"I'm not so sure about that, Bibi's fierce," he admired.

He really does love her, Margo thought as a tinge of disappointment cloaked her.

"I have to talk to you," he hissed again as Tavis approached.

"Hey, Gus, mind if we take you to get changed? We got some trucks—word on the street is they're your faves." Gus nodded enthusiastically. "Someone get a robe for Margo so she can take a breather," Tavis hollered. Brent rushed in, holding up a robe. Margo stepped in and instantly Matt pulled her and Chelsea into the offices.

"What's wrong with you?" Margo protested.

"I know how I know Mix," Matt said pointedly.

"If you tell me you slept with her, I will tell the internet right now we have broken up."

"Be serious," Matt admonished.

"She is," Chelsea said flatly and in agreement with her best friend.

Matt shook his head. "She's dating the CFO of my dad's company," Matt said.

"What?" Margo and Chelsea chorused.

"Last time I saw Rob I left early. When I was waiting for my car I watched her have a meltdown on the valet."

"Sounds on brand for her," Chelsea conceded.

"This is even worse than you think," Margo said frantically.

"Why?" Matt asked.

She looked at him and Chelsea and then blurted out, "Ford kissed me last night and Mix saw it."

"What?" Chelsea hissed as Matt chided, "Can't you keep it in your pants for one day around that guy?"

Margo's eyes narrowed. "First off all, I did keep it in my pants—he kissed me. And second of all....," she paused, stopping herself from saying, *You're sleeping with Bibi, so I don't think you should throw stones when you live a glass house.*

Matt and Chelsea looked at her expectantly. When she didn't continue, Matt asked, "How did your sister come to meet with Milles-Lade?"

"I don't know. Does it matter?" Margo asked worriedly.

"Yes. It's been bothering me that your sister hasn't met my dad. My whole life, he's said 'never give a dime to a person you haven't looked in the eye.' For her to be so far along and not have met him. It doesn't make sense. And now..."

"You're just telling me this now?" Margo interrupted, outraged. "Why didn't you tell me sooner that you thought something was off?"

"Sooner as in when? We just met Saturday, for crying out loud," he hissed.

"So, what now?" Chelsea hopped in, stopping their argument in its tracks.

"I don't know, but I'm going to find out," Matt said with certainty.

The sliding door slid open. Brent peeked his head in. "We need you on set." His walkie crackled, and he scurried off in search of Mix.

The trio emerged from the offices, putting on their best camera-ready faces, a façade Margo was finding easier and easier to shift into. Matt and Margo mode, as she'd come to call it, was becoming second nature for her. She stepped into the dress.

Jesus, she's gorgeous, Matt thought as Tavis zipped her up.

Carefully, he led her out onto the platform, Tavis adjusting the fabric of her dress, billowing it out around her. Then the colonial footmen waded into the pool, their velvet and adorned jacket tails floating up behind them. Meticulously, they unfurled the fabric of her train so it wouldn't touch the water, and Brent kicked up the fan to create a breeze for her hair. They cranked up the music, Beyoncé first, but then on Bibi's recommendation swapped to truck tunes to get Gus in the mood.

Within 30 minutes of shooting, the entire room was smitten with Matt and Margo and how adorable Gus looked with them. Clad in pink shorts with suspenders and pink knee socks, he took to Margo like she was a Bruder truck, hugging her and laughing as she tickled him, even posing like a right proper Ralph Lauren family.

"Matt, with Gus on Margo's lap, why don't you lean in and kiss her?" Simon asked as he clicked away on the camera.

"Sure," Matt said as he ever so lightly leaned down and kissed her on the forehead.

"That's nice. Margo, look this way as he does that," Simon directed. "Oh, that's great. Now, just for posterity and for your feed, stand up and give us a real kiss."

Both Matt and Margo froze. "What?" Margo asked, as she stood.

"Come on, you two, don't be shy. Simon says, kiss her," Simon cajoled.

So, Matt did and Margo was more surprised by the *kiss* than the fact that he was kissing her.

CHAPTER 33

Undertow

As soon as their lips touched, Margo shuffled backward, compelling her body to resist its natural inclination to lean in closer to him. His hands resting on her hips, Matt shuffled in stride with her, maintaining the connection of their bodies as Gus ran in circles on the platform making truck sounds. As she inched closer to the platform edge, the excess of her dress draped down into the pool, its voluminous taffeta absorbing the water like a sponge. The train began bearing more weight, pulling the footmen in closer toward the platform, inching Margo closer to the pink and white striped edge. Matt's hands moved to cradle her neck, the gravity of the fabric now pulling her in nearly as much as Matt's kiss.

She broke free grabbing at the train, breathless. "I'm going to fall in," she said as Matt pulled her closer.

Seeing the struggle, Matt reached around her and began hefting the fabric up out of the water, quickly realizing though there was too much.

"On second thought," he said, letting go of the fabric. Facing her he reached around her waist and unzipped the dress. As he did, she leaned in, her left ear resting against his left shoulder, her eyes downcast, her lids still wearing the haze of their lip lock.

As she held the fabric to her chest, Matt quickly slipped off his pink suit jacket and enveloped her in it, so she could let the dress drop and step out of it. He held her close and spun them away from the camera.

"I know you're a never nude, Valentine, but it's this or drowning in that silk pool cover Tavis calls a gown," he said smiling down at her.

Margo's insides went liquid. She carefully allowed herself to be spun as she gripped the lapels attempting to close the jacket tight around her. *Why did it have to be a slim cut suit,* she thought as her curves threatened to break free of the perfectly tailored cut.

"Can I get a robe?" Matt hollered over his shoulder as Margo peered past him at the audience rapt by the scene. Matt continued to shield her from their eyes as Topher and his team slid the plank of plywood across the water so Chelsea could run to Margo, who had just now become aware that Simon was still clicking away on his camera.

Matt hugged her in close, as they carefully slung a long silk kimono over her shoulders. "You're blushing, Valentine," he whispered in her ear, as his left arm reached up under the kimono, sliding the suit jacket free as his right hand deftly held the back of her neck steady to his chest. "Good thing pink looks good on you," he said as he kissed her forehead.

When he turned to help her across the plywood bridge, Margo saw all eyes on her. Simon looked lovestruck. "You guys were great. You have to see these pics."

He gestured to the large monitor. Margo peered over his shoulder as Matt continued to hold the back of her neck ever so gently. Simon clicked through a series of shots photo-capturing the removal of the dress and Matt hugging his jacket around her naked shoulders. Margo noticed that they looked like a perfect couple. She also noticed the way she was looking at Matt. She was almost breathless watching it, remembering the feel of the wool of his suit against her skin and his commanding touch as he carefully slid his jacket free of the kimono, for the briefest second her bare chest pressed against his crisp shirt. Matt squeezed her neck. Margo bit her lip.

"You think you got what you need, Simon?" he asked as Gus ran up to hug him goodbye.

"More than what we need. The ones for the campaign are amazing. I can't wait for you to see those when they're cut. And these, wow, you two have some pretty magnetic chemistry," he said as he shook Matt's hand.

As Simon hugged Margo goodbye, she looked over his shoulder at Ford, except *Ford* wasn't looking back at her. He was staring at Matt the way a fighter would at a Vegas weigh-in.

Forty minutes later, Matt, Margo, and Chelsea were pulling into their driveway, parking along the edge of the lane as Rita had demanded. They hadn't talked about the kiss. They'd just gotten down to the business of loading the car. Margo could tell that Chelsea was desperate to catch her eye, so she avoided it at all costs, letting her know that the kiss was not a discussion she intended to have. Instead they focused on Topher, who was helping them load in the extra ring light and equipment Kirby thought they might need on their trip.

"I can't believe you guys aren't going to be here for the rest of the shoot. You worked so hard," Kirby lamented.

"I know, we're off to Bora Bora in a few hours," Margo replied, as she hugged her sister goodbye.

"You were so great this morning, like *so* great. I'll send pics from the shoot and you send pics from your trip, deal?"

"Deal," Margo agreed as she piled in with Chelsea, who had raided the wardrobe closet, hoarding the bathing suits, Shop Ban.do towels, and Janessa Leone straw hats she thought would look good for their exotic content.

"Last night I grabbed all kinds of things from my own closet too, and I have a little surprise waiting for you at your place," Chelsea said as they pulled out of the B&B driveway.

It better be a barbiturate, cuz I can't handle any more surprises, Margo thought—the kiss ricocheting around her brain.

Sensing that Chelsea still wanted to ask about it, she pulled out her phone and called her mom to avoid the topic altogether.

As they neared the house, Margo saw Rita and the closet coven inside.

"Great," she said, feeling the bath she'd hoped for fading away.

"Don't be a Debbie Downer," Chelsea chided, pulling her inside. "You're going to like this, promise."

They walked in to find Rita pouting on the sofa as Dinah's style squad carefully folded and placed stacks of clothes into trunks. "What is this?" Margo asked as Matt took her bag from her hands.

"Some of us are going to Bora Bora in the morning," Rita said snidely.

Blanca rolled her eyes, "Now, Rita, we discussed this. You're here running the estate. Let the lovebirds fly south."

Rita pantomimed Blanca like a child would a sibling.

"Your maturity knows no measure," Clark said with a laugh.

"Now, Margo, we know you're headed off on your first major tour. Chelsea asked us to get you ready, since you were short on time," Blanca stated. Margo gratefully smiled at Chelsea. "Dinah gave us access to her entire closet, darling, including her '80s vintage Fendi luggage and we called in a few favors. These trunks are filled with everything you need. We have swimwear in a range of sizes along with cover-ups and hats in this one. Evening clothes and daytime options here. That one's Matt's. And this one's shoes, hair and makeup."

The trio presented each one like Vanna White would a letter on *Wheel of Fortune.*

"You guys, this is more than my entire wardrobe, like of my entire life!" Margo rushed forward to hug them.

"Now, to get your spray tan working," Eps said with a snap. "We have a tent down the hall."

"I call dibs, suckas!" Rita said as she raced toward the bedroom.

CHAPTER 34

Invested

Matt quietly closed the door to his room reviewing the materials that Leandra had sent over. The phone rang in his ear.

"Matthew, what a treat," Leandra sang upon answering.

"Hey Lee. Thanks for sending over the findings. Now that my trust is back, I'm considering making a few investments."

"I did as you asked. Kept it to myself, but Matt, I think your dad would be thrilled to hear that you're doing some real business. The expansion for this company is quite intriguing—it spiders out across mass and high-end retail, editorial content, and beyond," she said encouragingly.

"Thanks, Lee. I kinda want to get my ducks in the row before I consider running this past him. Has my dad been looking to invest in Blush & Bashful himself?"

"Not that I know of. You mentioning this company was the first I ever heard of them. Why? Should I ask around?"

"No. Not yet. Let me keep reviewing. I'll keep you posted as to where it takes me, promise."

They said their goodbyes and clicked off, but not before Lee gushed, "I've been watching your feed. So happy for you, Matthew."

Matt walked across the hall to grab Margo. He opened the door at the same time as he knocked. "Margo," he started when his eyes flashed from Rita's boobs to her pubes. She stood naked in Jimmy Cocoa's spray tan booth. Matt's hands flew to his face. He fell out of the door backward, stumbling to escape. He slammed the door shut.

"Margo!" he shouted.

She raced down the hall, still wearing the kimono he'd slipped over her shoulders. Now casually paired with her jeans and T-shirt, it fanned out behind her as she moved. "What? What's wrong? You look like you've seen a ghost!"

"Worse, I just saw Rita naked."

Margo burst out laughing.

"It's not funny," he demanded.

"Bet you wish she was a never nude," she said, stifling her grin.

He scowled and then shivered to shake off what he'd witnessed.

"Come on," she laughed. "The boys put a trunk together for you to take on the trip. Your packing's done."

Margo pulled him, gleefully, toward the living room. Matt registering how she absentmindedly laced her fingers through his as they walked.

That night the entire group sat out by the pool eating the feast Matt had ordered from Jon & Vinny's. They drank copious amounts of wine as Dinah regaled them with stories. "Mr. Salter, your third husband, swept you off to Bora Bora for a honeymoon, and while you were there you took up a lover...on your honeymoon?" Matt repeated again for clarification.

"Don't be such a prude, Matthew. My husband was having an affair. I thought I should catch up."

Matt smirked.

"But you, Valentine," Dinah said smoothly to Margo, "You won't have to look far to find your island lover." Dinah winked at Matt who blushed when he looked at Margo.

The next morning, the three of them got up early, Matt and Margo from their rooms and Chelsea the sofa. Rita was in the kitchen making smoothies.

"Morning, chickens," she crooned. "Car's on its way."

Margo couldn't believe that just one week ago, she had met Matt for the first time. And, in just a few hours they were going to board a private jet to fly halfway around the world. *What is this life?* she thought as she sipped her smoothie watching Matt make eggs for her and Chelsea.

As the porters loaded their bags, the three of them posed for pictures in front of the jet. They waved to Rita, who had insisted on driving them, which Matt deemed a ploy to tag along. So, he stood guard until the plane gate was closed. Once they were on their way, they ate and laughed. Matt mused that he thought his best friend, Ian, might drop in.

"He's a founding partner in Phame. I think he'll be there."

They pored over the pictures Kirby had sent the night before. "What an amazing concept and what a great shoot," Matt said, filled with pride for his two travel companions.

Then they slept. They woke up to an omelet bar and hot espressos as the flight attendants helped them sort through their arrival papers. When they landed, customs boarded the flight to check them in to the country, before a car on the tarmac swept them straight to their resort. On the drive, their handler Tegan, explained, "Phame trips themselves aren't that long, but many of our Phame Fam, that's what we call you, tack on extra days or go elsewhere to extend their trip. Are you guys headed anywhere luxe after this?"

"Nope, just here and back," Matt said.

"Well then, we have four days to light up your feed. You guys already got great engagement on the way here," Tegan said with so much joy one would think she had just discovered a new genome.

As Margo looked out the window she pondered, *Who are all these people following along in our lives? Certainly not my old friends—I've barely heard from them. And now everyone I care about is either in this car or out to dinner with my parents in Castle Heights,* she thought as she listened to Matt and Chelsea take Tegan through the content wish list they'd created on the plane.

Snorkeling, kayaking, fishing, foraging, hiking, and cooking lessons were all on the list of things they thought they could capture for their followers. At about hour four of the flight Margo offered, "I know we're fake," she said gesturing to Matt, not at all picking up on his momentary dismay, "but the things we do and what we say on our feed, *that* can be real. So, I want to talk about the fish we would have seen or caught before the waters started getting warmer, or the plants we would have found if the beach lands were better protected. Some of these other people like Dree—I follow her and I love her and her clothes. She's so amazing. And, that has its place, but that's not me. After this ends, I want what I did with you to feel like it lives up to who I am. We have a zillion people following us. Let's inspire them, not just make them want to buy my lip gloss. We can do both, right?"

Chelsea smiled. "You can *so* do both, and your posts are already so inspiring. The one you two put up today with the picture of *you* getting ready, Margo, made me cry," Chelsea reached for her phone and read the caption aloud. *"When I was 11 my mom died. She'd been sick for a long time. My dad and I watched her slowly lose her battle with cancer. My world crumbled, and I used the rubble to build a shield around my heart. This one seems intent on dismantling it. Find someone who wants even the broken parts of you,"* Chelsea's voice cracked as Margo's eyes swiveled to Matt.

"I didn't write that," she said, as a tear spilled over onto her cheek.

"You were busy. I thought I'd help out. Is it okay? I know you're the writer," Matt said with uncertainty.

"Oh, Matty." Margo went to hug him. "I didn't know."

"No one really does, I've never talked about it. Not once. Something told me today I should."

Margo looked at him with wonder, as she reached out her hand to touch his face. "You're a good man, Seven. Someone's gonna be so lucky to get you for *real*, cuz I feel so lucky to have you for *fake*."

CHAPTER 35

Wish You Were Here

From the minute they arrived Margo felt like she'd been dropped into an alternate universe. Lush grounds led to their private bungalow. It was gorgeous.

"Get changed. I'll be back in an hour," Tegan chirped.

Within a blink of an eye they were showered and following Tegan to the dock. There they boarded *The Lady in Red,* a 49-meter super-yacht and set sail to chase the sunset. As the boat pulled out, Margo realized just how out of her element she was. As a writer, she'd been trained to be an observer. Being at the center of attention wasn't her inclination, but lately it had become her norm. Tonight, she found herself relying on Matt. *He's so good at this,* she thought, watching him holding court, the warmth of his arm, protectively securing her waist. *Come to think of it, Chelsea's excellent at this too*, Margo decided. *They're like beacon lights set off in a room, drawing people toward them.*

"This is Ian. We've been best friends since boarding school," Matt gushed with pride to Margo and Chelsea.

"I feel like I already know you," Ian said as he leaned in to hug Margo.

Margo hugged him back, his alluring smell of sandalwood and vetiver hanging in the air.

"This is Chelsea, my best friend and work wife." Margo folded Chelsea into their horseshoe.

Chelsea's eyes went wide like a school girl meeting Harry Styles.

"I went to *Danica* five times," she said reverently. "I'm a huge fan."

"She's also an artist," Margo offered. Chelsea blushed.

"Critics might not have gotten it, but it changed pop art for good," Chelsea said deadly serious.

"Thank you. Means a lot," Ian replied with a certain humility that made Margo instantly like him. "Can I get you ladies a drink?"

"Do you have apple juice and whiskey?" Chelsea asked, winking at Margo.

"I'm sure we can rustle some up. Matt, care to help me?" With that, the pair ventured to the bar on the DJ Khaled-size party yacht.

"This is insane. He's one of my idols."

"You're one of my idols," Margo said sweetly, poking her friend in the side while admiring the drape of her one shoulder dress, emerald eye shadow, and enormous earrings, knowing that her own rainbow pleated, floor-length skirt and fitted tank were all Chelsea's doing.

"If you love me so much, then you're going to tell me about that kiss."

Margo groaned. "What about it?"

"Don't play dumb, it's not your color child," Chelsea retorted, giving her best Tavis impression.

"It was," Margo paused, "unexpected."

"Eeeehhhh," Chelsea said like a buzzer at a basketball game. "Try again."

Margo sighed. "Okay, it was kind of amazing."

"I knew it," Chelsea shouted. Dree Von Valle and Manuela Carrillo looked in their direction, sneering. "Not exactly friendly, are they?" Chelsea whispered.

"They must not have gotten the memo that we're Phame Fam." The pair laughed.

"Back to the kiss," Chelsea cornered.

"The kiss doesn't matter," Margo dismissed.

Chelsea began to protest when Margo held up one hand to stop her. "Matt is in love with Bibiana Romano. He told me they've dated on and off since he was in boarding school and Gus is like a son to him. This week he went off to see her *twice*. Twice, Chelsea. That kiss was him keeping up appearances, nothing more. He loves her. He's just playing a part with me."

Chelsea looked stricken, like she might either cry or smash something like Sally Field in *Steel Magnolias* when Clairee tells her to hit Ouiser. "Whatttt?" she hissed.

Margo realizing Dree and Manuela were Grid.Vid-ing the sunset, pulled Chelsea away from the railing.

"I look like I have a droopy eye," Manuela whined. Dree waved her off, "I'll face tune us tomorrow before I post it."

Now out of earshot Margo continued, "He's just very good at his role, I guess."

"Your wish is our command," Ian interrupted. "We had them press this apple juice just for you." Chelsea looked momentarily distraught. "Don't look so worried, Half Pint, we were happy to do it." She took her drink from his hands, her face softening at the *Little House on the Prairie* reference. "Matt told me it's a guilty pleasure we have in common. I, like you, was the only non-white kid in America who prayed to be Charles Ingalls's adopted son. Let's talk episodes," he said as he kicked back on a pool lounger, the invitation too good for Chelsea to resist.

She sat down as she glanced at Margo letting her know their chat was not done.

Matt and Margo took the lounger next to them. "Tired?" Matt asked.

"Exhausted," Margo admitted.

"I know you really don't drink so I had yours made heavy on the juice, light on the Jack. Snoop Dogg would not approve," Matt said as he folded her into his arms, her back pressed to his chest as he reached for a Hermès blanket to cover her outstretched legs.

"Christ, is that Hermès?" she asked.

"Should we steal it?" Matt questioned. "I feel like we have a few good weeks of this before we're found out. Let's Winona this whole yacht." He winked. Margo laughed out loud.

Two hours later, after a serious lip-sync battle pitting Ian and Matt's *Summer Lovin'* up against Chelsea and Margo's *Wannabe* by the Spice Girls, they were on land and standing in front of their bungalow. "Tegan told me you guys have more than sunbathing on your mind, so I set up a four-person snorkel. Thought it'd be cool if I tagged along. Hope that's not a problem," Ian said.

"Are you kidding me, buddy? We wouldn't have it any other way," Matt replied.

"Boat leaves at 7:30 a.m. Meet on the docks. I'll have breakfast and lunch set for the boat. Chelsea, can I walk you to your bungalow?" he asked as he gestured down the footpath.

Chelsea gave Margo a pinch-me grin as she walked ahead.

"He's nice," Margo said.

"And smart," Matt added as he keyed into their bungalow with its thatched roof and four pillars that it stood upon in the turquoise water below. "I can take the sofa," Matt offered as Margo headed to wash her face.

She peered around the bathroom door, "It's king size. I don't see any reason not to just share. We *are* friends, after all. And what if Rita really is here?" she questioned ominously.

"That's it, you're closest to the door." He feigned horror as he flopped onto the bed.

CHAPTER 36

Dive In

The next morning, they set sail on a snorkeling adventure that kicked off three days of sun, sand, and laughing. Tegan was right, the four of them were a Phame Fam, and that made the entire trip worthwhile. Margo adored Ian. He wasn't like the other influencers on this particular trip. They were nice, but Margo could tell they weren't looking to bring any outsiders in, especially ones who might not have earned their place at the table. Margo got the read that they felt a certain ownership over the fact that they had built their audiences through years of hard work, *earning* their million-plus followers. Grid.it had gifted Matt and Margo theirs. That made them the kids that no one wanted to sit with at lunch. Margo wasn't as upset about it as Chelsea. She was crushed. She idolized these people.

"I will make Joanna Chen like me if it is the last thing I do," Chelsea declared to Ian as they munched grilled octopus and sipped Vidal Blanc on day two.

"Is it really that important, Half Pint?"

She looked appalled, "Like the air I breathe," she said dramatically.

Their snorkel dive on day one had been next level. Sting rays, manta rays, reef sharks, and hundreds of brightly colored tropical fish captivated them each time they dove into the blue waters. Not to mention, Ian was chock-full of knowledge on nearly every topic. He continually astounded them with his tales, and his undeniable talents helped them art direct shots and videos that were out of this world. Paddle boarding, jet skiing, lying in the sand, cooking classes—all of it through Ian's lens made it major travel goals for their feed.

As their Phame Fam grew stronger, Matt and Margo's interactions became easier and more natural. Holding hands, Matt's arms around her waist, Matt leaning in to kiss her as they lay on the hammock, her feeling the undertow of the water, and his kiss again—all of it became effortless before the lens.

On day four, in between drinks, Margo and Chelsea leapt into the pool, sunbathing atop a giant red heart.

"You like her," Matt observed as Ian stared at Chelsea.

"I do," Ian answered.

Matt was shocked. Ian hadn't truly liked anyone in a long time.

"And, you like her," Ian said, nodding toward Margo. Matt followed his gaze. "You look distraught. Isn't that a good thing, to like the woman you're living with?"

Matt heaved a sigh, "It's too long a story to tell you today, but we're lying to everyone about being in love."

Ian looked perplexed. "Buddy, I've known you a long time. If you two think you're lying about being in love, the only people you're lying to is each other, because the rest of us see it plain as day." Ian stared at Matt intently.

"What are you two talking about?" Chelsea asked, suddenly standing over them reaching for her towel.

"My crush on you, Half Pint," Ian said as Chelsea turned the same shade of red as her pool float.

"Oh my, we arrived just in time," Margo said as she slid toward the pool chair where Matt was stretched out, her wet hair, getting his shirt entirely drenched.

"Excuse me," he said, pulling at the white linen.

"Oh, did I get you wet?" Margo asked as she purposely rung out her hair on his chest.

"Hey!" he shouted as he hopped up. He looked at her devilishly.

"Matthew Milles-Lade, don't you dare," Margo said sternly, stepping back from him.

"Sorry, Valentine," Matthew said as he grabbed her, throwing her back into the pool with him. She shrieked with laughter as they came up for air.

"Where's my high-five now?" Matt asked laughing. Margo jumped on his neck trying to pull him under. Instead his arms wrapped around her holding her tight, too strong for her to take him down. "Say uncle!" Matt demanded.

"Never!" Margo cried as she tried again to pull him under, when suddenly she leaned in and kissed him full on the mouth and more deeply than even she expected. His body went slack. Margo shoved him under the water. "Victory is mine!" she shouted as Matt came up for air, only then realizing *that* kiss was their first kiss for kiss sake – because no camera was pointed at them this time – and Margo had been the one to instigate it.

"C'mon, you two lovebirds, we have a last fish fry to get to," Ian said as he gathered their things, Matt and Margo staring at one another only a few inches apart, breathless.

"Right," Margo said as she ran for the steps.

"Chels, come help me decide what to wear," she commanded, knowing she needed someone else there to make sure she didn't kiss Matt again, because suddenly she was certain she wanted to.

CHAPTER 37

The Berry Best

As Chelsea helped Margo pick out her outfit for their last afternoon sail, she hissed, "What was that in the pool?"

Margo looked over her shoulder to see Matt on the deck talking on his phone. With his 5 o'clock shadow and furrowed brow, he looked handsomely rugged.

"I don't know. I did it without thinking. It just happened."

"Three minutes after you told me in the pool that you were excited to get back to Ford, *it* just happened? You, kissing like Noah and Allie in *The Notebook*?!"

"Keep your voice down," Margo hissed at Chelsea. They both leaned back from the closet to peer out the sliding doors. Matt was still engrossed on his call and completely unaware. "I think you're being dramatic, it wasn't that kind of a kiss," Margo admonished in a hush.

But, Chelsea wasn't wrong, moments before that kiss, Margo *had* told her about the late-night text session with Ford as Matt lay dead asleep in bed next to her.

"He texted me to say he missed me, and then he sent a pretty spicy description of what he intends to do to me when we get back," Margo shared as she splashed water up on her shoulders.

"Nuh uhhh," Chelsea said doe-eyed with surprise, as she foisted herself atop the float. "Show me!"

Margo handed over her phone. She then pushed them away from the wall and the boys, paddling them out into the middle of the organic shaped pool as Chelsea read the text chain. She knew when she'd gotten to the spicier spot because Chelsea blushed as red as the heart-shaped pool float she lay atop of. "Whoa, he certainly went for it, huh?"

"I think he's trying to be romantic."

Chelsea snorted. "Romance is red roses secretly sent to your room, which Ian did for me, by the way." Margo awwwwed. "*This* text is more Missy Elliot let me put that thing down, flip, and reverse it."

"Stoooppp!" Margo said with a laugh, "I think he's seeing all these pictures with me and Matt, and he's trying to keep up from afar."

Margo's justification indicated she was giving him a pass for what Chelsea knew Margo would never allow in any other man, *and not just the sexting, his horrible grammar,* she thought as she watched her friend from atop her heart-shaped perch.

"Honestly, Chels, I didn't even know the guy liked me until the day the news came out, so I'm freaking out," Margo said, her head swimming along with the rest of her as she tugged them both toward the pool steps.

"And you want that...this?" Chelsea asked, gesturing at the phone in her hand as Margo paddle-kicked them to the shallow end. "Because I sorta sensed something growing between you and Matt." Chelsea rolled off the float, holding the phone up above the water.

"Yesterday Matt FaceTimed with Gus and Bibi for over an hour. It couldn't be any clearer to me. He's with *her*. I'm not going to miss my chance to be with Ford, because I *maybe* have a crush on the guy I'm fake dating, especially when I'm witnessing him real-lifing it with Bibi Romano," Margo said as they climbed out of the pool.

Now back in their bungalow, as she and Chelsea decided on accessories next to the dress they had chosen—a vintage orange sherbet, strapless sun dress with rows of dramatic ruffles across the bodice and a large waist tie, Margo was totally confused.

"I think these, don't you?" Chelsea pondered aloud, stepping back, admiring the four petite gold chains and large statement earrings she'd chosen.

"First rule of Style Club: don't question your stylist, isn't that what you'd told me?" Margo joked as she scooped up the necklaces. Just then, Matt slid the glass door open and stepped back into the room.

"I should go get dressed," Chelsea said.

"Wait! You'll probably want to hear this," Matt declared stopping her. He gestured for them to sit. "My dad knows nothing of the Blush & Bashful deal, and Leandra said there's no money allocated from their funds to go toward an investment."

"What does that mean?" Margo asked confusion and worry crashing on her face.

"It means, we need to FaceTime Kirby right now and find out who she's talking to and what they've said, exactly. Something shady is going on, and it could mean your sister's going to come up empty-handed at the end of all of this. Based on all the money she and David just poured into that campaign, my guess would be that would be a hit they might not come back from."

Stress lined Margo's face. She and Chelsea exchanged worried glances. "I'll go press your dress. You two call," Chelsea said as she gathered up the sorbet garment.

The FaceTime call connected and Kirby appeared on the screen. "Gang's all here," she bellowed, raising the phone so Margo could see David and her parents in the background. Everyone waved. "We're all insanely jealous of your trip, Margo," Kirby crooned.

"We saw your pictures, M, you both look amazing," her mother beamed, cutting veggies for their Melon family meal. "Hi, Matt," she added.

"Hi, Mrs. Melon!" He waved at the screen.

"Maureen, please," she sweetly corrected.

"Well, we don't want to keep you; we actually wanted to talk to you and David, Kirbs," Margo hopped in. Kirby looked at the phone expectantly, prompting them to continue. "Alone," Margo clarified.

"Oh," her sister looked surprised as she went outside, David in the frame following behind her. Once the sliding door was closed, "Kirby, who have you been talking to at MLE?" Matt asked.

"Rob Rolle. Why?"

"It struck me as odd, when you said you hadn't met my dad. He's never given a dollar to anyone he hasn't met with personally."

"Maybe his team is still routing it," David offered.

"I don't think so. I asked the head of business affairs. It's her team that knows every potential investment on deck. I actually had her research you. She was impressed, but she just confirmed that there are no MLE dollars being funneled for any new investment and there's no investment for B&B on her books from any account. She has sign-off. She would know."

Both Kirby and David looked alarmed. "There must be some misunderstanding. We just spoke to Rob today. He said all the paperwork is coming along."

"Who put you in touch with Rob?" Matt asked.

"Mix," they said in unison, then David took the phone. "I had two other prospects when Mix came to me and said she heard I was doing a capital raise. She thought she had a better money guy in MLE. Everyone knows your dad's company and how lucrative MLE's investment board is. The terms we were getting out of Rob blew the other guys out of the water. So, we took them out of the running to focus on MLE." David paused, almost not wanting to ask the next question, "Matt, are you telling me that I may have tainted those other options and now MLE might not come through? I'm panicked here, bud." David's eyes pleaded at the phone screen.

"Don't freak out just yet. I have a plan brewing. Leandra Jennings, head of BA for MLE is involved, she's overseen every transaction MLE has carried out for more than two decades. When I wanted cash for a lemonade stand, it was Lee who gave it to me. Have you ever heard her name?" Matt asked. They both shook their heads no. "Okay, I need you to trust me here."

"But, do we trust them?" Kirby interrupted.

"No," Matt said matter-of-factly. "But, keep talking to them as if you do until I get this sorted." Kirby and David looked nervous. "You guys, it's going to be fine. I know how much you're counting on that cash infusion. I'm not going to let you down. I'm working on other options. You can bet on me. You might be the first to do so, but I promise I'm going to make certain you get the deal you deserve. I just need a bit more time to suss this out and actually get in front of Rob myself. For all we know he's making a play to leave MLE and make you his first venture. I'm not saying money's not there. I'm just saying it's not MLE money if it is."

"That's all well and good, Matt, but he's a dick. We're only dealing with him because we wanted to get in at MLE," David shared.

"I hear ya. Don't worry. This is all going to work out even better in the long run. Oh, and don't trust Mix in this. I don't know yet the extent of how they know one another. Just keep this all in the family," Matt said, Margo's heart squeezing at the reference.

"Now what?" Margo asked after they'd hung up.

"I'm not sure. But, until I figure it out it's business as usual." Matt stood. "I believe you have this sherbet confection to put on and I have a coordinating lilac number," Matt said to Margo. Then, looking at Chelsea, "if you go with something yellow we'll arrive looking like Apricot, Plum Puddin', and Lemon Meringue. Don't mess this up, Chels," he said very seriously.

"Care to tell me why a boy knows all the Strawberry Shortcake characters?" Margo asked.

"Wow, Apricot, that's mighty sexist of you. Just because I'm a boy doesn't mean she wasn't one of my *berry* best friends too," Matt admonished.

"You're ridiculous," Chelsea laughed, "and wrong. I'm more Angel Cake."

"Well, as long as you aren't the Purple Pieman," Matt said as he sauntered toward the shower, his lilac chinos in hand.

An hour later they boarded *The Lady in Red.* Ian and Margo set out to grab drinks as Matt and Chelsea snagged their favorite deck spot. Watching Ian across the bow, Chelsea looked like a girl saying goodbye to her first love at summer camp. "It's okay, he has a phone. You can call him," Matt poked fun at her forlorn look.

"I haven't even kissed him yet," Chelsea blurted out.

"Well, the night's still young, Angel Cake." Matt winked. Then, he cleared his throat. "Do you know who Margo was texting last night?" he asked casually. Chelsea knew he was anything but.

She paused, biting her lip. "Ford," she said, hoping to read his reaction. There wasn't one. Matt nodded. "Annnnd?" Chelsea said drawing out the word.

"And what?" he asked, now feigning ignorance. Chelsea stared him down. "She's a grown woman. I just wondered," he said as Ian and Margo strode toward them, laughing. *God, is she beautiful,* Matt thought, watching her, the grace of her arms as she spoke with Ian, the slope of her neck.

"Picture time," Dree and Manuela cried, "everyone up."

Margo pulled Matt to his feet. "Aren't you two coming?" Margo asked looking back at Chelsea.

"Mom and Dad? No we're staying here. Make us proud," she said.

"Mind your angles, buddy," Ian coached as he kicked back.

Matt took Margo's hand and spun her into place as she laughed. She stood there, when Anine Lee turned and tsked. "This dress needs you to show it off properly." She manhandled Margo, pulling her hips forward while simultaneously pushing her ribcage back like she were Kate Moss. She placed Margo's opposite arm on Matt's shoulder and began contorting her hand. "You don't want Shaq hands," she justified. Then, she posed her head and neck.

"What about him?" Margo asked as she held the scoliosis-like pose.

"Him? He's perfect," Anine purred.

"She has a point," Matt said with a wink. Margo let her head fall back in a full laugh.

The revelry ratcheted up after that, with Chelsea and Margo dominating the dance floor. Matt and Ian, however, remained in a hushed conversation, until a Salt-N-Pepa/TLC mash-up demanded their participation. When "Faithfully" came on, they coupled up. Margo rested her head on Matt's shoulder her face turned in toward his neck as they slow danced. She could smell his aftershave, a mix of lavender, sandalwood, and bergamot.

"Are you wearing my cologne?" she asked puzzled.

"I don't know what you're talking about," Matt said innocently.

"You smell like me," she observed.

"Like plastic, melted apricots?" he asked as he sniffed at the air. She used their interlaced hands to poke him in the chest. He smiled. "I like the way you smell, Valentine." He looked down at her. "Can you forgive me for borrowing some?" he asked apologetically.

"Maybe," she flirted, as he cinched her into him. Margo's eyes peered over his shoulder just in time to see Ian lean down and kiss Chels. Margo felt her heart smile for them. Then she felt Matt delicately brush his lips across her forehead, letting them rest there as he deeply inhaled her scent. Just as he was about to turn her face up toward his, the captain came over the intercom and everyone broke apart to clap, Matt included.

Margo felt bereft to not be in his arms but recovered quickly when Chelsea rushed up behind her. "There's a bonfire—are you two going?" Margo asked hugging her.

"I don't think so. I have to pack, and by pack, I mean make out with Ian...in case you didn't get that," Chelsea said conspiratorially.

"I got it, Angel Cake," Margo laughed.

CHAPTER 38

Just Add Water

Matt and Margo walked back to their bungalow. Ever the gentleman, Matt left his hand on Margo's lower back guiding her. When they got into the room, he dutifully helped her gather up all her clothes including the 18 swimsuits she'd worn throughout their four-day-stay. By the end they were in a complete sweat from the summer heat.

"Wanna skip the bonfire and go for a swim?" Matt asked eying their private pool, "We haven't used it yet."

"I don't really wanna get a swimsuit wet for the flight home," Margo concluded, eyeing the water.

"Me either." Matt winked. "Come on, never nude. Just once. I'll keep my eyes closed."

It is hot, Margo thought. She looked torn. "Okay, give me a minute," she said as she jumped toward the bathroom, taking off her makeup and piling her hair on top of her head. When she was done, Matt was already in the pool. "Close your eyes," she demanded. He did as he was told and Margo jumped in, water splashing everywhere.

"For a never nude, a cannonball is a bold choice," Matt said mopping his face.

"Well, I'm turning over a new leaf," she offered as she swam the length of the pool like a mom not wanting to get her hair wet.

"It's liberating, huh? Feels good on your balls," Matt said now swimming beside her.

"Gross," she cried splashing him with water. "And, yes, it does."

"Seeeee?" he laughed.

They floated in the pool for the next two hours, talking, laughing, and ordering late-night room service. The waiter delivered their meal right to the pool. Margo covered herself as best she could.

"She's naked. We're both naked," Matt declared as she splashed him.

"You're so immature!"

"Nothing we haven't seen before sir," their private butler, said with a slight blush.

As Matt mixed their drinks, Margo picked up her phone. She'd heard it ding at least eight times. The first seven were all texts from Chelsea. *Best trip ever* type of notes—the last one a picture of her and Ian in their private hot tub. *Bathing suits on,* Margo noted. *And yet here I am skinny-dipping.*

But then a tongue out emoji, water drops, and an eggplant from Ford arrived with a screen capture from her last Grid.Vid.

"Cat got your tongue," Matt asked just as she looked at the tongue emoji on her screen.

She jumped and her phone slipped right out of her hands and into the pool. "Shhhiiitttt," she said as Matt quickly dove in after it. He emerged with it in hand, coming up directly in front of her.

"Sorry," he said realizing they were inches apart. He put her phone on the deck and hopped out, grabbing their towels. "Quick, call the front desk and ask for a bag of rice."

Margo hesitated. He'd used both towels to dry the phone, the curve of his hipbone and his muscles contracting in his arm, back and thigh as he knelt down to do it.

"Margo, I won't look," he shouted.

She hopped out and ran toward the bathroom grabbing a robe for each of them, then hurrying in to call the butler back. He arrived with rice minutes later. "That was fast," Margo observed.

"Well, there are no pockets for phones when you're naked, so we're prepared."

It was Margo's turn to blush.

The next morning, they peered at her phone in the bag of rice. "Should we call it," Matt asked.

"The phone?"

"No time of death," he laughed.

"It might still make it," she offered optimistically.

"My phone would make it. But my phone doesn't look like a slasher film." He nodded toward her shattered and scarred screen. "How do you swipe anything with all those cracks? Pretty soon we won't be a high-fiving couple because you won't have fingerprints," he observed.

She hit him with a pillow. "Seriously though, I need a phone," she worried.

Matt paused. "Can you call your IT guy at the office to set up a new phone for you today? I can call Zinny to pick it up and drop it at our place so you'll have it when we land. They should be able to use your email logins to get it all downloading."

Margo nodded. "Good idea, you call Zinny and I'll use this rice to glue them a letter. How many grains to spell *Dear Brad in IT*?" she said mocking him for the fact that she didn't have a phone to call on.

"Very funny," he admonished. "But you do have a laptop to email them." He raised an eyebrow. Margo felt her stomach flip at his charm.

"You're right," she said begrudgingly.

"I'm right?" he said in mock surprise. "That deserves a high-five, while you still have your fingertips!"

CHAPTER 39

Home Sweet Rita

Sixteen hours later, the trio arrived at LAX. A town car on the tarmac whisked them through a private customs gate, where Rita was waiting in a giant Chevy Tahoe. "How does she reach the pedals?" Matt marveled watching her jump to grab the rear hatch.

As they approached, Rita swept her arms out for a hug.

"Rita, what are you wearing?" Matt asked, seeing their faces emblazoned across her chest.

"Just a side gig I started while you were away. Sold 29 of 'em so far."

"To who? Prison inmates and shut-ins?" Matt peppered her with questions the rest of the ride home.

"Well, look who the cat dragged in," Rita sneered.

Zinny sat on the bench in the courtyard as they pulled in. She waved as they got out but then stopped. "Matthew, what are you doing with this traitor?"

"Zinaida Katerine Bobrova," Rita said mimicking Zinny's accent.

"You two know each other?" Matt asked.

"She betrayed me," they both said at the same time, incredulously.

"Is this Lady D's house? You still work for her?" Zinny asked.

"Guess you wouldn't know since I fired you," Rita shot back coolly. They glared at one another.

"Should we do something?" Margo whispered.

"Make popcorn?" Matt suggested.

Margo shoved him playfully. "Ladies," she said, "I'm sure we can leave the past in the past."

"Ahhh, the naïveté of youth," Zinny scoffed.

"Something we can agree on," Rita echoed. Both women scowled at Margo.

"I bring your phone, Miss Margo," Zinny said as she handed it over. She took Margo's hands. "I am grateful to meet you," she said smiling. "Don't ever get on my bad side." She looked over her shoulder directly at Rita. "I never forget and you never see me coming."

"Okay, now that you're done threatening my girlfriend, I think you can go," Matt said taking Zinny by the shoulders as Rita lunged toward her and Margo held her back.

"She is tiny flea who should be drowned," Zinny said to Matt.

"Okay, well, I'll take that idea of homicide under advisement." He steered her toward her car.

"I see you tonight," Zinny said hugging him and giving Rita the finger over his shoulder.

"Tonight?"

"Yes, is family weekend in Malibu. Miss Tiff is very excited for Margo to come. You did not forget?" she demanded.

"No, of course not."

"Yes, you did."

"Yes, I did," he admitted, looking back over his shoulder at Margo. "But, don't worry, we'll be there."

CHAPTER 40

Hype Man

"My phone won't boot up properly," Margo noted as Matt navigated Kanan Road crossing to the PCH before heading up to Malibu.

"Maybe it needs a fingerprint and you no longer have one," he said.

"Hah," Margo said dryly, as she opened the center console in search of a USB port. She removed the CD that lay on top. "*Hyped,*" she read aloud on the front, then flipping it over and continuing. "Hold On" by Wilson Phillips, "Against All Odds" by Phil Collins, "Making Love Out of Nothing at All" by Air Supply?" Matt nodded approvingly. "Let me get this straight, your hype mix is all soft rock?"

"I will have you know that nothing will hype you up more than an *Endless Love* car concert."

"I guess we're about to find out." Margo slid the CD into the deck. Foreigner's "I Want to Know What Love Is" filled the car.

"This is a slow burn," Matt shouted over the stereo as he cranked it up. By the time they hit "Time for Me to Fly" by REO Speedwagon, both Matt and Margo were singing at the top of their lungs.

When they stopped for gas, Margo smiled as she watched him in her side-view mirror. His text dinged. *So*

excited to see you. Can't wait for movie night snuggles.
Margo's smile faltered. It was from Bibi.

Matt got back in, handed her a box of Red Vines, winked, and turned up "Hard Habit to Break" by Chicago. Margo spent the rest of the ride pushing that text out of her mind.

Thirty minutes later, they fell out of the car laughing.

"Well, don't you two look like you're having fun?"

"Hey, Tiff," Matt said coolly his mood dampening. "This is Margo."

"I know who she is, silly," Tiff said sweeping Margo into a hug. "Come on inside."

"We're just gonna head upstairs to put our things down," Matt said hauling Margo up the floating staircase.

The home was gorgeous, a modern-day beach house, very San Miguel meets Malibu. "Whoa, this place is huge," Margo observed, as Matt pulled them down the hall to his bedroom, which was camel and white, featuring woven tapestries and Peruvian embroideries all set off by sweeping views of the Pacific Ocean. "Wow," Margo observed.

"Mattttyyyy!" Tiff shouted up the stairs.

He sighed deeply. "Fuck, I hate when she calls me that. No one calls me that, especially not her," Matt said angrily, speaking aloud to himself, as he opened one suitcase stand.

"I call you that," Margo said quietly.

"What?" his voice muffled by the closet where he was reaching for a second stand.

"I call you Matty," she repeated softly. She looked worried.

He stopped what he was doing and pushed his hand through his hair. He opened the rack and grabbed her hand, pulling her down to sit next to him on the bed. "I don't mind when you call me that, Valentine. Tiff, I mind." He looked at her intently.

"Why?" Margo asked quietly.

Matt paused. "There was one person on this entire planet who called me Matty and then they weren't here and I just never wanted to be called that again." He looked down fidgeting with her rings. "But not you. You're fine." He looked at her.

"Your mom? Was that her nickname for you?"

Surprise registered on his face. He chuckled as if recalling a fond memory. "No, she called me Matthew, Mr. Matt, Buddy, Budders." He paused. "My dad. He called me Matty my whole life. Then my mom died and he stopped. After that, he disappeared into his work. My nickname kind of died with my mom. Suddenly I didn't feel like I had any parents." Matt searched her eyes. She reached out with her free hand and delicately brushed her thumb against the bottom ridge of his lip.

Matt started to lean forward, when suddenly, Tiff burst into the room. "Matttyyyy, I've been calling you!"

He sighed. "Everyone's downstairs, waiting for you two."

"We'll be right down, Tiff," he said through a clenched jaw, as he shut the door, knowing for sure the moment had passed.

Margo chastised herself for almost kissing him...*again*. Her phone dinged and she picked it up. "Even my rings are different," she observed as she used her thumb to bring the screen to life. "Who's Rob?" she said aloud.

"Hmm?" Matt said from the bathroom.

"Some guy named Rob is texting me and...," she trailed off.

Matt peered around the corner, stopping dead when he saw the look on Margo's face. "What's wrong?" he asked tossing his dopp kit on the bed and walking to her.

"Holy shit!" she said, then looking at him in wonder, "I have Margaux's phone!"

Matt nodded. "Well, honey, that would make sense since you are Margo." He spoke slowly as if she had a head injury.

"Nooo," Margo said shaking her head.

Matt nodded yes. "Are we in a Lifetime movie?" he asked.

"No, listen to me, I have Margaux's phone."

"Who's on first?" Matt asked, joking.

Margo shook her head adamantly and then grabbed him by his shoulders. "Listen to me, Mix's real name is Margaux. M-A-R-G-A-U-X. The IT guys must have programmed my new phone with her logins. I can see her emails."

Matt was stunned. The phone rang for a FaceTime call and Margo threw it like it had burned her. They both jumped back. Matt delicately reached out to flip the phone over. It was her mom. They both looked confused. "How is your mom calling Mix?"

"I think it's my number so I'm still getting my own calls and texts but because they programmed in her email, I'm getting her emails and some of her texts that are directed through her cloud." They peered at the screen.

"So, is she getting yours?" Matt asked as the phone rang again, causing him to scream, which in turn caused Margo to shout. It was Rob FaceTiming her.

"Holy shit!" Margo said.

Matt grabbed the phone. "First, silence this. We can't have him call her and have your phone go off. Second," he said grabbing Margo's thumb so he could reopen the phone. "We have to look at her emails."

Margo yanked her arm away. "We can't look at her emails. That's wrong. I don't want bad karma from Mix's emails."

"Okay, then I'll look at her emails. Think of it this way, it's because of your *good* karma that this gift fell in our lap. The universe wants us to look."

She relented. Matt started scrolling through the phone. Margo started pacing the room.

"Holy shit," Matt declared.

"What?" Margo hissed when suddenly the doors flew open again. They both groaned.

"Maaaattttyyy, we're all waiting," Tiff forced, agitated.

Margo walked up, grabbed her elbow, spun her around and deposited her back at the door. "Hey Tiff, we got something going on here. You guys toast without us. Also, my boyfriend doesn't like to be called Matty. It's kind of a nickname his dad gave him and it's really only for him to use. So, if you could go with Matt or Matthew, from now on, that would be preferred." Margo gently pushed Tiff out of the room. "Okay? Great. We'll be down in a few." With that, Margo closed the door as Tiff stood there blankly in shock.

Matt's jaw hit the floor. "Well, won't you be my Valentine?" he chuckled. "Tiff is gonna make a voodoo doll out of you!"

"Let her. We got bigger fish to fry," Margo said waving him off.

"*You* have no idea," he confirmed. "And that fish's name is Rob and he's *so* on our hook."

CHAPTER 41

Jackpot

Matt flew down the floating staircase, dragging Margo behind him like a terrified puppy attempting stairs for the first time. "Slow down!" she cried. "What did you find?"

"I thought you wanted plausible deniability for your karma?" Matt said as he careened to a stop, searching the backyard for Rob.

"I do, but I also *really* want to know the plan."

"The plan is, follow my lead." He ushered them through the massive living room and out the bifold glass doors. "Dad, meet Margo."

"Margo, what a treat." Brooks Milles-Lade said as he walked toward her with his hands outstretched.

"Mr. Milles-Lade," Margo beamed, trying to catch her breath from Matt's parkour course through the house.

"Brooks, please," he corrected. He clasped her one hand in both of his.

Tiff scowled by his side, *no doubt pickled in anger from my pushing her out of Matt's room*, Margo thought. "Tiff, your home is gorgeous," Margo offered, attempting to diffuse her pout. Tiff nodded coolly, using the index and middle finger on each hand to scissor and lift the part of her carefully beach-waved blonde hair. "I'd love to do a Grid.Vid tour," Margo charmed.

Matt watched Tiff momentarily melt at Margo's suggestion of her being broadcast to their quarter of a million followers. "That could be fun," Tiff considered, repeating the same scissored zhuzh of her hair.

Matt swooped in, grabbing Margo away. "Sorry to steal her," he said smiling. "Who are you?" he hissed as they strode across the pool deck.

"I believe the correct phrase is *a baller*." Margo winked. "She might be my fake mother-in-law someday, Seven. Gotta win her back."

Matt shuddered at the thought of Tiff being his stepmom, "You kiss your mother with that filthy mouth?" Margo let her head fall back in a full laugh.

"Hey, Rob, how's it going?" Matt asked as he and Margo approached.

Rob smiled slickly. "Good, buddy." *I'm not your fucking buddy,* Matt thought. "And this must be Margo? You two certainly caught the attention of Brooks. Seemed like it came out of left field if you ask me, but who I am to judge," he said tauntingly.

Matt laughed, the tin of which was completely fake. Margo noted it immediately because she loved when she made him laugh for real. Margo grimaced at Rob, not at his comments but at the amount of cologne he was wearing.

"Working on anything special?" Matt asked, as he casually reached for a beer behind the outdoor bar.

"Not really, same old same old. And, you know, the big things I can't really talk about with people outside the company," Rob offered as a jab.

"Makes sense." Matt paused. "I don't know if you know this, but Margo's sister owns Blush & Bashful. Kirby mentioned that MLE was looking to invest heavily in them."

Rob didn't even flinch. "What's that now?" Brooks asked as he walked up.

"Margo's sister, Kirby, told me that MLE is courting them for a big investment of her platform, Blush & Bashful."

Brooks looked reflective. "Rob, that doesn't ring a bell. Jog my memory."

If Rob's head was spinning, Matt couldn't tell. He looked cool as a cucumber. "I actually *did* know, that you two were sisters," Rob led with, looking at Margo. "Impressive company. Somehow, they fell onto my list of up-and-comers. I looked at them, but we're certainly not to the point where we'd bring you in, Brooks. Still researching. Lee's pulling stats. I guess our inquiry got them fired up, but everything has to go through the proper channels. They should know that. I can certainly take you through what I learned tomorrow, Brooks," Rob said dismissively as he grabbed another beer.

"Funny, I thought you could take us through it now," Matt said pointedly. Rob's eyes narrowed. If Brooks was surprised at his son's forwardness, he didn't show it. "Because I'm confused," Matt continued, "Kirby said the deal was pretty far along, but then I found out that you're actually building a new company helmed by Margaux Dubois," Matt said turning to his dad to explain. "She's known by her team at Blush & Bashful as Mix. She works there as the current director of communications." Matt turned back to stare down Rob. "Turns out she's planning to leave to start her own retail platform. The wireframes for it seem quite impressive. It lists you, Rob, as a founding partner. That's a new title for you on an MLE business. If this *is* an MLE business. Are you investing in

both with MLE funds?" Matt then innocently turned to his
father. "Seemed strange to me. Made me wonder if you,"
Matt said turning back to Rob, "were pretending a deal
was imminent for Blush & Bashful with MLE, knowing it's
not and knowing that once they realize that too and have
lost all that time, capital, and the funds they spent on
legal, they'll be immobilized. Perfect time for you and Mix
to swoop in and launch a competitor."

Margo inhaled deeply at this bombshell. She stared at
Matt wide-eyed, her face hot with anger. Now it was
Brooks whose eyes narrowed. "Rob, is this true, are you
posturing to this company that MLE is investing when I
know nothing of it? And, how is this Margaux Dubois—
Mix—tangled in all of it?"

Rob looked completely indifferent. *He's better than I
thought,* Matt decided, *not even a glimmer of a reaction.*

"Brooks, I have conversations all day long. You know
that. That's part of my job. And I don't know what Matt
thinks he knows, but he doesn't have his facts straight. I
would never pursue an illegitimate investment on MLE's
behalf. And if there was an opportunity for me to be a
strategic partner, you would know about it." Rob popped
a chip with guacamole in his mouth like nothing was
amiss before adding, "Matt, I'm embarrassed for you
buddy. This is a new low, which is surprising because I've
always thought you pretty much resided at rock bottom."

Brooks surveyed Rob. Then he looked to Matt.
Cockiness rolled off Rob, like heat off a desert road. *This
prick is certain my dad isn't going to question him,* Matt
thought, suddenly nervous, *what if he doesn't?* After a
long pause in which Rob kept munching chips as if his
head weren't on a stake, Brooks's line of vision swiveled

to Margo. "Margo, might you give me Kirby's cell? Mix's too? I think we should give each of them a call." Brooks turned his gaze back to Rob, "And don't even think about texting this Mix to get your stories straight, Rob. It won't matter. You're already fired."

With that Brooks began to walk toward the house, Margo and Matt stepping in behind him. Before Matt could even consider dancing on Rob's grave, Rob reared his perfectly V-05'ed head. Like a sudden cool front before a storm, his cockiness switched to a roiling, seething anger. "Are you fucking kidding me, Brooks?" he spat out venomously. "A decade we've worked together and you fire *me* because your fuck-up of a son pieces together some half-baked plot off a *Mr. Robot* episode?" Rob let out a barkish laugh at the preposterous thought. "You're smarter than this Brooks, aren't you? You have the chance to let me lead your *dinosaur* of a company into the future and you chose this pissant who's going to grind it into the ground? You really are a fool," he hissed, acidity dripping in his tone.

Brooks turned back toward Rob.

"Dad, it's fine," Matt said, stepping in his way.

"No, Matty, it's not," Brooks clipped. Margo squeezed Matt's hand at the use of his nickname. "Rob," Brooks said, "you're an asshole—you always have been and you always will be. And I'm not worried in the least about what you do or where you go. Start this company, start ten, come at me and Matty every day. Because while you're so focused on what me and my son are doing, we'll be focused on our business, slaying our dragons, building *our* empires. You'll be right where you've always been, ten steps behind me, watching *me* make every move, watching *me* make every dollar." Brooks turned to Zinny. "Mind taking out the garbage twice today, Zin?"

"It would be my pleasure, Mr. M."

CHAPTER 42

Nixed Off The List

Margo dialed Mix from her phone, knowing she'd be more inclined to answer a number she recognized. She and Matt sat on the leather chesterfield sofa in Brooks's office while Brooks sat across on a '70s Italian shearling club chair, all three leaning forward in anticipation.

It rang twice when Mix picked up. "Hi Margo, Rob said you might be calling." Her voice was lacquered with professionalism.

"Hi, Mix, you're on speakerphone with Matt and his father, Brooks Milles-Lade."

"Mr. Milles-Lade," Mix said cordially.

"Lovely to be chatting, Mix," he countered.

Mix launched in: "I'll keep this simple for everyone. Rob and I have known one another for years. I thought Blush & Bashful would be a great investment for MLE, so I opened the door to Kirby and David." Margo's jaw tightened at hearing her sister's name fall out of Mix's mouth. "In recent days I realized that maybe I'd done so because of my *own* dreams. I shared them with Rob, and he thought something was there so we started to explore it."

Margo cut her off. "You know what? Stop talking Mix. I thought you *stealing* my idea for the shoot was duplicitous, but you stealing my sister's investor and attempting to undermine her success shows me that it wasn't duplicity, it's just *you*. So, I'm done letting you talk." She looked up at Brooks, "Forgive me, Brooks, for interrupting, but Mix, you're fired."

Mix let out a barkish laugh and sneered, "First of all, sweetie, you should be the one to talk about duplicity. Don't think I don't know about you and Matt." Margo's eyes flew to Matt's with worry about what Mix might say next. "Second, you don't have the authority to fire me."

Margo's eyes flared with anger. "Maybe I don't, but if you really don't think Kirby will back me, call her and find out." There was dead silence on the line.

"Obviously," Mix continued. "none of *this* matters. Rob and I are well under way in our plans to launch the only good thing that came out my tenure at B&B, my nickname. Starting tomorrow we'll be helming our new property Mixi.com. Thanks to a few supportive friends who are super happy to see it launch, like Dree and Manuela, we've already loaded it with content. I think you met them on your trip, Margo." Mix's inflection insinuated something Margo couldn't put her finger on. "Like you said, Matt, our wireframes are amazing. Not sure how you saw them," she said icily, "but it doesn't matter because your little Fourth of July campaign doesn't hit for another week, and, when it does we'll have beat you to the punch with our own tagline of Mixi on Top. So thanks for the call, you three. Continued success," she added. Then, the line went dead.

"She seems like a real pussycat," Brooks purred sarcastically. Margo snorted a single laugh. "She and Rob are perfect for one another. All claws. No substance," he added. He stood and grabbed his own phone. "Margo, call your sister, fill her in, and tell her that MLE is going to front her the money to launch the remainder of her editorial platform today. Ask her what she needs right now to launch her ad campaign in the next few hours. I'll get Lee on the phone to make sure the funds are dispersed. Consider it our good faith offer to hold B&B exclusive 'til we get the remaining paperwork sorted out." Margo couldn't believe her ears. "And, Matty, let's figure out how you can helm this," Brooks said, his thumbs already typing on his phone.

"About that, Dad. I'd like this to be my first venture in a new company I'm calling Leni, think of it as an incubator for MLE. Leni's focus will be on new ventures, ones that aren't as big as the monster mergers and acquisitions MLE currently focuses on. They're more start-up level companies that need leadership to put them on the path to industry domination. I've been speaking with Ian about it, and he's on board to join as a special investor. Once I give him the green light, he has a few other key money folks he wants to bring to the table to sit on our review board. According to him, they've already invested in properties like Grid.it, Nav Cars, and Sit Spot Stay, all of which became huge earners but needed careful leadership to get them there." Matt looked confident as he spoke, with just a knife's edge of eagerness at having his dad's approval.

Brooks paused. "Sounds like you've really been thinking about this, Matty."

Matt nodded. Margo squeezed his hand, only then realizing she was holding it, something she hadn't recalled doing.

"Let's do it. And I can't think of a better namesake than your mother for such a big move. She'd be proud to have her name on the door."

Matt stood and they shook hands, his father then squeezing his shoulder. "I'm proud of you, son."

Margo's eyes drifted to the framed photo on the coffee table of a young Matt sitting atop his mother's lap, her hair dramatically short, her smile magnetic. *Brooks Leni & Matty* was engraved in the sterling silver of the frame. She hopped up. "I'm going to go call Kirby and let her know," she said stepping out, closing the door behind her. She paced in the living room, telling Kirby everything, she and David gasping in all the right places on the other end of the line.

"Margo, why didn't you tell us it was your idea?"

"Chelsea and I decided you'd made a big investment in Mix. Why upset the applecart when we could just figure it out? If I had any idea she'd do this, believe me, I would have told you."

Two hours later ads started to fill Grid.it and populate sites like Buzzfeed and Reddit. As they clicked across platforms, there they were, Matt and Margo resplendent in pink, with Gus and his pink trucks playing upon the cabana-striped platform. Their island in the aqua of the pool, in soft focus, as seven Founders in white sat fiercely behind them owning the shot. The image itself was compelling, but when you added the tagline of *The Founding Females. May They Rewrite History* and paired it with a carousel of images, the campaign felt paradigm shifting.

Margo shared the image on their @MattlovesMargo feed with the caption, *When your sister is a boss, this happens....* The likes flooded in and when they shared the video edit of these amazing women reciting Maya Angelou's words, the world took notice. In that moment, Margo realized for all the damage Mix had done, she had also fueled Margo's fire to make this happen. *Not that I'm giving Mix a pass, that feral cat will get hers,* she decided, but she felt grateful for just how turned upside down her life had been these past few weeks. *Because, when the deck got reshuffled, I got him,* she thought, looking at Matt across the kitchen mixing drinks with Zinny.

She slid off her barstool and went over to him. "Thanks for today," she said as she helped him roll glass rims in sugar for whatever drink Tiff had declared they needed to make to celebrate.

"My pleasure, Valentine," Matt said as Zinny rooted through the pantry looking for pineapple juice.

Matt licked lime and sugar off his hand. Margo turned to face him. She stood up on her tiptoes and kissed him. At first, Matt, not wanting to get the syrup on her face, left his hands where they were but as the kiss deepened, he instinctively cradled her face. *Our first real kiss,* Margo thought, *not for camera, not for show, just for us.*

Zinny cleared her throat behind them. Matt and Margo broke apart.

"Here, I'll take these," Margo said, placing the first finished drinks on a tray. She walked out, smiling, not registering the worry on Matt's face as he looked to see Bibi on the pool deck watching them.

CHAPTER 43

The Morning After

They'd stayed up laughing and talking to all hours of the night, a game of drunken charades breaking out at 1 a.m. and late-night swimming at around 2:30.

In the recesses of her tequila-addled brain, Margo thought she recalled a make-out sesh in the pool after Matt had thrown her in. She woke up in bed alone, her head pounding, to the dinging of her phone. She reached for it and read a text from Ford. *Heard the news. Need to see you. I can't get our night on that striped platform out of my mind.*

At first Margo didn't catch it. She was still foggy. But then it hit her, this text wasn't meant for Margo, it was meant for MARGAUX.

"You pig," she said aloud.

Then she broke her solemn swear not to look at Mix's phone. She scrolled through Mix's texts and there it was, an entire chain with Ford in which he detailed all the *50 Shades of Grey* ways they'd been fooling around at the office. "What a fucking dog!"

She got up and showered. Even though she was hung over, she felt light and breezy at the thought of what had happened with her and Matt yesterday. She smiled to herself as she walked down the hall but froze when she saw Matt and Bibi in the kitchen cooking for Gus. She watched them laughing and dancing, Matt dipping Bibi and then tossing Gus around like they were pro wrestlers. Bibi hugged at his waist and nuzzled his neck. She watched as Matt turned, took Bibi in a full bear hug, lifting her up off the ground. Her stomach knotted.

She pushed herself up against the wall and quietly backed toward the staircase when Tiff came around the corner. She looked at Margo and then past her seeing Matt and Bibi singing in the kitchen.

"Don't look so surprised, sugar. You never really thought you were going to break up that band, did you?" she purred. Margo got the sense that Tiff was enjoying this and not just because she'd hustled her out yesterday. "Bibi has a hold on the Milles-Lade men—that one especially. I suggest you make your peace with the fact that you'll never have his full attention."

Margo's eyes narrowed in at Tiff. "Thanks for having me." She pushed up the stairs past her host, not catching Tiff's sly smirk in the foyer mirror.

Pacing around the room, she felt so stupid. *He told you that he loves them,* she chided herself. *And, each time it's been you kissing him. You have to get out of here.* She texted him, *Hey, Kirbs needs me. I'm gonna uber. You can keep planning with your dad....*

Two minutes later, Matt was upstairs and walking into the room as Margo hurried around packing. "Let me drive you."

"No, you stay. Why should you leave when I'm just going to be in the office all day?" She crushed more things in her bag.

"I feel like something's off." Matt watched her worriedly zip through the room. "Is something off?"

"Don't be silly," she challenged as she breezed by him looking for her other shoe. He grabbed her by the waist, spinning her around.

"Nothing happened last night," he said. Her heart sank thinking of that kiss as nothing. "I mean, I know we kissed, but nothing happened here." He gestured toward the bed. "We'd all been drinking, so I crashed in the pool house."

"With Bibi," Margo pointed out, noting that in the room division Bibi had scored the posh sleeping quarters.

"Yeah, but…"

"I'm not worried about where you slept, Matt, why would I be?" Margo asked flatly. "Right now I'm just worried about getting back for my sister." She hefted her suitcase down. Matt nodded as she walked out of the room, not stopping her.

CHAPTER 44:

And then what...

"And then what?" Chelsea demanded as she munched the Szechuan beans they'd ordered along with the rest of their Joan's on Third Postmates delivery.

Margo had spent the past six hours detailing every minute of her Friday into Saturday morning with Matt and his family, the IT mix-up that revealed the cunning plan of Mix and Rob, the subsequent fight with him and the fallout with her, the launch of Mixi, the acceleration of B&B's campaign, Matt's idea for Leni, the fact that it's named after his mother, whose real name was Helen before Brooks gave her the nickname, the kiss, and then her discovering Matt in the kitchen with Bibi. Her current question was in regards to the text from Ford.

"And then what?" Margo repeated as she dished out some more spinach dip. "Then I called him and told him I knew about Mix and that he was an asshole."

"And?" Chelsea prodded.

"And he said, 'I told you not to keep me waiting.'"

Chelsea let out a gasp. "Dog!" she declared.

"I know," Margo crooned in agreement. "So, now I'm all alone in real life even though the internet still thinks I'm in love."

"Well, the internet's not wrong, you are in love," Chelsea observed, "and we don't know that he's not."

"You'd know if you saw him in that kitchen with Bibi," Margo said devastated.

The doorbell went off. "It's Raining Men," poured down from the speakers. Neither woman moved but both chorused, "Rita!" before breaking out in peals of laughter.

A few minutes later, there was a knock at the door. "Come in, Rita!" Margo shouted.

The door slowly opened, but it wasn't Rita. It was Bibi. Chelsea stood.

"I gotta go. I'll see you tomorrow morning," Chelsea said as she quickly gathered her things. "Ian's arriving tonight for a Leni board meeting. Expect me to arrive fully cherished." She swooned, turned, and made her departure. "Lovely to see you, Bibi," she whispered warmly as she passed her in the doorway.

"Come on in." Margo smiled, hoping it didn't look as fake as it felt.

"Matt and Gus are on their way," Bibi said as she stepped over the threshold and cautiously headed toward the kitchen, "Gus wanted to ride with Matt."

"That's nice." Margo began closing containers and placing them in the fridge. Bibi watched.

"I think you think something's going on that isn't," she began, cutting right to it.

Margo paused with her arms in the fridge. "It's okay, Bibi, I know you two are together."

"No, we're not."

Now wiping the island, Margo still averted her eyes. "Not together as in a couple, but friends with benefits together. Matt told me you two sleep together." She tried to sound casual as if she were cool about it.

"But that's just it, we're not. We haven't been, not since you arrived," Bibi said reaching for Margo's arm, stopping her cleaning. "Matt *does* love me. And I love him." Margo actually winced at the words. "But we are not in love. He's holding that place for someone else."

Margo slowly looked up. "But in Bora Bora he FaceTimed you constantly, and this morning in the kitchen..."

"Yeah, and you know what we talked about on every FaceTime and as we ate pancakes today?" Margo held her gaze, forcing the optimism that was trying to swell in her heart to die. "You. All he talks about is you, Margo. Don't break his heart because he has the biggest heart I know, and you're holding it in your hands." Margo felt as if her arms were numb. Bibi took her hands. "I know I can trust you." Margo nodded and swallowed the lump in her throat.

"Mooooommmmmyyy, Matt said you'd take me for ice cream!" Gus ran into the room, Matt followed behind.

"Did he now?" Bibi sang as she squeezed Margo's hands. Her kind eyes bore into Margo. "Well, he told me he was taking us to Hawaii for Christmas. Let's hope he keeps his promises too." She smiled slyly at Matt as she walked out.

Matt stood in the entry, looking at Margo as if she were a stray dog you're trying to capture in an alley before they can run by you. "Hey, Valentine, safe to come in?" Margo nodded. Matt walked toward her. "Wanna hear something crazy?" he asked.

"Does it start with two strangers pretending to be a couple on the internet to get a house, 'cause I think I've heard that one."

"No, it's crazier than that," Matt offered.

"Yeah?"

He nodded. "What if I told you *he* was never pretending?" Matt's eyes were suddenly vulnerable. Margo stood perfectly still across the island from him. "Margo Valentine, I fell in love with you the minute I met you. It's never been a lie for me. Not for one second."

Her entire body felt both heavy and light at the same time. As if sensing she was about to fall over, Matt grabbed her and for the first time, *he* kissed *her* just for kissing sake and Margo melted into the floor. They spun against the island and Matt hoisted her up onto the counter as their kiss deepened. Breaking apart breathlessly, Matt whispered, "Isn't this so much better than high-fiving?" Margo's head fell back as she let out a full laugh. *God, I love her laugh,* he thought.

As Matt began to kiss up the side of her neck, "Oh we're still high-fiving, Seven, and on very special occasions we are high-fiving *and* kissing at the same time," she shared matter-of-factly as she crossed her arms behind his neck.

"No," Matt demanded, standing back staring at her with a heavy-lidded smirk.

"Oh, yes," Margo said defiantly. She put both her hands up for a double high-five, which he begrudgingly participated in as Margo leaned in to kiss him. "Feels right, doesn't it?" she asked still clasping both his hands at the patty-cake position, their lips touching.

Matt let out a laugh as he let go of her hands, to help her jump down. "Come on, never nude," he said as he pulled her toward the hall. "Let's go find something to high-five about."

EPILOGUE:

Part 1:

Matt sleepily rolled out of bed, carefully extracting his arm out from under Margo. He walked across the bedroom, fully naked, the tiniest sliver of moonlight lighting his way, when he was suddenly aware of a shape at the edge of the room. It moved and he screamed. The shape screamed in response and flicked on a night watchman–size flashlight, shining it right in Matt's eyes.

Margo sat bolt upright in bed with a yelp, clutching the tangled sheets to her bare chest. "What the hell?" she shrieked, as Matt shielded his eyes in the flashlight glare.

The beam briefly leaving his face to point at his nether regions, "Mr. Miiiiiiiillllleeeesss-lade, indeed!"

"What are you doing in our room?" Matt snarled, the bright beam flashing back to his face, "Stop that!" he hissed as he blocked his eyes with one hand and held his junk with the other.

Rita tsk-tsked, "Don't be such a prude." She placed the light under her chin like a child in a school Christmas pageant. "Just keeping watch."

"You watch me when I sleep?" Matt spat out in shock.

"Noooo, I watch *over* you when you sleep. Someone had to. Until tonight *she* was across the hall." Rita gestured toward Margo. "Hi, Margo," she smiled.

"Hi, Rita," Margo laughed back.

Matt gasped, "Don't you *hi* her," he said pointing at Rita and then at Margo, "Don't encourage her." He turned back to Rita, "Go!" He pointed toward the door.

"Gotta make the rounds anyway." Rita slid the deck door open, looking wantonly back at Matt as she stepped through, then slid the door closed. When she was done, she pressed the palm of her hand to the glass and nodded for Matt to do the same on his side. He stood there defiantly. She looked stern and nodded again.

"I'm not doing that," Matt said through gritted teeth.

"She's just gonna stand there all night," Margo yawned as she flopped back down on the bed to go to sleep.

Matt stared harder at Rita. Rita's scowl deepened in return. "Oh for crying in the night!" Matt stomped over and put his hand up to hers through the glass. She smiled, winked, and then walked off whistling. "You are going to home depot and buying wooden dowels for every door and window today," Matt said, as he walked into the bathroom to pee, his original mission.

When he crawled back into bed, Margo slid close to him. "What are we going to do about her?"

"Nothing," Margo said dreamily.

"Nothing?" Matt said exasperated.

"Nothing," Margo repeated. "My dad always said, *You can't reason with crazy and you can't give crazy a reason.* So, nothing. She's just a part of this house."

"Maybe we should move," Matt offered up sleepily.

Margo flung herself around, almost head-butting him in the process. "Move?" she said outraged.

"Is that so crazy?"

"Yes," she said as she peered down at him from her one elbowed perch, "this house brought us together. We are meant to be here."

"Okay." He pulled her back down to sleep. "We stay, but if I go missing, check her pockets."

Somewhere around 9:30 a.m. Matt and Margo stirred awake. "We gotta get up. Got my first Leni meeting today," Matt said into the nuzzle of her neck. She groaned. "Come on," he cajoled. "Chelsea's coming with Ian in an hour."

She rolled over and he kissed her. "Do we have to?"

He hopped out of bed, then leaned in, kissing her again. "Yes," he said.

"Fine." She sat up. "Kirby wants me dreaming up more editorial ideas. I'm getting my first byline." Her silk sleep mask sat high on her forehead.

"Babe, that's amazing!" Matt said as he slid on pants. "You shower. I'll get breakfast started."

"Wow, Seven, real boyfriend looks good on you," Margo flirted coming up on her knees on the edge of the bed. They kissed.

"I know, right?" he smirked.

Around noon, the doorbell rang. Matt looked to see his dad, Ian, and Chelsea walking down the path. Matt gave his father the nickel tour, as Margo got a tray of coffees ready.

"What's going on?" Chelsea asked, nudging her friend as they stood in the marble kitchen.

"Matt and I are a couple, like for real." Margo smiled widely.

"Well, duh," Chelsea retorted as Ian got out his wallet and handed her a $100 bill. Margo nodded at their exchange.

"We made a bet about how long it would take you two to figure out what we already knew," Ian said.

Margo smirked at Chelsea, "Attagirl."

Ian took the French press as Matt grabbed the mugs from the kitchen. "Have fun, editor," he said.

"Have fun, CEO," she replied their eyes twinkling back at one another.

"Oh, please," Chelsea groaned at them.

Just as Matt called them to order, Rita and Dinah swanned through the door. Matt jumped up, but Dinah waved him off. "Brooks Milles-Lade, while I live and breathe! What a pleasure to meet you. I'm Dinah Robbins-Mackey-Salter-Joiner-Jenson." She floated through the living room toward him. Brooks took her hand and kissed it as he held her gaze. "Ohhhhh, I felt that," Dinah said, with a shiver of exaggerated ecstasy. "Don't break my heart and tell me you're taken, because I'm looking for lucky number seven!"

Rita stepped to Matt's side. "We might be brother and sister," she whispered, nodding toward Dinah and Brooks. "Then we can live out all our *Flowers in the Attic* fantasies." She wagged her eyebrows at Matt.

He grimaced as if he'd licked an airplane tray table. "That's not happening, Rita," he said flatly.

She shrugged, "You sure 'bout that Seven?" she pouted, using the nickname Margo had given him. Then, she leapt toward Ian.

"Guys meet my lucky pennies," Ian crooned as he swept Rita into a hug.

Part 2:

Hello Henrietta—It's been too long. I think the last time we saw one another was in Paris just before you launched Grid.it. We must fix that and have dinner soon.

I'm writing today regarding a topic that hits close to home. I'm attaching a video I'd like you to see. It was shot by Dree Von Valle on a recent Phame trip. She and another dear friend of mine, Manuela Carrillo, shot it, inadvertently, but brought it to my attention once they realized what they'd captured. In it, Margo Melon of @MattlovesMargo, one of your selected participants for your industry-shifting campaign, The 25 Must Follows, details that her relationship to Matt Milles-Lade is fake. She goes on to say that Matt is really in love with Bibiana Romano, the internationally acclaimed actress.

I recently left my tenure at her sister's company, Blush & Bashful, because I didn't find their business model to rise up to my level of expectation. When I watched this video and heard the lack of integrity that Ms. Melon has, it affirmed my decision to part ways. At first, I thought I would say nothing. To each her own. One's lack of virtue is not worth losing my focus over, but now that I am following in your footsteps and founding my own site, I have begun to wrestle with the personal toll it takes to know a truth and do nothing. This girl and her just-as-dubious partner are defrauding your hard-earned audience. Not only that, they are building a business upon a lie. Doing nothing didn't sit well with me. My conscience said I had to speak up. Doing the right thing is just who I am. So, on the eve of my own site launch, mixi.com, I am writing you.

I can't tell you what to do with this information in the halls of Grid.it, but I did want to let you know that in addition to bringing this to you, I am also bringing this to the public. In a few days my founding partner, Rob Rolle, and I are going on CNBC to talk about the impact a lie like this can have on the public who believes them and the businesses who compete against them. I wanted to give you a few days to decide if you wanted to un-verify their account, delete it all together, or find another measure by which to hold them accountable for their actions. I look forward to discussing the matter with you.

I think it bears repeating, it is not in my nature to go after another woman in the media. I believe there's room for all of us, but when something this egregious occurs, my moral compass compels me to act.

All best,
Margaux "Mix" Dubois

XOXO, moxie

Thank you to my family. Mom, you are a writer. I thank you for giving me the gift of words, including the ones you make up to win at Boggle. Thank you for pouring your love into me so that I might stand a chance in this world. Dad, you taught me the fine art of storytelling and how to make a friend anywhere, even in line for the bathroom. It's a skill that has served me surprisingly well. Phyllis, your support means the world to me, and I am grateful to have had your eyes on every page. You are a treasure in my life. Becky, you inspire me each day. Maybe you don't know it, but you do. Brian and Renee, thanks for making me an aunt and raising the best niece and nephew a girl could ever hope for. I love you, Noah, and Maggie beyond measure. To the rest of my family, I love you and am grateful to have my Ohio crew to return home to. You are spectacular humans and I am honored that every year it is you I battle for the last ham ball. To Erin, you are my work wife and one of my truest friends. I would be lost without your wisdom and support. I am so very lucky to have you. Thank you for quitting only that one time...so far. To Lindsay, how is it we never run out of things to say? I adore you and am so glad we are two peas who share the same pod. Katrina, Heather, James, and Holly, you are like a fanny pack—perfect, necessary, fashionable, and my truest treasures. I love you and can't wait for the girl's trips ahead of us. You have believed in me from the word Gucci, and I love you. To Jules, you are my family. Period.

The end. I adore you and the amazing way you are a mother to your son and a guiding force for all of your students and me. You are my biggest cheerleader. I can't wait for all this world holds for us both! I love you. To Stacia, you are my sister wife and forever #WCW. I am so very lucky that the universe brought me your way and we got to slay dragons together. Michele, here's to traveling the globe with you, *Bachelor* fantasy trip style, forever and ever, amen. I could not be more grateful to have you in my corner and in my life. To Lesley, thank you for always seeking out the girl with the clipboard. My life was changed the minute you did. To Maggie, my Gemini twin. Crystals brought us together but the glue of friendship made sure we stuck. You make my life sparkle with the way you support me. To Kelli, you read before anyone else and were in my corner from day one. Thanks for being my fake neighbor and real friend. To Jenni, I don't how I lucked out that out of all the kindred spirits in the world, I got you as mine. I am so thankful to have you as a friend and partner in crime. For all my other friends, Anthony, PJ, Sidd, Allyson, Dylan, Kyle, Brooke & Gabriel, Paige, Michelle, Brittany, Veronica & Kris, Heather, Becca, Jennifer, and too many more to name, I am intensely grateful for you. Thank you for the big and little ways you support and inspire me. I am overwhelmed with gratitude. To all my advance readers, you are the dream weavers who helped me keep the faith on the path ahead. I am soul-level grateful for the time you spent to read and the care you took with your feedback. Now, go write your Amazon reviews. To Kat, thank you for going to the distance to recreate and shoot the magical cover image. You look good on a book cover lady! To Natalie and

Rochelle, thank you for taking my vision for the cover and running with it. Your work brought me to tears, proof that my coal black heart still beats. To Sarah Christensen Fu, you are a publishing unicorn and book ninja wielding Wicken-level web sorcery like a right, proper witch. I am in awe of you. To Jessica Marlow, let's go run this town. I'm so very honored to have you on my team. And, finally, to the universe. Thank you for letting me throw this Hail Mary, but I'm not done yet. I'm going to need that three-pointer at the buzzer to give me just the permission I need to do this at least a dozen more times.

Made in the USA
San Bernardino, CA
22 November 2019

60276615R00219